A WHISTL

A. S. Byatt is one of Britai[...] fourth novel in her quartet which includes *The Virgin in the Garden*, *Still Life*, and *Babel Tower*. Her other novels are *The Shadow of the Sun*, *The Game*, *Possession* (winner of the Booker Prize in 1990), and *The Biographer's Tale*. She has also written two novellas, published together as *Angels and Insects*, and four collections of shorter works: *Sugar and Other Stories*, *The Matisse Stories*, *The Djinn in the Nightingale's Eye* and *Elementals*. Educated at York and at Newnham College, Cambridge, she taught at the Central School of Art and Design, and was Senior Lecturer in English at University College, London, before becoming a full-time writer in 1983. A distinguished critic as well as a novelist, she was appointed CBE in 1990 and DBE in 1999.

A. S. Byatt

A WHISTLING WOMAN

VINTAGE

Published by Vintage 2003

2 4 6 8 10 9 7 5 3 1

Copyright © A. S. Byatt, 2002

A. S. Byatt has asserted her right under the Copyright,
Designs and Patents Act, 1988 to be identified as the author
of this work

First published in Great Britain in 2002 by
Chatto & Windus

Vintage
Random House, 20 Vauxhall Bridge Road,
London SW1V 2SA

Random House Australia (Pty) Limited
20 Alfred Street, Milsons Point, Sydney
New South Wales 2061, Australia

Random House New Zealand Limited
18 Poland Road, Glenfield,
Auckland 10, New Zealand

Random House (Pty) Limited
Endulini, 5A Jubilee Road, Parktown 2193,
South Africa

The Random House Group Limited Reg. No. 954009
www.randomhouse.co.uk

A CIP catalogue record for this book
is available from the British Library

ISBN 0 09 944339 2

Papers used by Random House are natural, recyclable
products made from wood grown in sustainable forests.
The manufacturing processes conform to the environmental regulations of the country of origin

Printed and bound in Great Britain by
Bookmarque Ltd, Croydon, Surrey

For Steve Jones and Frances Ashcroft

A Whistling Woman and a Crowing Hen
Is neither good for God nor Men.

A frequent saying of my maternal grandmother.

'And just as I'd taken the highest tree in the wood,' continued
the Pigeon, raising its voice to a shriek, 'and just as I was
thinking I should be free of them at last, they must needs
come wriggling down from the sky! Ugh, Serpent!'

'But I'm *not* a serpent, I tell you!' said Alice. 'I'm a – I'm a –'

'Well! *What* are you?' said the Pigeon. 'I can see you're
trying to invent something!'

'I – I'm a little girl,' said Alice, rather doubtfully, as she
remembered the number of changes she had gone through that
day.

'A likely story indeed!' said the Pigeon, in a tone of the
deepest contempt. 'I've seen a good many little girls in my
time, but never *one* with such a neck as that! No, no! You're a
serpent; and there's no use denying it.'

Lewis Carroll, *Alice in Wonderland.*

Here, at the Fountains sliding foot,
Or at some Fruit-trees mossy root,
Casting the Bodies Vest aside,
My soul into the boughs does glide:
There like a Bird it sits and sings,
Then whets, and combs its silver Wings;
And, till prepar'd for longer flight,
Waves in its plumes the various Light.

Andrew Marvell, *The Garden.*

I

. . . 'This is the last tree,' said the thrush. The last tree was a dwarf
thorn, its black branches shaped one way by the wind, pointing back the
way they had come. 'Formerly,' said the thrush, 'there was a last tree
further out. And in earlier times there was a stunted wood, the Krumholz.
The waste is advancing.'

They looked into iron twilight. They could barely make out the bluff
where the wood had once been rooted.

'No one goes out there,' said the thrush. 'In former days, there were
travellers, until winter set in. But now they are afraid of the Whistlers.
The winters have lengthened. And in the light days the land is infested by
the Whistlers.'

'The place we seek is on the other side,' said Artegall. 'According to the
maps and the histories. We must go, and quickly, before winter sets in.'

'And before the hunters catch up with us,' said Mark.

'No one has set out, or come from there, in my life-time,' said the
thrush, fluffing out his spotted feathers. His life-time was not very long,
and his territory was small. He was a wiry, thick-quilted thrush.

'What is the land like?' asked Artegall.

'Scrub and stones, mosses, and lichens, deep pools with ice-covers,
frozen rivers. There are white creatures there, I've been told, that scutter in
the snow and hide in holes. And slick, grey efts, in the pools. They used
to say the lichens were edible, if not palatable. All hearsay. I haven't been
there.'

'And the Whistlers?'

'No one has seen them and lived,' said the thrush. 'Indeed, to hear
them is mostly fatal. They fly or glide like grey shadows and make a
sound — a sound —'

'A sound?'

'So it is said, a high, whistling sound, at the extreme edge of what any
creature can hear, yet all must hear it. A dog can hear whistles that you
hear as disturbed silence. But these creatures have the power to pierce any

I

ear – bird and man, bear and snowcock, even your sleeping stone reptile who appears to be lifeless.'

Artegall looked at Dracosilex, who had shown no sign of life since the Bale Fires of the last village.

'I could do with his counsel,' said Artegall. 'If he could be wakened.'

'If the Whistlers woke him,' said the thrush, 'you would not live to hear his counsel. And your bones would be picked in an instant.'

They built a shelter near the last tree, and set up their tents, before night fell. Noises howled and hummed round them, fine, glassy sounds and a regular quavering boom, and the icy blasts of the wind, blowing and flowing over the dry rattling twigs of the last tree. There were also shrill notes that could have been whistling, human or inhuman. Mark said that he had heard that the porpoises and the dolphins sang to each other in the blue summer waters of the south, from which they had come. 'There is needles and knives in this wind,' said Dol Throstle. 'And talons and claws.' They chewed dried meat, and sweet dried grapes, too few, gone too quickly.

In the morning a fine dry snow fell, gusting and eddying in the wind. They could not see very far. They discussed who should scout and who should stay. Mark asked if Artegall's geography books had contained maps of this land. There were a few maps of the Northern Empire, he said, vague shapeless spaces with a few rivers and many drawings of fabulous beasts, with twenty legs, or curving claws. It was written, White Waste. I remember one or two trails without issue, and arrows pointing out of the page, To the North. The pages were very richly decorated, bordered with golden apples and crimson cherries and emerald vine-leaves. And iron axes, and flakes of fire.

Dol Throstle remembered how Mark the page-boy had mocked the young prince at the outset, with his stories of the books of venery, history, geography, dutifully committed to memory in the study-prison of his white tower in the south. And how Artegall's knowledge had led them through forests, and his languages had made it possible to speak to strangers, and his books of tracking and stalking had found food in hard places. And Mark for his part had taught Artegall the knack of tickling trout, and stealing from bees, and chattering like a naïf lad to soldiers in inns. And now they were no longer prince and whipping-boy and nursemaid, but three leathery, weathered creatures, all muscle and quickened eyes, bundled in borrowed skins. A snake had taught Artegall the language of the beasts, but they were all, Dol thought, part of the animal kingdom now, they could melt into woodland like foxes, lie lost in grassland like hares, they could flow along hillsides like wolves.

Mark said they could not travel at night, using the stars, because of the cold.

And then they heard, for the first time, in the noises of the wind and the clack of the twigs, the whistle, that rose and fell and then rose and rose, out of pitch, so they knew they were still hearing it though the sound disturbed only their brains. And Dol's courage failed, and she thought she was a fool and a madwoman to bring two mere boys so far, in search of a kingdom that was perhaps only a fantasy out of legend. And Mark thought, numbed, that this time maybe there was no way forward, only snow-blindness and frost-bite, and behind were the steady hunters, beating them out of cover like fowls. And Artegall thought that the voices were terrible, and would destroy the brain in the skull. And then the sound died down, and released them. Artegall had the idea of making little balls of lambswool to put in their ears, under their skin hoods.

In the morning the two boys set out, leaving Dol under the thorn. 'If we do not come back within three days,' said Artegall, 'you must turn back. The soldiers may not harm you if I am not there.'

'Nonsense,' said Dol. 'I will come after you, whatever may befall. I am no mean tracker, by now.'

They found, after a mile or two of careful advance over characterless scrub and crackling frost, that they needed their ears in the ice-gloom, both to test brittle crusts over deep crevices and to listen to the land, for footfalls, for the snap of branches, for the beat of wings. They found a kind of goat-path, among the little junipers and ling, which widened into a track. They stumped steadily on; Mark singled out prominent stones along the track which might be pointers, put there by human hands. The cloud-cover was lowering and thickening. They examined the stones, and found scratches — an arrow perhaps, a bird's-foot, three-toed, on one, and then on another. They decided if they found a third to turn back, and fetch Dol, and their provisions, and try this road. A little wind got up, and blew ice in their faces, in sharp splinters. They could hear singing in this wind. At first they did not speak of it, taking it for an interior humming, that kept time with their footsteps and the beat of blood. Mark said, in the end,

'Do you hear sweet voices in the wind?'

'So you hear them too. Voices, thin and high, and a kind of flute, or maybe another voice.'

'Maybe an ice equivalent of a mirage in a desert.'

'Maybe the voices of the Whistlers.'

'Or the spirits of their victims.'

They struggled on, and the track became less definite. There were no more markers. The wind pelted them with frozen snow. Mark said

'The singing is unbearably sad, unbearably –' and fell over in the snow behind Artegall. As Artegall turned, the perfectly-pitched music in his head turned to an undulating whistle. He reached to put the bulb of wool in his ears, fumbling with his fur-gloved fingers, before he knelt by his friend. The wool did not wholly exclude the whistling, but reduced it to a whisper of a shriek. And he saw them coming at him through the gloom, one, two, three, five, eight, thirteen of them, sailing on outstretched grey wings, almost indistinguishable from the cloud, their long, slender necks held out before them like swans', their thin legs trailing like herons', their bright beaks like curving scimitars, pale red-gold. They landed in a circle round the two, and Mark saw with horror that their faces above their beaks were human, that they had dark, human, forward-looking eyes under arched eyebrows, that their feather-hoods covered, or flowed into, long hair, which they shook out over their shoulders, that the legs above the bird-talons that struck and gripped the icy stones were human above the feathered ankles, that the bodies inside the great cloaks of grey pinioned wings were human, female, with high breasts and slender waists, but covered in white down. Artegall found that he could not move, though he could see and hear.

The Whistlers began a kind of strutting dance, moving stiffly on their claws, winding their long necks gracefully like charming serpents, bowing and pointing and singing at the two humans, on the white earth in the gathering darkness. Artegall understood that they were singing, over and under the terrible whistle, but he could make no sense of the words. He tried to listen as he listened to the speech of birds, and heard cackle and hiss; he tried to listen as he would listen to women, and heard meaningless babble of airy syllables. He saw then that their song was somehow spinning a cocoon of icy threads round and over his friend's body, like a glassy shroud hardening into a coffin. His own hands and feet were threaded with filaments which he was powerless to cast off. It came numbly to him, he must understand their language, or speak to them, or he must die. He listened as he had never listened in his life, and began to make out that their language, like their bodies, was a dreadful hybrid, feather-words and skin-words grown into each other, beak-words and tongue- and teeth-words fused. He could hear it, he could even construct it, by some terrible *operation inside his own skull of simultaneous separation and stitching, so that he was, as it were, dividing the two fronts of a leather jerkin and then, between the two parts of his brain, threading them together with a thong of thought. 'Pity,' he said, in this strange new speech, his tongue like leather. 'Pity, women-birds, bird-women — kind — creatures — this — man — too — is — kind.' No hurt, he cried, small, promising and asking, no hurt. And one Whistler said*

'He hears us.'

'I hear you.'

'He hears words in whistling.'

'I hear your words, Whistlers. I hear, I speak.'

He said, in bird speech, 'The King of the snakes taught me this speech.' He said, in human speech, 'Do not hurt us, we are lost, we mean good.' He repeated, in their speech, 'I hear you, you hear me.' It was like a blade in the brain, dividing and touching both divided parts.

They stopped singing, then, and moved together in a circle, whistling to each other with bowed heads. They came back, and one, whistling hesitant and low, said

'We will carry you to a safe place for the night. We will not harm you. Do you hear me?'

'I can hear you.'

'We will carry your friend, too. He is not harmed. He will wake.'

They snatched up Mark, three pairs of claws, and flew away. Then Artegall felt the scaled grip, through all his furs, and the cold air inside his hood as they rose, and wheeled north, into the gathering dark and the blast of the wind. He knew no more.

He woke by a glowing fire, deep in a cave. Mark slept beside him, the ice-cocoon melted. The bird-women roosted on rocky ledges, preening grey wings with wicked beaks. They brought him soup, grey, bitter, gluey, in a tall jar. They gathered round and asked who he was, where he was going? He told them, for he saw no help in concealing it, who he was — Artegall, prince of Harena — and of his escape from the South when the black ships poured into the harbour, and of his companions, Dol Throstle, who was his nurse, and Mark, and some others, who had not survived. And he spoke of Hamraskir Kveld-Ulf, his father's legendary northern cousin, who Dol had told him might provide a sure refuge from the spies and assassins sent out from Mormorea by Barbasangue. He said doubtfully that maybe the Northern Kingdom was only legend. Dol had spoken of it with certainty when she hid him in the laundry-cart, but the certainty had diminished with the rough journey. Maybe there was nothing north of the wasteland except ice-floes, and cold dancing lights.

'It is there,' said one of the Whistlers. Her name was Hvanvit. 'In a valley in the ice-mountains, beyond this land. It goes by many names. Hofgarden, Harreby, Veralden. We call it Veralden. The kings of Veralden have always been powerful wizards. They are shape-shifters, who can become wolves, or bears, at will, and travel out into the badlands, watching the borders, talking to the wind-spirits, listening to the advances and retreats of the ice. In Veralden, only men were shape-shifters. Women stayed in the valley, spinning and teaching, tending fruit-trees and flowers. They never left the valley. We wanted to go out, we wanted the speed and the danger of the wind and the snow and the dark. We charmed a young student into parting with his knowledge, and we made feather-coats, as you see, and rode the storm-winds at night. We flew in, over the mountain-wall, before dawn, plaited our wild hair, put on gown and slippers, and went to sing sweetly to the fruit-trees. But we were spied on, by a traitress, and shamed. And an angry crowd burned our women's clothes outside the gates of Veralden, and almost burned us. But we put a little fear into them, and whistled in their minds, so that they merely drove us away like a flock of geese, calling us evil, and unclean. So we have lived here, where nothing lives, riding the winds, evading hunters and snow-eagles. We have grown angry because no one could hear our speech. Until you came.'

They talked into the night. Artegall listened courteously to their tales of grief and exile, and only then did he return to his own quest, and ask whether the king in Veralden was his kinsman, Hamraskir Kveld-Ulf. They said they believed so. They dared not approach the city. 'But we will set you on your way,' said Hvanvit, 'we will carry you over the wasteland and bring food for you. For we are not the most terrible danger you will meet on this journey – more terrible still are the ancient enemies, cold and dark and hunger. In all the time we have circled and swept over this land we have seen no one come across safely. We could show you bones, and men preserved in ice as though they slept, and proud horses, and sledge-dogs. When we tried to speak to them, our song proved mortal to their ears, until you came. Maybe you will speak of us, and our wanderings, to Hamraskir Kveld-Ulf when you come to him, if indeed you come there.'

And Artegall, daring, asked Hvanvit if she desired to be a woman again. And she said, no, she could never forgo the wind in the wings, and *the free racing through the stormskies. But she would like to be welcome in Veralden, to drink wine again, with her kinsfolk.*

So the next day, Dol Throstle saw shapes flying arrowswift, high against the iron clouds, one, two, three, five, eight, thirteen, and two were burdened and flying lower. She saw the long stretched necks, and the piercing beaks, and took a brand from her fire by the Last Tree, and prepared to lose her life hard, and make some of these creatures pay dearly for her. But Artegall's voice came out of the air, telling her not to hurt the Whistlers, for they were friends, and would help them across the badlands.

And so they journeyed, carried by the flock of bird-women, who shared the burden, murmuring and hissing to each other. They crossed the bitter scrub and icy marshes, sleeping in caverns that opened underground. Dol Throstle did not trust the Whistlers, though Artegall held long conversations with Hvanvit. Dol thought they were edgy, angry, nervous creatures, ready to take offence, ready to wheel away capriciously and leave the humans to their own devices. Although their dark eyes had silky lashes and arched brows, she could not endure their inhuman stare. She felt they were judging her, by rules and ideas she knew nothing of. They might, for no reason she would know, decide to stab and deafen, as they had decided to help and protect. She saw Hvanvit's eyes follow Artegall, as he went to and fro, and Hvanvit's sisters' eyes, in their graceful bird-heads, watched Hvanvit. But Dol could not see what, or if, they were thinking.

After many days of this laborious progress, they saw, wavering in the cold mist, the distant shoulders and icy head of a great peak, thrusting up from the ground. They saw, as they flew closer, tall stone markers, and then carved gateposts, defining a scarce visible road, winding in between the shoulder hills. The Whistlers set down the three travellers, stretching and flapping their wings, making small cries of what might have been relief.

'We can go no further,' said Hvanvit. 'On pain of death. But you may go into the mountain. Watch your backs, and speak courteously to any creature you meet, from worm to wolf, for nothing there is simply what it appears to be.'

Then the three travellers thanked the Whistlers, and Artegall would have embraced Hvanvit, but she drew back, curving her long neck.

'I shall not forget you,' said Artegall. 'Ever.'

'We shall see,' said Hvanvit.

The gatepost was carved with an ascending spiral of forms, wolf and dragon, snake and albatross, hare and snail, and strangest of all in that cold place, butterflies on branches. They went in, hurrying a little, for night was falling. Behind them, the flock of Whistlers were like arrows in the dusk, and then like a swarm of bees, and then gone.

As they went on into the mountain pass, the night thickened, and they noticed, on the mountainside, little lights appearing and vanishing, like eyes, or like lanterns with the shutters flicked open and shut, watching or signalling. It was like walking willingly into a trap, Mark thought, clutching his knife-hilt, stepping soundlessly, as the mountainside rose sheer and black before them, and the light of the stars above them narrowed and diminished. For they were going down, in a looping spiral, into the dark heart of the mountain. After a long time they rested, huddled together, wrapped in their skin tents, and dozed fitfully.

They were awakened by the crow of a cockerel, clear, repeated and unafraid, saluting an invisible sunrise. Then they saw the thin pale line of grey-gold dawn, across the rim of the cleft. And as the sunlight spread out, they saw that though behind and around them was an icy pass of black basalt, in front was a white city wall, closing the valley, with battlements, on which black cocks strutted and crowed. There were human faces between the battlements. There was a huge barred gate, made of treetrunks, with bright hinges and great locks. Now Artegall, at the outset of his journey, had imagined crying proudly

'I am Artegall, son of Barbadoria, prince of Harena, and the Southern Isles, come to see my kinsman.'

But he said

'We are three weary travellers in need of shelter, if you will take us in.'

And the cocks crowed in a wild chorus, and the great door rolled back and Artegall, Mark and Dol Throstle, three lean, tattered, bundled figures, bearing the sleeping Dracosilex, walked into the unimaginable city.

Inside, time and space were not the same. There were wide white streets, and houses with the windows flung open, and great fountains playing, and flowers, scarlet and gold, purple and blue, tumbling from the balconies, and trees spreading leafy branches in what, when they looked up amazed, was summer sunlight. And Dracosilex, who had been no more than a burdensome stone since the Bale Fires, gave a start of fierce life, spread his wings and tail, claws and nostrils, blinked his scaly eyes and stepped out of Mark's pack lightly to the ground, where he began a sinuous leaping and prancing of which they would not have thought him *capable. They walked through many fair streets with a crowd gathering behind them, but not approaching. Dol Throstle felt constricted in her furs, and after a time stopped to discard her hat, and her hood, and then her heavy coat, and the young men did likewise. They went on more lightly, their cold skins drinking sunlight, into a great square, with a pillared hall, a circle of fountains, and swallows darting. On the steps of the hall stood a tall figure, the largest man Artegall had ever seen, with a huge sable beard, and black curls like heaped grapes, and black eyes under branching black brows. His black robe was embroidered with green and gold snaking vines or climbing snakes, with jewelled flowers and inky-blue glittering stars, with moons and suns and golden apples. He wore also a heavy sword in a battered sheath. And he came down the steps and took Artegall in his arms, and then Mark, and then, in an embrace at once a bear-hug and full of respect, Dol Throstle.*

'Welcome,' he said. 'Welcome, Artegall, Mark, Mistress Dol. You have been waited for. I am Hamraskir Kveld-Ulf, and you are safe and at home in this city. First you must wash, and then you must eat, and then you will tell me your adventures.' He repeated, 'You are safe in this city.'

And for the first time since they set out, fear left the cave in the back of their minds, and they felt that what he said was true. They were safe in his city.

'And that,' said Agatha to the assembled listeners, 'is the end of the story.'

There was an appalled silence.

Leo said 'The end?'

'The end,' said Agatha.

It was the summer of 1968. The telling of the story had begun two years ago, and had continued, almost every Sunday, until that day. It was long and intricate and had seemed endless. The first listeners had been Agatha's daughter, Saskia, now eight, and Leo, the son of Frederica Potter, who shared Agatha's house in Hamelin Square, in Kennington. Then the two Agyepong children, from across the Square, had become regulars – they were Clement, and Thano (short for Athanasius). Frederica herself always came, and most of the time Daniel Orton came too. Daniel was a priest (without any uniform) and Frederica's brother-in-law. He was a professional Listener, employed by a telephone-answering service for the desperate, in the crypt of St Simeon's Church, in the City.

The last two members of the audience were the Ottokar twins, John, who wrote computer languages, and Paul, who preferred to be known as Zag, and was the lead-singer of a group known as Zag and the Syzygy (pronounced ziggy) Zy-goats. All these people were both shocked and affronted by Agatha's brutal exercise of narrative power. She closed her notebook; her face wore its usual mild, composed look.

Leo's red eyebrows knit in a ferocious frown.

'That isn't the end. We don't know everything. We don't know what happened to the Whistlers. We don't know what his uncle was like. We don't know where his father is. We've waited and waited and waited to know these things, and now you say, now you say . . .'

Saskia stared, and opened her mouth. No sound came out, but her pale skin purpled and dappled. Then the howl came, primitive and outraged. Tears spurted out between closed eyelids, bounced on her cheeks. Agatha put her hand on her shoulder. Saskia flung away, and burrowed her head into Daniel, who closed his large hands over her.

'Why?' asked Thano.

'What did you stop there for?' asked Clement.

There was no satisfaction in the end of the story. It was as though they had all been stabbed. Agatha looked shaken by their vehemence; but closed her mouth, and closed her hands on the book.

'That is where I always meant it to end,' she said. Her voice was not completely steady.

'Tea,' said Daniel, making his way into the kitchen. Putting on the kettle, he heard Leo's clear voice, absolute as his mother's.

'But it wasn't an end, it wasn't a *real end* –'

'What's a real end?' said Frederica. 'The end is always the most unreal bit . . .'

'No, no, no,' said Leo above Saskia's sobs, 'There are good ends and this isn't one, *this isn't an end* . . .'

They were not exactly a family, the two women and their children, who were both in the same class at the William Blake Primary School. They had come together for convenience, after Frederica's flight from her husband and hard-fought divorce. Both

were highfliers, although Agatha was the more obviously successful, rising fast in the hierarchy of the Civil Service, a woman with
a solid place in the world, a secretary, a telephone, colleagues, an
office. Her private life was secret. No one had ever been told who
Saskia's father was, although Agatha occasionally remarked wryly
that only in the British Civil Service had a woman a right to three
illegitimate children before questions were asked. There were no
signs of any more children, and she was unnaturally uncommuni-
cative about her personal life. This was good for Frederica, who
in the company of another kind of woman might have talked too
much about her own problems. Or felt competitive. But Agatha's
reticence and dryness brought out the best in her. They supported
each other in practical ways. Leo went home to his father's
country house on visits. But the two women were able to help
each other with childcare, with shopping, with book buying, with
a new kind of necessary efficiency. And out of that sprang a kind
of new and different domestic comfort. Leo and Saskia were
friends, and quarrelled much less than they would have done if
they were siblings. Agatha and Frederica were calmer together
than if they had been sisters. Daniel, who had been married to
Frederica's dead sister, Stephanie, thought often about this, but
did not know whether Frederica did. Agatha never appeared to
see any family she may have had. It all worked much better than
they had expected or hoped it would.

Later, Frederica thought, as she put Leo to bed, about real
endings. What endings made you cry with happiness? In her own
case, reunions of parents and children, separated by danger. The
ending of *Peter Pan*, when the children flew back into the nursery
and the real world. The climax of *We Didn't Mean to Go to Sea*
when Daddy was seen unexpectedly in the Dutch harbour, on the
other side of the stormy water. She poured water down her son's
solid spine, and put her nose in his damp, flaming hair, and
thought of Saskia, who had as good as no father – none had been
mentioned, no name, no history, nothing. Even a discovered
uncle, Frederica thought, appeared to be too much for Agatha.
But what would become of the Sundays? They would have to
resort to reading. She herself was no storyteller. She wondered if
Agatha had thought of publishing her tale. She might try to show

it to Rupert Parrott. A publisher might even induce Agatha to take the tale further, perhaps in a sequel . . .

Endings. Frederica sat and waited for her lover, and wondered what the end of the affair would be. She had begun to think that there was always only an unreal moment's grace between the beginning of a love affair (the phrase was already old-fashioned, but she had a growing distaste for the word relationship) and this steady self-questioning about how and why and when it would end. The moment's grace was the moment of being 'in love', which brought with it a clear, driven purposefulness, an impersonal *directed* energy that was desired in its absence, and frightening in its presence. (Not least because at thirty-three a woman knew that the dreadful belief that it was possible to prolong this state forever was the most tormenting aspect of the illusion.) For days, or weeks, or months, as the case may be, Frederica thought, putting on a short white cotton nightdress, brushing her red hair, we do nothing without the accompanying image of the loved face, the imaginary limbs, and then, one day, we notice it's gone, there is no more, love is over. And what kills it? Often enough (she put out all the lights except the bedside lamp, she turned down the cover) a failure in oneself, or in the beloved, to conform to an ideal pattern put in the mind long before these particular two have met. I want a man who is stronger than I am, who will contain my anger and my folly and make me feel safe. He – John Ottokar – wishes to be such a strong man, but somehow we have arrived at a point where he needs *me* to reassure and to comfort him, and if I do this, it saps what I think of as Love, which is diminished to affection. (She stopped in front of the mirror and looked at her bony quick features, twisted her mouth in a grimace, touched her bright hair.) It is a dance. It has a formal pattern that friendships don't. It is a made-up story, *Love*. Something else, fiercer and harsher and hotter (Life?) needs us to believe in Love for purposes of its own, which are not ours. And we collude. She remembered playing the young Elizabeth I in the garden, the virgin queen whose power was the recognition that separateness and solitude were safety.

All a bit metaphysical, Frederica thought, waiting for the tap on the area window, from the basement steps down to the flat where she lived. All a defence against him not coming, which we always fear, even if really we are indifferent as to whether he comes or not.

But a month ago, six months ago, I wasn't thinking in language about what (if anything) is love. I was thinking about his mouth, and his arse, and his hands. People like me, who think too much, are so glad, so grateful, at least at first, to be overcome by thoughts of lips, hands and eyes.

And when the tap sounded, there was the usual tingle of terror as she went to look out. There was the mass of pale hair, the wide face, the tall body, the smile against glass.

The problem was, was this recognisable person a lover or an invader? With glass between, Frederica could not tell John from Paul. Sometimes she could not tell them apart without glass between, for brief moments, and sometimes, when Paul was clever, for longer. Paul made a third, visible or invisible, at their meetings, Paul dogged their footsteps when they went out and came in, the thought of Paul – because Paul chose that it should be so – mingled with the scent of sex in the bed, and swarmed in the quietness after.

They had secret signs, which they had instituted without ever discussing them, by which Frederica would know John was John and not Paul. He breathed on the glass now, and wrote in the mist a capital L, which Frederica knew was for Leo, not for Love.

It was probably only a matter of time before Paul, who had a cat-like capacity to creep up, detected this too, peering down through the railings. She opened the door, and John and the night air came in, and he opened his arms. And immediately she knew that he was someone, not her idea of her own lover, nor her *idea* of John Ottokar, but a complicated troubled breathing man, with ruffled hair and an erection. She closed the blind and with four quick hands they undressed him, and tumbled into the bed.

Later, they talked. Most of their talk was in darkness, because of John's work, and even more, because Frederica was fastidious about including him often, or much, in Leo's life. This was for all their sakes. Disaster (possibly) lurked if Leo became too attached, or too opposed, to John. It lurked if John found Leo a nuisance or a responsibility, it lurked if she herself didn't like the way the man spoke to the boy.

They had reached the stage (a beginning of an end?) where

much of what they said was repetition of what had been said before. John was a man of few words, diminishing to no words, in any case. His eloquence was an eloquence of finger-tips and tongue. And the new languages of the huge computers also, perhaps, Fortran and COBOL, but Frederica was mathematically illiterate.

This time, John said something new. He said that he had been offered a post in the University of North Yorkshire. Writing computer programs for the scientists. Running his own computer department.

Frederica said 'But that would mean living up there.'

'It would.'

Panic rose in her.

'When would you begin?' she asked, with exaggerated practical calm.

'I'd need to give three months' notice. They want someone right away.'

A primitive Frederica thought, he doesn't want me any more, he wants to leave me, he wants to end it. And her idea of his idea of an end made an end a disaster.

'We shan't see each other —' her reasonable voice said. He said simultaneously — it was not clear he heard her —

'It's a real step forward. An enormous amount more responsibility and space to have ideas of my own ...'

You are thinking of yourself, her mind snapped, but she didn't say. She repeated 'We shan't see each other.'

'Not like this. No. Is that too bad? Where are we going, Frederica?'

'Nowhere at all,' she did finally snap, 'if you go to the other end of the country, just like that.'

'I thought perhaps you wouldn't mind too much,' he said.

She could not think quickly enough of a truthful answer to this. Would she? At the moment she felt like an abandoned child in a forest. John Ottokar said in his hesitant, unused voice

'And if it turned out you did mind, we could work something out. You've got family up there. It's not an impossible place.'

'I *escaped* from it. I left the North. I live *here*.'

'Well then,' he said, peaceably, meaninglessly.

Frederica had an image of her several selves, the child, the woman, the mother, the lover, the solitary, tangled like coiling snakes in a clay pot, turmoiling. She said, changing tack

'I wondered if you wanted to come to the Science Museum with Leo and me on Sunday. You tell him things I can't –'

'I can't do that. There's a meeting of the Spirit's Tigers. Paul needs me to go.'

'Why does he always need *you*? He's got all those groups – the Tigers, his psychotherapy group, his Zag and the Syzygy Zy-goats, why does he always need *you*?'

'You know why. I'm the other half of the original group of two. You know that.'

This was part of their usual repeated talk, something they went over each time they met.

'No one appears to consider what *you* need. Not the Quakers, not the music-people, not even the psychoanalysts.'

'That's true. I'm the strong one, you see. Contrary to appearances, I'm the strong one.'

'That doesn't give them a right to see you in terms of *him*.'

'I see myself in terms of him, Frederica. I try not to, but I do. I always have. That's how it is.'

'I know.'

'If you don't want me to go to the UNY, I won't.'

'I don't have an opinion. Or a right to one. You must do what's best for you.'

They were not quarrelling, they were sad. John Ottokar gave up the effort of talking, touched her breast and her belly until she turned to him, and they made love again.

Frederica thought, the next day, this will all reduce itself to a few mnemonics. His face on the glass, an image I have of our four legs like two pairs of scissors. Why do I have to be *in* this hurt, when I'm not sure there's any real reason to be hurt, when I can imagine afterwards with clarity and probably accuracy?

Was the fact that she was put out an indication of Love, after all?

She thought of Leo. Another man's son, a man himself now partly reduced to manageable mnemonics. Also, her own son. She got on with Leo in her own odd way because she wasn't motherly. There wasn't an ounce of cuddle or home-making in her thin body. But the person she was recognised fiercely and absolutely the person he was, and respected him.

She thought, if she had to, she might even die for Leo. It was silly to think about that, it either happened or didn't. But the readiness was there, and surprised her.

II

Snails are best observed at dawn, after rain. The light on Gungingap Scar was full of water, trembling and iridescent. The valleys, like the fingers of a giant glove, which radiated out from Mimmer's Tarn were full of veils and scarves of wet mist, evaporating in twists and flourishes. Moving through this liquid atmosphere, the searchers – however well they knew the terrain – had a pleasant sense that the hills were flowing, changing shape like waves, that solid stones and wind-twisted hedges loomed suddenly out of wool or spume, where a moment before there had been nothing. The water-drops on thorns and thistles were glittering prisms, full of many-coloured lights. And across the wet turf, over the dry-stone walls, the snails slid fluently, creating an intricate net of silvery ribbons, their shells glistening with water, their dove-grey translucent bodies glistening with their own secretions, their fine horns wavering before them, testing the air, peering quietly around. Their shells were variegated and lovely, some a delicate lemon, some a deep rose, some a greenish soot-black, some striped boldly in dark spirals on buff, some with creamy spirals on rose, some with a single band of dark on gold, some like ghosts, greyish-white coiled on chalk-white. Most of these were *Cepea nemoralis* and had rich black lips, but some – not many – closely resembling the *nemoralis* in other ways, were white-lipped *Cepea hortensis*. Several also bore glossy blue, or green, or crimson dots on their shoulders, placed there by the latest group of researchers to track their movements and their fates.

The snail populations of Dun Vale Hall, and the surrounding moorland of the rich limestone of Gungingap, had been studied by several generations, beginning with a Victorian vicar, Richard Hunmanby, and an Edwardian schoolmaster and distinguished amateur conchologist, Joseph Mann. Luk Lysgaard-Peacock and

Jacqueline Winwar were attempting to study the population genetics and the biological diversity of the creatures who obligingly carried their histories, written like hieroglyphs, on the coiling, brittle houses on their backs. They compared the incidence of one, two and three stripes, of dark and light shells, with the records of their predecessors. In the days of Hunmanby and Mann, the snails had been known as *Helix,* not *Cepea, hortensis* or *nemoralis.* Hunmanby had been of the opinion that *nemoralis* and *hortensis* were distinct species. Mann was not sure. He had observed that the creatures lived together and intermingled, but had more than once observed large numbers of both kinds clustered, intertwined, high in the branches of beech-trees.

'My object in climbing amongst them – in the case of those individuals who were very high in the trees I used a pair of powerful field glasses, discretion being the better part of valour – was to ascertain whether matrimonial alliances between these two forms are usual or not. In one avenue of beech-trees, decked with shells, I counted sixty happy couples, twenty-five of which were *hortensis,* the rest *nemoralis.* In all my observations I saw no single instance of such cross-marriages – the "black-mouths" invariably paired with "black-mouths" and "white-mouths" with "white-mouths". There is also the smaller variety *H. hybrida,* smaller with a pink or brown mouth and rib, which I have never observed to mate at all.'

The object of Jacqueline Winwar's thesis – which was nearly completed – was to ascertain whether the changes in the populations – fewer striped shells, more single-coloured – were influenced more by heredity and Darwinian selection, or by immediate changes in the environment. Did woodland dappling favour stripes? What effect was the recent diminution in the thrush population having? Luk Lysgaard-Peacock's concerns with population genetics were larger and more varied, but his field-work with these snail populations had been continuous for some years now, and was beginning to show some interesting (if anomalous) patterns.

They worked well together, moving quietly across the wet ground, charting the numbers and positions of this and that colour and form. They worked at snail-level and snail-speed, interrogating tufts, turning over stones. Jacqueline stopped to count, to piece together, the smashed and picked-out shells by the thrush's anvil –

there was a preponderance of dark and striped, including several green-spots which had been marked not in the wood, but in the hedgerow between the field with the hen-houses and the open moor. Luk went on, into the field. And as the sun sucked up the mist and warmed the earth, he saw and smelled burning. Someone had made a huge, widespread fire against the wall, had scorched the whole field and burned deep into the wall and the earth. Fragments of charred, tarred planks were scattered round the edges of the conflagration. Luk lifted out two or three indistinguishable blackened shells, which crumbled in his fingers. It was a mess, whatever it had been for. It had happened just at the place in the wall where the snails particularly liked to congregate and hibernate. He had been studying them to see whether they came back to the same places. He called Jacqueline, who came up and stared.

Both of them saw the ash, the bubbled creosote, the scorched earth, as vandalism and desecration. They were accustomed to working inch by inch, and this conflagration had destroyed almost half a small field. Luk said

'That will skew all our results nicely.'

Jacqueline said 'It's absurd to grieve for a few snails.'

'There were a hell of a lot more than a few. In that particular wall.'

Jacqueline sat down on a rock. Luk put his arm round her shoulder. Jacqueline removed his arm, and took up her notebook. She began to make a drawing of the burned area. Luk looked up and saw someone in the distance, crossing the next field. This was a small woman, in breeches, accompanied by a black and white sheepdog, and a sheep. She walked with an unpractised limp. As she came nearer they could see that her face was badly bruised and her lips swollen. She was carrying a large basket of eggs, laid neatly in rows, but still with smears of blood and nest on them. She was Lucy Nighby, owner of Dun Vale Hall, and of the land they stood on.

'Dr Peacock. Jacquie. Morning.' Her voice was amiable.

Neither of them remarked on her injuries. Luk said

'You've made a hell of a mess of our research, with your bonfire.'

'That wasn't me. I helped of course, but that was Gunner. He's built a brand-new battery, where the water-meadow was, with corrugated walls. So we burned the old chicken-sheds. They were rotting. I didn't stop to think about the snails. There are snails all over the place, wherever, anyway, aren't there? I mean, not here more than anywhere else —'

'Well, as a matter of fact — because of the wall —'

'I'm so sorry. Anyway Gunner —'

She did not finish the sentence. There was no need. She called the dog, whose name was Shirley, and the sheep, whose name was Tobias. They trotted up together. She said 'You get a lot of eggs, in a battery.' Her eyelid was rapidly swelling round her eye so that she appeared to be winking. This prevented Jacqueline from saying anything about hens in batteries. Lucy said, a little grimly, 'You could call Gunner an act of God, I dare say, in your researches.'

'I'd rather have live snails,' said Luk.

'Acts of God don't care what you'd rather have, that's what I mean,' said Lucy Nighby and went on her way towards the Hall. The Hall stood in the pocket of the longest finger of the glove, next to Mimmer's Tarn, dark and deep, with a reedy shore. Lucy had been born Lucy Holdsworth and had inherited the Hall. She had married Gunner, who came from a seafaring family from Staithes, north of Whitby, when he came to help to manage the riding stables she was trying to run. He now managed the farm, which was mostly moorland sheep, with some hens, ducks and geese. Recently he had installed turkey pens like penitentiaries. They rented out ponies for excursions. Thin ponies. Lucy was a thin woman, faded fair. There were three children, Carla, Ellis and Annie.

'Sometimes,' said Luk, 'I think this whole project is going to be inconclusive.'

'Well — it can only be open-ended, unless someone slaughters *all* the snails with a nuclear bomb or something.'

'Your thesis data are collected anyway.'

'I know. I've been thinking —'

Luk's hand still remembered her firm fingers, patting him away.

'I've decided to ask Lyon Bowman if he'll take me on as a researcher. I want to do hard science. I want to study the physiology of memory. I thought you could work on snails' giant neurones — studying conduction — I want to do something *very precise*, like that.'

'I see. Why?'

'I don't exactly know why. I just know that that's what I have to do. Why is something to do with Konrad Lorenz. Or at least, it came together in my mind when I was reading him. His defence of the idea of instinct, against modern ideas that everything is a product of environment — of nurture — not of inherent reflexes. And I wanted to be part of that, of looking into that. And he wrote — I read — that we have "*an absolute ignorance of the physiological mechanisms underlying learning*". And I thought, that's it, that's the next thing. And Bowman's done all that good work on pigeon-vision . . .'

'That sounds all right to me,' said Luk. 'He's not a nice man.'

'That doesn't matter.'

'It does. It always does. It always has to be taken into account. I shall miss you.'

'Miss me? I'll still come out and follow the snails —'

'There are things I want to say.'

'Don't.'

'You can't say *don't*, until you've heard what I have to say —'

'I can, I can. Don't. Let's just go on, as we are.'

Luk put out a hand. Jacqueline backed away, a little, made the gap between her body and his reach just that bit too great. It was the reverse of a mating dance, he reflected, it was a ritual move of avoidance, perfected by her, recognised by him. He thought of Lorenz's studies of the behaviour of other creatures. Most unreceptive females bit, or scratched or snarled. This one just took a step or two out of reach. The signs were quite clear. She did not want him. What puzzled him as a scientist, given the unambiguous clarity of her discreet messages, was how much he wanted her.

She bent down again, to her notebook, making a precise drawing of the scorched earth. Luk stood by the wall, and stared out over the moorland. You could turn yourself, he often thought, into a kind of scientific experiment on love, or desire, gone wrong. A scientific explanation of his own behaviour would be that males of similar species — baboons, apes — thought of little but sex and competition, were driven to collect and compel. But then, that didn't explain his own certainty that Jacqueline was *the one* for him, his own inability to make a rational decision to find another, more compliant, more receptive woman. He had known almost the moment he saw her that she was the one, though she was then only just out of girlhood, neat and unexceptional. He wondered if the mechanisms were akin to imprinting. You could receive a wave of a pheromone that sent you mad with desire, but it didn't put you into a state of hopeless waiting for year after year? He thought about swan chicks emerging from the shell to suppose a goose, or a duck, or a luggage-trolley with a honker, were their parent.

He considered Lucy Nighby's sheep, Tobias, which she had hand-reared, who certainly considered himself to be something between a human and a sheepdog. But human beings who went in for hopeless love usually fell into it when they were reasonably independent beings. Maybe there was some primitive brain-cell waiting to be fired by a face, or the sight of haunches, or the cadence of a voice, which was already imprinted from birth, and waiting to be triggered? Jacqueline's movements were quick and neat, her brown gaze direct and lively, but she was not Helen of Troy, she was no queen who drew the males of the species like honey or violet light drew moths. Indeed, her only other suitor appeared to be rather half-hearted, rather self-contained, exhibiting a nervous male version of what Luk had just characterised as the ritual move of avoidance. Jacqueline had 'always' been attached to Marcus Potter, since before he, Luk, had known her. Marcus looked vaguely, Luk thought uncharitably, as though he needed a woman to make sure his shirt was buttoned on the right buttons, and his socks matched. Vague and thin and pale. It was impossible to imagine him, in bed, doing more than *poke* feebly and blindly. He did not believe Jacqueline was a virgin but he didn't believe she slept with Marcus Potter. Another mystery. On the other hand, she *looked at him* tenderly, or hopefully . . .

Another curiosity about unsuccessful love was the way it set itself against reason – the reasoned observation of instinctual behaviour, that was – by waiting patiently for a change in circumstances. Luk had not observed many cases – he was not sure he had observed *any* – of the objects of hopeless passions suddenly doing a *volte-face* and learning to love the rejected. He had observed one or two cases of sad and resigned decisions to accept second-best (both by men and by women) which had more or less worked, but left whole areas of the fiercest, secret selves of lover and beloved forever closed away, inert. And how did he know all that? Because he watched. You could do experiments in human love, as you could in the choices of apes or rabbits, tomtits or red deer. You could infect or inoculate yourself with various strains of it (once you understood how it 'took') as doctors did who were their own experimental subjects for vaccines. Did he want to be cured? No, he wanted Jacqueline. He observed wryly that both pure reason and the instinct of blind self-preservation (to say nothing of the need to spread his seed to become an ancestor) required him to give up this clearly futile pursuit. The sun rose higher over the moortops, and Luk looked at Jacqueline, crouched in burned grass and heather, with love.

Jacqueline tried to concentrate on her drawing. She did not like upsetting people. Luk most of all. This thought was, however, peripheral to her concentration on the idea of electrical conduction and practical ways of examining the activities of giant neurones. Jacqueline Winwar, like Frederica Potter, was an ambitious woman. But she had come upon her own ambition almost casually, as one thing led to another. She had grown up in a suburb of Calverley, with a pharmacist father and an infant-teacher mother, who had been pleased that she did so well at school, but had never said to her 'you will go to a good university', let alone 'you will be a scientist' or 'you will make discoveries.' Nature studies had seemed wholesome, and Jacqueline's ability to throw herself into them showed she had a nice, uncomplicated, enthusiastic nature. Jacqueline's parents, and Jacqueline, supposed that these were interesting hobbies. They assumed that she would marry, and bear children, and the hobbies would come in useful for teaching the children about the world, keeping them occupied. Jacqueline, unlike Frederica, was not always top of the class, and did not expect to be. But she did well, and it became clear that she must go to university – the school expected it, and by then a certain blindly-working greed for knowledge in Jacqueline required it.

She still had a conventional vision of herself, some day or other, meeting the 'right man' and being joined to him in a flurry of white veiling and organ music. In the interim, she had various student affairs – partly at least out of physiological curiosity, partly also because she wished to do what was expected – and continued her desultory but deeply rooted connection to Marcus Potter, with whom she did not sleep, and towards whom she felt an exasperated maternal responsibility combined with a complete respect for his closed-off, humming mathematical mind. Marcus was not quite of this world, not quite real, and Jacqueline, as she began to understand the extent of her own ambitions, began to suspect that she had chosen him for this reason. He was so clearly an impossible candidate for the orange blossoms, veilings, and organ, let alone for tenderly cooked little dinners by candle-light, or electric brushings of naked skin in the bathroom, that it was possible for her to go on working, to put her exams, her thesis, the snails, and now the physiology of memory first, without thinking of herself as a freak. She needed to appear unobtrusive and ordinary. She did not even have to think about that. You got on better (at least if you were a woman) if no one noticed you.

Frederica the schoolgirl had known she would be *someone*, had known eyes would be on her, fame would touch her, people would know who she was when she walked down a street. She had wanted everything – love, sex, the life of the mind. She had tried marriage, and had Leo, and made a small living as best she might. Jacqueline thought of herself as a lesser, more shadowy being than Marcus's brilliant sister. But she was beginning to recognise the inexorable force of her own curiosity, her desire to know the next thing, and then the next, and then the next. It lived in her like a bright dragon in a cave, it had to be fed, it must not be denied, it would destroy her if she did not feed it . . . The next thing was to explain as much as was necessary of all this to Lyon Bowman. She wanted to say to Luk 'you are too good for me, I won't ever give you enough attention.' But she knew that silence was better. Luk, she thought hopefully, would transfer all that to someone else, and then they could go on comfortably.

Luk had a repeating dream about Jacqueline. In it she was – some of the time – a brown bird. Most often, she was a bird of that wonderful dusky, brown-black of female blackbirds, and had a sharp gold beak, and gold eyes where her own were brown. Often this bird was more the size of a large pheasant than that of a blackbird, proud and quick. It would appear amongst the *Cepea nemoralis* where he had been expecting to see the woman, and would busy itself with gathering the shells and piling them on the anvil-stone. He would know (it was a simple dream) that he should not creep up on it, and yet would, and it would watch him, its dark feathered head on one side, its gold beak glittering. Sometimes, not often, it would extract the snails from the shells, and they would dangle, squirming and stretching, from the bill. Once he closed his hands round it, and for a moment it seemed almost to nestle there, warm and feathery. Then he felt its heart go faster and faster, and knew he must let go or kill it, and woke, in the sweat of the decision. It was a very simple dream, he considered. But that wasn't the point, it couldn't be reduced to its simple meaning. The brown feathers, the watchfulness, the fine twig-legs, the rapid thrum of the over-excited tiny heart changed him, changed her in him. He thought scientifically about this, too. When she got into the memory-stores of the brain would she find how a woman can become a bird in the skull of a sleeping man?

III

The Vice-Chancellor was up early, as usual. He sat behind his vast desk (he was an abnormally tall man, nearly 6 feet 5 inches) and looked out at what he thought of as 'his' lawn, knowing it was not. His Lodgings were in one corner of the ground floor of Long Royston Hall, the Elizabethan house given to the new university by its owner, Matthew Crowe, who still inhabited part of it. From one window Sir Gerard Wijnnobel could see the formal terrace where Frederica, in shift and farthingale, had strutted as the young Elizabeth, in Alexander Wedderburn's *Astraea*, in 1953. From another, beyond the yew hedge which bordered 'his' garden, were grassy slopes and the towers of the University, connected by walkways, plazas, and little canals. He could see the Evolution Tower, a spiral of glass and steel, and the Language Tower, a modified ziggurat, in brick.

He was planning a conference on Body and Mind. His desk was covered with neat lists of possible speakers (and listeners). His mind drove towards inclusiveness. There would be linguists, philosophers, biologists, mathematicians, sociologists, medical men. There would have to be physicists, there would have to be discussion of the way modern physics saw the observer affecting – changing – the observed. Embryologists, psychologists, psycho-analysts, Freudian, Jungian, Kleinian. He smiled at himself. He was desiring a biological-cognitive Theory of Everything, which would not be even remotely possible in his life-time. He supposed he must also include students of religion. He was descended from theologians, Dutch Calvinist and Jewish. He had been in his time both a distinguished mathematician and an innovatory grammar-ian. He believed strongly that universities should be what their name implied, places for the study of everything. He had, with passion, cunning, and meticulous determination, constructed a revolutionary syllabus for his institution, which required *all* students to study some science, more than one language, an art form.

Probably there should be artists also at the conference. But for the most part, they talked badly, they explained themselves foolishly and inadequately.

Not that he did not care about art. Across the lawn, which was mazed with shining spider-threads and brilliant with dew, was his Hepworth (purchased by the University, at his instigation). It was a large, pierced white oval stone, strung with crossing wires. He saw the shadow of the threads on the glimmer of the stone, the yew-dark through its centre. He had known Hepworth in Hampstead, in 1938, when he had just arrived from Holland, braced for the war to come. They had talked maths. She had described to him the interest of pierced forms, the way the hole incorporated air and light in the solid stone. She described the sensuous pleasure of working hand and arm into and through a spiralling tunnel.

He saw also a few white fantail pigeons, at the base of the plinth, their breasts pleasantly and fortuitously echoing the curve of the marble. Then he saw his wife's Abyssinian cat, Bastet, a brindled shadow lurking under lupins. The pigeons took fright and went up. He loved to see them fly and tumble. He loved the light through the creamy-white of their tailfeathers. Those that were left were canny and hardened. They were fit survivors. Bastet had regularly found and devoured their squabs.

He kept his books elsewhere. In his study were his Rembrandt etchings and his Mondrians. Some of the Rembrandts had come with him from Holland, and others he had bought after the war, when they could still be had very cheaply. He specialised in single figures meditating in profound shadows – old men with fine beards, lined and composed old women. His favourite, perhaps, was 'Student at a table by candlelight', with a pit of darkness and a bright small flame. He had Rembrandt's only etched still life, a conical shell, *Conus marmorens*, its spiral closest to the onlooker's eye, its surface patterned like a dark net thrown over bone. He also had a copy of a work known as 'Faust in his study'. The old man in his cap looked through gloom at a lit window, where a mystic hand pointed. It pointed at a floating apparition of three concentric circles, scattering brightness. The inmost one was crossed with the Christian INRI in its segments. On the outer ones was written

+ ADAM + TE + DAGERAM + ARMTET + ALGAR + ALGASTNA ++

No one had ever explained this writing. Wijnnobel's cabbalist grandfather had tried and been baffled, like the rest. He himself had an idea about it, from time to time, but they never worked.

Mondrian, too, had been in Hampstead in 1938 and 1939, painting severe black and white grids with discrete peripheral rectangles of red, yellow and blue. Mondrian believed that everything – the sum of things – could be represented by these three colours, with black, white and grey, within the intersections of verticals and horizontals. The colours were signs, denoting all the colour in the world, symbolising everything, purple, gold, indigo, flame, blood, earth, ultramarine, even green, which Mondrian could not bear to look at. The straight lines represented the refinement of spiritual vision. They were the intersection of the infinite flat horizon, and the infinite vertical, travelling away from earth into the source of light. They avoided the tragic capriciousness of the dreadfully particular curves of flesh, or even of the changing moon. The vertical line was taut, and was the tension in all things. The horizontal line was weight and gravity. The figure of the Cross was the meeting of vertical and horizontal, an intrinsic form of the spirit. The movement of waves on the sea, the form of the starry sky, could be represented with patterns of little crossings. Diagonals, according to Mondrian, were not essentially abstract, and should be eschewed. He had had trouble stabilising the chemistry of his red, and had in fact changed it often. Wijnnobel thought this system was mad in its man-made purity, and yet found it endlessly beautiful in its own implacable terms. There were many triads of 'primary' colours, of which, for historical reasons, Mondrian had picked one. It was one vision of necessity, of the building blocks of the universe. A theory of everything.

Also, like the Rembrandts, it represented his country in his own mind. A kind of stubborn plainness and exactness, shot through with spiritual extremity. The English amongst whom he lived, were averse to extremes. He respected that, but he knew there was danger, as well as power, in their unawareness. He liked Yorkshire, he felt at home here, because it resembled his own land in some ways. But there were differences.

★

Vincent Hodgkiss, who was Dean of Students, arrived at 9.00 to discuss various matters, including the Body–Mind Conference. ('There should be a more elegant name,' he said. Wijnnobel replied that this one was accurate.) Hodgkiss was a philosopher, a student of Wittgenstein. Wijnnobel admired him because he worked on Wittgenstein's maths as well as his ideas of language. He was a square-shouldered, spectacled man, balding slowly, who spoke little and carefully. They discussed the form and the composition of the conference. Wijnnobel said he had given further thought to the 'star' speakers – *primi inter pares* – and had two names to put before Hodgkiss. 'In your capacity as Dean of Students, as well as in your Conference capacity.'

'I thought,' said Wijnnobel 'that we could create a historic encounter – a historic debate – between Hodder Pinsky and Theobald Eichenbaum.'

Pinsky was quite young, American, and called his discipline cognitive psycho-linguistics. He used computers to explore what he believed to be the deep and universal structures of linguistic competence. Eichenbaum was elderly, German and called himself an ethologist. He had made delicate studies of imprinting in young dogs, foxes and wolves, had worked on the group behaviour of rats-nests, wolf-packs and shoaling fish. The two shared a belief that certain biological structures were innate, but differed as to what these were, and as to the nature of the learning process, and the growth-patterns of human and other societies. Eichenbaum was suspect because his past was cloudy with compromises with Fascism (he had continued to teach in the Schwarzwald throughout the war and had uncompromising ideas about the survival of the fittest). Pinsky's politics were democratic – he was a regular presence at the ceremonial burning of draft-papers (not his own, for he was almost blind) and aligned himself with those who wanted to rewrite the constitutions of the universities and jettison much of the accumulated intellectual junk in them. Everything could, in his view, be put together again from scratch, gleaming and almost infinitely improved. Eichenbaum, on the other hand, quoted with approval Konrad Lorenz's dictum that it takes only two generations to kill a culture that has taken centuries to evolve.

It was difficult to imagine them liking each other. Vincent Hodgkiss said that it was also possible that the students would demonstrate against both of them. Eichenbaum because of what his politics were thought to be, and Pinsky, whose politics were impeccable, because of his uncompromising stand about innate intelligence. He said that he'd been informed that there were students visiting the campus who were not students of the University, but veterans of the Paris protests and the Anti-University.

Wijnnobel said an Anti-University sounded interesting.

'Well, *in principle*, yes,' said Hodgkiss. 'In practice, I believe it is somewhat disorderly and confusing.'

'Do we know,' Hodgkiss asked 'if either Pinsky or Eichenbaum would be interested in coming?'

'I took the liberty of writing to both,' said Wijnnobel. 'Both were intrigued but cautious. I have their letters, here . . .'

He was searching as he spoke in the wire tray on his desk. The papers in it were neatly piled, but as he turned them, his fingers became sticky and blackened. It became clear that the pages had been layered with a kind of oozing black pitch. They came up together, and dripped. Vincent Hodgkiss watched Wijnnobel try to prise the papers apart. He offered to help. Wijnnobel laid one illegible page on his blotter. 'How very odd,' said Hodgkiss in his Oxford voice, which some of the northerners found affected. 'What can have happened?'

Wijnnobel detached another two illegible pages.

'It looks quite deliberate,' said Hodgkiss, consumed now by pure curiosity. 'Do we have a student trickster . . .'

'I don't think so,' said Wijnnobel. 'I fear I know the perpetrator. Do not bother yourself with the matter.'

He tapped his black fingertips on the blotter. His face was expressionless. Hodgkiss watched the fastidious fingers detach another illegible paper. He offered a paper handkerchief.

'I hope none of this was of great importance.'

'Some was, some was not. Some personal letters. Pinsky's latest paper.'

He leaned over to put an envelope in the waste basket. Its black contents had been carefully smoothed and arranged in a pointlessly orderly pile, pinned together with a kitchen skewer.

'Witchcraft?'

'Not exactly. Shall we say, a barbed joke? Please forget this matter. I assure you it is my problem.'

'Certainly,' said Hodgkiss.

When Hodgkiss had left, Wijnnobel went to look for his wife. The messages were from her. They were not the first, and would not be the last. Every now and then they preceded acts of greater violence. The waste paper was frequent and therefore normal. 'I have read your letters,' the message ran. '*I know.*' The pitch, or whatever it was, was new. When his work was hurt, it was serious.

He found her in the guests' cloakroom, a room with rose-pink curtains and wallpaper sprigged with unreal Jacobean flowers, in pretty pinks, golds and terracotta. She was standing on the closed lavatory, holding a dripping paintbrush. Beside her was one of the Lodgings' genuine Jacobean chairs on which stood a large can of thick black paint. She had painted two walls and most of the ceiling. There were smears of black paint on the carpet, and a ghostly black naked footprint. She was wearing a shapeless black cotton dress and over it a white, vaguely medical overall, smeared also with black paint. She was a large, heavy woman with dark hair, cut with a square fringe, like an Egyptian painting. She wore gold charm bracelets, on each wrist. On the part of the ceiling which had dried, she had fixed little fluorescent stars, in a pattern. Gerard Wijnnobel worked out that it was the constellation of Scorpio. He stooped in the low doorway.

'What are you doing, Eva?'

'You can see what I am doing. Brightening things. Taking them and cutting them out in little stars. Bringing this mausoleum into the real world.'

'Black is not brightening, Eva,' said Wijnnobel, foolishly and reasonably.

'It is modern, I think, and stylish. I am making a dazzling darkness. I shall put stars all over, over all of it. Cancer here, and Capricorn there. And Aries over the cistern. No one will have anything like it. I am using the few talents I have, for the benefit of this place, which is where I live, indeed where I am the mistress. I thought,' she said, staring at him with large multi-coloured eyes, gold and brown, 'that you would be pleased that I had found something creative to do with my time.'

It was always just possible that she really meant what she said.

'I think there are — I think this is a listed house — I think there are things we may and may not do in its rooms —'

'I live here. When I am dead, it will be a matter of a few hours to restore the soulless chintz. I have to live here, Gerard. I would like there to be meaning, even in the bog.'

She made a sweep with the brush. She said 'I dreamed of a cavern with the starry heavens for its only ceiling.' She had a heavy mouth, that went down, sadly, at the corners. She said

'You are a person of no imagination, Gerard, a person with a closed soul.'

'Maybe,' said the Vice-Chancellor.

'Love has made his mansion in the place of excrement,' said Eva Wijnnobel. She looked to see the effect of this on him, and a flicker of calculation passed across her face. 'Have you had breakfast, my dear? I quite forgot breakfast. We could take it together, and then you could return to your important papers and I to my decorative task.'

Wijnnobel had had breakfast, but said he had not. He took her hand, and helped her down from the pedestal. Her brush flicked black across his pale blue tie. They went together into the dining-room, where Lady Wijnnobel began to slice wedges of toast too thick for the toaster, humming to herself. There was congealing bacon, in a chafing-dish. Lady Wijnnobel's dogs, two border collies named Odin and Frigg, shimmied in, agitating their sterns.

'Ask Daddy for some bacon-rind,' said Eva Wijnnobel to Odin, who was wall-eyed like his namesake, with one eye blue and dead, one brown and calculating. Odin was grey-blue and golden, with white ruff and plumed tail. Frigg was black and white. Both were fat, and had the ingratiating squirm of outdoor dogs compelled to sit around in houses. 'Mummy hasn't forgotten you,' said Eva Wijnnobel, handing them bacon and squares of fried bread. 'There ought to have been nice fat kidneys for you. I must speak to the cook.'

'You should take them for a long walk, Eva,' said Gerard Wijnnobel. 'Those sorts of dogs need exercise.'

'I know, dear. You are always telling me. I am always trailing up and down with them. All the time. I know about dogs, don't I, my darlings?'

Odin grimaced. Frigg abased herself. Gerard Wijnnobel sipped black coffee. He knew she had not been out with the dogs and would not go out. He believed that all this – stars, paint, dogs, the ravenous dove-destroying Abyssinian cat, Bastet – was his fault. He had no idea what to do. He was, in this, entirely dependent on the kindness of others, a housekeeper, a secretary, a doctor. He decided it might be possible to live with a black, starry cloakroom. He would ask the housekeeper to remove the antique chair, tactfully. To clean the carpet. Perhaps even to consult Lady Wijnnobel about a replacement carpet, more in keeping with black walls.

He had met Eva Selkett during the war, during his time at Bletchley. He was thirty-four and had had one love-affair, with a Dutch Jewish art historian, who had been shot in Amsterdam. Eva was twenty-four, a stenographer. She came from an English family that had been settled in Alexandria, she said. She said she was an Egyptologist, and had written a thesis on hieroglyphs, this was how she had come to be working with the code-breakers. She said that this research had been done in Oxford, and then said that she had given the wrong impression and she was about to take up a place in Oxford when the war broke out, her serious research had been done in Alexandria. In 1942 and 1943 she was beautiful, with a great mass of dark hair rolled over her brow, and another rolled under, along her shoulders. She said very little, and gave the impression of sadness and private withdrawal. Bit by bit, she revealed that all her family had died in the German invasion; that she had also lost a lover; that she had been very ill, but was now better. She listened, when he took her out to dinner, occasionally offering an enigmatic and appropriate quotation. She quoted Yeats and Vaughan, Jung and Hermes Trismegistus. Wijnnobel was naturally a sparse talker, but in those days he talked to her, over dinner, over warm English beer, sitting by their bicycles in a field, listening to the planes go over. He told her briefly about Liliane. He talked to her about Mondrian, Hepworth, Gabo, the spiritual meanings of horizontals and verticals. She spoke – quietly and cogently – about number symbolism and spiritual forms. It was in the air, amongst the code-breakers, the Platonic world of pure maths. He was awkward with women, because of his height. He was afraid of her creamy beauty. One day, as they leaned on a gate, she took his hand, gravely, and put it on her breast, over her cotton shirt. She said, a week or two later, 'When we are married we will have a dovecote, and doves.' The future seemed brief, in those days. He wanted children. He wanted to lose himself in the curves of that warm skin. They married quickly – there was no family to invite, or so he thought. Later he discovered that Eva's orphaned state, like her degree in Egyptology, was not what it seemed. They had a honeymoon in a country farmhouse in Oxfordshire.

He knew quickly that he was disappointed – he did not then say, deceived. He tried to overcome his disappointment. After the war, he had university posts in Durham and London. He worked. Eva grew fat. He hoped, once or twice, that she might be growing heavier because she was pregnant, but no children came. He retreated into Fibonacci spirals and a study of word order in sentences in several languages. Eva in a white nightgown walked out of an upper window in Durham and crashed through an apple-tree, breaking her wrist and her nose. She was, she said, the scorpion goddess, Selket. She was also drunk. She was also sick. Remedies were tried – a Jungian analysis, group healing sessions at Cedar Mount, periods in nursing homes. She told anyone who cared to hear that she was a sacrificial victim of her husband's ambition, his self-absorption, his worldly success. She told everyone that he had mistresses in foreign parts. In his Calvinist soul Gerard Wijnnobel believed her, even though his reasonable mind could put the contrary case with his usual clarity.

★

Another man, not far away, sat on the edge of his bed in Cedar Mount and tried to make plans. He was supposed to be in the Association Room. It was thought desirable that those who were able should associate in groups. He was due for an interview, an assessment, with the psychiatrist, Dr Kieran Quarrell. These were rare and had to be made the most of.

He watched the blood run down the walls and seep up mildly round the edges of the linoleum. It was clear red blood this morning. It burst through the wall-covering – washable vinyl, with a cheerful pattern of two-dimensional sunflowers – in small bright gouts and bubbles. From there it descended in trickles, which joined to form a clear red sheet towards the base of the wall. Round its edges, as sheets of blood do, it coagulated and browned. Round the edges of the linoleum it pulsed a little, as though some system of veins under the floorboards were pumping it out. He watched it soak into someone's white sock that had been left lying around. He felt calm. The blood, that morning, was an interesting phenomenon. He would have liked to discuss it with someone. Was it there or not there? He was certainly seeing it – with his eyes – noting its viscosity and flow. He was not making it up. It wasn't a projection of his state of mind, which was calm, not bloody. It was not a metaphor.

On the other hand, he was almost entirely certain that if he picked up the soaked sock, it would be white wool, and would not drip red. In certain *hectic* moods, he saw blood falling through the air itself, in sheets, like rain. Then sometimes he lost, lost, lost his head a bit, lost what the male nurses called his cool.

He thought, if he failed to mention the blood – and he was under no obligation to mention or not to mention things – then he might talk himself out of there, out through the gates of the enclosure. He was almost entirely sure he wanted to get out. His life had a purpose. It was meant to flow on, towards its goal, not to eddy round this anchored bed. An obligation was laid upon him, to *live* his life, which he was not doing. Those who spoke to him explained that, not entirely patiently, over and over. The voices, like the blood, were *there* and he himself did not produce or control them. They were different from the hum of chatter in the Association Room. They were not in his head. He listened to them. He knew no one else heard them.

He had hidden his pill in his shoe. A clear head was required. His head was old and young. His hair was a bright white mass. His beard bristled brindled, black and fiery, with touches of steel. He was a big man. He sat quietly on the edge of the bed, and waited, and watched the blood.

IV

Frederica gave up teaching because she wanted to teach. All that summer in 1968, the students marched and held meetings, made banners and discussed the nature of things. They barricaded the administrative offices. They wrote long documents with endless clauses, demanding both to be released from the oppression of imposed ideas and establishment-structured concepts, and to be better prepared for the 'total environment' they were to enter. 'Total environment' meant the world of employment. The art students at the Samuel Palmer School were particularly hostile to the newly-introduced courses of Liberal Studies, which included Frederica's literature, as well as some philosophy, sociology and psychology. A note was pushed under the door of the Liberal Studies Office. 'We Demand that courses in Literature and Philosophy be made *conceptually relevant* to Jewellery Design.'

The past was to be abolished. Someone put all Alan Melville's Vermeer slides in a bath of acid, and displayed them with a notice 'The Lady Vanishes'. Richmond Bly, the head of Liberal Studies, and a Blake enthusiast, was very much on the side of the students. At a passionate 36-hour meeting, in which he urged the students to become Tigers of Wrath and do away with the Horses of Instruction, he agreed that there should be no more authoritarian lectures, that all meetings of students and teachers should be open-ended explorations, or interchanges, and that difficult and irrelevant things like Frederica's classes in Metaphysical Poetry should be abolished. Frederica's classes in contemporary fiction became a series of repetitive attempts to find out the first principles of why art students should bother themselves with literature at all. Frederica had no answer. It was clear to her that it was better to be interested in things than not interested in them, and that included literature, as it might have included botany or nuclear fission. But she found it increasingly difficult to retain her own interest in the transient phenomenon of being a student, especially a student who didn't study, but talked and talked. She suggested that the contemporary fiction class agree a topic on contemporary fiction and discuss it. Someone proposed *Lady Chatterley's Lover*. After lengthy debate this proposal was adopted. The seminar took place. Frederica sat at the back, in a non-authoritarian position. No one spoke. No one spoke. Frederica asked if anyone had read *Lady Chatterley's Lover*. No one had, or no one would admit it. Frederica stood up. She said 'If I had lectured on this book, I should have learned something. One or two of you might have learned something. As it is, we breathe a bit, and it gets to be lunch time. I have my life to live. I'm going.'

She glared at them. They stared back, critical and recalcitrant. She walked out. She walked along the corridor, and tapped on the door of Richmond Bly's office.

'More trouble?' he said, with a kind of pleasure, sensing the electric field of Frederica's rage.

'Not really. I want to resign. As of now.'

'You don't want to be too rigid, Frederica. These are exciting times. You don't want to be hide-bound and *old*. There's a lot to learn from the passion of these young people.'

'Yes,' said Frederica. 'But not the things *I* want to learn, that's the point. I'm in the wrong place, at the wrong time. OK, I accept what you say, I'm too old to be here. Who the hell wants to be twenty forever? I need to *learn* something, and it isn't how to be a Student.'

'OK,' said Bly, equably. 'As of now?'

'As of now.'

Why? she wondered later. It was true that she wanted to learn something, to *think*, and it was true that she was a good teacher because she was more interested in the books she taught than in the students who listened – which is not to say that she wasn't interested in the students, only that she had her priorities. It was also true that she had no idea *what* she wanted to do. There was the projected thesis on metaphor, impossible now – she would never get a research grant as a single woman with a small child. She envied Agatha, who had a career and made real decisions that changed people's lives. But Agatha had said, once, that she felt that she was becoming her job, that a civil servant was what she *was*, whether she liked it or not, which she wasn't sure about. Agatha was defined. She herself – though still undoubtedly in her own mind, and in other people's, 'brilliant' – was somehow a scrappy structure lacking outline and architecture. She considered her options. She had to, there was the problem of no money, and perhaps she had meant to drive herself to action by creating a financial crisis where there had been a bare sufficiency. Like most freelance persons she had become addicted to opening envelopes containing cheques. Cheques from newspapers for small reviews. Cheques from Rupert Parrott for reading the slush heap of Bowers & Eden. Cheques for extra-mural teaching. Pink cheques, grey cheques, duck-egg blue cheques for £3.7.6d or £1.12.7½d meaning trousers for Leo, a pair of tights, an Iris Murdoch novel, washing-up liquid, apples, roses, wine.

So, how to replace the art school cheques? What did people do? She asked her friends Tony Watson, who had his own column now in the *New Statesman*, and Alan Melville. Tony said he would talk to the editor. Alan said he was entirely with her in her decision but couldn't help. She talked to Hugh Pink, the poet, who worked part-time for Bowers & Eden. Hugh said there were almost no women in publishing, though there were women *authors*, he had always supposed she would eventually be a writer. Frederica said that the writer in the house was Agatha Mond, and she wanted Hugh to get Agatha to send the fairy story to Rupert Parrott. 'Now it's come to an end,' said Frederica. 'Then she'll have to write a sequel. Saskia and Leo are languishing. I can't write a fairy story for them. I appear not to be a writer.'

'You do write,' said Hugh. 'I saw.'

'That's not writing, that's a game,' said Frederica. She was defensive.

Hugh was the only person to whom Frederica had shown her book of jottings, cut-ups, commonplaces and scraps of writing, which she called *Laminations*. She had only shown him certain bits, as illustrations of jokes or literary points.

'It's a contemporary game,' said Hugh. 'Like Burroughs and Jeff Nuttall, only quite different, of course, because it's you.'

'It's got intimate bits in, bits of me. Only a few lines long.' She didn't show him those bits.

She had had the word, *Laminations*, before the object. It referred to her attempts to live her life in separated strata, which did not run into each other. Sex, literature, the kitchen, teaching, the newspaper, *objets trouvés*. She did not put Leo into *Laminations*, not because he was not part of her fragmentary life, but because he was not fragmented. Lately, however, she had begun to put in odd passages from the books with which she was trying to teach him, too late, to read. How do you interest a boy with the vocabulary of a sophisticated adolescent in Daddy cleaning the car and Mummy making cakes?

She took the exercise books out of her desk and showed them to Hugh. Her last entry was a collection of graffiti from the Samuel Palmer School.

> *Turn on, tune in, drop out.*
> *Art is Orgasm which blasts away Civic Walls and Bourgeois Frames and BURSTS OPEN the locks and chains of Capital.*
> *Student-networks for relevance to the total environment.*
> *Teaching is oppression.*
> *We Demand you make Literature more relevant to Jewellery Design.*
> *Shut up and listen for a change.*
> *Use pricks and cunts not brains. Use tongues for Human Delight not syllabubbles.*
> *Prescribe mushrooms not Shakespeare Texts. Learn folly to be wise.*
> *Paint all the walls every day with everything that comes to hand.*

Hugh flicked back through the pages. Frederica hovered nervously. He laughed. He smiled. He noted the cut-ups of Lawrence and Forster. 'And those are the cut-up letters from my ex-husband's solicitor.'

'It's like a private I Ching,' said Hugh. 'Well, not private. A particular, an individual I Ching. Can I show it to Rupert?'

'It isn't finished.'

'That's its nature.'

Frederica gave in. Hugh was part of her laminated system. He was a friend, in many ways *the* friend, as far as writing and reading went. It was important that he should never be confused with possible lovers. He had not always quite seen it that way himself. Frederica thought, thinking about not thinking about sex, about John Ottokar. Who had accepted the Yorkshire job, starting in the autumn term.

★

The person who produced real work, real cheques, for Frederica, turned out to be Edmund Wilkie.

Wilkie, who was still professionally interested in the activities of the brain, and the nature of perception, had somehow also managed to become part of the then small, curiously open and anarchic world of BBC Television. People had good ideas (and bad ideas) and put them into practice, without too much bureaucratic consultation. One of the series he had inaugurated was a kind of literary guessing-game called *Gobbets*. The idea was simple. Four guessers, a chairman and an actor sat round (or along) a table. The actor read out quotations and the guessers guessed where they came from. At the time, many people assumed that this was the way television would go, or one of the ways – civilised, after-dinner mind-flexing, the reader's version of snooker or tennis. Frederica didn't have a television. She was beginning to see that this was an impossible state of affairs, for Leo wept with rage that his friends could see *Batman* and *Dr Who*, and he could not. She was not unusual in this. She did not consider television to be *important*, despite her journalist friend Tony Watson's excited speeches on how all elections from henceforth would be won and lost on the small screen. She had a vague idea that it was sinful to spend one's evenings passively staring, whether at news, satire, discussion or whatever. All these things could be better and quicker experienced by other means. And then, there was the old individualist's supercilious fear of becoming part of a *mass*. Which was thought, by the producers of *Gobbets*, to be interested in the attribution and discussion of literary quotations.

Wilkie told Frederica that she could come and be part of the team, for a trial run. 'We can never find enough women to go on the programme,' he explained. 'They won't play. You do some reviewing, we'll class you as a journalist.' The programmes were recorded in blocks of four, sometimes in the Television Centre, sometimes in Manchester. There was an atmosphere of party-going and an illusion of a complex cultural life which was going on, on and off the screen. Frederica guessed Marvell's 'Garden', and Henry Green's *Loving* and Auden's 'September 1939' and an obscure passage from *Sense and Sensibility*. She failed to guess a passage from Byron, whom she had never got on with, and a passage from *Dombey and Son*, which made her briefly furious. She was surprised to be invited back – despite the difficulty of finding women. Wilkie said to her 'You're not scared of the camera. That's very unusual. You just say what you think.'

Frederica thought about being scared of the camera. If she wasn't, it was because she didn't take it seriously. She didn't see herself and didn't want to. Small cheques arrived. She travelled to Manchester in a carriage full of poets, historians and thinkers and listened whilst they talked about how to write about war.

Then Wilkie said casually that he wanted her to audition for a new series which was partly about television itself, about what it did, what effects it had. On everything from politics to science to art. 'I've put you down for an audition,' he said. 'To do interviews on it. To ask questions. You'd be good.'

'No, I wouldn't. I'm not an interviewer.'

'You're not scared. You think fast. It'd be a good idea to have a thinking woman. They don't go in for them.'

'I don't think so.'

'Come along to the auditions anyway. For the experience. You don't know where it may lead.'

'I don't know.'

'And what else are you doing at the moment, Frederica?'

'I don't know.'

'Well, then.'

Wilkie's new project was called *Through the Looking-Glass*. The auditions took place, not in the Television Centre, but in some large warehouse or temporary studio in Islington. Frederica went to be auditioned without enthusiasm, and therefore without preparation. She wore a dark green shirt, with white collar and cuffs. She had learned from *Gobbets* not to wear black, or stripes. She had also learned to mistrust the girls with little trays of make-up, rouge and sponges, eyeliners and thick mascara. She looked, in the mirrors, she thought, like a fierce doll. It stirred a memory.

What? Who? The Wicked Queen, in Disney's *Snow White*. The lights would bleach her, they said. There were about ten candidates, sitting in the gloom, two Sunday journalists, a lady novelist, an actress. Television presenters in those days were still sweetly-spoken women with immaculate, dressed hair and excellent, trained elocution, or men with *gravitas* and Broadcasting House resonance.

The auditions were arranged in pairs. Frederica was surprised, and annoyed, to find Alexander Wedderburn, who had moved from radio to educational television, as part of the BBC team. He explained to Frederica that each pair would interview each other – 'First A will interview B, and then vice versa, five minutes each way.' He said 'We've tried to put men with women and vice versa. I'm afraid you've drawn Mickey Impey. He's a pop poet.'

'I know. Leo recites his stuff at school.'

'He was on our committee on teaching English. Dreadfully cocky. That may help, of course.'

Frederica nodded. Mickey Impey was a pretty young man with a lop-sided mass of golden curls. He wore a tee shirt printed with Blake's *Ghost of a Flea*, surrounded by a ring of buttons. *Frodo Lives. Make Love Not War. Ho Ho Ho Chi Minh.* FALL OUT FALLOUT. *Psychiatry Kills. One Law for the Ox and the Tiger is Oppression. Down with School Dinners.* He rattled when he moved.

They tossed a coin for who should go first, and Frederica lost. If she had been thinking she would have seen that this was a disadvantage, since the second questioner has time to sum up the first during his own interview. They were in canvas chairs, facing each other. The poet put on a friendly, mischievous grin. Frederica considered him. The clapper-board clapped.

'When did you start writing poetry?'

'I piped ditties in my pram. My pram was my chariot of fire, my cloud where I piped away. Everything was poetry. Still is.'

'They must have been pleased with you at school?'

'I was teacher's pet as a tiddler. Spouting nursery-rhymes. Later, 'I got ground down by the system.'

'The system?'

'What they *force down* you. What *kills the imagination*. Facts and figures, kings and queens, weights and measures, eggs and skeletons and stuff, lumps of shit. Oh dear. I'm not supposed to say that, am I?'

'I've no idea. I shouldn't think so. Couldn't you find any good in anything?'

'They shut me in a mental prison-house, girl. It was torture.'

Frederica thought, there are five minutes, I should get away from education, and on to his poems. But he was displaying an attitude, like a butterfly opening its wings in the sun.

'So how would you educate the young?'

'I wouldn't. I'd give them their freedom. To find out *what* they want, *when* they want. You only learn what you *desire* to learn.'

'And things like science? That need technical knowledge —'

'Listen, darling, science is a Bad Thing. The planet is going to kill itself dead with science. Probably they'll blow us up with nuclear mushrooms, and if they don't, they'll burn away the earth's crust with napalm and extinguish the fowls of the air and the fish in the sea with pesticides. Oh yeah. Science is for two things, human greed and human blinkered arrogance. Don't teach little kids science. Teach them human things, making love, painting pictures, writing poems, singing songs, meditation. I wrote a poem against science. Do you want to hear it?'

'OK, if it isn't too long.'

> The metal men in coats of white
> In shuttered rooms with shuttered eyes
> Make metal death with metal claws
> Block out the sunshine from the skies.
>
> The children dance in forests free
> They smell the sunshine and the rain,
> They dance and sing the roots and flowers
> Weave magic circles whole again.
>
> The metal men are full of hate
> They bind the children with a chain
> They clang the institution's gate
> And box the children up in pain.
>
> The children's eyes are red with rage
> They burst the prison-gates and chain

They burn the spectacles and coats
The men go naked in the rain.

The children teach the men to play
They teach the body's ancient truth.
The naked men kneel down and pray.
Rainwashed to innocence, and youth.

'So you think the young may be able to save the world from the scientists?'

'Listen. I *know*. They *are* saving it. It's happening. They're saving it by *natural spontaneity*. They are putting the blast of the orgasm against the radioactive spout of the bomb. They can do this by just not giving in. By changing our consciousness completely. *We will make everything new.*'

'You will change politics?'

'Politics for a start. No more dead men in deadly dark suits. Singers and sayers and hearers in lovely colours. No adversarial debating. Meditation together. A way through.'

'But there are difficult decisions. Population. How to feed the world.'

'If you change the *mind-set*, darling, you change everything. There will be new fabrics created, new colours brought to light, new styles, new ways of – of growing things, you know. New ways of sharing what there is on this earth. Yeah.'

'But the young won't stay young forever?'

The poet frowned.

'That remains to be seen. I think we may find that being truly young is a matter of being, so to speak, *in the truth*, in the truth of youth. I do believe in mind over matter. I do believe you get old and die because you secretly *want* to, you can't resist because you don't know how. But we will learn how. We will learn to live in infinity where we belong.'

'CUT,' said Alexander.

Mickey Impey had done even less preparation for his interview than Frederica. He leaned back in his chair, closed his eyes, swayed to and fro, and after a time intoned

'Well, what do you want to talk about, then?'

'Well, we could talk about my idea of education. It's different from yours. I believe in learning things, and knowing things. I don't think it all just comes without work.'

'You're uptight, I knew it. I could tell when I saw you. I expect you've had an awful lot of it.'

'An awful lot of what?'

'An awful lot of education.'

'Quite a lot. I went to university. I studied literature. I happen to believe you think better for yourself if you know something about what other people have thought, and the ways they have thought it.'

The poet swayed faster, without opening his eyes. Crash, creak, crash, creak. He said indistinctly

'All that junk. History. The past. Bad, bad, a bad trip, all that. Like copulating with corpses, girl, whatever-your-name-is. Now, you want to copulate with the living. A *lot*. Like I do. Then you get spontaneous poems, spontaneous *overflows* as the man said, I expect you thought I didn't know that.'

'I like your poems,' said Frederica. 'They amuse me. They amuse my son.'

The canvas chair lurched to a standstill.

'Listen. Stop the roundabout. Sing to the Lord. O all ye stars sing together. The lady likes my poems. Ring the bells. The condescending bitch likes my poems.'

'Have you any idea who I am?'

'Vaguely, vaguely. You're a teacher sort of person, a condescending bitch, a po-faced inerlectual, I know your sort.'

'But this particular version of it – of my *sort* – whom you are supposed to be interviewing –'

'*Whom*. Listen to her. Listen to the condescending bitch con-condescending-descending. Her descant. She puts in definite object pronouns. I expect you didn't know I knew *that* either, did you? They made me learn it. You don't need grammar.'

'I have noticed you use it very elegantly in your poems.'

'Did you say *elegant*? You fink my pomes are *elegant*. You are full of shit.'

'No, you are. But it doesn't stop you writing interesting poems.'

The rocking increased in tempo.

'CUT,' said Alexander.

The poet fell over backwards and remained lying on his back

45

with his legs in the air, wound in the struts of his chair. His expression was beatific.

Later, Wilkie invited Frederica to the Television Centre to watch a playback of this interview. They sat in a windowless room, and watched the box in the corner. Wilkie said 'As I said, the quality you have is a complete lack of fear of the camera. If you watch any of the others — including your garrulous partner — you can see fear in the neck-muscles, in the roll of the eye. The onset of Medusa. Not you. Look.'

Frederica said that she probably didn't look anxious because she took the precaution of not looking at herself. Wilkie said that if she was going to be professional she would *have* to look, and then to retain her insouciance.

She hardly recognised herself. The cameras were kind to her sharp bones, her large mouth. They made her sandy quality richer, gave her hair a dark red depth, her eyebrows, so carefully dusted and patted by the make-up artists, a winged arch. Mickey Impey's eyes had a fishy glare over his chirpy grin. But Frederica's eyes, on screen, glittered with interest and amusement. Her mouth had an intriguing wry slant.

'Do you remember, in the play, when I was Elizabeth, I recited that ballad? The woman whose skirts were cut off. Lawks a' mussy on me, this is none of I.'

'It isn't anybody else. You have all the ingredients of being a *personality*. Including what I would once have thought unlikely, a capacity to listen to other people.'

'We all grow older. I'm a teacher. I'm a mother.'

'The job's yours. Everyone agreed.'

'But I don't *want* to be a personality —'

'Oh, Frederica. I want, I want, like a bird in a nest. This is the future, wouldn't it be interesting, for a time anyway? I live two lives, I do my research, I do this. What *do* you want, anyway?'

'I don't know. Rupert Parrott thinks he'll publish my book of bits and pieces. He says it's of the moment, it's a book for *now*. I don't know that he knows. Anyway, it isn't a book, not a real book, I'm not a writer. I seem to have had an education designed to incapacitate writers. Mickey Impey wasn't so far wrong.'

'Well, then. If you know. We could pay you a retainer, the

programme doesn't start for months and months, but there'll be lots of consultation, I'd like your input, as they say here. You'd be at the cutting edge of what ought to be the new form of thought, maybe a new kind of art.'

He ran back the tape and started again. Frederica gazed at her own face. What she liked in it, she saw, as Impey recited his youthful credo again, was that it was a woman's face, not a girl's. Alert, watchful, grown up. Attractive, even to its owner. She was not used to this.

Wilkie explained his idea of *Through the Looking-Glass*. Frederica thought later that this was the first time she had given him her complete attention, and also the first time he had addressed her completely seriously, as though she was neither audience for wit, nor satirical sparring-partner. She had lost her virginity to him, back in 1953, but that had been (and had been designed by her to be), a casual and unimportant happening. He had always been known as a brilliant man, a student of perception and cognition who managed to have a public career also, designing programmes. At the auditions, Frederica remembered, he had worn a pink shirt with a white collar − a rose-pink shirt with a black and white optical tie with little boxes whose perspective was unstable, and could be read many ways. His glasses now had large, heavy, squarish rims. His dark hair was longer. He was slightly too plump for this style, but not unpleasing, she remembered.

The television, Wilkie said, very seriously, was going to change everyone's consciousness. In large ways and small. The large ways were more obvious. It was already clear to everyone who mattered that the politics of the future would be conducted in these small boxes. 'You have to learn to *charm* people when your face is a few inches across and you're talking into the intimacy of their fish and chips, or their fondling their girl-friend's breasts, or shoving mush down their yowling infant . . .' Rhetoric would go, must go, was going. If you were going to sway the masses you must be able to do it one by one 'sight unseen' as the lovely phrase has it. 'It will look more honest and *be* more insidious and dishonest,' said Wilkie.

And then, television was going to change the larger world. Television was making the Vietnam war impossible for the Americans. It was revealing the images of napalm there, of starvation elsewhere on the earth. McLuhan's 'global village' was one way of putting it. He preferred to think it had shrunk the earth. You'll notice, he said, as we go on, we'll talk more and more about 'the planet' because from out there in space it seems small, a unity, lonely up there with its colours, the swirls of blue, and ochre, and green.

Frederica said she'd already noticed that contemporary novels tended to mention the fact of the box flickering away in the corner of the room, with its grey other-life, soldiers and tanks or other sinks in other kitchens. She said she thought it might take the place of the hearth in nineteenth-century fiction, the coals where Dickens's characters saw the generation of fantastic images, the warmth around which stories were read aloud, or told, or lived.

'You are still thinking in terms of novels,' said Wilkie. 'But yes, that's just, that's very just. I was thinking also of Plato's Cave, with the fire and the shadows.'

'Novels won't go away.'

'That remains to be seen.'

'We *need* images made of language.'

'Indeed. But we are entering an age when language becomes subordinate to images. At the moment, what passes for the art of the television is bastard forms of other art-forms. Puppet-shows for kids, kitchen-sink drama squashed into three piece suites, cramped epic *films*, talking heads reciting poems after midnight.

'Now we have colour – remember the colour,' Wilkie adjured Frederica, his black and white tie following the contour of his small belly under the rich rosy shirt – 'they will think of showing films about paintings and films about films, but they should be making works of art designed to be seen in small boxes with the light constructed in pixels, magenta, green, cyan blue. And the subject-matter of that art should be everything that can be thought about in coloured images, from politicians' lips to craters on the moon, from blood-corpuscles under the microscope and the slow growth of embryos to the unfolding of flowers and the seeding of forests, and all this can be woven together, as the technology advances, into one great living tapestry. Also, it can and must be *about itself*, which is suggested by your idea of flickering grey hearths in the corner of real rooms. It can show how it changes the way we see the world. It can analyse the way we respond to stimuli – whether babies seeing faces, or gannets seeing beaks, or people on sofas being induced to want – *now* – ripple ice-cream with chocolate coating. It can always show and, if it chooses, always simultaneously think. What is the use of going on and on filming music-hall and nigger minstrels, who need a proscenium arch and the body chemistry of a live audience, when you can magnify nematode worms and make new forms of beauty with infinite cubes of coloured light with infinitely varied images moving in them . . .?'

Through the Looking-Glass, Wilkie said, was going to be the very first television about television. And he didn't just mean a critical chat-show. He meant a new form of thought.

'In the meantime,' he said, 'since you are going to be the visible face and audible voice of my project, you must have a television. You must have a brand-new colour television. And you must look at everything, from sport to cartoons to Vietnam.'

Frederica asked about the colour. Black and white cinema films still seemed more complex, paradoxically. Colour was comparatively shrill. As with photographs. Black and white somehow was more analytic.

Wilkie said that Leonardo had been suspicious of colour as transient illusion. Line and light and shadows were more essential renderings of reality. 'But whether we like it or not,' he said, 'we are now going to live with light-boxes full of mosaics of transmitted coloured light. People will forget what this moment was like, the moment when we had coloured light-boxes having not had them. I'll send you one round.'

'Leo'll be pleased.'

★

Later – much later – when Frederica who had felt old at thirty was surprised at how she did not feel old at sixty – she looked back on this time of youthful turmoil, of overturning and jettisoning, as something very far away and finished, as the mild, indefinite, tentatively hopeful 50s were not finished.

For one thing, historically, it takes a few decades to learn that younger generations than 'the young' sprout like mushrooms, that if the young of the 60s could not remember the War they were followed rapidly by generations who could not remember Vietnam, who were followed by generations who could not remember the Falklands. The face-paint, the hair, the head-bands, the bells on fingers and toes came to seem both tribal and *vieux jeu*, though Leo's generation harboured a nostalgia for a 'freedom' so frequently proclaimed and sung that it must have existed, *in illo tempore*, in some other place. Or perhaps, Frederica thought, considering how sparse her own precise memories of that time were, this was the case with all thirty-year-old memories, whether you were thirty in 1868 or 1968? You were exhausted by trying to make a life, trying to make sense, and by the life of the young, which depended on your own no-longer young energy for its existence. Her idea of her own youth was a densely patterned carpet of mnemonics and rhythms, from T.S. Eliot, first tastes of banana, melon, whalemeat, lobster, exam questions recalled in total irrelevant detail, minor humiliations, dreadful, unfocused, unsatisfied sexual desire. The carpet of the 50s was woven of many colours, in fine threads, even if much of it was pastel, or fawn, or dove grey. Whereas the 60s were like a fishing-net woven horribly loose and slack with only the odd very bright plastic object caught in its meshes, whilst everything else had rushed and flowed through, back into the undifferentiated ocean.

She remembered John Ottokar's legs. His double face on the window, his and Paul's.

She did, also, remember the first weeks of colour television. Not because of Wilkie's words about it, but because of the colour. She sat before it on the end of her mattress, or curled on her side and stared into it. What she remembered of it at sixty was:

Tennis on green grass with white figures and the geometry of the court contained and constantly in movement in the geometry of the box.

A programme which watched a hand drawing, which watched the movements of eye to object, of hand on paper, as black and white unreal edges and contours and shadows grew out of nothing, and the photographed face became the analysed, placed, disposed pattern of marks.

An educational programme on the uses of a microscope, with prepared slides in gels of aquamarine and violet.

The first colour transmissions of snooker. The gleam of the pink ball, the perfect sky-blue of the blue ball, the trajectories of vermilion, the ivory-white of the cue-ball, the eye-expanding green field of the table.

An early film by a herpetologist in the Amazon who was able, with colour, to show a lethal bushmaster camouflaged in decaying forest debris, a golden poisonous toad amongst glittering water-drops on glossy quivering leaves, the flap of the blue wings of the brilliant Morphos in the canopy, the swarming of army ants, the perfect disguise of the bee orchid . . .

Also the plumes of smoke and towers of flame in the rainforest in Vietnam.

These she remembered, when her own clothes and furniture had gone from her, reviews she had written, lunches she had eaten, hopes she had entertained.

Most of all, from that time, she remembered a woman, to whom reading had come as easy as flying to a sparrow, trying to teach an articulate eight-year-old who stared at simple words as though they were mazes or traps. She remembered, as they sat together, she and Leo, how in her own childhood the words had seemed to dance into meaning as the elements in a kaleidoscope danced into geometrical forms. She remembered, like the taste of honey, or vanilla, the pleasure of mastering *ch, qu, wh,* and quickly after, *its* and *it's, who's* and *whose,* the delightful logical order of it, the sense that her own mind already knew these things which were there like a carpet to be unrolled and danced on. She could not quite imagine what went on in the head of the clever boy who could not read. What did he see, or *not* see, what connections did he not make? She tried to think analogically – her own sums at school had always gone wrong, she could not get the decimal point right by thinking, though she had got reasonably good at placing it by simple common sense, in adult life. But she couldn't get her imagination inside what he couldn't see. She *couldn't help.* The school said it would sort itself out, and she did not believe them. Her own head became full of stopped-off electric currents. She could do it. She couldn't pass the capacity to do it to him. She could teach almost anyone to see in a poem something that they hadn't known was there. But she couldn't see what Leo didn't see.

What do you remember of 1968? Snakes and snooker and a set white face, with a frown, and tears brimming in proud eyes.

V

Jacqueline Winwar went to see Lyon Bowman at the end of the summer term about doing post-doctoral work in his lab. He was working on the visual cortex of kittens and pigeons. He was in his early forties, a brightly-coloured man, with a lot of shiny dark hair, long lashes over large brown eyes, round cheeks with a red-apple redness, and a full mouth, which could also fairly be described as red.

Jacqueline said she wanted to work on the physiology of memory. She wanted to find out how the neurones changed after learning had taken place, how memories were preserved in the cells. She had an idea for an experiment – a series of experiments – with snails, which had giant neurones that were relatively easy to dissect and observe. She thought it would be possible to do a kind of Pavlovian training on snails. She thought, she said, that they could be both habituated to shocks (as Kandel's work with *Aplysia* was designed to show) and also sensitised to good and bad flavours in their food. She wanted to be able to measure pre- and post-synapsal changes after learning. She wanted to study the neuro-transmitters, and the electrical signals.

Lyon Bowman said he didn't really believe you could train a snail. It was true, the neurones were promising. If she was going to measure action potentials she would need sophisticated maths. How good was her maths? He had the look of a man who assumed that a woman naturalist had probably underestimated the problems of changing to hard laboratory science.

Jacqueline said she knew a lot about snails, and had kept them, and practised already on training them to eat and refuse certain foods. She thought she had evidence. She handed him her records. She said that the maths was a difficulty, but could be learned.

'Why study memory this way?' said Bowman. 'Why not follow

Jacobson and suppose that the way to study memory is to study the molecules of the RNA, or Ungar's idea that it's communicated in protein chains?'

Jacqueline said that she had always been interested in Hebb's idea that the remembering brain actually constructed new links, new reinforced joins between stimulated neurones. He'd seen the brain as a system of flashing lights, building electric links which caused the flashes to be more definite and more prolonged. He'd had that idea in 1949 when it wasn't possible to study how neurones and synapses behaved. But it was now – in simple ways – beginning to be possible. She wanted to see if he was right. If the brain grew and shaped itself. 'And how.'

Jacqueline continued to explain, citing various elegant experiments of the Japanese neuro-ethologist Hagiwara, and J.Z. Young's work on the eyes and mind of the octopus. She was describing a world in which she wanted to be, in what she thought was the appropriate formal and academic manner. Lyon Bowman was shuffling the papers on his desk. He said that no one in his lab was working on snails, particularly, and mentioned San Diego and Plymouth.

Jacqueline heard herself say

'It would be an interesting physiological experiment to find out what it is in people's eyes that shows you they aren't really interested in you. It's like photographs. There's a moment when the face dies, and if you click the shutter just after it, the photo's dead. I don't know what it is. Eyes are eyes, and if they're alive, they're alive. How do we read that they're looking or not looking?'

'I see. I'm not looking at you. Or rather, I'm looking at you, but not attending to you.'

'Yes. And it's *my life* we're discussing.'

'Why should I have to worry about your life more than the life of any other well-qualified – *better* qualified – post-doctoral candidate?'

'No reason. For you. I – I can feel you thinking, I'm a dull good competent student. I'm not. I'm obsessed. I work. I want to do real science. I want to do your sort of science.'

'Obsessive women make bad members of teams, in my narrow experience.'

'They don't get much chance. I wasn't really asking you to take me because I'm obsessed. Just to *see* me.'

'I see you.'

He laughed.

'Another thing, Miss Winwar. Women often vanish with half their work done, to attend to their own physiology. How do I know you won't?'

'You don't. But I won't.'

'Have you a boy-friend?'

'No.'

She could see him not asking, why not. She waited. They had been playing some game with eyes and other minute, involuntary movements and probably with smells, she suspected, that she couldn't have played if she'd been a man, and also wouldn't have had to play, of course. She tried to see her sex – with some success – as a problem and an obstacle, to be solved and surmounted. She thought, she probably had her place, her space in the lab, unless some better candidate turned up and erased the impression she'd made, the memories that had somehow or other arranged themselves in the soft grey matter behind Lyon Bowman's now smiling eyes.

She thought, we shan't *ever* be able to sort out all of what happens when two people talk to each other.

She thought, each of us can put a building-block into the wall of understanding it.

In the event, Lyon Bowman offered her the place, for the autumn of 1968.

★

Cedar Mount
Hospital for the care of the Insane and the Mentally Ill
Calverley

From Kieran Quarrell,
Senior Psychiatrist, to Elvet Gander, M.D., Psychoanalyst

Dear Elvet

I got yr letters and yr paper on the Spirit's Tigers, for wch many thanks. I was agreeably surprised at yr level tone in reporting all these spiritual stirrings. You don't go overboard, as some of yr profession lately have done, but you don't automatically reject. I remain sceptical about spiritual journeys to hell (or heaven) in general, but I don't think filling people up with pills and inducing vacancy is the answer either. Part of the problem you and I are both dealing with is that genuine spiritual seekers (whatever the 'spirit' is) do bear some resemblance to the truly batty whose wiring has short-circuited. We can say that, even if we aren't at all clear – who is, really? – what the desirable definitions of 'sane' and 'normal' are.

I've been thinking about all this – and yr paper was opportune – because I've got a patient who troubles me and might interest you. And indeed he might interest yr Tigers, since he presents what are certainly some sort of 'spiritual' problems.

He's called Lamb. Josh Lamb, he calls himself. He's about forty, with a North Yorkshire accent of an educated kind. He's impressive to look at. Tall, with a mass of very straight bright white hair, *long* lined face, big, wide-set dark eyes under dark brows and lashes. An hairy man. He wears a beard, straight and bristling, like a bush. His beard isn't white, it's multi-coloured, blacks and browns and reds.

He's cagey about his life, and sometimes claims to have no memories, or to be unable to distinguish memories from lying visions sent by the devil. (He tells you these things pleasantly and reasonably.) He's been a teacher, so much is clear, also a verger, and a hospital porter. He's also spent long periods as a tramp, doing odd jobs in farms, and begging – like a sadhu with a begging-bowl (his own analogy). This isn't his first stay in Cedar Mount. He's been in and out; his first stay dates back to before I came here.

He presents auditory and visual hallucinations; he goes through phases when he can do nothing but lie flat on his back and weep silently. He seems to forget to eat and he doesn't make a fuss, he just doesn't eat. When the hallucinations are strong, he stands in a corner, with his back to the wall, arguing and gesticulating. Or bowing, repeatedly and rapidly. Sometimes he insists on wearing a wide-brimmed oilskin hat, and becomes threatening when it is taken away. (I don't know why it ever is. It calms him. I make them give it back.)

It isn't easy to establish any personal history for him. He says his parents are dead. He says he simply doesn't remember them. Sometimes he cunningly ascribes this loss of memory to electric shock therapy, which is half-plausible. Why am I so sure he *does* remember his parents?

I ask how old he was when they died. Mostly he says he doesn't remember, but once, when he was perturbed and haunted, and his guard was down, he said 'Eleven.' I asked on that occasion if both parents had died together. He replied – I took it down as he said it, exactly – 'Oh no. Absolutely not together. But at related times, not very far apart.' I couldn't get any more out of him. He has a way of looking at you as though he's offered you a *vital clue*, on a plate, but you are much too much of a fool to follow it up. It isn't offensive. He isn't offensive. He's rather dignified.

He was in one of my groups, for a time. What I called the sticky group. The group full of bellyachers and obstinate mutes and moaners. They could all simply glare and sulk for a whole session if I abdicated the 'leading' rôle. He didn't – doesn't – have that disconnectedness that goes with classic schizophrenia. I noticed early on that he was a noticing man. He knew, often before I did myself, where the next outburst was coming from, who was simmering, who was upset. So when I abdicated, he took charge. No, I'll correct that. The others gave him charge, they turned to him. I thought, in the early days, maybe it was just that he looked enigmatic. And clean, spick and span, unlike many of the others. There was a woman whose husband had bashed her to jelly and who cried a lot. Another woman, superficially no-nonsense, a great avoider of depth or difficulty, kept having a go at the jelly-woman, implying she'd asked for it. I was going to write 'Lamb suddenly said –' but actually, that would be a mis-statement. *She* said to Lamb 'What do you think, what would you do?'

And he said 'You must give up the arrogance of supposing evil is your fault, or begins with you. It's out there in the world. It's active. It got you. I say simply, get out of its way. Forget blame, that's of the least consequence.' And she thanked him, as though he'd given her something precious. You could argue, of course, that an idea of *active evil*, for which no one is responsible, is actually quite dangerous. He gave it, so to speak, a consoling gloss. I always refuse to suggest particular courses of action, of course. That is emphatically not part of my rôle within the group. So they turn to him, and he obliges. He does it pretty well. But not as though he's involved himself. Maybe he does it well for that reason. That's *his* rôle. It may be part of my rôle to put his pronouncements in question, but it makes me uneasy.

He had an appointment today, for his regular assessment. He says he wants to leave the hospital, but when I ask where he'd go, what he'd do, he simply smiles and says

'I would say, the Lord will direct me, but you might take that for a sign of madness, and I do wish very much to leave this place.' I asked why he should think that this would be taken as a sign of madness. He replied that St Joan had been burned, but also sanctified, for seeing and hearing things. Whereas now, as he pointed out agreeably enough, we shut them up.

He is reading St Augustine and Kierkegaard. I asked him why these two, and he said they knew evil. I asked him what evil was. He replied 'Roast lamb.' He likes puns. He says Cedar Mount is transfiguring him into a walrus. This I think is to do with blubber. Largactil tends to make the patients fat, and also perhaps there's a reference to blubbing. (He weeps frequently.) On the other hand his education might not include that prep-school locution.

Dr Shriver wrote in his case-notes that Lamb's conversation was inconsequential, not to say meaningless. He was trying hard to be chatty, at the assessment, because he wants to get out. I asked him if he felt he had a religious vocation. He said 'Many are called but few are chosen. I was despised and rejected.'

Why? said I. 'Because I told them I could see Christ's blood stream in the firmament,' said he, composedly. 'It does, you know,' he added, pleasantly. Again that sense of being handed a clue on a plate, and proving inadequate. (Me. I suppose it's good for me, to feel inadequate so often. As long as it's balanced by occasional self-approval for possible adequacy.)

I tried to pursue the topic of St Augustine. I don't know much about the Saint − a ferocious old African predestinarian, I vaguely believe, courtesy of the excellent novels of Anthony Burgess. Lamb said he (St A.) had betrayed his Master. Jesus? I asked. No, said Lamb, the prophet Mani who had understood the true nature of the world. The true nature of evil, he glossed that statement. Augustine betrayed him, he said again. The Manichees were in the Truth and he abandoned them for milky Christianity. (Milky? What does a good Freudian like yr good self make of that?) He then said something I couldn't follow or record about how there would be understanding of those things, also of 'the testament of my father who burns like the cherubim in heaven or the fiends in hell, he will show the way . . .'

I asked if he meant his real father. He said 'What do you mean by real?' and wouldn't say any more.

He has no record of violence − though he does create, so to speak, an *atmosphere* of the possibility of violence. You get religious language about blood and fire every Sunday in church. No one thinks vicars are odd or should be shut up.

He *deserves respect*, I feel instinctively.

If he was amongst your Tigers he might (I am being fanciful, *of course, but*) discover who or what is speaking to him. He says no one is. (He wants out of here, he knows he has to *look* normal.) But I watched him listening-in (without letting-on that I was watching) and *something* was talking to him − from the region of the air-vent – all through our conversation. He wasn't letting-on, and I wasn't letting-on.

I think he deserves better than a bed in a ward and the company of the amiable and disgusting mad.

I haven't got him across to you, really, I see, re-reading this, tho' I was making a meticulous attempt to reproduce his presence. I should like you to meet him. I have to decide what to do about him.

Yours as ever
Pontius Quarrell

From Elvet Gander to Kieran Quarrell

My dear Kieran,

Yr Lamb sounds full of possibilities – not least because I've not known you desert yr normally dry style for so long in the description of any other patient. It may well be that he may find a niche among the Spirit's Tigers (dreadful mixed metaphor, tigers don't nest) – we'll see. I'll reply in kind with a description of the patient who is exercising my own mind, and who is indeed the proximate cause of my own participation in the Meetings of the Spirit's Tigers. They call them Meetings because the group grew from Quaker origins – indeed, the founding members are Quakers, and they named the group, in a characteristically self-deprecating way, from a rather good angry poem by a Quaker poet, Christopher Levenson, who asks where is now the *Fire* and the *vision* which inspired the early Friends literally to quake in the presence of the Light. Levenson writes

> *Hand to which earth was volatile as flame*
> *And every bush responded to God's name*
> *Might find the spirit's tigers have grown tame.*

'Genteel and tidy' he says the modern Quakers are, and describes their God finely

> *Their God is just? That only! Too domesticated*
> *Vast social worker, not conjured, but stated,*
> *Too timid a lover, too well-bred!*

You, wise friend, and I, in the days of the wisdom of Erving Goffman on the self-regulating Asylum, know what it is to be constrained by the mercy of a vast social worker (for whom there is nevertheless *something* to be said!). And to be truthful, despite their aspirations to spiritual fieriness I do find the founding members of the Spirit's Tigers 'too genteel and tidy'. They may wish to prowl and roar and glitter in the jungle but it is beyond them. On the other hand, they have attracted to themselves some wilder, less predictable spirits, including my patient, who calls himself Zag, though his birth-name is Paul. He is himself what's known as a 'birthright' Quaker. He's also, most significantly, a monozygotic identical twin. He sings in a musical group called, rather wittily, 'Zag and the Ziggy Zy-goats'. (Sometimes he spells Ziggy, Syzygy.) The twin, John, is a very respectable mathematician, who wears an anonymous white coat and programs soulless computers. Both claim to be illiterate and un-literary, largely because they spoke a private language in childhood, and communicated through mathematical symbols and music. They used to live in Welwyn Garden City and go on the great CND marches of the 50s with their parents, singing and playing – he plays guitar and trumpet. John plays the clarinet. John, according to Zag, took to going to an extra-mural class in literature, taught by a girl, called Freda or Francesca or something. His intention was to 'learn ordinary language' by this means, Zag says, and he started an affaire with Freda or Francesca, from whom Zag stole a copy of *The Birth of Tragedy from the Spirit of Music*. Nietzsche suited Zag, and he found in there that Zagreus is the name of the dismembered sacrificial Dionysos. Accompanied by satyrs, the satyr-dance of the undifferentiated. Hence Zy-goats. Not bad for an illiterate singer. He's manic-depressive, into drugs and not sure of his own sexuality. All over the place. He's psychologically not properly differentiated from his twin, I think. He's *very* narcissistic, but the face he sees in the pool, so to speak, is John's not his own. He tells me John is his parent and his other half; he read somewhere that identical twins are a form of virgin birth, of asexual reproduction, and he is convinced that he, Zag, is the 'bud' which formed on the primary zygote that was John. (He likes to think about Dionysos sheltered in the thigh of Zeus.) Sometimes this causes him to fantasise about being a special hero – not of woman born, etc. etc. – and sometimes he says he is nothing, John's shadow, John's seed, John's ghost, John's emanation (like all the Tigers he's superficially familiar with Blake, and one of the Tigers I'll come to, an art historian called Richmond Bly, is a bit of a Blake expert). Anyway, as you may imagine, the analyst–patient dyad is a peculiarly unsatisfactory place to treat such a convinced half-soul. He isn't interested in me – everything is very simply projected on to the absent John. I think I'd do better if I were treating both twins, but John is resolved against this course. Paul-Zag, I think, is predominantly and possibly unconsciously homosexual in his own double-narcissistic way. John has made a resolute bid to be 'normal' (dreaded word) and has, as I said, picked the said Francesca or Freda, who seems a pompous and superficial sort of a clever girl, with a failed marriage behind her and a ready-made child for John, a little boy growing up without a father.

Zag is both superficially and profoundly very *charming* (I use that word in its ancient, magical sense). He has a real presence, what you could call charisma, when he sings. I've seen him. He has authority when he sings. Since he discovered Zagreus he sings in bits of leopard-skin and festooned with gold and silver snake-like things. His followers fling bits of bloody flesh (giblets and so on) around on the stage. Off the stage, he is all-over-the-place, a disintegrating ego, given to tantrums and weeping and despairing immobility lasting days, or weeks. He says he is dangerous without John. 'He is the earth and I am the lightning.' (There is ambiguity in these phrases, of course. He wishes to *strike* John.) (Or penetrate him, even.) It is possible that if I were treating both twins I might see John's withdrawal as necessary, or beneficial, but from the point of view of Zag's peculiar agony (wch I have not presented very clearly, only skeletally) John's behaviour is appallingly destructive.

It was Zag who suggested I come to the Meetings of the Tigers to 'meet' John, whom he persuades (blackmails, I fear) into attending some of the Meetings. I have to tread very carefully, and have not made much progress in breaking down the defences, or penetrating the reserve, of John. I do sometimes imagine (a professional hazard, I am aware) that the 'sane' twin is more profoundly disturbed (mad) than the ostensibly abnormal one. I do know that Zag makes him suffer. But he doesn't wish for the help I would like to offer.

There is a Meeting of the Tigers this weekend. They meet at Four Pence, which is a Bedfordshire sort of farmhouse without a farm belonging to Frank and Milly Fisher, two of the founding members. The Tigers recently formed a link with a much more dubious entity, the Joyful Companions (the inner community of an entity called the Children of Joy, run by a charismatic C. of E. clergyman called Gideon Farrar). It's rather like watching two amoebas extending their pseudopodia to swallow each other. It's a fact of our time that we have rediscovered the need for communal consciousness, for breaking the bounds between I and Thou, but it does (as all primitive religions do, and I think that that is what this is) take some odd forms. I am in it, and out of it, as you may imagine. I'll report back, after the weekend, on whether I think the new marriage-bed will make a seed-bed for the soul of your Lamb.

Zag has *coerced* John into promising to come. Can a man (yours truly) with a sharp eye for the gladiatorial combat of two-and-one *also* be open to any true spiritual awakening that is going on? I do believe so, but if you hear no more, believe that I have been struck dumb, or blind, for my presumption. Why do I dare make such dangerous jokes? I am queasy/uneasy. You signed yourself Pontius. I would not be a psychoanalytic Caiaphas or unregenerate Saul. We must not become an Orthodoxy. We must be open to new wisdom. But this is for my next epistle.

Yours fraternally,
Elvet Gander

Well, Kieran, here is the promised report on the weekend with the Tigers. It had its *hairy* moments, a new word I'm beginning to use without quite understanding all its connotations. Most of the ones I know fit, anyway. I'll try to describe it all like a case-study (you know my deep aversion to false 'objectivity' and therapic claims of 'detachment' wch are bound to be bogus. But you don't want to hear too much of the grinding and shrieking of the soul of Elvet Gander M.D. I know you, gruffandgrum craggyface, drawing horrors but always on tidy graph paper.)

The cast. Frank and Milly Fisher, birthright Quakers, well-to-do, early fifties, veterans of the Friends' Ambulance Unit and the CND marches. He is a bank official, she an assistant headmistress. In the world of work. There are two more regular Quaker Tigers − a fortyish lady (maiden? I'm not sure) called Patience Coope, and a youngish man, Brinsley Ludd, some sort of social worker. They all display the same symptoms. They are on the one hand, profoundly *unsatisfied*. They want to have a revolution, and what they want to rebel against is sweet reason and kindness. This is hard for them, for they are all sweet, reasonable, and kind. By nature or culture, it doesn't matter, that is what they *are*, I don't think it's a mask. So the dissatisfaction is peculiarly pure and naked. You will say − or anyway, most of the Tigers wd say, sweet reason and kindness are deeply suspect. I say you (and the Tigers) shd be careful. Sometimes these things are real, or almost real, or partly real.

Then − the Tigers are ecumenical − there's the C. of E. contingent. A regular bod called Canon Adelbert Holly. Preaches the Death of God, Deus Absconditus, and the Impossibility of the Church as she is constituted. Author of *Within God Without God* and *Our Passions Christ's Passion*. Describes himself as a 'trained sexual therapist'. V. shifty about who trained him. Aet. fifty-nine-ish. Over-excitable, smoke-stained teeth, straggly hair, spitty speaker. And

then Gideon Farrar, whom I mentioned, founder of the Children of
Joy, and its inner sanctum, the Joyful Companions. A spade-shaped
yellow beard, blue-eyed *honest* charisma, bonhomous in a slightly
nauseating way. (OK. I can explain that *undetached* adjective, and
may later. Meantime, take 'nauseating' as read, the response of the
not-unsubtle but not wholly longsuffering Elvet Gander, and reserve
a little judgement.)

Farrar brings his patient sweet wife, Clemency, and an acolyte
called Ruth, an alarmingly docile young person (ex-nurse) from the
resident community. Lovely 'calm' face. Long golden plait down her
back. Her will resigned to God's (or Gideon's). No opinions.

Clergyman no. 3, this time with a big black beard, and also a
black sweater, a portly person called Daniel Orton, who runs a
suicide-line in a telephone centre in the City. (He works with Holly
in a crypt.)

An art historian called Richmond Bly, student of Blake's
prophetic books, driven to fear, trembling and soul-searching by the
student revolution in the Samuel Palmer School.

A patient of my own, called Ellie (she named herself for the dead
little girl in *The Water Babies*), who is clothed all in white, including
a nun-like veil and bandaged arms and legs.

The twins I wrote you of. The Quakers have always been good
at absorbing the mentally disturbed and treating them kindly and
with respect. Look at the humane understanding Mary Lamb,
matricide, had amongst them in the days of Romanticism. They are
nice to Ellie. They extinguish the little fires Zag lights on their
staircases, when he isn't looking, and without comment. (This may
not be what he *wants*, but that is how they do react.)

Have I forgotten anyone? Yes, as usual, I have forgotten the
forgettable Brenda Pincher. She arrives with the Farrar contingent,
but I do not believe she is a Child of Joy. She is small and brown,
and you don't hold her face in yr mind from one meeting to the
next. I don't know what she does.

It will be borne in upon you that all these seekers after uprising
and mind-blowing (soul-blowing) come from the Caring Professions.
Sometimes I think the whole human world is a vast pool of carers
caring for carers caring, creeping through a jumble of capitalists,
exploiters, masters and oppressors whom we can't see, and
automatically loathe, another SPECIES.

The Weekends have a designated shape or form, from which we
occasionally deviate. I'm not against imposed forms myself – I
believe in the finite psychoanalytic hour, timetabled and paid for.
Freud showed us the benefit of that. Some of the Tigers find the

whole idea of structure ludicrous, however, in what should be a primary blaze of spiritual violence – why a *weekend only*, let alone a timetable of sessions?

We begin and end with a Meeting for Worship. The idea is to sit in a meditative silence, and for those to whom the Spirit (or ego, or id?) calls, to speak their message, which is then accepted by the group and made part of the silence. I have argued for a third Meeting, somewhere in the middle. I like the silence, the *hum* of togetherness. The hope is, that over the weekend, the group will deepen its understanding, will see new lights and sing new songs, so to speak.

There are other sorts of session. The most basic are problem-solving sessions (like Maoist self-criticism, at times) where 'little' difficulties are brought into the open and cleared up. You'll immediately recognise the nature and the pitfalls, pratfalls, of this kind of thing. An example. Holly smokes particularly pungent yellow cigarettes. Milly Fisher thinks he ought not to, in Meetings. He said he could think of nothing but the cigarettes if he hadn't got one. She replied that she was asthmatic, and could think of nothing but her lungs. Then they decided simultaneously to make little personal sacrifices and reversed their positions. I don't smoke my pipe and I don't mention my pipe. You will appreciate the sacrifice that involves. But one shouldn't parade sacrifices. (A v. Quakerly position.)

A third kind of group encounter we decided to call 'ludic' sessions. We play what you might call spiritual parlour-games, mostly devised by Farrar, who excels at them. The idea is to get closer to each other, and also to shake ourselves out of routine ways of seeing the world. (Zag advocates LSD but the Quakers are against that.) I think Farrar wd like the ludic encounters to be more rumbustious than is generally acceptable. His Children go in for what's known, I believe, as 'touchy-feely' Christianity, bodily rubbings and exploratory huggings. He did manage to institute a kind of greeting ceremony where everyone had to embrace everyone, to break down barriers. (The English reluctance to touch anyone else at all is very odd, when you think of the bulk of human beings and their habits.) I admired Farrar's technique – genial backslapping for the men, a delicate protective enfolding for the women. He's immensely narcissistic and immensely outgoing. I was touched by everyone. Gales of Holly's bad breath across my nostrils, courteous brief hugs from the Quakers, a gangling giggle from Bly, with an evasive wriggle (he is not at ease in his body), a brisk hand-shake from B. Pincher (who appeared not to understand the purpose of the greeting), a soft kiss on the cheek from Ruth, a cringe from Ellie, a slap across the cheek from Zag and a positive backwards lurch out of my arms from his brother. The fat Daniel, who you'd think would give a man a great bear-hug, rested his hands as brief and light as hoverflies over my shoulders. The idea was to do the whole circle again, at the end, to see if we'd relaxed (or stiffened, of course, theoretically possible).

Another 'ludic' exercise was a primitive experiment in deliberate thought transmission. We picked 'transmitters' who wrote down, or drew, what they were transmitting and then we meditated and tried to receive the image. I pointed out that this was fairly standard in scientific ESP trials. I was mildly told off. Mixed results. Holly managed to 'transmit' a burning bush to two of the Quakers, Zag, Ruth and (this is a bit doubtful) Richmond Bly.

Another ludic exercise was the drawing of 'spiritual images' of oneself. John was quite unable to conceal the fact that he and Zag had drawn identical geometric patterns – a highly complex series of polyhedrons inside other polyhedrons. John said, this was a game they often played as children. He also said, rather surprisingly, that God was 'to be seen' in mathematics. 'God is mathematics, the form that's in everything.'

Zag said the polyhedrons represented 'everything being *in touch*, all these points of contact, infinite touch'. John didn't like that. He said it wasn't surprising, both of them drawing the same pattern. 'We've both drawn this one often enough before.' Zag said 'We've both drawn *all sorts* of forms and figures before. This is the Complicated One, admit it.' John said 'So. If I do admit it. We would both naturally choose the Complicated One. Don't make a supernatural happening out of a statistically probable coincidence.' Zag said 'There are hundreds of figures you could have chosen. I *felt* it would be the Complicated One.' John said 'So you were second-guessing me. Nothing surprising in that.'

Daniel Orton drew a leafless tree, with deep roots. Gideon drew an angel with a flaming sword. Holly drew the Cross, with a black, man-shaped hole in it. Ellie drew a minute circle. Like so, o. O, and Miss Pincher produced a nice studentish sketch of three apples, nicely shaded-in and hinting at three dimensions.

I can see you thinking – And Elvet Gander. I drew my pipe, of course. I put it next to my own version of Van Gogh's drawing of his pipe. (The dead-ash one, next to the sprouting onion.) I wrote under it Ceci n'est pas une pipe. Ceci n'est pas Elvet Gander. Farrar said, writing was cheating. I said, it was a pity if there were rules to preclude wit. Richmond Bly (who had drawn a *sad sheep*, I think he meant it for Blake's Lamb) said that if William Blake cd combine image and word in one icon, so cd Magritte, and *ipso facto* so cd Elvet Gander.

This group has a remarkable variety of natural leaders, who change rôles. The Fishers have a quiet authority – it's their house, and their idea – which they're at great pains to disclaim. Farrar is a born Leader – his need to lead is pitifully blatant – his own people love him, and bask in his warmth (and he in theirs). Holly doesn't mind. He's a loner, and comfortable with it. He so to speak gets his pleasure from *theorising* the others' behaviour. My Ellie, and Farrar's Ruth, *hurtle* to renounce their Selves for others. Ruth is distinctly the handmaid type, Richmond Bly wd like to be a leader, and knows he won't make it, so follows. He needs to be part, either way. To sing the same song as the others.

Zag has more *charisma* than everyone else put together, but it don't shine out like splendour from shook foil unless he's asked to sing, and then he's the snake-charmer. He cries 'Share my passion.' Gideon Farrar says 'I'll give you what you want.' (Implying, what you want is *me*.) The Tigers holds the two together, to its credit.

These are the leaders, and then there are the Watchers. Elvet Gander, psychoanalyst. Always one step out of the arena, looking to see what other people's utterances mean, cover, *can be translated into*. Trained, God help him (!), in suspicion and scepticism from the dark days of his studenthood, and wryly watching his own tentative hand-claspings and drawings-back. Daniel Orton's a watcher. He doesn't appear to be watching according to any rules, or for any power-intrigue that I can see. Does he have a deep, quiet faith, or is he a Priest of No God, like his colleague? You don't learn much about him. I asked him if he was married and he replied, 'My wife died in 1959.' End of conversation, end of topic. End of him, he implied. He was stalwart at washing-up, clearing up, closing shouting-matches. He sees Ellie's invisible fence, and keeps to his side. She notices this. Miss B. Pincher is a watcher, *I suppose*. She looks so damned ordinary, it's as though she's an emissary from another planet, pretending to be human.

The final Meeting was 'inspirational'. When these things work, they work like poems, or orchestras. First one takes up a note, then another, and they build on it. The Quakers began – they are usually 'called' to speak first – with biblical quotations about those who are born of the Spirit. 'The wind bloweth where it listeth, and thou hearest the sound thereof, but canst not tell whence it cometh, and whither it goeth: so is every one that is born of the Spirit.' We must give up our wills and go with the wind, was the message. Zag suddenly made up a beautiful little song, a lilting wind-song, in a minor key. Even Ellie said something. She didn't stand to speak, indeed she sank her head with its coverings a little lower, and held it with her bandaged hands, and said 'There should be a safe place where we wouldn't be afraid to hear.' Did I speak? I did not. I don't. But I did hear a vague rushing in the silence. Afterwards, everyone was all solemn and so to speak *rainwashed*, after a storm. They agreed that they (we) must do more to make Ellie's safe place. The Fishers want to found a therapeutic community – like Laing's Philadelphia Association, with differences. They said they admired Laing but weren't quite sure about his *praxis*. (The word 'hairy' came up again, tho' they can't have uttered it? Who did?) They said their community wd have open doors, but a core of residents who would both care and be cared for. No 'patients'. No 'doctors'.

Farrar asked why the Joyful Companions were not already the desired community, and the others found it hard to answer, for the reason was, that they do not trust *him*. This caused them to turn to me, and say that my insights, my wisdom, were as necessary as the wisdom of the churches. I was suddenly the centre of attention because I wasn't Gideon Farrar. I said I would think about it. God knows, Kieran (God!!!). (We write, God, exactly when we least believe in It. Natural theologians, of course, use this involuntary cultural reflex as evidence of G's persistence.) OK, *God knows* I want no part of Farrar's huggy-bunnies and happy-clappy-chappies. I wonder, cd one use his undoubted energy differently, like earthing electricity? What do we want people *to be*? Holly's Jung wanted healthy Aryan spirits in Aryan bodies, mandalas and sun-worship. But our deliciously earthy Freud was earthed in pre-war Bourgeois Vienna, bleak and musty with antimacassars and three-piece suites, quite like our front parlour in Stockport. (Did you know I grew up in Stockport?) I don't want to perpetuate the Normal bourgeoisie. So what, where? If we did start such a thing – with an imaginative psychiatrist (or two) and a few sensible visionary Quakers, we cd make a real safe house for people like Ellie, and your Lamb.

Young Ludd went round the Tigers asking who would be prepared to put time in, to take the idea further. John Ottokar said he wouldn't. He said he wouldn't have the spare time. Then he added 'And I might be moving away. That is, I *am* moving away.' First I'd heard of it, and, as it turns out, first Zag had.

The other non-starter was the man I'd picked for the possible king-pin, the solid Daniel Orton. He's got experience in plenty, and good sense, I intuit. He just said 'No, I don't think so.' Holly said 'That is strange, Daniel. This would seem, on the face of it, to be your work, your calling, precisely.' Orton repeated, no, I don't think so.

I asked him, as he was leaving, catching him privily in the entrance hall, why. He looked at me with a look I interpreted as *crossness* – I don't know what else it was. He said 'I'm not a community animal, Mr Gander. I know myself so far.' I said 'But you belong to a community –' He said 'That's how I know.' At this point there was shouting behind us, and John Ottokar *rushed past* and flung himself on to a motor bike, on wch he must have come. I asked Zag what had happened. Zag said 'He's a turd, he's turning himself into a pure turd.' I am too tired to analyse his choice of metaphor (unless it's literal). This is a dreadfully long missive to inflict on you. Take it at yr own speed – foolish advice for what I *must make* the last sentence.

Yours ever
Elvet

★

The snail-searchers were scattered in a triangle. Marcus lifted his head and noticed it was briefly equilateral, before Jacqueline moved away, attenuating the connections, pulling both invisible lines after her to a fine point.

All three, spread at silent, companionable distances, were preoccupied with mathematics. All three were thinking about order (and disorder) in mathematical terms.

Marcus, the only natural mathematician, picked up an empty shell of *Cepea nemoralis*, a fine-lined coil of chocolate brown on shimmering horny-gold, and puzzled again about the way natural patterns of growth constructed themselves along the Fibonacci spiral. Snail-shells, ramshorns, spider-webs, branches of trees and twigs on branches, sunflower heads. Take a number, add it to its predecessor, add the number obtained to its predecessor. 1, 1, 2, 3, 5, 8, 13. It grew in starts, not smoothly. Kepler had noticed that the ratio of these numbers to each other became closer and closer to the ratio of the Golden Section as the series progressed. As though 0.618034 was a mystical constant in the geometry of life. Marcus had discussed with Luk, a merely journeyman mathematician, but an imaginative naturalist, the possibility of working out the maths of the dynamics of phyllotaxis, or the increments of the snail-shell. The one in his hand – and all the others around –

seemed constructed on a Platonic skeleton of the ordering of things, a glassy web informing matter.

Jacqueline's mathematical problems were only just beginning. She was trying to master the differential equations needed to map and measure the action potential of the symmetrical giant cells on the ventral surface of the snail-brain. The idea was to insert micro-pipettes into the prepared cells, to inject potassium chloride, and to pass pulses of electricity through them. She was having trouble with the dense layers of connective tissue around the cells, which were hard to soften with enzymes, and hard to dissect by hand. The electrodes were hard to insert, and hard to keep in place. She had to readjust both the chemistry and the mechanics, and then to readjust them again. Her work disintegrated into mess and failure; the beauty and order of the creature's nervous system became mash and inert stuff. Beyond the preparation were the problems of the oscilloscope and the problems of constructing a voltage clamp to make the delicate measurements possible. Somewhere in all this cutting and stripping and splaying lay the thread of a clue — perhaps — to the biochemistry of learning and memory. The snail knew how to move, to choose and avoid foods, to mate, to hibernate. In these neurones were a map of part of that process of knowledge and learning. A ghost-dissection hung in her imagination on the moor. The snails on the wall before her slid forward on contracting and expanding feet, opened their delicate, miraculous mouths, extended their shining horns.

Luk Lysgaard-Peacock's maths was simpler. It was arithmetic — six pink, twelve wide-striped, two chalk-white, a yellow — becoming statistics meaningful or maybe meaningless, as his numbers were added to the numbers recorded by his Edwardian predecessor and the original Victorian clergyman. The beautiful idea that snails carried their genetic code on the coils and colourings of their shells, which had acquired a happenstance metaphorical elegance with the discovery of the helical nature of the DNA, was about to become redundant as a useful tool. The discovery of electrophoresis — the grinding and mashing of snail-flesh (or any flesh) to be stretched and measured and mapped on a gel in an electric current — had provided a quick way in the lab to replace all the local observation, recording and guesswork. Luk knew this. He was using electrophoresis to analyse both snails, slugs, and other creatures. But this was not a substitute for the precise observation of what creatures did, how creatures related to each other, in the world of living things.

He measured the world from inside the balance of his own body – he was a creature among creatures, out here amongst heather and tough grass and thorn-trees. He noticed the sharp, peaty smell of the air; fresh earth at the opening of a burrow; exposed roots, scraped by what? Things moving – sheep on the horizon, a long, slender, dark coral worm, a spring bubbling in a reedy patch, moss, snails, snail-trails, a majestic golden slug.

He noticed the variable human triangle, too. He could feel Jacqueline's purposeful progress without looking at her. He asked himself how, and registered the faint electrical crawl of his own sexual interest, mingled with the naturalist's scanning for anything moving. It was his nature to be shadowy. He wondered if Jacqueline's body registered Marcus as his registered her. Would he pick up those currents? He could not feel that they were there. Marcus was not charged.

A sheepdog trotted towards them, making small whining sounds, from the direction of Gunner Nighby's new hen-battery in the water-meadow. It was Lucy Nighby's Shirley. She ran up and wreathed herself round Jacqueline's ankles, snorting and nipping at her calves. Jacqueline looked for Tobias, the sheep who thought he was a dog. He was trotting towards them along a sheep-track. Jacqueline whistled to him; she was fond of him, and approved of his resolutely confused ambitions. He came up, a little wearily. Jacqueline put out a hand to pat him, and found her palm smeared with blood. Blood was seeping up from his skull between his stubs of horns. Blood was wet, Jacqueline also saw, all over his fleece, red-brown and tacky. A lot of blood. Jacqueline knelt down and ran her fingers through the wool. The wound on his head was nasty but superficial. The blood on his flanks and rump did not appear to be his own.

Jacqueline cried out. Luk came over and looked at the trembling beast. Jacqueline said they should perhaps take him back to Dun Vale Hall in the car. Luk said he wasn't sure about that. Perhaps they should reconnoitre the battery? Shirley appeared to be urging Jacqueline in that direction, nipping and butting and whining. There was blood also on Shirley's silver-white ruff, but it could have come from Tobias. They decided against going back for Luk's car. They went towards the battery, in the brightening morning, along the sheep-track with the dog and the sheep. Over a rise, beyond a knot of thorns, they saw the large, ugly box, with its galvanised roof and creosoted walls. They went on.

In front of the building Lucy Nighby was picking up eggs. She had obviously dropped a full basket. There were intact eggs rolling around her, and a mess of yolk and albumen and shell, in which she was picking up pieces. She was kneeling on the concrete in front of the building, her hair over her face, picking up eggs. When they came up, they saw that her hair was full of blood and spattered yolk. She looked up blankly, one eye completely closed by a huge, swollen bruise, her nose dripping blood on to her shirt and breeches. Her cheeks were bashed and swollen. Her movements were jerky. She was not distinguishing, as she scrabbled in the mess, between empty shells and slippery, filthy, unbroken eggs.

Jacqueline ran forward, took hold of her, and tried to keep her still.

'What's happened? Lucy, what's happened? Who hurt you?'

A voice from the battery door said

'It's not her as is hurt. Get in here, I'm bleeding to death, the silly cow's done for me.'

Luk went to the door. He could hear the rows of hens making alarmed cluckings and rattling their cages. There was a smell of chickenshit and feathers. It was dark. Gunner Nighby sat inside the door, crouched over his leg, gripping. He was also bloody. His hands and face were smeared, his shirt splashed, his trousers, when Luk touched them, soaked.

'Went for me,' said Gunner to Luk. 'Wi' a trowel. My *good* trowel. Stainless steel. Bloody sharp. Gashed my leg. Gashed my rib. I'll get her for this. Get a doctor. Go on, do something, or I'll be dead.'

'What did you do to Lucy?'

'I didn't take a sharp trowel to her, any road. *Do something*, you cunt.'

Luk did something. He took off Gunner's disgusting trousers, ripped off Gunner's shirt and vest, made a pad, and a tight bandage, round his groin, and saw that there was indeed a nasty

70

triangular rent in his left rib-cage. He made him a pillow of sacks, and went back to Jacqueline, pursued by wheezy invective.

Lucy was in a pitiful state. She sobbed steadily, a metronomic, gasping sobbing. She would not be dissuaded from gathering up the eggs. When they questioned her, she made only an almost inaudible keening. When Luk suggested fetching his car and driving both Gunner and Lucy to the doctor, she shook her head violently and pushed him away with dripping fingers. Jacqueline said they should get the car, go to Dun Vale Hall and call the ambulance. Someone should stay with Gunner. She looked at Marcus. Luk was already running down the track to the road. He was fit, he ran fast. Lucy moaned and rocked. Jacqueline said that perhaps Marcus should stay with Gunner, until help came. Keep an eye on the bandage.

Marcus didn't answer. His face was white, his shoulders hunched. He opened his dry mouth and closed it. Lucy picked up an unbroken egg and dropped it. Marcus flinched at the splatting sound. Jacqueline said

'You can't afford to faint. There's only three of us, we're all needed. Gunner won't hurt you.'

'No,' he brought out, with difficulty.

'Maybe you'd better go with Lucy and Luk.'

She couldn't think. She was sure she herself would be more use at the Hall. She knew Marcus was not afraid of Gunner. He was afraid Gunner would worsen, or die, and he wouldn't know what to do. She didn't wholly know what to do herself although she had done various First Aid badges, as a Girl Guide. She had done all the things respectable girls do. Marcus's glasses were full of steam. She put an arm round his shoulder. 'You go with Lucy. Take care of Lucy. I'll stay with Gunner.' Luk drove back up the track. Marcus, trying to overcome his own trembling, put out a hand to Lucy.

'Come with us,' he said.

Lucy rocked back on her heels. Marcus hated touching people. He took hold of her bloody, slimy hands. His own were insubstantial. He gripped. Barely perceptibly, she gripped back. He brought her to her feet – she was a slight woman, feather-boned – and half-carried her to the car. The first touch was the worst. He went into her atmosphere of blood and sulphur and mess. He kept hold of her hand. She didn't take hers away, though she flinched. Luk drove them away.

Jacqueline went back to Gunner, who was drowsy and truculent. He said they shouldn't go off without him, he could very well die. He didn't believe that, Jacqueline saw, though she thought he might be right. She put a hand on the tight bandage, to add to the pressure where the blood welled up.

'She ought to be locked up. She hurt my kids.'

'Hurt? How?'

'Beat them up. Battered them. They were trying to help me. They tried to take the rake away. She went for me, wi' the rake. She turned on them. She meant to finish me. She meant to do for me. Wi' th' rake. Should be locked up.'

'What did you do to her, Gunner?'

'Told you. You can see. She went for me. I didn't stab *her*. Not with rake. Not with trowel. You can see who went for who, it's bloody obvious, *bloody* obvious. She hurt th' kids. She's not fit . . .'

He muttered. 'I was just telling her off . . .'

His voice trailed into silence. His chin fell. Jacqueline felt his pulse, which was faint. His blood pumped quietly, in and out of his body.

Luk swung his car into the farmyard of Dun Vale Hall. The yard was enclosed by outbuildings, all in sombre grey stone, like a fortress. The house was seventeenth-century with modern additions, milking-sheds, storerooms, loose-box, and old dairy, slate-roofed. The back door was open. The buildings were quiet. Lucy gave a little moan, and stiffened. Marcus made himself put an arm round her. She gave a whicker of rebuff, and shrank from him.

'Stay there,' said Luk. He had a bad feeling about what was behind that unsnecked door. He got out of the car and went in.

He tripped on the steps, which were worn and hollowed. The back door opened straight into the kitchen, which had small deep windows, heavy beams, and white-washed walls, spattered and smeared with bloodstains. Luk sniffed the scent of violence and listened to the silence. He could feel, in his own ribs, someone somewhere in the house, breathing in pain. The light through the uneven window-panes was grey. He crossed the kitchen, stepping thief-soft, and went through a wicket-gate, and a pair of split doors, like a stable-door. He was now in a long paved stone corridor. On the stones blood-splashes glistened, damp in the centre, skinning over at the edges. These flagstones too were hollowed by generations of bootsteps. Luk stepped lightly through the door which divided the servants' quarters from the Hall, and found himself in a square entrance space, two storeys high, still grey-paved but lit through stained glass windows beside and over the low heavy door, so that pools of violet, amber and green light lay amongst the blood-spots. He listened. He could hear the breathing now. He could feel the presence of bodies.

There was a wide shallow-stepped staircase, going up to a landing with a balcony. At the top Luk found all three children, Carla, Ellis and Annie. They wore interlock pyjamas, printed with white lambs and white daisies on sky blue. All three were blood-smeared, and one, the smallest, Annie, was soaked and dripping. Carla and Ellis sat with their backs to the wall, which was panelled. Carla was eight, Ellis five – both, like Gunner, were white-blond. Annie was lying across their knees, her face invisible under a mask of blood. All the white hair was laced with red, all the small fingernails dark with it. All three were breathing. Carla and Ellis stared at Luk out of shocked, expressionless blue eyes. Carla's small hand gripped Annie's shoulder; her knuckles were pale with force. Luk asked them where a telephone was. They stared, shivered, were mute. He bent and listened to their breathing, ran downstairs and found a kind of office, its chair overturned, its phone off the hook and shrilling. He reconnected it, called 999, and explained where he was, where the children were, where Gunner was. He went back to the children, listened again to their breathing – Annie's was laboured and faint – and found blankets in a nursery bedroom, which he put round their trembling shoulders. He thought of going out to Marcus and Lucy and decided against it. He sat down next to the children; Carla and Ellis, he saw, had scalp-wounds; Annie's looked worse than that.

Luk stared down at the stained glass. The left-hand window showed a man with a sword in a dark valley between pointed peaks. Descending upon him from a dark sky was a leather-winged, sabre-toothed demon, horned, hoofed and clawed. On the right-hand side, under blue sky, a man in a helmet like a magnified snail-shell swam across a blue and purple river towards a golden castle-wall, through slits in which protruded, a little

73

awkwardly, several long golden bronze trumpets. Over the door were four circular lights, arranged like a four-leafed clover, depicting the seasons. A new lamb, skipping in a green field. A striped bee, travelling from a sunflower to a hexagonal honeycomb across cobalt. A spiralling stook of corn on a deep gold ground. A holly-tree in snow, crimson-berried, emerald-leaved, with a fire lit beside it, the scarlet tongues of flame moving up in a spire.

He heard from a distance, the sirens and horns of the approaching police and the ambulance. They came in, they gathered up the children and took them away to be washed, and stitched, and examined, inside and out. They took away the bloody rake from the nursery and the bloody trowel from the battery. They took away Gunner, on a stretcher, scarlet-swathed, and Lucy, dishevelled and tight-lipped. They went over the farmhouse, measuring, recording, bloodstains, breakages. Luk and Jacqueline and Marcus were interviewed, and their shock and efficacy equally became part of an orderly narrative.

Luk thought, closing his vigil away in the dark of his mind, that this was the end now, of loose violence at least. But it was not. It was a halt, only. The real beginning, indeed, was still to come.

★

The man who was called Josh Lamb was one of the few residents of Cedar Mount who read the local papers put out in the Association Room. He sat in a slippery tan arm-chair and read the *Calverley Post*'s account of the events at Dun Vale Hall. A violent attack on the family had taken place, the paper said. Both Mr Nighby and the three children had received serious injuries. All were in hospital, as was Mrs Nighby, who was suffering from severe shock. The police were investigating. They were waiting for the children to be well enough to help them with their investigation. They were not at present seeking to interview anyone else about the attack or attacks. There was a photograph of Dun Vale Hall, nestled peacefully in the moorland. There were no photographs of the Nighbys.

The new woman sat on a chair, with her hands folded in her lap. She spoke to no one and looked at nothing. The staff belittled everyone with a kindly use of Christian names, and 'dear'. The new woman was Lucy dear. Her face was roundish, her cheeks pink and weathered, her eyes a little sunk. Her hair straggled but Josh thought it probably normally did not. There was blood, clotting in its strands. There was blood running down those soft round cheeks and into her mouth corners. There was blood soaking her blue shirt over her breasts, and dripping into her composed lap. In the old days he had taken the intricate realism of its drip and flow for proof that it was real. Now he knew that it was not there, and that there was nothing he could do about the intricacy, the redundant detail, with which he saw it.

He thought he should speak to Lucy dear, but his hands and his knees were trembling. Old pictures tried to surge up; he knew what they were, and knew that the veil of blood that clouded his retina was drawn across, mercifully, to close them out. But they unnerved him. He was not sure he could stand. He prayed for strength. The blood grew redder and swifter.

The nurse came up to him.

'A cup of tea, Josh? You look a bit off colour.'

She was in a red mist.

'That woman.'

'She's a bit shocked. She's had a bad time.'

'You're right, I'm off colour. The colours are all bad, bloody colours.'

He liked jokes that only he, their maker, could untwist. He liked sounding as though he was swearing, when he was being exact.

The nurse laughed. 'Cup of tea cures all ills.'

'I hate tea.'

'So you do. I should remember, shouldn't I? Horlicks, then.'

He loved Horlicks, sweet, white, malty. He had a sweet tooth. He thought of Ezekiel the prophet, eating the inexpressibly sweet rolls of the scriptures, like honey.

He put the Largactil that came with it, into his sock. The right moment to speak to the woman would be opened to him. He need only be patient.

★

From Kieran Quarrell to Elvet Gander

My dear Elvet,

I am growing suspicious about the extent to which I need yr permission to have feelings about my patients. Clinical detachment is a profoundly unnatural state of mind, and all sorts of evil can come of it. It was useful enough in my early days – and nights – in Casualty amongst all that battered flesh and wild and hopeless hangers-on. It was a survival tool. So it gets carried over into psychiatry. We offer our patients what appears to be human contact, human warmth – and we give them a calculated simulacrum of human contact, with no flesh, no blood, no love, no desire. It's not only medical decorum, of course. It's primitive egalitarian justice – all my patients have a *right* to all my attention, potentially, only I'm not equally interested in all of them. And honesty counts for something in squaring up to the world? It must?

Anyway, this preamble is my excuse for telling you I've spent time recently poking about in the case history of the man I told you about, Josh Lamb. He's had a bit of a relapse. Started seeing things and hearing voices again. Talked away furiously for 3 days to what sounded like a whole jury of inquisitors. I wish I didn't have my job to do. I'm sure there's some sort of sense, if one had time to listen, mixed up in all this stuff about light and dark, smudges and stains, aeons and twins, teeth and claws he goes on and on about. We had to put him in solitary. He wasn't sleeping and neither was anyone else. You'd need to listen *for days* to sort out the sense, the scenario. A lot of it's static, just babble. Well, I say that. How do I know?

Anyway, he calmed down. I am commanded to be still, he said. So I took a bit of a risk, and invited him back into the therapy group. The group seems to do him good, steady him.

We had a new member, a woman in her thirties, who's with us since a violent bust-up with her husband (who's in hospital). She's a quiet – indeed, totally silent – sensible-looking sort of person. Stabbed her husband with a stainless-steel trowel. He was in the habit of beating her up, that's known. She has three kids, all of whom were injured in the final set-to. One, the youngest, looked likely to lose an eye, it was *bad*. They're in care, now. The husband claims his wife made an unprovoked attack on him and the children with a rake. He says she just went berserk. The problem for the police is that one of the two elder kids supports that story, and the other says, equally positively, that the father hit the mother with the rake, and she then grabbed it. Same with their injuries. One says dad did it, one says mum. Lucy doesn't speak at all. Hasn't opened her mouth since the incident. At all. She's quite docile. She's been charged with causing 'actual bodily harm', and placed in Cedar Mount until the trial. She agreed to come to the group – at least, she went where she was led. One of the other women – an irascible type – tried to provoke her into speaking. Accused her of not pulling her weight etc., etc. – just trying to look superior and make a nasty atmosphere. Lucy just sat. I wd say she didn't know where she was. The irascible woman (her name's Mira), appealed to Lamb – as they do – saying, didn't he agree, it wd only work if they all made some effort to speak. He said – as near as I can remember – I daren't write down what they say, at the time, in case I get taken for the Leader or the Recording Angel of the group – he said

'You can be in another world where there's too much space and too much meaning to speak. You hear wicked winds blast, you smell snow, you see blood, ordinary speech is like scales of dead skin falling from your scalp at your feet. She can only hear your complaining like dead leaves rustling. What you say may have force here, but not where she is. You should listen to her silence.'

And Mira said, I'm sorry, which was a first time.

And Lucy looked at him with tears in her eyes, and opened her mouth, and licked her lips, but no sound came out.

And he said to Lucy

'What you need to know, is that the good and the evil in the world are equal. You need to know that evil is not subordinate. It is a power, it can overcome. You need to know that you are not evil in yourself, but you are a battlefield, where it can fight and overcome.'

Or some such thing. It looks a bit flat, written down, what he said. But the atmosphere was electric. Lucy's tears ran. My own eyes prickled (I record this clinically). The word for the effect he has on the group is 'charisma'. I'm beginning to think I'd like to write a paper on charisma. You have it, of course.

I don't, I think. I know.

Anyway, Elvet, I have as I said been doing some research into his history. And found nuggets of sheer gold. He let fall once that he'd been treated by Sam Krabbe, at Newcastle. So I got hold of old Krabbe's case-histories – with lots of trouble, I'll spare you the details. And I finally located him, because of old Krabbe's meticulous cross-referencing.

He was born, not Josh Lamb, but Joshua Ramsden. Born in Darlington, 1928. His father was an elementary school teacher and a Methodist lay preacher. Joseph Ramsden. Joseph Ramsden was hanged in Durham gaol in 1939 (May) for the murder of his wife, Nellie, and his daughter, Ruth, aged six. Krabbe's notes say he claimed to have seen an angel, who told him to smother his family, that they might not see the coming holocaust. He appears (Krabbe's notes are exiguous) to have compared himself to Abraham sacrificing Isaac, and to Jephthah, sacrificing his daughter. He refused to plead insanity. These are the bare bones – Krabbe gives no more details, though I guess I might find more, if I went through the archives of the local papers. Krabbe gives no indication, in the notes I have, of what Joseph Ramsden was like, or what, if anything, Joshua said about him.

During the war, Krabbe says Joshua says, he was 'evacuated' to live with an 'auntie', called Agnes Lamb. (Is anyone? Is it not overdetermined?) National Service as an airman, invalided out with some illness that left him hospitalised for about two years – records not clear. He started a theology degree in Durham in the 1950s, again giving up because he was ill. Krabbe says he thinks he still feels called to the priesthood. He reads, as I think I told you, St Augustine and Kierkegaard. He says he has always been a 'wanderer' (tramp) and chooses to live in poverty. I don't know whether or not to tell him I've found out all these things he has resolutely refused to tell me.

The thing is, Elvet, the thing is, *imagine that man's life*. You can't. One day there is a family. (Maybe a perfectly ordinary-seeming one, maybe not, we don't know.) The next, there isn't. Mother and sister horribly dead. Dad in prison. Young Joshua possibly *intended to be dead* – or possibly not. Krabbe doesn't say how he escaped, or indeed how much he knew, or didn't, of what had happened. Then, after the long-drawn-out process of justice, Dad is dead too, even more horribly dead. I don't know what he knew of that, what he was told, what he guessed. In my experience you can't keep that sort of thing wholly secret, it seeps through. What did he think? Who did he think he was? How – you have to ask, in our profession – did he survive, even as disturbed and strange as he is?

I have to say, he is one of the kindest and gentlest men I have ever met. He has – in the midst of his whirlwind, a comprehensible explicable whirlwind – what seems to be a real wisdom. I do not know how to proceed, but if ever there was a man I wished to help, to cure, to enable, it is him. Which brings me back to where I began. We don't treat all our patients as equal. This one is slightly phosphorescent.

All this explains, of course, his interest in the fate of Lucy Nighby and her domestic mayhem. Her arrival coincided with his return to exhibiting deluded and hallucinated behaviour. It would, wouldn't it? If he knew her story (which was in the papers) and it seeped into his mind.

Maybe – just maybe – both he and she could benefit from yr Quakerish therapeutic community. How is it all going?

VI

A rash of stickers and posters appeared on the surfaces of the campus. They varied in size and design, in colour and style. There were small, square, white printed ones, usually verbose.

An intellectual minority remains totally inefficacious if it submits to, or even becomes complacent in, the ghetto prepared for it.

Where the bourgeois economists saw a relation between things (the exchange of one commodity for another) Marx revealed a relation between people. V.I. Lenin.

Mao-Tse-Tung-thought, like all true theory, claims to be true before it has been realised, and to be realisable, because it is true.

These, and others like them, were characterised in very small print as 'A preliminary pre-publication of the Anti-University of the Moors'. They were arranged in well-glued patterns on doors, pillars, blackboards, notice-boards, like hop-scotch grids, crosses of Lorraine or schemata for tic-tac-toe. There were also long plastic streamers, in dayglo pink, lime green, banana yellow, attached to window-frames, the branches of trees, goal-posts, rubbish-bins.

These bore messages such as

Be intolerant of repressive tolerance.
Syllabus is oppression. Get out from under the juggernaut.
Students are the new proletariat.
Teaching is exploitation.
Do not submit to e-ducation. You need not be led by the nose. Sit still, stare around, expand your mind.

Then there were the art-works, painted on sheets and draped

over lecterns, painted with gaudy flowers, naked humans, exploding volcanos.

Pop pills. Stop all ills.
All you need is your navel.
Freedom lies in the right use of the arsehole.
Try not to think.
Art is orgasm.
Knowledge is an illusion people have.
Come into gone. I do assure you. The dreadful has already happened.

Heaps of leaflets blew between the towers.

The Anti-University is coming. Anti-knowledge, anti-ignorance, anti-teaching, anti-students, anti-knickers, anti-Christ, anti-Buddha, anti-spinach, anti-bourgeois, anti-art, anti-anti-art, anti-transport, anti-plastics, anti-meat, anti-psychiatry, anti-Wijnnobel, anti-phlogistin, anti-tealeaves, anti-capitalism, anti-hamburgers, anti-fizzy-beer, anti-overweight-currencies-in-your-pocket, anti-white-or-any-other heat of technology, anti-being-anti. (Naturally.)

Wijnnobel and Hodgkiss met to discuss these manifestations. There was a touch of frost in the autumn air, and the lawn outside the Vice-Chancellor's window was crisped with it. He poured coffee from a Bauhaus silver pot for Hodgkiss, to whom he was attached, because they were both reasonable, reticent men. He liked the shape of the movement of the streamlined pot, and the curve of coffee, in front of his uncompromising Mondrian. These were the minimal refinements of a complicated civilisation.

'Where do you think all this is coming from, Vincent?'
'I don't know. I haven't heard of this Anti-University having any physical location. I don't know who runs it, or will run it.'
'You don't have an intelligence service.'
'I don't. I don't believe it's coming from the Student Union. We have a meeting with Nick Tewfell later this morning. He hasn't mentioned it.'
'Curious how put out I find myself to be singled out, by name, for attack.'

'Not precisely *singled*. You are lined up with Christ and Buddha.'

'And spinach. There's probably no harm in it.'

The North Yorkshire University had been relatively untouched by the first wave of student revolt. Wijnnobel and Hodgkiss had taken the unusual view that there was much to be said for the student demands for representation on governing bodies, and had accordingly invited Nick Tewfell, the Union President, and one other student-elected member, on to the Governing Body. They did not always make an appearance at meetings.

Hodgkiss said 'If it's coming from outside, of course, it could escalate into something else.'

'I think we should do nothing to provoke that. I would even suggest leaving the stickers in place. Then they will have to stick over their own messages. No laws are being broken. Universities should defend liberties.'

'Pop pills?'

'It doesn't say which pills, does it?'

'It doesn't mean iron jelloids.'

'Some of it,' said Wijnnobel peacefully, pouring more coffee, 'is quite funny.'

He turned to the subject of the Body–Mind Conference now scheduled for midsummer 1969, at the end of the academic year which was just beginning.

'I have letters, I am happy to say, from both Eichenbaum and Pinsky, accepting our invitation. Eichenbaum's provisional title is "The Idea of the Innate and its part in a Theory of Learning". Pinsky says his will be something like "Artificial Intelligence and Cognitive Psychology. Order from Noise".'

'Students have been known to object to both of them.'

'Indeed?'

'Eichenbaum was pelted with eggs and rotten fruit in America. And Pinsky was howled down with loudspeakers in Paris.'

'A university must uphold free speech. It is dangerous to prevent anyone from being heard, *anyone*. Which is why we must let this Anti-University have its say. Until and unless our own students are not following our own courses, and therefore failing.'

'I agree. We may turn out to be complacent.'

'Better than being provocative.'

'I agree. We agree. We might, most delicately and unobtrusively, sound out Nick Tewfell on both these issues.'

Wijnnobel poured more coffee.

'You will give a paper yourself, Vincent?'

'Would a paper on "Wittgenstein and the Dangerous Charm of Mathematics" be acceptable? It would connect logic, language, Cantor's ideas on infinity, Wittgenstein on Freud . . .'

'I shall look forward to it. Now, let us look at what we should bring up with young Tewfell.'

Nick Tewfell was a neat, dark man, who wore a corduroy jacket, a checked shirt, and a red tie. His hair was cut short, clipped up the back of his narrow head. His preoccupations appeared to be more to do with canteen and bar improvements, than with the flamboyant slogans of the Anti-University. His father was an official in the Boilermakers' Union; he came from Sunderland. He was studying History – he was not an outstanding student, it had simply been his best subject at school – and spent much of his spare time working for the Calverley Labour party, and addressing the Calverley Young Socialists. He was, for a student politician, a pragmatic and accommodating man.

He sat in Wijnnobel's study and discussed forthcoming speakers, at the Union (Michael Foot, R.D. Laing), at the University (Anthony Crosland, Ernst Gombrich). The subject of the Body–Mind Conference arose. Wijnnobel, in a neutral voice, named the principal speakers. He said that the Conference would put the University firmly on the map, as an important centre of learning. Tewfell expressed polite enthusiasm for this idea, and volunteered that both Eichenbaum and Pinsky should attract a large audience. Hodgkiss smiled to himself. He asked Tewfell if he knew anything about the so-called Anti-University.

'I know where it is, I think. I know one or two of the people involved.'

'Students of the University?'

'Some. Not all. Some are graduate students.'

'Do you know anything about their proposed activities?'

'I don't know that *they* do, really. I don't think any of us have been approached – beyond the posters and things. I've not seen signs of any actual *classes*. Just notices.'

'I see no harm in notices. But I would naturally feel differently if classes were disrupted.'

'I'm sure you will be told of further developments. If there are any. We believe in free speech.'

'So does the University.'

Tewfell reported the concerns of the last Union Committee meeting.

'Students are asking for syllabus changes. They feel we have to do more work – spread ourselves wider – than students in other places.'

'You have one more year to do it. You chose to follow this syllabus. It is meant to be taxing.'

An edge of iron came into Gerard Wijnnobel's clear voice.

'Students are specifically asking if the requirement to study another language could be made optional.'

'Indeed. Why?'

'Because – because it is very hard, for some of them. And they want time to study important new things. Theories. Literary theory, political theory.'

'I have always said, no man understands his own language who cannot follow the forms of another language.'

'I should answer that,' said Tewfell, 'by saying that no student can do *everything* in a first degree.'

'And I should have to accept that. But I believe certain things are essential to understanding the mind, and others come subsequently. I would argue that literary theory is meaningless without knowledge of more than one grammar and more than one syntax.'

'Grammar is élitism; grammar is a control system.'

'Nonsense.'

'I was quoting one of those posters, Vice-Chancellor.'

'How can grammar be élitist? You are confusing it with Received Pronunciation.'

'Not me. The posters.'

Hodgkiss said 'It may become necessary to *explain* the language requirement to the student body.'

'It should – to the student mind, or any mind – be self-evident, beautiful, and clear,' said Wijnnobel.

'You are a perfectionist,' said Hodgkiss.

'A *practical* perfectionist,' said the Vice-Chancellor.

'It might be practical to put the case. With which I agree, entirely.'

'English Lit. students, particularly,' said Tewfell, 'resent the time spent on languages. They say it's like going back to school.'

'As we all should, all our lives.'

'And,' said Hodgkiss pacifically, 'they cannot say languages – living ones at least – have no use in the real world.'

'I didn't say I agreed with them,' said Tewfell. 'I see what you mean. I report what they say. A significant body of opinion. I was mandated to say so.'

'I am disappointed,' said the Vice-Chancellor.

What had begun well had dampened down.

The Anti-University did in fact have a base. This was two caravans and a dormobile, parked at a place oddly known as Griffin Street. Griffin Street was an almost derelict row of labourers' cottages at the edge of the original Long Royston Estate, where parkland met open moors. The University proposed, when funds became available, to make the renovated cottages into graduate accommodation. One was already inhabited by two graduate students, Greg Tod and Waltraut Ross, a political historian and an anthropologist.

The dormobile belonged to Avram Snitkin, an itinerant ethnomethodologist. Snitkin had told Tod and Ross that he was writing up an indepth study of law-court procedures in Britain, which he was. Tod and Ross suspected him of studying themselves at the same time. This didn't bother them. Ethnomethodology meant studying the world of the studied from inside that world, as it comported itself. They thought he had a right.

One of the caravans was horsedrawn, a real Romany caravan with shafts and high steps and curtained windows. This was inhabited by Deborah Ritter, who was not a student of UNY, or indeed of anywhere, though she had from time to time and place to place studied comparative religion, anthropology, folklore and psychology. The other caravan had once been white, and was oval-shaped like an egg, balanced on an axle and a strut. It was pulled by a landrover. The landrover belonged to Jonty Surtees, who was older than the others, and had been on Haight-Ashbery, and with the Nanterre students, and had visited the communes in

Copenhagen, and liaised with Kommune I in Berlin. The caravans were just beyond the old park fence. They were not technically on University land. Deborah's horse, Vivasvat, fat, placid, dapple-grey with hairy fetlocks and an unkempt mane, grazed on a long tether. Deborah and Jonty Surtees were a kind of couple, both large and smiling, both with flowing red-gold hair over their shoulders. Surtees also had a fine red-gold moustache. He wore dark shirts, embroidered with flames and roses, open to the navel. Deborah wore Indian silky tunics over long skirts and bare feet; her brow was bound with a multi-coloured woven ribbon. Tod and Ross wore jeans and tee shirts, with varying slogans and faces. The Anti-University was taking shape in the five unused cottages in Griffin Street. Desks had been made from bricks and breeze-board. Typewriters clacked. In the kitchen Deborah cooked great cauldrons of beans, rice, herbs and floating curls of tomato skin. There was also a perpetual porridge-pot.

In curious synchrony with the Vice-Chancellor's invitations to Body and Mind, and at this stage unaware of the synchrony, the nuclear Anti-University despatched invitations to potential teachers and students. Greg Tod wrote to disaffected idealists from the LSE and Essex, Waltraut Ross wrote to student leaders in Europe, and Deborah Ritter wrote to various communes, hospitals, art schools and groups. Bring your own food and bedding, they said. We shall make a free space for self-expression, for the breakdown of artificial limits. Whilst they waited, they painted the caravans. The walls of the Romany caravan became a forest of silver and pine-green trees, overlapping, hung with gold and silver fruits and crimson pomegranates. The egg-shaped caravan was bedizened with coiling streamers and funnels and snakes and ladders and vines and creepers, inch by inch, in orange and shocking pink and pretty blues and many different greens. They argued for a whole evening about whether it was right to suggest topics of possible courses to potential instructors, and decided it was not. If by any chance everyone chose to give the same course, that only proved it was truly needed, and truly inspired. Leaflets were printed, saying, come and share your knowledge, however profound, however elementary. All can be studied, from cosmology to marmalade, from so-called madness to vegetarian cookery, from mantras to armed resistance to the death of capitalism to growing sweet-peas. The world is multifarious, so is the Anti-University. We can elucidate Karl Marx, set you on the way to Mao-thought, read your palm or open the secrets of the Tarot. All human life is here, or if it is not, it will be. Bring yourself (& food & bedding & music & art).

Late one afternoon, Ross, Tod and Deborah Ritter were sitting in the kitchen, smoking, burning incense, chopping onions, and discussing the withering of the bourgeois state and the transfiguration of the proletariat. Deborah was humming, which annoyed Greg Tod, who was talking. A figure appeared between the trees in the parkland, coming from the direction of the university. It was a black figure, female, heavy, tall; its progress was urgent and ungainly. Waltraut Ross watched out of the kitchen window, as the woman approached. Ross herself was small and skinny, and dressed usually in tight black sweaters and leggings like a resting ballerina. She had the very thin woman's contempt for the buxom or the heavy.

'It's a fat woman,' she said.

'Do we know her?' said Greg Tod.

'She looks sort of familiar. But I can't place her. She's got dogs with her. Fat collie dogs, with a fat woman.'

'Fat white woman,' said Deborah Ritter, unable to resist the quotation, 'whom nobody loves.'

'Not necessarily,' said Greg.

'Certainly *very* bourgeois,' said Waltraut.

The woman knocked. Heavily, several times.

'Shall I?'

'May as well.'

They were working by candlelight. When Waltraut opened the door, the black figure for a moment filled it, and the flames danced in the cold draught that came with her.

'Shut the door,' said Greg Tod. 'We like our fug.' There she stood, resolutely not part of their lolling, smiling, companionable world. She wore a large black coat that was a semi-cloak, with slits not sleeves, well-cut, with braided button-holes, suggesting both academic dress and witchcraft. Beneath it, she was a bundle of tunics and robe-like cardigans. Her black hair was heavy, and glossy, her brow lost under the fringe.

Her lips were dark crimson.

'What can we do for you?' said Greg.

'I saw your messages. I have come to offer my services to your – your community.'

No one invited her to take off her cloak.

'My name is Eva Selkett. I propose to offer instruction under that name. I have other names, but I shall teach here under the name of Eva Selkett.'

'And what will you teach? Not that we're sure we want anyone to *teach* anyone anything.'

'I shall demonstrate and show. Ancient Egyptian wisdom, the reading of the Tarot, astrological arcana, and the cosmology of the Kabbalists.'

Deborah Ritter heaped several branches on to the open fire, which flared and blazed.

'I think we've got quite a lot of that already. I can read Tarot, I can read palms, I can cast horoscopes, myself.'

Eva Selkett was sweating. Her face shone. She put up a hand – covered with large rings, amethyst and opal – and wiped it.

'I should like to take off my coat.'

'I know who you are,' said Greg Tod. 'It comes back to me. You're his wife. You're *Lady* Wijnnobel.'

'Well?' said Eva, formidable and melting.

'We don't want you,' said Waltraut Ross. 'You're the enemy.'

'I thought you were – open to all comers. I have certain skills, certain knowledge. Not desired where I find myself.'

'Nor here, I'm afraid,' said Greg Tod. 'No Ladies here.'

Odin and Frigg, who had been shut out, could be heard scratching at the door. Eva Wijnnobel appeared not to know what to do. She seemed to suppose that if she stood, resolutely enough, the company would see things her way. It was clear that she had not foreseen any outcome except acceptance.

'You make us uncomfortable,' said Deborah Ritter. 'There's something not right about you coming here. We – we feel you shouldn't stay.'

The dogs scratched.

'*Please,*' said Waltraut Ross, 'go now. Nothing has started. We'll be in touch when we're up and running. But as you can see, we – there isn't anything *happening.*'

'I understood there was.'

Greg opened the door. 'You understood wrongly. We'll be in touch, that's what they say, don't they? We will, probably. Please, go home now.'

'I shall come back,' she said. Her hot face crumpled a little. They knew they should have been sorry for her, and were not. They very badly wanted her to go.

After an awkwardly prolonged silence, she went.

Jonty Surtees came in later, when it was dark. Deborah ladled bean stew into faience dishes. They told him of their weird visitor and her proposal. 'I saw who she was,' said Greg Tod. 'She was *Lady* Wijnnobel. Just marched in and said she was going to give courses on tarot and astrology. A mad old bat. Just *stood* there.'

Deborah hummed.

Waltraut said sharply 'It would be nice to have something that wasn't beans. They explode your gut.'

'Farty,' said Greg Tod. 'Farty and tasty,' he added, pacifically.

Jonty Surtees chewed thoughtfully.

'Pythagoras said they were soul-food,' said Deborah. 'And they're cheap. And tasty.'

'Meat would be nice, meat would be tasty,' said Waltraut, who believed human beings were carnivores and that was that.

'Meat is murder,' said Deborah, placidly.

'What did you say to her?' said Jonty Surtees.

'We got rid of her. We made it quite clear she was unwanted.'

'I'm surprised.'

'There was something – not nice – about her,' said Waltraut.

'I'm surprised. You missed a trick there. There is nothing more useful if you're trying to disrupt – to overthrow – an oppressive structure, a self-constituted power-centre, than a sympathiser – a convert, an ally – *inside* that structure. Oh, yes, you missed a trick.'

'She wasn't a convert or an ally,' said Deborah. 'She was doing her own thing.'

'It doesn't matter – politically – what she's like *at all*,' said Surtees. 'She's the Vice-Chancellor's *wife*. She could have all sorts of uses.'

'So is the Anti-University a deliberate revolutionary act?' said Greg Tod. 'Part of a grand strategy?'

'Oh, I thought that went without saying. Part of the sniping, the attrition, the destabilisation that will bring the whole thing down. When the time comes. You have to be opportunist. You have to be vigilant. That woman was a weapon and a loophole. You should have welcomed her in.'

'You didn't see her,' said Waltraut. 'Or you wouldn't be so keen.'

'War is not a question of personalities,' said Jonty Surtees, and farted, long and loud.

'I told you,' said Waltraut. 'Beans explode your gut.'

The next morning, the Wijnnobels' housekeeper came to the breakfast table, and said

'There's a young man outside wants to see you, my lady.'

Eva Wijnnobel was in her dressing-gown, crimson velvet.

'He may come back later.'

'He's got a bunch of flowers. A big bunch.'

Eva followed the housekeeper to the dining-room door. Jonty Surtees was standing in the hall, with a huge bouquet of wild flowers – foxgloves, arum lilies, cow parsley, late buttercups, marguerites, festoons of bryony and nightshade – gathered in the park.

He smiled. He had a huge and friendly smile. He said 'These are for you. You came to visit us yesterday, and some of us were discourteous. We are very sorry. We were unprepared and disconcerted. We hope you will accept an apology, and some wild flowers, and come back when things begin to happen. We want you to know you will be welcome and valued.'

Eva reached for the flowers. Gerard Wijnnobel came out after his wife.

Jonty Surtees smiled at him, too.

'I was just bringing a peace-offering. One or two of my friends were – well – a little impolite. I hope there are no hard feelings?'

'No hard feelings,' said Eva, slowly.

'Who was that, Eva?'

'I don't know. I'd never seen him before.'

'What was he talking about? Who was rude to you?'

'Only students. It wasn't important. It was exaggerated to bring flowers. Kind, of course, as well as exaggerated. They are all right, really. Just young.'

VII

From Elvet Gander to Kieran Quarrell

My dear Kieran,

Do you have a Jungian interest in coincidence? Here is a rather elegant sample. I received two letters, this week, in the same post, from the same place, both inviting me to give a paper. One was from the Vice-Chancellor of your new University, asking me to be part of a multi-disciplinary conference in June on the multifarious relations of Body and Mind. There are to be chemists, philosophers, linguists, neurologists, literary men, sociologists, psychologists etc. etc. I am asked to speak – in any way I choose – for psychoanalysis. 'An essential strand of our discussion' the V-C says. (I believe he himself is a Grammarian.)

The other letter was from a group designating themselves as the Anti-University of North Yorkshire. They say they are instituting periodic and intermittent gatherings to discuss what isn't discussed by the Establishment, and they want me to talk – or otherwise communicate, in any way that pleases me, at any time of my own choice – about psychic regression-therapy, for instance, as an example, without restricting me. Changing the mental set of the establishment they say is urgent, is desperate. The University letterhead is red and black and has rearing dragons, symbolic mound with tree (a cedar?), and something I think is a fountain. The Anti-University communication is on greenish paper and is decorated with a kind of spotted-Dick effect of painted unlidded eyes – I never know if they are the Evil Eye, or an eye designed to stare down the Evil Eye, or an Evil Eye to counteract the Evil Eye.

They are not so far apart in their arcane symbolism, it strikes me. Maybe not in their undertakings, also. The Vice-Chancellor says his keynote speakers are Hodder Pinsky and Theobald Eichenbaum. He is a brave man. Both are thought to be raving determinists, and even if Pinsky's political views are impeccably Left, his psychology isn't. And there are nasty smells about Eichenbaum's German past.

Anyway, it is clearly my duty, and will be my pleasure, to accept both invitations. It wd obviously be convenient, and dramatically amusing, to accept both at the same time. But my courage may fail me. As you will know, those of my profession are reluctant to speak in gatherings not composed of our own faithful. I feel it is a matter of honour to overcome this flocking instinct.

A man must act in the world that exists (universe and anti-universe) and a properly analysed man shd feel no fear of philosophers or neuroscientists. Or of activists. I shall come North and prospect. I shall hope to discuss yr Lamb with you.

It is difficult indeed to imagine the effect of such a history on the survivor. You say the boy was eleven. You say he has never spoken of his parents (or sister). He was almost certainly in a pre-pubertal state at the time of those horrific events, and his coming-to-know them must have coincided with the outbreak of war – and the general perturbation of an entire population, which may have been a blessing in disguise. It is even possible that he remembers nothing. That is, that he is in a state of intense denial. And if we disturb that deadness, and take him back to that horror and beyond it, do we have the skills and the love to help him make a place in the world? He has not made his own – or he would not be where he is, hearing voices, seeing whatever he sees.

I should like to meet him.

We as a profession believe in truth and knowledge. But my first flinching feeling, at that history, is, better for him to forget. But that cannot be right?

Yours ever,
Elvet

★

Joshua Ramsden had not forgotten. He remembered everything, he thought, and never spoke of it, had never spoken of it, to anyone. This was the sentence he said to himself, when he was thinking in words, which meant that he knew *in words* that he did remember, but was not having to go through the act, or perhaps the infliction, of memory.

In fact, remembering everything was different from total recall. The things he remembered were lumps, or raw gobbets, of what his body – eyes, ears, nose, nerves – had taken in. They would rise up at him, or swim up inside him, without warning, after all this long stretch of time, interrupting his breath, and the beating of his heart, arousing dancing malevolent inkspots in his vision. He *felt* these memories like bright lights through holes in a blanket, or slimy underwater roots grasped through mud. The rest – the blanket of time, the mud of consecutive events – he had put together in safe words, which he used for protection against the glare and touch of the horror. He knew that once the bodily process of memory had been set in action, he was helpless to stop it. One gobbet was threaded to another, like a dreadful necklace. Age had made the throttling grasp of the necklace a very little more bearable, because he could confidently expect the moment of forgetting again. The horror lay in wait for him like a malignant bully, cunning enough to wait to pounce when he was again inattentive and unprotected.

What often started it was the flesh of his thighs. He had still been in short trousers, a big boy whose trousers were tight. Covered with puppy fat. He remembered standing there with all that solid flesh juddering and dancing, alive and uncontrollable, hot, cold, wet. Over all those years he had been so sorry, and was still, for that lumpen boy with great naked thighs who did not know what to do.

He remembered also, in his body, *their* flesh. They were lying side by side. Someone had crossed their dead hands on their breasts, and someone had closed their eyes but neither the bodies nor the faces were peaceful. Their mouths were open. His mother's mouth was twisted. Her false teeth had slipped. One of her breasts, much scratched, slipped puffily through a tear in her pink nightdress. His sister's eyelids and brow were horribly bruised and swollen. His mother's hands were helplessly clawing, in their clumsy propped position. His sister's thin feet looked as they always did, blue-veined, transparent, white. He was so sorry that this woman should have been fixed in his mind with extruded teeth. He was so unbearably sorry for his sister's feet. He was so sorry for the stains on the nightdress, and the candy-striped pyjamas.

His body remembered the smell, sweetish, corrupt, and every change in that smell during the time he stayed alone in that house with those two.

He came to understand that this remembering had destroyed much of the plump boy's past in his mind, eradicating it more ruthlessly than electric shock therapy, which jangled, stabbed and fragmented. Nothing 'came to mind' when he tried to recall the woman, or the little girl, who had become the things on the bed. He remembered, with the pity he extended to all memories of that awkward, stumbling boy, later attempts to imagine them doing things like walking, or eating, or touching him. Not immediately, but after about a year, he had created puppet mother, puppet sister, smiling and usual, and had seen them for what they were, wavering shades who automatically called up the solid flesh, the artificial teeth, the flaccid toes and fingers.

Most of all he pitied the moments when the boy might have known what was there, and was innocent and ignorant. He could see him coming home, letting himself into the house, after his first-ever night staying with a friend from school. He remembered that his mother had let him go, without reference to his father, who was strict and might have forbidden him. The boy had not had many friends – it was difficult, because he was not allowed out to play, because he spent his weekends in religious classes, in Chapel. But another boy had invited him, and he had gone. He could not remember the boy's name. Or his face. He remembered saying 'thank you' politely to the boy's mother, when he left, and he remembered her saying 'come again soon'. He remembered feeling cautiously pleased with himself – he had done nothing odd or foolish, he had been made welcome, he had behaved like a real boy and not been found out in any failing. He remembered this because part of himself had gone on being pleased with this success, had still basked in the warm smile of the other boy's mother, had still hoped – expected – to take up the now-impossible invitation. He had had to teach the naïve plump boy to remember all the time that all that was now over and done with for ever and ever. It was like missing a step – no, like expecting another step, when you were already at the foot of the stairs. All the veins shrilled and had to be made quiet.

Over and over he watched in his memory as the plump boy called in the hall 'I'm back,' and ran, with the energy of confidence, up the stairs to look for them, to tell them about it. *The pathetic ignorance of him.*

93

When he had found them, for some reason, he decided to wait until his father came back. After a time, he wandered (must have wandered, this part was occluded) into his own bedroom, where he lay on his bed and must – it seemed to the remembering man – have passed into a deep sleep.

When the plump boy woke, it was deep night, and very dark. Swimming up out of sleep, he thought, he really thought, *the poor fool*, that he had had a bad dream. His room, his things, seemed for the last time ordinary to him, daily, in their shadowy solidity in the darkness. His dressing-gown was his dressing-gown, his skeleton leaves skeleton leaves, his money-box in the shape of a pillar-box simply a red tin. He stayed in there with his things for a time (from then on no remembered time was measurable, only the succession of night and day). The man could not remember, when the boy went out of his bedroom to check whether he had dreamed, whether his father was back, what the boy had hoped, expected, or felt. He saw him in his memory *creep* along a landing, with vacancy roaring around the strip of linoleum he trod on, he saw him – *the poor thing* – tremble so violently he could not open the bedroom door he must have closed.

When he did, they were still there, of course. And his father, from whom help might have come, was not.

He saw himself standing, with his back to the death-bed, staring out into the night. He saw the pitiful shaking boy, and he saw himself. That is, his present self inhabited that memory.

It was very dark out there. The dark was not uniform. There was liquid ink, there was sluggish pitch, there was sooty veiling. It was as though the outside was woven of strips, of moving belts, of surging waves of black-crested blackness, some creeping, some sliding, some hurtling. The window was no protection, the house and its bricks were flimsy. What howled and pranced out there, what swallowed and gulped, was what was real. Inside his head was a jar or cave full of that soft and violent black which was trying to get out and mingle with the rest of the mass. The bony fence of his skull, the warm mat of his hair, were crumbling and flimsy like the bricks, the mortar, the roof-tiles of the poor house.

He saw the moon. It was the last, slender sickle-edge of the waning moon. He saw on the rushing blackness the globe of black matter that was the unlit face of the moon.

He saw the glass of the window-pane. It was a sash-window. In or through the glass of the window-pane he saw the face of the poor boy at the window. It was a nobler face than the blemished, puffy face he avoided in his mirror. It had fine, sloping planes, and smoke-dark eyes under frowning brows. Its hair was colourless. He could not now remember, when his hair had not been white, what colour it had been. He remembered the moment of seeing the other, standing there on dark air, as the moment when he had been bleached. The other was wearing white, too, a white which gleamed slightly amongst the blackness, and had wonderful folds and flutes which at their deepest opened on infinity. The other stood easily out there in the turbulence. He said, the poor boy heard him say

'Hold out your arms.'

So he held out his arms.

And was given to hold a sooty sphere, dreadfully dense, warm as though it had been taken like a cinder from a furnace that had gone out.

'You will have to carry it,' said the other. 'This is how it is.'

He couldn't hold it up, it was so thick, so heavy.

'You can. We must,' said the other. The other pointed at the side of the ball of dark, and he saw that a sliver of light ran round from pole to pole. It was a mild, cold, pale light. It was like a window into an empty shining, it was like a strip of daylight through a dark curtain, it was like a slash in the rind of darkness.

'This is what is,' said the other.

He did not know how long he stood there, holding up what was too heavy to hold, but holding it, whilst outside the inordinate roared and precipitated itself. He knew that if he could hold it up, he could continue to exist out there, where he now had to be.

At dawn, the other told him to go downstairs. When he reached the kitchen, the other told him to go further down. So he went down the stone steps into the coal cellar.

His father looked as though he had tried to burrow his way to the centre of the sloping hill of coal. The early light came in through a circular hole in the pavement above the coal-hole, which was its only window, and the orifice through which the sacks of coal were emptied. So the cool dawn light came down the slope of glistening black chunks, spangling here and there off their sheen. The whole floor of the place was spread with coal-dust, which also glittered, less silver than the coal, more iridescent with rose, purple, green, indigo, like pools of oil in the street. His father had smeared this dust over his face and hands, into his thick white eyebrows and his bushy moustache. His eyelashes were full of soot. He was wearing the black suit which he wore to preach on Sundays. He wore also a white shirt, now smudged and sootstained, but no collar and tie. He had a huge Adam's apple, which had always throbbed dynamically in the pulpit and which now trembled and twitched, under the coal-dust, black over dull red. He was sitting with his knees under his chin. He coughed. He had always, Joshua remembered, been asthmatic. Now his lungs were full of dust and ashes. He cleared his throat, several times, and then spoke, in a husky squeak.

'Where have you been?'

Like any accusing parent. Like this one, who believed the outside world contaminated an inner purity.

'I stayed out. I stayed overnight.'

He could not remember if he had said, or thought and suppressed, the dreadful sentence, 'Mummy said I could stay out.'

'You should have been here,' said the scarecrow on the coalhill.

The man remembered again the boy's vulnerable thighs at this point. They too were now streaked with coal-dust. He did not meet his father's eye. He looked down into the dust, hearing a dodged or deferred death sentence, as he would have heard a dodged or deferred smacking.

Because he could not meet his father's eye, he stared at his red neck, his Adam's apple, above the disorder of the collarless shirt.

'Get on with you,' said the man in the coal. 'There may have been a purpose to it.'

He stood, like thick clay, heavy as the smudged ball of dark he had held up at the window.

'Go away,' said the man. 'Get the police.'

He couldn't move or speak.

'I told you –' said his father, and wheezed and coughed and spluttered.

The boy turned and clambered up the stairs on all fours. He went out into the street, which looked like a street in which boys walked with satchels to school, and mothers went shopping and posted letters, and little girls dragged at their mothers' hands and lingered by doorsteps or peered down gratings into coal-holes. He took his instruction literally. He walked and walked, along the sooty streets, until he saw, at the High Street crossing, a policeman. He went to this man's side, and tugged at his pocket. The policeman was very tall, and his helmet made him taller. He waved his arms, directing the flow of traffic. The man could not remember the policeman's face.

'My father says you have to come.'

He couldn't remember the policeman's answer.

'My father says you have to come to our house, now.'

Something in his voice, something in his dirty face, must have convinced the man, for he came.

He must have gone back to the house with the policeman, but of this he had no memory. He did not sleep in that house again, but where he had slept, before his Auntie Agnes came for him, he could not remember. He remembered a pervasive surging and sickness of dark in his body, a knowledge that he would only gain consciousness to lose it completely, so must be numb, must not feel or know.

Of the subsequent time, some of his memories were dreams, or fantasies, and some were not. He had known, he was sure, all the time, what would happen, and then what had happened, to his father, though how he had known he was not sure. His Auntie Agnes, in fact a remote cousin of his mother, had taken him away to where she lived in a mining village in County Durham. She treated the boy as though he was in some way dirty and had a bad smell around him. She stood at a distance, and perpetually ordered him to tidy and wash himself. She had a small, round, querulous, frowning face, and iron-grey hair in curled rolls above her ears.

He could not remember that she had ever spoken to him about the events that were the cause of his being there.

The days of his father's trial, condemnation and execution had passed, as far as she was able to make them, like all other grim northern school-days. Hitler's tanks had rolled across Poland and Belgium, and were tearing into France. Because of the popular obsession with News, the boy, now known as Lamb, had seen newspapers. He remembered places where he had seen newspapers – a bus shelter, the village store – because he had vomited in both, and had been spanked for dirtiness. His father's face and Adolf Hitler's had been on the same page. 'Ramsden refuses insanity plea. The Lord commanded me to do it. A Holocaust is Coming.' 'I was ordered to take a short cut to Salvation.' And much later, 'Ramsden Will Not Appeal. "I am prepared to hang."' He had remembered his father's neck in the cellar. Neither aunt nor newspaper had made it possible for him to know when the hanging took place. Had he wanted to know? He had flinched from knowing. At times his aunt turned the radio off, quickly, quickly, when she heard him coming, immediately after the War news, and he supposed she was keeping it from him, keeping him from hearing it. He had never spoken to anyone at all of those weeks and months. He had occasionally, as a grown man, wanted to discuss with someone his aunt's iron resolve to preserve the normal, metronomic regularity of his tedious days. For in her limited way she was admirable. She wanted to make him dull, ordinary, unexceptionable. No flicker of expression in her pasty little mask had betrayed to the boy that this day was different, this day was obscene.

Occasionally, in various hospitals and churches, he had believed he remembered visiting his father in the condemned cell. He certainly remembered a dreadful debate in the heavy boy's head as to whether, when the call to make the visit came, he would be able to bring himself to go to that place, or to look at that man, who was alive, and would not be. How could they face each other in that knowledge? How did they? He remembered it all so clearly, the man behind a black table, the stiff, silent, heavy-breathing guards, the cup of nasty tea he was offered, his father's inability to swallow what he had supped from his own cup, the shaking of that larynx. He remembered seeing his father's Bible –

his personal Bible, with the soft leather cover and the plain gilt Cross – and being glad his father had something of his own in that place. He remembered a high window, a small source of grey light in black shadow (varied by institutional spinach green) like the round window in the stone above the coal-hole. He thought, when he was thinking clearly, that this confrontation had never taken place, but was merely a product of the poor boy's torment, of his religious desire, bred and inculcated in him, to love, respect and forgive his father, seventy times seven, and to share his fear with him, to *help him somehow* in this extremity. And crossing that like the dark wave rolling back from the stones where it has broken, was the memory of the dead flesh on the bed, the smell, the indignity. Those two were beyond help.

He was inclined to believe that the scene had not taken place. His memories of it nevertheless consistently gave him a powerful sense of defeat, of having failed his father. He could remember no word either had spoken, only the nasty taste of the tea, the grimy cracks in the pottery, the voice of the guard saying 'I'm sorry it's time to go now.' He believed he had constructed the memory out of a desire to have done, or tried to do, a good, the right, thing. He had constructed it from scenes in films and scenes in adventure stories. His father had always been against invented stories, and had urged him to read his Bible, which was sufficient, which answered all needs. In a school class reading *Oliver Twist* Josh Lamb had disgraced himself by having a fit during the reading-aloud of the gruesome description of Oliver's terror of Fagin's terror in the condemned cell. Taken to the cinema – by whom, not his aunt, he could not remember? – to see *Kind Hearts and Coronets* he had disgraced himself again, vomiting over the shoulders of the boy in front of him, as Dennis Price sat composed in the condemned cell, writing his confession. He had come to agree with his father. Telling stories, like making graven images, made loopholes for evil and the Father of Lies to enter the world.

That his father had tried to communicate with him, he believed he knew. He had picked up two postcards addressed to himself, on days when he had come down to breakfast before his aunt. He had immediately secreted them amongst his homework. They were greyish, furry cards. The ink had bled into them. They had ruled lines, which his father did not need. One had a biblical reference. Genesis 22, 6, 7 and 8. It was not signed. Possibly his father felt that 'love from' him would be unacceptable or appalling. The second said 'I want you to have my own Bible for your use, and to remember me, if you will take it. I have written a letter, which I hope will be given to you, or kept until you are old enough to read it with understanding, whether or not you can forgive.'

In his imagination, these writings were not brave, or firm, but quavering and slanting, as though every letter had been formed with extreme difficulty, by a trembling hand. No letter was ever given to him.

He kept the cards for some time, moving them from book to book in his small library – *The Boys' Book of Nature, Lives of Heroes, True Tales of Christian Mission*. He never kept them either in his Bible, or in the prayer book. He did not look at them often. They were like slivers of dead, contaminating matter, but it was his duty to preserve and contemplate them. One day – he was not sure when, it was in his teens, he had been ill – he looked everywhere and could not find them. Over and over again he opened book after book, not exactly wanting to see them, but wanting most desperately to stop searching, to be reunited with the fragments of which he was the keeper. He never found them. He knew his aunt went through his things regularly, looking for dirt, for cigarettes, for naughty notes, for wickedness that was only her imagination. He didn't speak to her about the matter, ever, and she never spoke to him.

Genesis 22, 6, 7, 8.

> *And Abraham took the wood of the burnt offering, and laid it upon Isaac his son; and he took the fire in his hand, and a knife; and they went both of them together.*
>
> *And Isaac spake unto Abraham his father, and said, My father: and he said, Here am I, my son. And he said, Behold the fire and the wood: but where is the lamb for a burnt offering?*
>
> *And Abraham said, My son, God will provide himself a lamb for a burnt offering: so they went both of them together.*

The message had a shocking ambiguity. Was his father telling him that like Abraham, he had unquestioningly obeyed a command to make an offering of his son – and in his case, his wife and daughter also? Or was he saying, that he had not trusted God enough, but that God had saved this son as he had saved Isaac? They went both of them together. They were together. His impotent spirit did try to accompany his father into the horror. Here am I, my son. Where?

Holocaust meant burnt offering, the boy knew, before ever the word became used for the wickedness that had not yet come. His father had been right, even, events proved, that another kind of holocaust was coming. The empty house in which the sacrifice had taken place was reduced to dust and ashes in a German raid on the steelworks and railways. They would have died then, who had died earlier. As for himself, the heavy boy, Joshua Ramsden, Josh Lamb, he was twice plucked from the burning. He was, as he would not have been, evacuated.

The fact of the general evacuation of children from threatened cities at the end of 1939, made it easier for Agnes Lamb to describe her nephew as an 'evacuee'. He was not the only boy to appear parentless in those village communities – parentless, and with no personal belongings, moreover. He could be made invisible amongst the other lost souls in the grammar school to which they travelled from several villages in brown buses. Many boys were mocked for strange accents, or teased because of odd habits. Josh Lamb did not stand out. His teachers were all old men, or women, for the young men had been called into the Forces. The man did not remember the boy having spoken to anyone, though he thought he must have done. He remembered some lessons, Latin, which was taught by an old gentleman called Mr Shepherd, a white-haired hunchback with gold-rimmed spectacles, and Scripture, which was taught by an energetic fiery woman called Sibyl Manson.

He thought of these as his years of 'grubbing' and pupation. He had known – it had been made clear to him – that he was singled out, cast out, chosen. These were the years in which, for a long time, he did not see the other, who had spoken to him out of the dark, and given him the weight of darkness to hold in his arms. He moved around in the grey fog of normality and unknowing that his aunt had tried to weave to preserve him, or herself, from the memory and the knowledge of the horror. He did experience himself as being closed in a tight skin, which held him together in the vacancy in which his true self tumbled and fell, a skin like horn, or parchment, in which he was formless, like the yellow-milky liquid that spurts out of cocoons and pupation caskets which are prematurely broken into. Now and then – stumbling on a paving-stone, slapped on the back in a coughing-fit, hanging from a bar in the gym, where he had swarmed up and could not come down, he saw the dark open again, great crevasses where the busy warp and weft flailed and hurtled. Or looking into a shop window in the street he would see his own reflection, and behind it, not the odd car, no ordinary passers-by, no policeman, but the roaring and rushing of the loom of the inordinate. There was no mirror in his bedroom, indeed, there were no mirrors in his aunt's house. She was against Vanity. So he saw himself little. He had ceased to be plump. He wore long trousers.

'Scripture' in the War Years meant Bible-reading. In that sense, it was storytelling. Latin was dry, was the learning and chanting of words. Both Miss Manson and Mr Shepherd were good teachers, who knew how to make what they taught not only unforgettable, but part of the foundation of the selves that were building in the more or less attentive boys. Miss Manson talked of the love of God the good Father, and told them the tales of the Old Testament, the man and woman in the innocent Garden, the snake, the apple, the fig-leaves, the walls, gates and angel with the flaming sword. She told them about Noah and the Deluge. They painted wooden Arks floating on blue waves, on the lined paper of their exercise-books. Josh Lamb was praised for imagination, when he painted his ark on a stormy night in inky water, with a lantern at the prow, and a sliver of moon in the sky. They also drew Lot's wife, turning into a pillar of salt as she looked back at the conflagration of Sodom and Gomorrah. They drew angels with huge white wings. Miss Manson brought in pictures of angels, by Van Eyck, by Giotto, by Fra Angelico, for them to see the beauty of the other eternal world, as men had glimpsed it. She passed over the drunkenness of Noah, and the precise sins of Sodom. They all painted rainbows, however. God had promised Noah that he would always care for the earth and its inhabitants. On the railways and steelmills, and on town centres, the bombs fell. Men were evil, said Miss Manson, but there would be a reckoning.

She came, as she had to, to the story of Abraham and Isaac. They all drew Hagar in the wilderness, and yet another Angel, making the mother turn back to her baby, whom she had abandoned because she loved him too much to watch him die. You must trust the Lord, said Miss Manson. Hagar's faith was weak. Abraham's ninety-year-old wife bore him a son, Isaac, when he was an old man. They may have counted differently in those days. They came, as they had to, to the tale of the sacrifice of Isaac.

And it came to pass after these things, that God did tempt Abraham, and said unto him, Abraham: and he said, Behold, here I am.

And he said, Take now thy son, thine only son Isaac, whom thou lovest, and get thee into the land of Moriah; and offer him there for a burnt offering upon one of the mountains which I will tell thee of.

Here was another picture to paint, the boy with the wood on his back, the man with the knife, the angel, the ram caught in a thicket by his horns.

The man was to wonder about the need for a natural explanation of the presence of the ram, when all the story was full of supernatural will and arbitrary power. The boy was compelled, for the first time, to argue. He never argued. The man believed he remembered that the boy never spoke. But he sat without drawing wood or angel-feathers. Miss Manson stepped between the desks, and saw his empty book. She bent over him. She had blazing red hair sleeked into a page-boy, lifted into almost-horns on her brow with tortoiseshell-spotted slides. She had a funny tweed suit, flecked rust and green, and smelled of mothballs. She wore glasses with tortoiseshell rims.

'No inspiration, Lamb? Usually so diligent.'

'I don't like the story, Miss.'

'It is the Word of God, Lamb. It isn't up to you to like or dislike it. You must understand, interpret, and learn from it. What worries you?'

'Why did the Lord tempt Abraham, Miss? I thought the Devil

was the tempter, like in the Garden of Eden. Why did he order . . . why did he ask . . . how could Abraham . . . kill . . .'

'His son whom he loved? The Scripture takes very good care to say that Abraham loved his son, at the moment when the supreme sacrifice is asked of him. We are all asked to make sacrifices, Lamb. It isn't a sacrifice, if it isn't something you love. Abraham was asked to make the greatest sacrifice possible, his son, whom he loved. It is happening all round us, young men are going off to fight for our freedom, and their wives and mothers must be cheerful, because it is needful.'

'But –'

'Still "but", Lamb?'

She was a good teacher. She did want to know what troubled his mind. She carried, he later thought, a small lantern of charisma, as Mr Shepherd also did. But its light fell bleakly into his dark.

'*But*, I think, the word "tempting" is right. You *tempt* people to do what they shouldn't. He shouldn't have.'

'The Lord's Prayer teaches us to ask the Lord, "Lead us not into temptation." Temptation here means "trial".'

'It still means *not* doing – things. We have to ask Him to *stop* us going into temptation. Not to tempt us.'

'We are not all as good, or as strong, or as holy as Abraham. We do not have the purity to dare to submit ourselves to God's Will.'

'I think –' the boy said slowly.

'Go on, Lamb.'

'*I* think the Devil had got into God, and was winning. I think – I think it was evil to ask him to do that –'

'No, no, it is wickedness and weakness ever to think God can do evil. God is goodness itself. He made all well for Abraham. The sacrifice was provided, the Angel stayed his hand, Isaac survived.'

'Isaac hated him forever, perhaps.'

'No, no, because he too was chosen, was a holy man, who was able to trust, both his earthly and his Heavenly Fathers. There is no merit in obedience if obedience is easy and pleasant.'

Black boiled inside and outside him. He smelt mothballs and wool. She showed him, then, the art postcard she had brought to help them see the scene, and understand.

Later, he knew that it was Rembrandt's version of the Sacrifice of Isaac. The angel leans out of black thunderclouds. Its right hand grasps Abraham's strong wrist. The curved knife, sharpened horribly clean, hangs forever in free fall across the landscape. Abraham's bearded face, intent on what he has set out to do, startled in his nerves by the apparition, is turned up to the angel, away from the boy. The boy, naked except for a loincloth, lies back on the firewood. He has no face. Abraham's left hand, brown skin on white, is clamped like a sucker, over the whole upper head of the boy. The head is forced back, smothered, so that the man cannot see the boy's face and the boy cannot see the knife. What can be seen is the stretched white throat. Murder and pity. The boy, Josh Lamb, seeing this picture, was filled with that overwhelming and appalling pity with which the man now regarded the distant boy. He stared, and then all his muscles clamped into spasm, he vomited, he foamed, his bowels gave way, he went into the dark, which was busy and roaring, which was not peace. God was bad, bad was God, his voice squeaked as he went, whether into the air or only into the cavern of his head he never knew and could not ask. For no one spoke to him again of the episode. That he remembered, at least.

In later years this episode became part of the rigorous and rigid account he made for himself of his ineluctable destiny. All human beings tell their life-stories to themselves, selecting and reinforcing certain memories, casting others into oblivion. All human beings are interested in causation. 'Because I had a good Latin teacher, who caught my mind with incantatory grammar, I became a theologian, and because I chose Latin, I put aside the sciences of earth, flesh and space.' All human beings are interested in pure coincidence, which can act in a life as surely as causation, and appear to resemble that, as though both were equally the effects of a divine putting-on. Most of us know the flutter of the heart which comes when, out of a whole library, we put a random hand on the *one necessary book*, and – unerringly we should say, but what does that *mean*? – open it, at the *one necessary page*. In the *Arabian Nights*, it has been said, a man has his Destiny written on his forehead, and his character, his nature, is that Destiny and nothing else. A boy, a man, like Josh Lamb, Joshua Ramsden, who has found himself tumbling in the dark sea outside the terrible transparent mirror of the fragile window-pane, persists perhaps by linking moments of conscious survival into a fine suspension-bridge of a personal destiny, a narrow path of constructed light, arching out over the bulging and boiling.

During Josh Lamb's school-days the battle flamed in the air and descended screaming and incandescent from the sky to earth. Everyone was quick with a small sense of destiny, everyone had their 'luck' which had saved their house, or their doom, which had seen their daily life battered to dust and rubble. Little boys ran, arms spread like dark wings, humming and burring, Spitfires, Hurricanes, Beaufighters. All life had a glaring 'reality' which was unreal, and different from the normal (ordinary).

He found old storybooks in which serpents strangled the shores and the impotent gods were defeated. He read them as the bombers growled and churned over his bedroom roof, close, close. He knew that they described the truth of things. The little children in Hamelin Square in 1968 listened to tales of dark fate and world battle, sitting on safe sofas by the fireside, eating toast and honey. They inhabited the darkness briefly, with a thrill and a shiver, like swimmers advancing into the cold water, drenched by the roaring breakers, scuttling back to sand and sunlight, sleeking their wet hair and skins. Leo and Saskia, Thano and Clement, were not without their own wounds and destinies. But they could believe in cushions, fireside, bread, milk, and honey. The boy Josh Lamb took comfort from the old myth because it was an adequate description of the world he inhabited, by necessity.

He linked his father's lost postcard, with the Genesis reference, to the Rembrandt painting and his classroom fit. He was ambivalently chosen for sacrifice and saved from the burning. Much later, in one of his asylum incarcerations, he was encouraged to do 'Art Therapy'. He took pleasure in painting wild skies with a full moon covered by a five-fingered cloud, like a hand clutching it to quench it. He knew by then what it represented, what it was a Sign of. The Smudge. But as a boy he had not understood that.

He began to hear voices, so his tale of his destiny told him, shortly after the fit in the Scripture lesson. They were not 'in' his head, they were somewhere out there, like Hagar's Angel, and Abraham's. Sometimes it was as if he 'overheard' them. They quarrelled with each other, as his father and mother (rarely) had quarrelled. He got into trouble with his aunt, and with teachers, for cocking his head to catch what they said. He learned to listen without moving a muscle. When the voices were talking, he didn't hear the ordinary world. There was one particular voice that he called the tempter. It gave orders, in a clear, incontrovertible, no-nonsense tone. It told him to step into the road in front of the school bus. It told him to open the window and step out on to the darkness. He had seen that the other could stand up in it. What had he to lose? said the voice. There was a very strangled voice, which spoke in fragments only, which said 'No, don't', and 'Get *on* bus', and 'Remember', though it didn't say what he should remember. Sometimes they all shrieked and whistled together, and he put his hands to his ears. He might, in some other world, have told his aunt about the voices, but the voices themselves reminded him that his aunt already thought he was nasty.

The tempter always spoke clear English. When the other returned, the twin who had given him the dark to hold, he did not at first know him or acknowledge him, for he spoke in Latin. The man believed, the man *knew* that the boy had heard Latin he could neither understand nor construe, which, written down and looked up, had sense and meaning.

Languages, said Mr Shepherd, show us that our way of seeing the world is incomplete. You must learn to translate English into Latin, and Latin into English, precisely and beautifully, but you must never suppose that the one is the *same as* the other. A man thinking in Latin is not thinking the same thoughts as a man thinking in English. For one thing, the shape of the words, and the shape of the sentences, changes the shape of the thoughts. For another, some words cannot be translated, they exist only in the language that made them. For another, later languages are partly based on the forms and words of Latin, which they have absorbed and transmuted. To know Latin, boys, is to know part of the history of this country, which we are defending, part of its roots and origins. Latin is like one blue-print of the forms of thinking and speaking, across which another Germanic form has been placed. The word translate comes from Latin – *trans*, across, *latum*, from *fero, ferre, tuli, latum*, I carry, carried. The word transmute is formed in the same way, from *trans*, across, and *muto, mutare, mutavi, mutatum*, I change, changed.

What are known as the Romance languages, he told them,

French, Spanish, Italian, Portuguese and others, come from Latin more directly than English. English has two ways of saying many things precisely because it is a deliciously mongrel language, with its Anglo-Saxon, Norse and Germanic roots.

It is my hope, boys, to be able to make you – or some of you – however fleetingly – *think* in Latin.

This should cause you never again to take English for granted as the language of common sense.

The boy, who knew he himself was double, inside and outside, formed the idea, half drawn from Mr Shepherd's observations, of a different world, out there, described in a different language, with different rules. It felt like a way to slip out of his bonds, to reform himself. He listened.

They chanted prepositions which took the ablative, to a tune invented by Mr Shepherd.

> *A, ab, absque, coram, de*
> *Palam, clam, cum, ex and e*
> Sometimes *in, sub, super, subter*

They talked about words made up with prepositions. Many of you are evacuees, said Mr Shepherd. That comes from *e*, meaning out of, and *vacuus*, meaning empty. *Vacuus* connects to vacancy and also of course to the word vacuum, meaning emptiness, from where we get vacuum cleaners, which suck up dirt into an emptiness and vacuum flasks which keep fluids warm inside a silvered wall of vacancy.

The boy had made his own description of his destiny, which included the word evacuee, which until that moment had meant to him that he had been ejected into emptiness. Now he saw that it could mean the opposite, where he had come from was empty.

There was some classroom sniggering about the corporeal (from *corpus*, body) meanings of evacuate. Mr Shepherd said he was glad to know they were so well informed, and that yes, you could evacuate your bowels, or your stomach, through various orifices. He told them the derivation of orifice. *Ora*, mouth, *facio*, to make, any opening, which had the form of a mouth, such as a jar, a tube, a wound. *Orare*, to pray, to speak. *Orator*. *Ora pro nobis*, said a Catholic boy. You are thinking in Latin, said Mr Shepherd. Good boy.

They were sent away to find words beginning with *e*, or *ex* for homework. First, said Mr Shepherd, write down those you have thought of *without* the dictionary. Then use it. Connect your words. Connect them. It is more interesting than Lotto, I think. Is 'Lotto' Latin, sir? asked a wit. No, said Mr Shepherd. It is Old English and comes from Llot, or Fate, or Destiny. It is to do with drawing lots – bits of wood, or short straws. It may be related to Old Norse, *hlant*, blood of sacrifice. In this interesting case the French and Italian appear to derive from the English. The Latin is *sors, sortis*. The *sortes virgilianae* was a kind of fatal lottery which consisted of opening Virgil's writings at random, and reading the fate *allotted* to you on the page. A *sorcerer* is expert in *sortes*. He makes, or divines (*divinare*, to conjure, French *deviner*, to guess) fates.

The boys came back to class with words, like blackberries at harvest, like lots, or *sortes*, or pieces of an infinite jigsaw. Elicit, evolve, eliminate (from *limen*, threshold, a magical word, good boy), excrescence, exaggerate, exempt, exigent, exgurgitate, extrude, educate ('*to lead out*, boys, I lead you out of your darkness into the clear light of knowledge'), exculpate, erupt, emit, extrapolate, exceed, efface, effusion, exude . . .

Eject, he had said, thinking, an evacuee is ejected. From *jaces*, I throw, as with javelins, said Mr Shepherd.

Then Shattuck, the dark boy who captained the rugby 15 said 'Execute'.

The whistling in his ears began again. He remembered this sometimes, not always.

'From *Ex* plus *sequor*, to follow out, to carry out. You may execute a command, human or divine, Shattuck.'

'And a man, sir. You may execute a man.'

'By derivation. You may execute a command or a sentence which has come to mean, to take the life of a man. Sentence, from *sententia*, opinion, judgement.'

Eject, evacuate, execute. Educate.

No one has found eximious or egregious, said Mr Shepherd. Eximious is a delicious word, meaning, outstanding. From ex + *imere*, to take out, to make an exception of. And egregious I am particularly attached to, since my name is Shepherd. For it comes from *ex + grex, gregis*, a flock. It means also, the exceptional, the outstanding, that which stands out from the mass. It may be good, or bad. An egregious act of kindness. An egregious falsehood. Solid objects, like sheep, like thresholds, like hands and mouths, are behind many abstract words, boys. It is the way the human mind works. Our ancestors were all shepherds, or farmers, or masons.

Or warriors, sir.

Or warriors, Shattuck.

The Latin for shepherd is Pastor. Hence, pastoral, to do with the countryside. Hence con*gregation*, *flock* of people, gathering.

And here – not at the discussion of the word, execute, during which he had gripped his desk and endured, but here, with Shepherd, with egregious, he had again glimpsed his own eximious lot. For something that wove languages on two looms, the visible commonplace and commonsense, and the inordinate, the extra-vagant (outward-wandering) invisible underside of the tapestry, was letting him glimpse messages. Agnes and Lamb were no accident, and his proper nature and name were Ramsden, the lair of the horned egregious beast. Not for nothing was the ram caught in the thicket, the egregious, extrapolated, ejected, eliminated, evacuated Ram. And Miss Manson was Christianity, she spoke for the mild Lamb, the Son of Man, but he, secretly, was the Ram who knew the dreadful truth, that the orders executed by both his father (Abraham) and the bewigged monster who had condemned him on behalf of the Son of Man were the orders of a god who was possessed and conquered and inhabited by Evil. Impotent angels, horned beasts helplessly tangled in thickets, were eternally opposed to Powers they might never master, powers who could make of him evacuated dead matter, eliminated *shit*, ejected *bolus*, if they turned their baleful attention on him.

VIII

The man remembered less of his late adolescence than of his childhood; it appeared that the shock treatment had burned away more of what he still knew to have been a troubled and a tormented time. He matriculated in 1943 when the war-tide was turning, and took his Higher School Certificate in 1945 as the nation erupted into peace. In 1949 he had become a theological student in Durham. These things were on record, he had certificates, he had an exiguous history. The form of his memory was woven differently.

His aunt took him to Morning Prayer every Sunday at the local church of St John the Divine. She was an assiduous attender, a church mouse who scurried away after the service in case anyone asked any inconvenient question. To her, church-going was part of the grey flannel of normality in which she chose to secrete the boy, hiding him away in a back pew, rebuffing overtures from other church-goers. He remembered confusedly how deeply ashamed she had been of him. How she had flushed darkly and thrust her chin into her chest when he sang, loud and clear. He liked singing. The church was small, and for a time he had been in the choir. He knew his aunt hated to see him up there, in his white gown. (The man remembered the boy as having had white hair above the white flowing pleats. When had his hair changed?) He himself felt less conspicuous under the enveloping white, with its clean, starched smell, than he did in his thick ill-fitting grey blazer. Once, he remembered, he had sung solo, *Agnus Dei qui tollis peccata mundi*. Something had gone horribly wrong. He could not remember what. Only the Vicar's pale, kind, confused eyes.

He was very confused about the Church. He felt that it was a place in which the dangerous vacancy in which he was forced to wander, was real and acknowledged. Sometimes he felt that the

Church was a fortress against the dark demons outside, and sometimes that it was itself a source of energy to them. By admitting their existence it fed and strengthened them. It was an old building, with a square tower and a rounded porch. It had two coloured windows, and the others were plain greyish glass. One of the coloured windows was old, and showed the Crucifixion. The man hung thin and twisted, his thorn-bound head fallen sideways, his rib-cage stretched, his feet and hands nailed with great bolts to the dark wood. Blood ran in festoons, over his face, out of the gaping orifice in his side, down the black tree from his shattered feet, out on to the dark cobalt-blue sky from his pierced palms. His face was a still mask. There was a black sun above him. It was a small window; he was alone; no mourners, no torturers, no angels. It was a very dark window; only in exceptionally bright weather, at noon, was it possible to distinguish much detail in it.

The other window was in the style of the Pre-Raphaelites, and was resolutely cheerful. A smiling, gold-haired figure stood in white robes with outspread arms, involved in a whirl of twining foliage, emerald leaves, bunches of grapes glowing ruby and amethyst and an unnatural dark blue. 'I am the true vine, and my Father is the husbandman' was written on a fluttering streamer under the elegant, etiolated bare feet. There was a suggestion that the figure was a foliate man – his fingers flowed into the branches, the curling tendrils of creeper wound themselves into his hair and beard, wandered around his neck and waist, and wrists.

If the outside violence were to break in, it would come seeping through the old window, like the outreaching fingers of a flood, probing, bursting. *There* was the darkness.

The Vicar's name was Denis Little. He was small, slight, blond, and a bachelor. He was timidly inclined to a High Church interest in ritual. Joshua Ramsden detected in him no real spirituality, only a kind of anxious yearning. He did not know, Joshua concluded (without knowing he had concluded anything) what forces were loose in the universe. The thick walls of his church were a dubious protection. Joshua Lamb dreamed, more than once, that the church was like a paper bag full of air, puffed out, sealed at the top, which the dark could clap in its hands, like a boy bursting such a bag, releasing a soft explosion of trapped air into the larger, violent currents. Denis Little had a framed reproduction of Van Eyck's Adoration of the Lamb from Ghent over the altar.

The Ram or Lamb stood, benign but judicial, on a scarlet table, its head emitting effulgent gold in rays. Lovely angels knelt around it. From a neat hole in its breast a spout of blood poured itself neatly and perpetually into a gold cup, a crimson pool rimmed with bright yellow sparkings. The sight of the round hole in the fleece and flesh made the boy feel nauseous. It was, the man believed, round about this time that he had started to see the blood running down surfaces in gouts, in clotting rivulets, in fast-moving sheets. Over the white-washed walls of the church, over the glass in the frame covering the Mystic Lamb.

Denis Little liked Josh Lamb. He encouraged him to be confirmed. Agnes Lamb was against this step – Morning Prayer and the church bazaar and whist drive were good enough for her, and therefore him. No need to take things too far. Josh Lamb didn't know if he wanted to be confirmed or not. He began at that time to be addicted to the different language of the church services and the Bible. He liked to repeat to Mr Little the old phrases like worn coins, like the Bun pennies of Queen Victoria with a half-obscured youthful female head, which turned up from time to time in their change, in those days. 'I pray unto God, that he will send us all things that be needful both for our souls and bodies; and that he will be merciful to us and forgive us our sins; and that it will please him to save and defend us in all dangers ghostly and bodily; and that he will keep us from all sin and wickedness, and from our ghostly enemy, and from everlasting death.' He learned easily, and recited with feeling. Denis Little patted his shoulder in approbation. His nervous fingers fluttered and played over the blazer shoulder with its stuffed padding. Inside the boy's flesh registered, and ignored, a faraway whisper, a ghost of an appeal. Once, the quavering palm of the spiritual hand brushed his cheek. He pushed it away, eyes down. The gesture was never repeated.

He began to write holy books at this time. 'This is the word of Joshua, who was evacuated from the place of the Ram, and exempt from the Offering that was made. I have held in my arms the heavy globus of Dark and have seen with mine eyes the blade of Light that shall part it.' The voices spoke to him as his hand rustled over the lined exercise-book. Don't write, not yet, writing is dangerous, desist. The time is not yet. The writing was not comforting.

He read the book of Joshua in the Old Testament, looking for signs. He was looking for signs of why he had been called Joshua. The name, it was true, had been chosen by his father; his preparation for the Confirmation included mild reference to his naming at his Baptism. If he had had godparents as an infant he did not know who they were. He told Denis Little his parents were dead. He was adept at preventing questions about them. Parts of his own substance became numb and withered every time he turned these questions away.

Joshua was an angry judge. He spoke with a man with a drawn sword, who stood over against him. Art thou for us or for our adversaries? Joshua asked. And found that the opponent was the captain of the host of the Lord, an angel, Josh Lamb supposed. The Lord led Joshua to smite, and slay, to stone, to burn, to circumcise and make mountains of foreskins. Joshua spoke gently to Achan, the son of Carmi, and asked him if he had taken the accursed thing. And Achan confessed that he had taken a goodly Babylonish garment, two hundred shekels of silver, and a wedge of gold, and hidden them under his tent. So Joshua and all Israel stoned him and his family to death 'and burned them with fire, after they had stoned them with stones'.

Joshua had an affinity with stones. He hanged kings, and closed them into caves with stones. He made an altar of whole stones 'over which no man hath lift up any iron' and offered burned offerings on it. He wrote a copy of the law of Moses on stones. He caused the stone walls of the city of Jericho to fall, with the sound of rams-horn trumpets. He caused the sun and the moon to stand still, whilst Joshua and his people slew the enemy with great slaughter. And the Lord came to help Joshua with his killing; he 'cast down great stones from heaven upon them unto Azekah, and they died; they were more which died with hailstones than they whom the children of Israel slew with the sword.'

And the sun stood still, and the moon stayed, until the people had avenged themselves upon their enemies . . .

And there was no day like that before it or after it, that the Lord hearkened unto the voice of a man: for the Lord fought for Israel.

The book of Joshua did not say what the enemies had done, who were slaughtered. They were enemies, it was enough.

Joshua was a heavy name to carry, heavy as a stone. His one act of gentleness was to appoint cities of refuge for involuntary murderers.

'That the slayer that killeth any person unawares and unwittingly may flee thither: and they shall be your refuge from the avenger of blood.'

The avenger of blood stalked in the dark. He had taken his father and was his father, who was the instrument of the avenger of blood, who heard the voice that exulted in pitiless stoning and burning. The refuge was only for the unwitting. He himself was somehow bloody. On bad days he could smell it, drying in the folds of his clothes, crusting in the locks of his hair, darkening under his fingernails.

Denis Little believed that reading the Bible was wholesome and consoling for growing boys. There was a divine purpose in things, good would prevail, he told them, goodness would work out its way through the darkness of history. The Lord was with our brave pilots and sailors, with the Red armies sweeping across eastern Europe. A just peace was coming, the Lord would not let his people fail. The bloodthirsty Nazis were being overcome.

Joshua would stone them. And then burn them.

Gentleness was a slack mouth, scratched, with false teeth half torn out.

He was asked to believe that God had become the impotent hanging man on the dark tree, the ghostly friend had breathed himself into flesh and blood and had become a burned offering, a sacrificial Lamb, the bloody food not of the 'ghostly enemy' but of the Lord of Hosts, the avenger of blood, who, sated with this flesh, would stop stoning, and burning, and burying alive.

It was, the boy had thought, not Joshua's God, but he himself, who was evil, who could not see clearly, who read wrongly. The Church was a cool, kind refuge from the storm. He himself brought the storm in from outside. The ghostly enemy sang in his ears that Joshua's God was evil. He needed sustaining, sustenance, a rite, an offering.

He presented himself for his first communion. A voice cried in the church, a clear, golden, strong voice, 'Don't eat flesh. Don't drink blood. This is the wrong way.'

And what was being held out to him was, he *saw*, a morsel of bloody muscle and fat, a cup of stinking, gravy-thick blood.

He pitched forward on to Denis Little's feet. He was ill for quite a long time, that time, it was his first time in the hospital. His memory of it was largely lost. He felt pity, terrible pity, for a child who had become a cosmic battlefield. He also felt an energetic ironic contempt for the church life, in which *all* children were said to be, were, cosmic battlefields, and yet one who heard and saw the horrible forces on the other side of the pane, pain, membrane, brain, that separated him from their full impact, could only be hustled away into a hospital ward, where madmen hummed, and caught at imaginary flies, and hid under their beds, and made missiles of their food.

A bull is weakened, he had read, for the *coup de grâce* with the sword, by the repeated blows of the picador, by the banderillas which lodge in his muscle, and send his warm blood streaming down his living flanks. The man saw that the boy had been weakened into 'normality' in the hospital, had been shocked, and argued, and drugged into shambling slowness – and half-starved too, for he knew for certain that much of the 'food' he was offered was poison, he remembered the clear, golden prohibition of flesh and blood, he subsisted on boiled vegetables and apple-tart, worrying sickly about the possibility of lard and the permissibility of milk. But in those days he had no idea whose the golden voice was. It was not time to learn. It was possible that the slow sleepwalker who left the hospital had been weakened by destiny enough to be able to die a little more (pretend to be 'normal' a little more) so that he was able to take communion (saying in his head, this is bread, this is bread, this is flour and water, is *bread*) and present himself, a pale simulacrum of a man called by some divinity, to study theology.

For even in his dead days, when he felt his inner flame quiescent and damped inside a kind of rubbery suit of the numb and withered matter of his body, he knew that he was his father's son, and must go in for the dangerous vocation of confronting the demons and the dark.

Durham was stony. The stone cathedral and the stone castle of the Prince Bishops rose on a stony promontory in the river, visible from everywhere in the compact city. The stone did not soar or aspire, though it had grace, in an immensely heavy way. The streets were cobbled, leading up to the cobbled paths leading to the Palace Green. Joshua Lamb, who connected everything increasingly with everything, and forgot those things which could not be connected, imagined holding those worn cobbles in his hand to stone sinners. He imagined them, reasonably enough, running with blood when Cromwell's soldiers were billeted in the great Nave. Nave, *nave*, *navis*, ship. The Ark on Ararat. Grounded. The stony city had two male populations, the cathedral and the miners. The university students were predominantly male, too. The cathedral, the theological colleges, the Deanery, had their own orderly life among the stones. The miners came up out of the earth, once a year, with bright banners, gathered in the cold dawn and swarmed down over the cobbles to the racecourse for their Gala.

The theologians did not go to the gala, and did not eat or drink in the dark, smoky public houses in the town. They gathered in their own common rooms and refectory. Some, Joshua Lamb saw, had a pallid spirituality in them. Some were dutiful and some were anxious. The young man had moments of what he believed was happiness, and these distracted and overthrew him. He remembered sitting in his small study-bedroom on the Bailey, and taking stock of the fact that he was not – for the first time since his Evacuation – oppressed by his aunt's disgust with him. He felt cleaner. He felt less fleshy, less obscene. He ate very little, to increase this feeling of lightness. Voices spoke to him, and told him not to touch flesh and blood. Walking to a lecture, he passed a fishmonger's shop. He saw the glittering flame-ringed eyes of the fresh herring, he saw the slate and peridot ripples, on lead and mercury sheen, of the gleaming mackerel.

His stomach turned. He imagined milk, issuing from the warm, squeezed, *handled* teats under the odorous cow-belly, and he drank water. He felt lightened by these decisions. The voices sang now, curving past him like bird-flight down staircases, humming like power-lines between the great pillars of the cathedral.

He had not expected to be able ever to have friends. He had had a friend whose living mother had smiled as she closed the door in his last moment of dailiness. He had known, as he stared out of the dark window with the bed and the bodies behind him, that here was the end of friendship. He had set himself to go on grimly, on his own, always on his own.

But the other young men in his college did not know that, and did not see him, as his aunt did, as a crawling thing. They were Christian young men, they included him as a matter of course in walks to see Hadrian's Wall, or visit Mithraic temples. They asked him to drink after-dinner cups of coffee or cocoa, and then asked his opinion on moral matters – the celibacy of the clergy (there were several High Church aspirants), the nature of sin, the truth of the resurrection. He discovered a strange circumstance. He spoke little, but when he spoke, the babble of voices always hushed, faces turned towards him like opening flowers, eyes widened. He could hear the silence of their attention, and he liked to hear it, he existed as a force, in the connection between his mind, his voice, and their listening. This airy electricity was his first dangerous happiness.

The second was his reading. For some time – at least a year, his broken memory could not reconstruct an image of those vanished orderly days – he was a good student, an exceptional student. He sat in the library, amongst the books inherited from monks and divines, and read proudly in Latin, as well as in English. He wrote thoughtful essays on points of doctrine and the history of Christian belief – essays which he was later commanded to burn and disperse to the winds, but which gave him, he remembered as a chill warning, such a sense of order, of belonging to a community, of voices rising to gather in a choir of language and harmonious sound. His pen travelled over the paper of his notebooks, and inside the library and outside it seemed to be balanced, to be part of a divine and human order. He read the Venerable Bede, in those days. There was a romantic piety amongst his fellow-students about the great men who had worked, or died, or been buried, in this sacred place. Bede's tomb, black and plain, stood in the Galilee Chapel. *Haec sunt in fossa, Bedae venerabilis ossa.* He read Bede's image of the sparrow, flying from the dark into the lighted room, and out again into the night. He found it touching.

The voices sang, Adeodatus.

Given by God. He thought it meant himself, the gift of God, chosen to be a priest.

He discovered it was the name of St Augustine's dead son, dead at fifteen, with whom the saint had written the *Dialogue of the Master*. The man in the Cedar Mount hospital kept two heavily marked books under his bed. They were Kierkegaard's *Fear and Trembling* and St Augustine's *Confessions*. Both were interleaved with pages of his own writing. Both were, as he saw it, then and now, riddling messages addressed to him personally, ambivalently designated for his rescue and his perdition. Both had been recommended to him by his tutor and instructor, Dr John Burgess, who liked to be known as Father Burgess.

This man had the charisma of Mr Shepherd and Miss Manson, but more formidably, for his training had led him to be aware of it, to know how to use it, and most delicately to refrain from using it when necessary. He was dark and ascetic, buttoned into black clothes; he wore a wide-brimmed black hat, and had a neatly trimmed squared black beard. He sensed Josh Lamb's trouble, without knowing anything of its cause, and set himself to finding out the secrets of Lamb's soul, by methods often quiet and negative, by *not* asking, by *not* insisting, by listening to every word. Now and then – sparsely, and therefore memorably – he would say definite things. 'Men, like you, with an undeniable vocation . . .' or 'I know that your spiritual life is a strong current, with much turbulence.' Or 'You will make a good priest. I have noticed that others confide in you, because you have a proper reticence, you keep confidences.'

Until Father Burgess said this, Josh Lamb had not supposed he was peculiarly favoured with the trust of others. It was true that one fellow-student had asked him to spend an evening listening to his doubts, and another, walking beside the River Weir, had laid his hand on Josh Lamb's arm and asked whether nightly visions of the bodies of young men was in itself evil? It was true also that his fellow-supervisee, a cricket-player called Reggie Booth, read aloud to Josh Lamb his letters from his fiancée, a student in Reading, who took pleasure in recounting advances made by other men, and in making frantic attacks on the hypocrisy of the Church. Josh listened, and turned round all these problems in a clear vacant space that hung inside him, where he isolated them and imagined them *through*.

It was not 'sympathy' he felt, since nothing in his body stirred in response to these problems, nothing in his single self put out a metaphorical finger to touch the hurt. He spoke truthfully from his absence to his interlocutors. He told the first that he must let himself hear his doubts, not stifle them, or they would become demons. He told the second that he must know the difference between real and imaginary young men. He threaded his way like an embroidery needle through the tangle of expostulation of the fiancée in Reading, 'This bit says she is *really worried*', 'This bit is designed to hurt *you*. Don't answer it.' How do you know? asked Reggie Booth. I simply listen to the feel of the words, said Josh Lamb.

But he was not going to bare his own soul for Father Burgess to listen to. It was swaddled and wadded from human prying. From somewhere inside his thick insulation he offered tantalising clues, or frantic fragments – he himself did not know which. He came back again and again to Abraham and Isaac. Why should a good God tempt his chosen servant to murder?

Father Burgess suggested he read *Fear and Trembling*, in which Kierkegaard examined the story of Abraham and Isaac, and presented the patriarch as the knight of Faith, to be praised not for his resignation to the will of God, but for the leap of complete trust, which in the ordinary human would come close to madness.

The pity the man in the hospital felt for the thigh of the fat boy which trembled as he stood and stared at the bed, was the same pity as he felt for the young student in the cathedral library who was writing his paper, *Credo quia absurdum*, to please Father Burgess. The student, because of his sparing eating habits, had become thin, though not broomstick-skeletal as he was later to be. (Lamb-Ramsden always had the uneasy capacity to see himself from outside, from some far place.)

Kierkegaard's speaker recognises that faith and madness are close, like two sides of a membrane, the thin student wrote. He quoted 'I can put up with everything, even if that demon, more horrifying than the skull and bones that put terror into men's hearts – even if madness itself were to hold up the fool's costume before my eyes and I could tell from its look that it was I who was to put it on; I can still save my soul so long as it is more important for me that my love of God should triumph in me than my worldly happiness . . . But by my own strength I cannot get the least little thing of what belongs to finitude; for I am continually using up my energy to renounce everything.'

The thin young man, in a cautious ecstasy of understanding, explained in his paper, which he later read to a gathered audience, the difference according to Kierkegaard between the tragic hero, the knights of infinite resignation, and the knights of faith who, like Abraham, are content to rest, narrow-minded, trusting, on the mystery, ready equally to lose Isaac or to receive him back again.

He explained Kierkegaard's horror at Abraham's faith.

'He knows it is beautiful to be born as the particular with the universal as his home, his friendly abode, which receives him straight away with open arms when he wishes to stay there. But he also knows that higher up there winds a lonely path, narrow and steep; he knows it is terrible to be born in solitude outside the universal, to walk without meeting a single traveller. He knows very well where he is and how he is related to men. Humanly speaking he is insane and cannot make himself understood to anyone. And yet, "insane" is the mildest expression for him. If he isn't viewed thus, he is a hypocrite, and the higher up the path he climbs, the more dreadful a hypocrite he becomes.'

The most daring thing about *Fear and Trembling*, the thin, white-haired young man said to his listeners, was the sudden likening of the knight of faith to the philistine bourgeois. This satisfied person 'takes pleasure, takes part, in everything'. He looks just like a tax-gatherer. He minds his affairs. He goes to church as a matter of course and sings 'lustily' for the pleasure of using his lungs. 'In the afternoon he takes a walk in the woods. He delights in everything he sees, in the crowd of people, in the new omnibuses, in the seashore . . .'

Consider, said Josh Lamb, who had lived more than half of his short life out in the whistling waste, how unusual in fact *it is* that a human being should look at the world with such pleasure, like God on the working-days of the Creation. And then consider Kierkegaard's next cunning joke. He goes on describing this unpoetic, untragic, finite person.

'Towards evening he goes home, his step tireless as a postman's. On the way it occurs to him that his wife will surely have some special little warm dish for his return, for example roast head of lamb with vegetables . . . As it happens, he hasn't a penny, and yet he firmly believes his wife has that delicacy waiting for him. If she has, to see him eat it would be a sight for superior people to envy and for plain folk to be inspired by, for his appetite is greater than Esau's. If his wife doesn't have the dish, curiously enough he is exactly the same.'

The young man paused, his hands held up, like the paintings of Cuthbert and Oswald in the cathedral, palms out to his hearers. As he remembered the fat thigh, so he now remembered, or thought he remembered, the almost-transparency of those bony hands. You could see red light around the fingers, between the webs. He felt pity for the raw knuckles. The young man, in his sermon, repeated the sentence. 'If his wife doesn't have the dish, curiously enough he is exactly the same.'

The cheerful bourgeois is to eat what. Roast *lamb*. Not only lamb, *lamb's head*. How can this not recall the ram in the thicket who is the substitute for the slaughtered son, but might never have materialised at all? There is the banal tasty head-on-a-platter with vegetables, and there is a man salivating at the thought of eating it who is 'exactly the same' if it doesn't materialise.

Here is the mystery of this text, said Josh Lamb. The closeness of the unthinking cheerfulness to the unthinking, unanxious calm faith, which does not question and takes no thought for the morrow. Consider the lilies and the sparrows falling. It is appallingly difficult. Tragedy is easier, as Kierkegaard knew.

'The tragic hero, the darling of ethics, is a purely human being, and he is someone I can understand, someone all of whose undertakings are in the open. If I go further I always run up against the paradox, the divine and the demonic, for silence is both of these. It is the demon's lure, and the more silent one keeps the more terrible the demon becomes; but silence is also divinity's communion with the individual.'

And there the suddenly eloquent young man became silent himself. (*E* + *loquor*, speaking out of.) He was aware that he had caused a trembling in his hearers, that he had stirred them, that his words, and Kierkegaard's, had lodged in their flesh and blood. Father Burgess said to him

'Well said. But always remember that one map of another man's thought always runs the risk of becoming a string of shortcuts between arbitrary landmarks.'

He had not understood at the time. But later, he had realised that 'his' Kierkegaard was made up of the lamb's head, the jester's costume, the demons, the winding path. He tried to reread, to rerember. They went on destroying his memory. A man cannot even *read* well, whose memory functions intermittently only.

There was a time, long or short, when he believed he had faith. What a gap, in cold fact, between the verb, believed, in the quotidian world, and the gold girdle, faith, which shimmered and dissolved. He walked and walked, in the cathedral, along the river, touching the stones of the great pillars in an ecstasy of sensing that his faith was solid. He saw the Sanctuary knocker, on the North Door, with its bronze face of fiery beast or demon, and laughed aloud at the meaningful coincidence that he, Joshua, was here, where someone had built a stone hiding-place for those running for dear life from the avenger of blood, to whom respite could be given, and a way out.

He was writing a required essay on St Augustine's concept of the nature and origin of evil. Augustine believed that an infinitely good, infinitely powerful Father had made the universe, and that some flaw in human will, some terrible perversity in human desire, had let in the forces of darkness. The human will was infected. 'There is indeed, *some light in men*; but let them walk fast, walk fast, *lest the shadows come*.' Augustine's spirit inhabited 'a limitless forest, full of unexpected dangers'. The saint was a man caught in the toils of the net of his own memory, to which he had imperfect access. 'This memory of mine is a great force, a vertiginous mystery, my God, a hidden depth of infinite complexity; and this is my soul, and this is what I am. What then am I, my God? What is my true nature? A living thing, taking innumerable forms, quite limitless ... For there is in me a lamentable darkness ...' Habit, infected memory, make virtue impossible. Nevertheless, the all-powerful God knows who will have faith and who will not, who will ascend to heaven and who will burn eternally.

Joshua Lamb read about St Augustine's misspent youth as a Manichee. The Manichees believed that evil was as powerful as, or more powerful than, the Good. They believed that the Ruler of Light, in a kingdom outside time and space, shone eternally to himself, until the forces of Dark and Matter invaded the borders and swallowed the particles of Light. The Light called up the First Adam, and sent him out to do battle. He was defeated, destroyed, and devoured by the demons, who confined the Light in Darkness, and created the world, including human beings, who did not know that they had Light in them, vainly trying to escape back to its own undifferentiated shining. The Suffering Jesus was another Messenger sent by the Light, and crucified, throughout the visible Universe. He was the fruit, on every tree, that was plucked and eaten. The Light had to be allowed to separate itself again completely from the dark. It had to flow back. To that end, the human children of Light had to forgo both procreation and the consumption of flesh and other solid creatures, both of which prolonged the entrapment of Light.

The Redeemer was in the very process of being redeemed, and the outcome was still very much in doubt. The same battle for the release of the light particles was taking place in every conscious human soul.

St Augustine repudiated his Manichaean youth; he was a doughty, battling saint, and he came to feel that the Manichaean sense of the passivity, the quiescence, the acquiescence of the Good, was an insult to God the Father, as the Manichaean sense of an incorrupt scattering of light particles in the corrupt body and mind, was a wrong description of the Fallen Soul. *All*, all was Fallen; all that could be redeemed was redeemed by the powerful and terrible Son of the Father. He fought his old allies with passion and ferocity.

Joshua Ramsden read the Manichaean psalm about the violated divinity of which the individual mind was part.

I am in everything; I bear the skies; I am the foundation; I am the life of the world; I am the milk that is in all trees; I am the sweet water that is beneath the sons of matter.

His newly-acquired Christian faith was ecstatic and brittle, shining like a fine bubble of glass.

He ate little, and slept only in snatches. He lay awake in the dark, spreadeagled on his back, and the spiritual currents spun through his veins like shoals of lethal air-bubbles, or scattered sphericles of quicksilver. He was running with airiness and slippery brightness. He lay awake and listened to the humming. Whenever, briefly, he slept (or so he remembered) he would wake suffocating, with the sense of a heavy hand, clamped over his nose, bruising his mouth and nostrils. He would smell raw meat, and a faint rottenness. He would thrash around for freedom. And the particles of brightness in his blood would wheel in terror, turn back, drain his heart.

The night came, the night of the return of the other. He woke under the fleshy pad, and struggled free, and a voice told him to stand, and look out. So he went to his window. The moon was full, silver, platinum, etched with shadowy lakes and mountains, brimming over with brightness. The other stood outside in the dark and smiled at him, from under his own flowing white hair, which caught the moonlight. His face was blanched, its shadows a delicate blue-grey like the shadows on the moon. Come out, said the other, beckoning. The moon shines bright as day. Come out.

So he went out into the street, stopping only to put on a raincoat and slippers. He followed the other, who walked, gliding, along the Bailey, up Dun Cow Lane, on to Palace Green. And there, walking, dancing, on the Green between castle and cathedral, under a dark indigo bowl of space full of moonlight, were hundreds and thousands of creatures made of light, men, women, winged things and swimming things, like sea-serpents or sinuous fish, all dripping with brilliance as though they were phosphorescence rising from the deep, as though they were made of scaly coats of brilliance that shone in moony colours, green, blue, silver, violet. They swarmed up and down towards the moon, in great dancing columns like gnats on a river-surface, like clouds of starlings drained of black and made of brightness, like sparks from a fire. They melted into pillars and causeways and branching forests of undifferentiated light and then took form again as dancers, swimmers, soaring wings. He could have watched forever and never knew how long he stood. The other stood beside him, and said 'Loose thy shoe from off thy foot, for the place whereon thou standest is holy.' So he took off his slippers, and his feet felt the cool light flowing over and through them, and the quiet life of the shorn grass and clover under them.

The other said he was the Syzygos, the Heavenly Twin. He was the Word. He had returned at the syzygy or conjunction of the bodies of light, the sun and the moon.

He put into the thin man's arms the heavy weight of things, the almost unbearable sphere, but this time it was made of cold light, it was fluid and fluent, and simultaneously it was infinitely weighted and ready to float up and away with the spiring crowd of creatures. And his fingers dabbled in its liquid surface, where wavelets lapped as on a shore, and yet also it had the gloss, and sheen, and cold sliding of metal. And the young man staggered a little, and splayed his bare feet, to hold up better. He felt he himself was molten metal in the intense pleasure of the presence of the Syzygos, whose smiling lips mirrored his own, whose eyes were dark blue wells under springing white brows. And the Syzygos told him, quietly, as he stood there holding the weight of things, that he had been walking in a wrong direction (though his deepest inclinations had been true). He was chosen to follow the true prophet, who was Mani, who had been flayed and martyred for understanding that light was fragile and the dark was fanged and full of energy. Mani had known that there was no certain outcome, and the cruel God of the Old Testament was inhabited and controlled by the Dark. This god's desire for flesh and blood sacrifice was inspired by, was *part of*, the loathsome greed and ogreish carnality of the Dark. Christ's death in time and space had been in vain and had compounded the original evil and increased the horrible energy of the original invaders. In the days of Mani himself, the true believers had thought that the Light particles went back from pure men – who abstained from flesh and desire – into the moon, and from there into the sun. And from there, back to the closed-off kingdom of Light.

More he was told, as he stood there watching the play of colour and the spinning of threads and weaving of shimmering curtains of lovely light.

St Cuthbert, who is buried here, said the Syzygos, saw the ascending spires of light also. But his description was partial, and darkened by the misguiding Book. You must read *our* books, which are scattered and fragmented, like our bodies and history, you must reweave our story and carry it forward, until the Light and the Dark are no longer involved in each other, until purity is pure and corruption is a bolus excreted, evacuated, eliminated.

And the thing in his arms shattered spontaneously, and took flight as a myriad splinters of brightness, like shooting stars, like arrows aimed at the full moon, where they vanished.

He walked home barefoot over the cobbles, which had rills of light and puddles of silver, eddying and flowing over them, as though they were the bed of a river.

After this, he heard more, more coherent voices, a chorus of guides, and instructors. He heard also demonic, tempting voices, which the guides and instructors told him must happen, as once the 'pathways' were open, the dark creatures would try to swarm in. He must suffer, there was no help for it.

For an uncertain length of time, as he remembered, he hurried like a shadow between his bedroom, the Cathedral and the library. He ordered books about the Manichees and discovered the various cosmogonies of the Gnostics, Marcion, Bardasanes, the Egyptian Valentinus whose kingdom of Light was the Pleroma, made of twenty-eight Aeons arranged in *Syzygia*, or heavenly pairs.

Sophia, the youngest of these Aeons, envied God's power to generate without partners, and brought forth an abortion, without form and void, since the male nous gives form to female matter. The abortion, ejected from the Pleroma, took form and was known as 'Sophia Without', daughter of heavenly Sophia. And Sophia Without made a psychic solid of her fear, grief, perplexity and entreaty – fear became a psychic essence, grief a solid material, perplexity a demon and entreaty a thread of repentance.

From this psychic substance the Demiurge created the solid cosmos, below the psychic sphere, and below that lay chaos and darkness. Joshua Ramsden read, and read. Light and dark flashed and clanged in the battlefield of his skull. Serpents coiled, and tusks and fangs struck. The fragile light shivered and retreated. He held on to the heavy pillars of the nave, to keep him upright in the storm where he staggered.

He did not write his essay on St Augustine's corruption of the origin of evil. He tried to write what he had been shown, the world of Aeons and demons, and became entangled in networks of interconnecting, interrelating, contrarily similar, reinforcing, contradicting, systems of names and names and names and qualities. As though theologians generated the language of proper names as easily as demons generated flesh, blood, sinews, plasma, piss, shit.

The Syzygos told him that the plethora of words and names were snares of the demons, for language was man-made, it belonged to the veil of flesh which separated him from the Light. It told him to do as Mani said. To eat no meat, to thwart and constrain no vegetable, to abstain from sex, to kill nothing. To respect the light particles in the whole of the creation. To try assiduously to set them free, to separate them from the dark.

Father Burgess said his essay on Gnostic cosmogony was incomprehensible, and advised him to desist from that course of study. It splinters the mind, like the Book of Revelation, he told the thin young man. Both are temptations, at certain points in a spiritual journey. Both are psychic mirrors for wild thoughts, both make circles of self-reference and echo chambers. It is normal to be seduced by these ideas, at a certain point along the way, he told the young man. The young man was desperately offended by the word, 'seduced'. He imagined fleshy fingers, lips and juices, the exact opposite of the bright threads and ribbons that made both the maze he was in, and the clue to the way through, simultaneously.

The voices told him the moment had come when he must speak. He must speak on the Green, where he had seen the pathway of light. He must tell people of the division of the Light and the Dark, of the things needful for the good life.

When he stood up to speak, his voice seemed to him a ghostly wail, a thin fluting. It was a grey day, with a cold wind, which ruffled his white hair, and seemed to him to blow through him, as though he had become merely a bone-cage. A few people gathered, of whom a few mocked, and a few shuffled. He felt the great earth-bound bulk of the Cathedral reared against him to hurt him. He stared up at it, faltered, and seemed to see its stones falling, heavy, heavy, to crush him. He choked. He fell on his hands and knees, he shielded his head from the blows of falling matter. They took him gently to the hospital again. When they let him out, they said, it was clear that the course of study was stressful to him, and possibly inappropriate. He should go home, they said, meaning, he should return to Agnes Lamb, and reconsider his vocation. Father Burgess put him on a train to Darlington. He said

'You overtaxed yourself, with too much enthusiasm – in the old sense of that word. You are a spiritually violent man. I am sure a way will be given to you to use your power for the best. I am sure you must now try and be peaceful, eat and sleep and do ordinary human things – go to the pictures, play football, make friends, drink beer – anchor yourself to the earth, and wait until your strength is renewed.'

'I am not a Christian,' said Josh Lamb. 'I am a Manichaean.'

'All of us have Manichaean moments,' said Father Burgess with unjustified blandness, as the train drew out in a cloud of soot and smoke and flying pellets of burning ash.

Josh Lamb got out at the next station. He packed a satchel of essentials, from the suitcase he left on the platform, and set out, on foot, into the countryside.

He was set against Agnes Lamb and her grey armchairs, her bowl of dripping and her thick curtains against the light.

He walked. He did bits of gardening. He found seasonal work on farms. He walked, he wandered into libraries and sat amongst stinking tramps. He looked after vegetables and fruit. Now and then he vanished from himself and found himself in hospital. He saw blood running, and great brimful seas of moonlight. Sometimes he thought he was nothing, flotsam, jetsam, a scarecrow. Sometimes, he knew his time had not yet come.

★

The gardens at Cedar Mount were closed, of course, inside a high wall, with spikes, and shards of glass. Inside, there were winding paths, and hedged alcoves, and lawns both expansive and enclosed. On fine days those inhabitants who could be trusted were encouraged to walk on the gravel paths, or to sit out on the stone seats and wooden benches that were disposed around the grounds. In one corner, at some distance from the main hospital building, was a mound with a kind of tufted grove of evergreens, and a swing, creaking on ropes from what looked like a scaffold between the yews and laurels, under the single imposing cedar, which might have given its name to the place.

A service path for gardeners ran to a compost heap behind a copper beech hedge between mound and wall. It was gloomy and overshadowed, but someone had nevertheless put a seat there, under the mound, with no view but the woven beech-twigs and the wall beyond. This dark place had always provided a refuge for the solitary, which was perhaps why it was there. Possibly some gardener even knew about the importance of hiding-places in closed communities. Lucy Nighby sat there whenever they were allowed out. She sat and stared at the dead beech-leaves, which were a drained gold, and rattled, and at the jagged edge of glass that glinted at the top of her horizon. It was almost winter, with a frosty brightness. She had her coat on; it was stained with the moss of the wet wooden seat.

She had decided to die, and had been secreting and saving pills to that end, without really knowing what the pills were, or what effect they would have. She had them in one pocket, in an envelope. She had a plastic bottle of water. Her practical concern was whether she had enough pills. And for that matter, enough water to get them all down. It was the end of the afternoon. A pale-blue sky was becoming thicker, greyer, rosy. She looked at everything very intently, because it was the last time, noting the slow diminishing of the greenness and the sharp brightness of the broken glass as though it was important to do so, noting too the smell of leaf-mould, of resin, of cold and damp. Her hands were cold. She fumbled with the bottle and the envelope. She would put herself out, like a candle, only it was more difficult.

She ate a pill, and sipped, and ate another.

There was a faint movement in the leaves behind her, a step no heavier than a bird disturbing a twig. She turned a little, her chill fingers holding the emerald and scarlet capsule to her lips. He was stepping silently down from the top of the mound, and his crown of white hair appeared to be giving out light in the gloom of the yew-branches. He appeared to be all white, his beard, his shirt, even his pale trousers. He wore no overcoat. He said

'I have been sent to fetch you.'

She didn't speak. She had found life simpler (at least) though not better, since she stopped speaking. The white figure formed and reformed before her eyes; it had rainbow edges, which might have come from her own tears, and it shimmered.

'Something told me,' he said. 'Not them, a voice I heard. To look for you here, now. I know how it is. I know where you are because I walk there. We have things to do, before we can – take ourselves out of the world. You must help me. And I will help you. I can help you.'

She sat there, the small woman, hunched in her camel coat. And felt herself coming back to herself, her untidy bunch of hair, her face pink with cold, her tired eyes, her heavy feet, her finger with the capsule arrested at her dry, cracked lips. A small wind rattled in the beech-leaves. The earth exhaled mild vegetable decomposition. The man looking down on her had the wind in his white hair and shirt and seemed to shine cold and white.

'Look,' he said 'there is the full moon, in the end of daylight. I shall tell you about the light. You know, and I know, about light and dark and what it is to be outside, where both are strong. We have things to do, but you don't know what they are, because you haven't yet been told. But I shall tell you. And you will listen.'

She held the capsule to her lips. Her eyes were wet. She knew – how? – he was a man who hated touching other people. But when he saw no help for it, he came, and with bright cold fingers took the capsule from her red ones, and folded her two hands in his. The sky darkened slowly. The round disc of the moon brightened. He sat down next to her and told her to look at the moon. In the moonlight, the glass spikes looked like a flowing beck of water over stones.

'We must be wise as serpents,' he said. 'We must go in now, and find a way out of here, and I will tell you what I know, and how we must live. Do you have more of those pills?'

She held out the envelope.

'No, I shan't take them. I have my own store, too. Keep them, in case the need is too strong. Because I know that if you and I know we have the means to go, we can find the courage to stay. Put them away.'

She made, now, one little gesture towards him, like a child asking for an embrace.

She felt him overcome his reluctance, give up his distance. Briefly and gracefully, he took hold of her, held her to him, put his cool lips to her brow.

'I am here,' he said. 'Remember, I am here, I know, I am watching for both of us.'

'Who are you?' she said.

'I shall take my name, later, when I am told.'

IX

Leo said 'Thano said, I saw your mum on telly.'

'He should have been in bed,' said Frederica defensively. They were walking back from school into Hamelin Square.

'I expect you didn't tell me you were on telly because you didn't want me to stay up to look at you *either*.'

'I think I probably did tell you. You weren't listening, as usual.'

'If you say, you *think* you *probably*, you know you really didn't.'

'Well,' said Frederica ludicrously, 'it's private.'

'Ha, ha,' said Leo. '*Private*.'

'Lovely to see you in your lovely flower-garden,' cried Marie Agyepong, Clement and Thano's mother, across the square. Victoria Ampleforth appeared on her renovated doorstep and called out congratulations.

'Very *original*, Frederica. I do admire your *nerve*.'

Frederica smiled briefly in her direction.

'*They* all saw you,' said Leo. 'Only I didn't.'

'*I* didn't,' Frederica told him.

He stopped on the pavement and looked up at her.

'Why? Why didn't you?'

'I was afraid I might not like the look of myself. I was afraid I might think I looked silly.'

'Thano didn't think you looked silly. He thought you put your hand in your hair too much. He liked your eyelashes.'

'Thano said he liked my *eyelashes*? He's only seven.'

'He thought they were funny. Like furry caterpillars. He said there were furry caterpillars on the programme, but he didn't explain very well.'

'When I was your age,' said Frederica, as they opened the front door, 'we used to get terribly upset when our mothers came to things at school in embarrassing hats. The thing is, looking back, all hats are embarrassing. Every child finds its particular mother's hat embarrassing. Too big, too small, too flowerpotty, too dishy, too veiled, too jokey. As many children, as many mothers, so many embarrassments. We didn't want to be children whose mothers didn't turn up, but we didn't want anyone to see our mothers.'

'I don't *mind* you being on telly, I think. I think I'm pleased, rather than not. People are impressed. They make jokes of course, but that's OK. They always make jokes about something. Like they always laugh at hats.'

Through the Looking-Glass was, from the beginning, a rapid and elaborate joke about the boxness of the Box. As it opened, the box appeared to contain the hot coals, or logs, the flickering flames and smouldering ash, in the hearth which had been the centre of groups in vanished rooms before the Box came. The fire in its shadowy cave was succeeded by a flat silvery mist (or swirl of smoke), in an elaborate gilded frame. The mist would then clear to reveal the interior of the Looking-Glass world. There was a revolving Janus clock, with a mathematical and a grinning face. There were duplicated mushrooms and cobwebs and windows. At the back of the box was what might have been a bay window, or a mirror reflecting a bay window. In the middle was a transparent box within a box, in which Frederica sat, into which the camera peered and intruded. All through the programme, round the edges of the contained space, from time to time, animated creatures and plants sauntered, sped, shot up and coiled. Roses and lilies, giant caterpillars and trundling chess pieces, multiplied by mirrors, made by students from the Samuel Palmer School of Art who had worked on the Blue Meanies and banana-bright funnels of the Yellow Submarine.

These were the early days of Laura Ashley's long dresses, in cottons and corduroys, spattered with rediscovered Victorian posies, with discreet frills at neck and wrist. Frederica wore blood-crimson rosebuds on a moss-green ground, or pale primroses on indigo. She began the pilots with a carved Vidal Sassoon bob, and grew her red hair longer and longer as the hugely successful sequence of programmes went on. She looked like a sharp, and knowing, and very adult Alice.

Wilkie's idea, like Lewis Carroll's chess-board, had a precise and arbitrary schema that could contain and proliferate thoughts, images, and connections. Frederica herself was the constant. Each week, three things were discussed – an object, an idea, and a person, living or dead. The intention was to avoid the normal categories of journalism – current affairs, politics, arts, science, popular titbits, satire – and mix things in new ways. Each programme had a guest for all three items, and a second guest who discussed one or the other.

There were three pilot programmes in the last quarter of 1968. The first, setting the scene, discussed Charles Dodgson, Nonsense, and an antique mirror. The second discussed Doris Lessing's idea of Free Women, in *The Golden Notebook*, George Eliot, and a Tupperware bowl. The third was about 'creativity' and discussed Sigmund Freud and a Picasso ceramic. Later programmes sprouted inventively in all directions, both visually and intellectually. They fed on the amiable eclectic parodies of the 60s. Frederica appeared as Snow White in a glass coffin, as a mermaid holding a looking-glass in a glass tank in a raree show, as the Witch in the sugar cottage, and, in a programme whose topic was sex, in a glass box sealed with seven padlocks, like the wife of the Genie, who escaped easily to seduce Scheherazade's husband-to-be and his brother, under a palm tree. They were to discuss DDT and astrology, memory and revolution, the death of the past and schizophrenia, nurture and nature, teaching grammar, Shakespeare, Dostoevsky, Mrs Beeton and D.H. Lawrence (who went with sex and the padlocks).

Frederica's guests on the first programme were Jonathan Miller and Richard Gregory, whose Royal Institution Lectures, in the Christmas of 1967–8, on the 'intelligent eye' had been full of visual puzzles, mirror games, and conjuring tricks. He had used the television to test its viewers' perceptions and preconceptions about how the brain constructs the visible world. Miller talked about many things: the child's-eye view of Victorian behaviour in the Alice books, psychoanalytic interpretations of tiny doors, lost keys, hidden gardens, mathematical games, verbal overexcitement, photographs and mirrors, surfaces and depths, self and other. He spoke of the surrealists' passion for Alice's dream world, and of Carroll's interest in doubles and twins.

Alice, he said, is the Victorian child putting together the wild world of grown-up rules and hidden intentions and violent feelings and incomprehensible conventions. She is an English empiricist, said Frederica. She doesn't get baffled or deceived or disconcerted. She is sure she exists, however she is stretched or shrunk or told she is a Serpent. Carroll saw things from a child's-eye view.

They took off from empiricism and discussed sense, and non-sense. Richard Gregory was presented with the first week's object, a Victorian hand-mirror, backed in silver, which was ornamented with bunches of silver grapes, wreaths of silver vine-leaves and trailing tendrils of coiling silver feelers and claspers. Mirrors, he said, had ancient meanings. The Victorian glass put him in mind of the ancient mirrors used in their religious ceremonies by the Manichees, who believed it was their duty to release the light trapped in matter, and saw grapes as one of the plants which were vessels of trapped light. It was not clear what the Manichees did with the trapped or reflected light, he said. Aristotle, the reasonable scientist, told us that a woman looking at a mirror during a menstrual period would cause its surface to become clouded with blood-red. This was because, according to Aristotle, there was an affinity between the bright eye, full of blood-vessels, and the smooth bright bronze mirror. Influences passed through the bright air. Sensual nonsense, with meaning.

The table was set for a kind of tea-party. A huge silver teapot could be shown to be mirroring the three faces, like a distorting mirror in a gallery, making Frederica into a beaky witch, Miller into a curly Bacchus with great cheeks, and Gregory into a cavernous Pluto. On the tea-table were various dishes, silver and glass, which turned out to contain caterpillars walking on mirrors, segmented, striped and bristling, with sooty eyes and horny probosces, orange, gold and green.

Richard Gregory explained that there were actually *two* Alices, Alice Liddell of Wonderland and her cousin Alice Raikes whom Dodgson had teased with an orange, held in her right hand, perceived in the glass in her left. 'Supposing I was on the other side,' that intelligent Alice had said, 'wouldn't the orange be in my *right* hand?' And from there, said Gregory, came the idea of going *through*, of seeing from the *other side*. He elaborated on the logical trips and blips of mirrors, which reverse left and right, but not up and down, in alphabets as in faces. Dodgson's friend was John Henry Pepper who used part-reflecting mirrors on stage to make actors appear, disappear, double, become transparent wraiths like the Cheshire Cat. Mirrors had their own illogical logic. Miller spoke of the happenstance of mirrors and photographs, both of which, independently, were first made apparent on a silver mist on glass. The camera showed ghosts of Frederica, of Miller, of Gregory, in mirrors behind the glass box they were in. The caterpillars whirred in their kaleidoscope.

Frederica said that her two guests made her think of how often Alice was between two benign creatures talking over her. The Gryphon and the Mock Turtle. Or not so benign. Hare and Hatter, Hengist and Horsa, Walrus and Carpenter, Red Queen and White Queen. Tweedledum and Tweedledee, she said, casting her eyes down, remembering briefly the mathematical Ottokars and their faces in her basement window. But Jonathan Miller had taken her up and was racing onwards, describing the disorderly order of the compulsive doublings of Carroll who was Dodgson, who invented word-games and Doublets and Syzygies where Walrus was introduced to Carpenter in segments of syllables, or Demand to Cormorant, or COOK to DINNER.

The first programme was fortunate. It was fortunate because the two very clever men, at ease with the camera and themselves, benign and gentle with Frederica, brought out the best in her. In the BBC cab which carried her back to the basement where an empty (unmade) bed awaited her, and her small son slept, she looked at her own ghost in the dark window, and gave herself a tight, triumphant grin. She thought about Alice, and herself. She *felt* like a clever child, with those two, who had their own knowledge, vastly greater than hers. Since she had done nothing much, she liked the sense they gave her of things – endless things – to be discovered and discussed. She felt briefly her undefeated childhood energy. I want, I want, I want, she had cried, like a bird in a nest with its gaping mouth. She had thought she had wanted womanhood and sex. Knowledge had been there, and she had swallowed it wholesale, because she was greedy and had a good digestion, but it hadn't seemed to be what mattered. Now, perhaps after all, it did. Those two delighted in the motions of their minds like Keats's sparrows full of themselves, springing on the gravel.

She looked through herself, in the black window of her black carriage, and liked the sparseness of the marks that made her up, a highlight, a smudge, a dark line of mouth, a glint of copper. She thought with a kind of quick horror of Aristotle's bloody mirror as a kind of mystery. Women and blood, blood and sex. Aristotle, Gregory said, believed semen and menstrual blood were the same. That spry confidence of Alice the essential child wavered and crumbled. She had wanted so much to be an actress. She had wanted to act, to go through the elegant motions of what she was not yet. She had been Alice, and had wanted, foolishly, to be Juliet, to be Mary Queen of Scots, to be Cleopatra. She had wanted to be full of Shakespeare's words about life – and love – like a vessel. The great teapot and the mirror-dishes of larvae came into her mind and her ghost laughed at her in the window. Oh no, thought Frederica, who was about to be refracted across a nation into thousands of splintered and glittering Fredericas, I don't want to *act*. I want to think. Clarity. Curiosity. Curiouser and curiouser.

The idea for the second Looking-Glass pilot was Frederica's own. She thought of it when Leo, refusing to eat a navarin she had taken some trouble over, began to quote *Alice in Wonderland*, pointlessly, in a sing-song, teasing voice. 'Alice-Mutton: Mutton-Alice,' he chanted. 'It isn't etiquette to cut anyone you've been introduced to. *Remove* the joint!' he cried. He added 'I don't think it's right to eat creatures. I am going to become a vegetarian.'

'I'd rather you didn't. I'd rather you were properly nourished. Look at your teeth. You evolved into an omnivorous animal. Look at your canine teeth, Leo. Please eat at least the vegetables in the sauce.'

'I don't like boiled vegetables.'

'You are pretending to be a nasty child, winding me up. I spent *hours* cooking that sauce, cutting the meat off the bone –'

'Did you think about how the poor lamb was killed, whilst you cut it?'

'Yes, I did. I always do. I cut it for you. So you'd get protein, and vitamins, and grow strong.'

'One dead sheep, one live boy.'

'Exactly.'

'Did you make rice pudding?'

'I did.'

'I promise not to introduce myself to that. I promise not to sing it's lovely rice pudding for dinner *again* if you let me go straight on to the pudding. If you don't say, just eat a bit of your nice stew, first.'

He knew she knew she was a parody of a mother. She ate her own navarin, which was delicious.

'I think you ought to let me be a vegetarian if I believe it's right.'

'You'd have to live on beans and nuts.'

'I don't like nuts.'

'No, you don't.'

'Beans make you fart.'

'They do.'

'Anyway, you *like* cooking. It relaxes you. I heard you telling Agatha. It's hands-on, you said.'

'Nobody likes cooking if people sit and grin and reject what they've cooked.'

Leo ate a few mouthfuls. 'Are sheeps worse than shrimps, are shrimps worse than accidental grubs in plums or slugs in lettuces?'

'I don't know. It's interesting that we all ask.'

'I bet you couldn't kill a sheep for yourself.'

'I certainly couldn't.'

'Or even a hen.'

'Or even a hen.'

'We don't have to kill hens. They give us eggs.'

'Give is the wrong word. They don't have much choice.'

'But if we *take* their eggs they aren't dead. I could live on eggs.'

'You'd be bored.'

'You could think of lots and lots of eggy things. Are there eggs in rice pudding?'

'No. Rice and milk. And sugar.'

'How pure,' said Leo.

He was a master of spoken English. He took a long time to read eggs, milk, mutton. He stared, and flushed, and sweated.

The second *Through the Looking-Glass* was called 'Free Women'. Frederica took this title from the sections of the *Golden Notebook* about Molly and Anna, the women living alone, or with children, without men. Her guests were Julia Corbett, a novelist, and Penny

Komuves, who worked on a new women's magazine called *Artemis*. Penny lived with Frederica's old friend Tony Watson, the Labour Party journalist and commentator. Tony wrote sometimes in *Artemis*, which aspired to be about everything that interested women, not only feminine things like love, and make-up, and fashion and fat. Tony wrote articles for them about comprehensive schooling, and the advantages and disadvantages of single-sex education. He wrote a piece on the First Woman Prime Minister, an imaginary figure who would rise to power in about 2020, redbrick educated, a northerner, an industrial tribunal lawyer, a mother. 'I cannot see in my crystal ball, what her husband is like,' Tony wrote. 'Maybe he is a quiet schoolteacher. Maybe he is a successful surgeon. Maybe he too is a politician, a journalist, a union leader. They will believe that what both of them do is of equal importance. Neither will walk two steps behind, like a royal consort.'

Penny Komuves was the daughter of a Hungarian political thinker who had fled in 1939. She had read politics, philosophy and economics at Oxford, and specialised professionally in articles about the new anxieties of female graduates, who found themselves alone in kitchens with infant children, admonished by experts like Bowlby that any prolonged separation between mother and child might damage the latter's development irrevocably. Their heads were full of Lawrentian ideology, or particle physics, or the sociology of leisure, or the labour theory of value, and their hands were full of suds, and soufflés, and strained purées and stained nappies. Is this all, they asked, and as yet found no answer. Penny Komuves's other interest was cookery. She researched, in her spare time, receipts for borscht and salmagundy, cock-a-leekie and cassoulet, pigs' trotters and confit of cockscombs. She was a culinary scholar and a culinary scientist. She wrote, in *Artemis*, every week, a suggested menu for a five-course dinner. Everything, the bread, the petits fours, the soups, salads and terrines, were hand-chosen in markets and delicatessens, home-brewed, home-baked, home-made.

Julia Corbett, a generation older than Frederica and Penny, was somewhere between a lady novelist and a woman novelist. Her subject was the lives of women. Her titles were the titles of her generation. Witty variations on confinement. *The Bright Prison.* *The Toy Box. I Cannot Get Out, Said the Bird. The Cold Frame. Life in a Shoe.* These trapped titles connected to a series of semi-savage ironic uses of nursery rhymes. *The Pumpkin-Eater. Daddy's Gone A-Hunting. Lucy's Pocket.* Phyllis Pratt, Bowers & Eden's successful blackly funny thriller writer had added darker versions. *Her Indoors. Come into My Parlour.* Julia Corbett was the author of *The Toy Box* and *Life in a Shoe.* Her latest novel was called *Just a Little Bit Higher.*

> Swing me just a little bit higher
> Obadiah do!
> Swing me high and I'll never fall
> Swing me over the garden wall
> Just a little bit higher
> Obadiah do!

It told the story of a happy marriage, where the teacher-husband encouraged his gently devoted wife to take a degree by correspondence, to train as a teacher herself. He then left her, qualified, pregnant, and 'free', for a younger, prettier, frailer student. Like all Julia Corbett's books, *Just a Little Bit Higher* was tartly bittersweet. Its edge of aimlessness frightened Frederica more than the ferocity and violence of *The Golden Notebook.*

The set for 'Free Women' turned the inner glass box into a transparent doll's house, with windows and doors of many kinds scrawled on it with a childish simplicity. There was a multiplicity of keys and keyholes. Inside, the three women sat round a kitchen table with a pink and white, imitation damask, plastic cloth. On the table were earthenware bowls heaped with eggs, or full of rising dough under teacloths. There was a tray of jam tarts, pastry flowers with scarlet eyes, ready to go into the oven. There were egg cups in the shape of hens, wearing knitted cosies like bobble-caps. There was a heaped collection of precise silver instruments (mostly tarnished) for performing arcane operations – marrow-scoops, button-hooks, sugar-tongs, toast-racks, tea-strainers, forked cheese-knives, along with impregnated dusters and pots of jewellers' rouge. There were whisks, and wooden paddles, jam cauldrons and thermometers. Can-openers, corkscrews, whelk-prods, and other instruments for poking and prying. The whole gallimaufray suggested, as the camera zoomed, a gynaecological theatre as much as a *batterie de cuisine.*

The cartoon creatures who sauntered and bobbed across the screen during the discussion were mainly from kitchen scenes in *Alice*. The leg-of-mutton, crowned with his paper frill, dripping with basting-fat, bowing and grinning. An animated capering cruet, salt, pepper, mustard, on spindly legs. A serenely floating flounder on a transparent serving-dish. The master-stroke, visually, was the mixing of these creatures with a bevy of Victorian childish cherubs' winged smiling curly bodiless heads, who occasionally melted into diminishing Cheshire Cats, and buzzed across the corners of the screen kitchen like swarms of flies.

With the two savants Frederica had been Alice, the clever and questing girl. With the two women, Wilkie said, he wanted her to create a kind of elbows-on-the-table *kaffee-klatsch*, the kind of talk women did when not overlooked. And how could they do that, Frederica asked, when they were overlooked intimately by a male camera-crew and studio staff, and even more intimately by the unseen millions? It will be surprisingly easy, Wilkie assured her. I picked you because you aren't frightened.

In fact what ensued was a knowing parody, a send-up of a *kaffee-klatsch*.

Frederica began with the question Sigmund Freud put to himself, and said he could not answer. What do women want?

Love, said Julia Corbett. Love, certainty, a family.

Sex and naughtiness too, said Penny Komuves.

Only sex is a long thing said Frederica. Because it leads to childbirth and all that is one long biological process. Except that now – with the Pill – women can pick and choose amongst men, and pick and choose whether to breed, or not.

They discussed whether this would change the way women saw men. Julia said women judged men on things that weren't apparently sexual, like kindness, like listening, like keeping appointments on time. Like courtesy. Frederica said Darwin had said that male beauty was determined by female sexual selection. So it was odd to live in a world of women's magazines, women's advertisements, with women's bodies decorated for men to look at. Penny said she thought it was mostly women who noticed other women's clothes. Frederica said, there is Miss World, and the perfect pneumatic body in swim-suit and stilettos. There is pornography. Penny Komuves said that since the peacock and the mandrill had tail-feather and buttock designed to attract females, it was odd that we did not have male beauty parades.

What would women look for? Julia asked, with mock timidity. Men wrap themselves up in customary suits of solemn black, and cut their hair and shave away their beards.

Not any longer they don't, said Penny. They grow it flowing, they wear flowery shirts, they dangle jewellery round their necks. The balance is shifting.

They discussed the aspects of the male body on which a hypothetical female jury would mark. Y-front advertisements were briefly mentioned. Male buttocks were timorously, and then gleefully, debated. Frederica described an art student whose close-fitting jeans had strategic holes revealing soft, brilliant purple knickers. The three women laughed. Modern women were free to choose, they agreed. To pick and choose. Like their primitive ancestors. Unlike their grandmothers, or even, in most cases, their mothers.

And where did it get them? Julia Corbett asked. The problem was still there. Women wanted children, women had to care for children, and in a way this only made all the sexual possibilities *stressful*.

The Pill, said Penny Komuves, meant that men could insist on sex because an impediment, a danger, had gone.

The body, said Frederica, wants to be pregnant. The woman often doesn't. I think of the Queen in *Snow-White*, seeing the drops of blood on the snow. We fear their appearance, we often fear their absence, worse. We are at war with ourselves, perhaps. After the choice provided by the Pill, there could be the choice of abortion. To decide to separate sex and children, to move both into the area of choice. Could either of you choose abortion?

No, said Julia. I might think I ought to be able to. But I couldn't choose it. Or so I think, now.

Penny Komuves looked briefly frozen, shook her head, and turned the question back to Frederica. Well, would you, she asked. Would you?

Frederica saw Leo's face in her mind's-eye. I might, she said. I might like to feel I had the right. I might not.

There was a shiver of silence. An angel passing, said Julia Corbett.

The cartoon cherubs fluttered. The pig-baby peered out of its swaddling-bands.

The screen showed a series of portraits of George Eliot, the chosen person of the programme. There was the heavy-awkward horse-face, the difficult teeth, the younger woman awkwardly bowing her gross head under the inappropriate ringlets. Tenniel's ugly Duchess flashed across the screen. Frederica remarked tartly that she had known a man who had felt that an exam question could be set on this great writer, quoting a description of her as a 'gaunt, moralistic Dame'. Discuss. Nevertheless, for most of their own discussion, and perhaps because they were on the screen, they circled round the subject of female beauty. Eliot punished her beautiful characters, Julia said. No, said Frederica, she punished those who *exploited* it, who *lived by it*. Hetty, cold Rosamund, chilly, terrified, power-crazed Gwendolen. Her warm-blooded heroines were beautiful too. Dorothea, Maggie. But they wanted something else out of life besides sex and marriage, and sex and marriage defeated them. She punished them, said Julia. She punished Dorothea for high-mindedness and Maggie for throbbing with emotion. She made Dorothea decline into marriage with a second-rate journalist, and punished Maggie for sex, with drowning. She couldn't make a model of a woman who could be free, and creative, and sexy. She couldn't give her readers any hope.

'She was free and creative and sexy,' said Frederica. 'She must have been the most public adulteress in England, and in the end Queen Victoria commissioned a series of paintings from her books and they tried to bury her in the Abbey.'

'She had no children,' said Penny. 'She knew about contraception, sponges and vinegar.'

'She looked after G.H. Lewes's sons,' said Frederica. 'She earned their school-fees.'

'Like a man,' said Julia. 'She earned money. Like a man.'

'She couldn't let Dorothea found a university, or Maggie write a book,' said Frederica. 'She was telling it how it was. How clever women's lives *were*.'

'The pretty women,' said Julia, 'are made to want *things*. China and damask, a bottom drawer full of sheets and tablecloths, a casket full of pretty ear-rings, like Hetty's. It's like the advertising world now. Everything still heads towards a rite of passage in a froth of white veiling with an attentive crowd trying to see the face underneath, and imagine what the body under the white lace, or satin, or organza will be doing when it's naked. And you have a great table of *things* – like we've got here – people have lovingly given you. And afterwards, you see the *things* were like the cheese in the mousetrap, and there you are in the kitchen, surrounded by them. Staring out of the window – women in novels are always staring out of windows, thinking how to get out, how to be free.'

'And *things*,' said Frederica, 'brings me to this week's object, which is: A Tupperware Bowl. Actually, we have three examples for you, because we couldn't choose which colour.'

The screen showed three pudding-basins, side by side, one in a pearly rose-pink, one in a duck-egg aquamarine, one in a soft lemon yellow. They were photographed against a white background. They were softly translucent, yet thick-skinned. Their lines were clean, pure, machined, repeating. Their shadows were beautiful, dove-grey, and identical. They had the elegance of an abstract painting.

Julia said they were lovely. She said they were clean-lined, they were light, they were useful. They were liberating. Look – she gestured – at all that mess on the table, all that fussy silver-cleaning, all that enslavement to objects. I remember hideous bakelite things in the war. These go with machines that do give us time, if we can use it. I put on my washing-machine – which has clean pure lines like this – and it washes, and I write. I agree, it would be useless if I wanted to be a forensic lawyer.

Penny Komuves said they were hideous. She said she liked traditional earthenware and brilliant Polish enamel. She said the earth would be piled up with these semi-indestructible shells, peeling and floating. That the Pacific Ocean was bobbing with plastic cups. That they were inhuman.

Frederica said they were beautiful and empty. They reminded her of rooms with blinds. Of female archetypes. Containers. Grails. Empty until filled. The question was with what.

Penny Komuves said they were sterile. And reminded her of Dutch caps. Or childhood buckets and spades. But these are not toys, said Penny Komuves.

Little girls, said Julia, are expected to play with plastic cups and sand and water, and make cakes and tarts and puddings. Boys make bridges and buildings.

Imaginary cakes, said Frederica, are so much more enticing than real ones. The ghosts of cakes. These are ghost-bowls.

It was odd, she observed finally, thinking of kitchens and things, that female characters in Victorian fiction are wise, and attractive, and human as little girls, and become monsters, demons, or victims, when they become women. Jane Eyre and Maggie are *diminished* by womanhood. The Queen of Hearts shouts Off with her head, the Duchess cringes, and Alice, 'loudly and decidedly', says 'Nonsense.' Carroll said he pictured the Queen of Hearts as 'a sort of embodiment of ungovernable passion – a blind and aimless Fury'. The Cook and the Duchess are no better, and the Looking-Glass Queens are seriously defective. Perhaps we shouldn't grow up.

The three women stared at the three blank, bland containers. Do we want to live on our own? Frederica asked the others. More and more of us do. What sort of creatures would we be if we were independent, if marriage didn't come into it, if men were optional? Julia said, we wouldn't be like the great virginal heroines of the last century. Florence Nightingale, Emily Davies. We might live as Mary Wollstonecraft wanted us to, in separate establishments, lovingly visiting chosen males, in charge of our own space, our own time. Penny Komuves said that recent scientific research appeared to prove that ice applied to the ovaries could in certain conditions produce parthenogenesis. Then, she said, we wouldn't need them at all, we could *really* choose. What would we choose?

Frederica tapped the Tupperware and produced a hollow rattle. We'd need servants. If we had children. What would *they* choose. You can't labour-save *all* labour.

Penny said: if we were really free, men would be different.

Like what? said Julia.

Softer. Kinder. More *fluid*. I don't know.

The programme ended with the three, faintly baffled, faintly ribald faces, and a nervous gust of laughter.

Frederica thought, seeing them later, that they were all girl-women. It was in the air, at the time. Penny Komuves had a small, square, slightly puppy-like face, with large dark eyes under a Quant schoolgirl fringe and bob. Julia Corbett, a generation older, had delicate crowsfeet at the corners of her luminous eyes, and a knot of fading red hair, skewered through with enamelled silver pins. She wore a large number of pretty silver rings and bracelets, and a necklace of silver and enamel hearts and flowers. But her dress was girlish – a pale flame-coloured shift, tied prettily under the breasts and cut above the knee. Her make-up was elaborate and faintly doll-like – spiky black lashes, domed cream and frosted blue eyelids, sugar-pink pale lips, and a dab of blusher on the elegant cheek-bones. Penny Komuves was in the wine-dark mode, with blackish lips, grape and silver eyelids, a white mask of a pugnacious face. She wore a skinny jumper under something resembling the gym-slip of Frederica's school-days, pointed little breasts at the lower edge of a pinafore yoke. Frederica herself wore a semi-transparent indigo shirt with a severe white collar and cuffs – also imitation schoolgirl, also half provocative – and was experimenting with an Alice band (indigo) in the coppery hair she was growing out. Below the shirt, she had a governessy grey long skirt, in poplin, a wide black elastic belt, and little, heeled boots. There were equal elements of dressing-up, parody (of what?) and mask. The carefully made-up faces appeared to hide, not reveal, the thoughts behind them. The frequent laughter was a little eerie. Wilkie said he was pleased. He would get letters of complaint, he said. Frederica said she couldn't see why. Indecency, said Wilkie. Drops of blood and iced ovaries, not nice. He was right, to Frederica's surprise. The audience grew.

X

What do women want?

Frederica at seventeen would never have believed that she could want celibacy. Since John Ottokar's departure for Calverley she had slept alone. Her most intense physical pleasure had been to take her tough, angular son in her angular arms, and smell his instantly recognisable hair and the living warmth of his skin. The discussion of sex on *Through the Looking-Glass* had caused her to wonder, in the abstract, why she didn't think about it more, or thought about it – she was an honest woman – with a new edge of apprehension. The body wants to be pregnant, she had asserted, and so it did. She had caught her body looking at Wilkie, wondering if he would 'do', considering his incipient portliness critically and his intelligent face with affection. But Wilkie liked young girls. They waited for him, in mini-skirts with swinging hair, at the end of filming. They rode off behind him on his Lambretta, their arms clasped round his waist as hers had been on their one motor-bike journey, in 1953. It seemed like yesterday, and was fifteen years ago. She was led to remember the days of *Astraea*, and her forcedly chaste, remote desire for Alexander Wedderburn. This was reinforced by an invitation to hear Flora Robson play Elizabeth I at the National Portrait Gallery. The memory led her to invite Alexander and Daniel to come with her.

On the day before the reading, John Ottokar telephoned from Calverley. He was coming down for the weekend, would she be there, he wanted her. The telephone was suddenly full of sex. Leo was away at his father's. John is coming, said Frederica to Agatha. Because Agatha never confided in Frederica about her own personal life, or problems – beyond Saskia's education, or her hopes of promotion, or her impatience with the Permanent

Secretary – that is, because Agatha never spoke to Frederica about her sex life, or even said if she had one, Frederica had taken on an air of unnatural discretion with Agatha. John had once said, in a moment of bitterness 'I suppose you discuss me –' and Frederica had said, no, as a matter of fact, we don't. She had added, to reassure him, 'Agatha doesn't talk like that, you can imagine, if you think about it.' And John had laughed.

So he came, and the small flat was full of heat, and tension, and pleasure, and tension, and concentration on usual, and unusual, suddenly reactivated bits of two rediscovered bodies, stroked, and dampened, and joined, and sucked apart, and Frederica had the usual feeling – this is the *real thing* – and the new, niggling feeling: 'This is the *usual* feeling.' Now I feel this is the real thing. And outside all this, I am something else, someone else, I walk alone.

'What are we going to do?' asked John Ottokar. 'We can't live apart like this, it tears you up.'

And Frederica looked at the beloved head – certainly beloved – on the pillow – and did not know what to answer. For she remembered wanting *a beloved head*, in the abstract, in the way in which Julia Corbett had said they had all wanted the froth of veiling, the triumphal progress, the virginal white dress over hidden flesh.

And she did not know what to answer, because she saw that she was happy to live apart, to have times of sex like this, naked, total, fierce times, and times completely without it. And John was unhappy, she thought with unjust malevolence, not because their two heads were not side by side all night every night, but because she evaded him, because he sensed there was more of her when he wasn't there.

They had a minor quarrel over Flora Robson and Elizabeth I. John said he was there for so little time, she didn't need to go. Frederica said she wanted to go. John said, you just want to see those people, Alexander whatsit, Daniel. Frederica said, don't be silly, I want to see *Elizabeth*. A Tudor tyrant, said John. You can see her any day.

Don't, said Frederica. *Don't* make pointless jealous noises about nothing. *Don't* try and shut me in one room. If we do that to each other, it's the beginning of the end.

Isn't it anyway?

No. You know there's only you. You know there's no one else.

He came with her to the Gallery. He kissed her on parting, and made a beautiful, possessive sweep of his sure hand, down her spine and round her bottom, claiming her as he let her go. She felt briefly weak, and gave herself a little shake, and went in to see Elizabeth.

'*Creativity*', the third pilot, the last before Christmas, was Wilkie's idea. Hodder Pinsky, the cognitive psychologist from La Jolla, already invited to Gerard Wijnnobel's conference, was giving a paper in Oxford on 'Order from Noise: the construction of meaning'. It would be a good plan, Wilkie said, to invite him with Elvet Gander, the psychoanalyst. 'Is the unconscious mind a system of circuitry and binary gates?' said Wilkie, 'or is it the Id, a turbulent beast raging in the dark?'

Frederica said she was afraid of Elvet Gander. She said she had seen him in action, like an orator, at the trial of *Babbletower*. His voice throbs, said Frederica. He radiates self-satisfaction. She did not say he was trying to analyse the Ottokars, and that for this reason she herself was part of his mental life. Wilkie said both scientists were *prima donnas*, both had style, they were natural for Television. Fire and Ice, you'll see, he told her. You will rise to the occasion.

The glass box for this programme had been rhythmically divided into ghostly cells, which could be seen, on closer examination, to be the plastic wells of egg-boxes. Behind the three chairs at the table Tenniel's Humpty Dumpty sat precariously on his gridded wall. There were eggs on the table, and cartoon eggs-with-legs ran across the foreground, pursued in an endless circle by cartoon chickens and cartoon disembodied eyes behind spectacles, observing which might come first. There were also modern versions of the slithy tove – something like badgers, something like lizards, something like corkscrews – and the mome raths – flying green pigs. There were ostrich eggs and Fabergé-decorated eggs and neat drawers of egg-collectors' eggs.

The subject of discussion – agreed in advance by both speakers – was Freud.

The object was a Picasso ceramic. It was not a real one, but a good copy. The studio did not run to the insurance, even in those days, of a real Picasso.

Elvet Gander looked, with his high bald crown and his long marbly face, like another variation on the egg theme. The heavy studio make-up accentuated this pallid look, and also the deep oval lids over his deep-set eyes. He had two characteristic expressions – a brooding stillness, with the lids dropped, and a flashing mesmeric attention when he raised them, and his dark eyes glittered. He was mobile and labile, he gestured with his long fingers, he shrugged and hunched his shoulders, he pursed his big lips, or stretched them in an alarming grin. He was wearing a flowing shirt in tie-dyed blue Indian cotton, embroidered with little stellar mandalas of mirror-glass, and round his neck a silver crescent moon on a leather thong.

Hodder Pinsky was tall, white-gold, and extravagantly symmetrical, Frederica immediately thought, taking his large hand in the Hospitality Room. His hair was a Nordic blond, his face chiselled, his cheek-bones perfect, his long mouth exactly held between control and relaxation. His fingernails were square and elegant. He wore a charcoal flannel suit, a sky-blue shirt, and a tie patterned with a design of reversible cubes, in black and white. His eyes were invisible, because he wore glasses – heavy-framed – with very thick blue lenses. He explained – it was almost the first thing he said – that he wore the glasses not as an affectation, but because he was 'purblind, that is, I can see my computer print-out, I can read, but you are an elegant blur.' His voice was American, East Coast, easy. He watched them – Wilkie, Frederica, Gander – with parts of his body that were not his eyes.

On air, Frederica asked them both to say what they thought creativity was.

Pinsky gave a definition in scientific terms. Creativity was the generation of new ideas, new explanations. He was, he said, in agreement with Noam Chomsky that the human mind is born, to use a metaphor, *wired* to construct grammar, and other forms of thought, as beavers are born wired to make dams, or birds to make nests. A human child can make endless new sentences it has never heard before, precisely because it is physiologically formed and ordered to be able to do so. A creative person makes a new idea as a child makes a new sentence. Some are more useful, or more surprising, than others. Some make previously unsuspected connections between things in the world. Part of his own work was to devise computer programmes, and laboratory experiments, to study the thought processes by which new ideas might be generated. To simulate thought. To examine choice.

Gander said that scientists always took scientific discoveries as their paradigm of creativity. Whereas the great work of art – at once unique and universal, at once open to explanation and resistant to categorisation – showed us the true extent of human powers. You would never, he said, make a laboratory programme that would 'explain' *King Lear*, you would never simulate in a laboratory the sublime pathos of Beethoven, or the perfect balance of mathematical precision and cosmic understanding in Piero della Francesca's *Baptism of Christ*.

Pinsky said Gander had to explain not only how he recognised 'sublime pathos' but what it was, and how people came to agree that they had identified it.

Gander said the great work of art was a raid by the intrepid conscious mind on the inchoate seething mass of the undifferentiated unconscious. The unconscious, Freud has shown, is without any sense of time or space. Its energy is the energy of the pleasure principle, desire, not reality. The great artist descends like Orpheus into the abyss, embraces the demons of his unspeakable desires and fears – of all our unspeakable desires and fears – and returns them to consciousness where he makes an image of them which allows them to be contemplated steadily. So Sophocles went and stared at the Oedipus – lascivious and murderous – who inhabits all infants – and brought back the knowledge of it, so that we might experience the horror as beauty and order. So Shakespeare went with Hamlet, to look at the roots of fratricide, patricide, incest and inhibition – and even deeper, at the desire of all life *to return to inertia*, the secret that the life instincts are all indifferently *death instincts* – and clambered up from amongst the dark roots of time and space to the ordered organic world, to make iambic pentameters which contained the terror – sluggish or stabbing – in the rhythms of time and space, of the conscious mind.

I am a Freudian, not a Jungian, said Elvet Gander. But I have recently come to the conclusion that the Master's religious scepticism was a little limiting. I think Jung may be right in seeing the great work of art as a mandala, a formal design which enables us to contemplate truth.

Pinsky, smiling whitely, said his ambitions were more mundane. But he did believe that cognitive psychology – as opposed to psychoanalysis – which, if Dr Gander would forgive him, was itself a poem, used language with poetic imprecision and resonance – he did believe cognitive psychology might have something eventually to say about the geometries of mandalas and indeed the regularities and irregularities of iambic pentameters. He was interested in the multifarious, simultaneous operations of the mind, in the way consciousness pictured and ordered the patterns it worked with.

There is, he said, an interesting computer programme called *Pandaemonium*, which is psychologists' everyday comic poetry, not sublime, though it takes its name, I suppose, from the industrious underworld of *Paradise Lost*. This programme has a hierarchy of mechanical demons who are devised, or designed (by us, their masters), to recognise patterns in rushes of random information, to create order from noise. It depends on what we call 'parallel processing'. There are the 'data demons' who recognise images, and shout. There are the computational demons who recognise clusters of recognised images, and shout. There are the cognitive demons who represent possible patterns, and collect the computed shouts. And there is the 'decision demon' who identifies the stimuli by the loudest shouting. The system can learn. It can identify printed letters, and morse code. It may one day understand what is so – unrepeatable – about *Hamlet*, or Beethoven's *Third*.

It will hardly save lives, or sanity, said Gander.

It may organise cities and communities of scientists to make justice – and art – said Pinsky. It may make us wiser about what we are. It may teach us not to misdescribe ourselves. I am not sure that your Freudian unconscious – however beautiful your poetry – exists. I think it is a reification of a fear, or a wish.

Frederica directed the conversation towards Sigmund Freud, whose bearded, bespectacled face, dark-eyed, wise, apprehensive and somehow uncertain, she thought, which was the best thing about it, filled the screen briefly, replacing Humpty Dumpty.

Gander spoke of Freud in much the same terms as he had spoken of Freud's understanding of Oedipus and Hamlet. He used the image of the dauntless hero, his self-analysis an unprecedented feat of discovery. He said the Master had changed the whole cultural world of his time, had changed the way everyone saw their bodies, their minds, their desires and their fears.

Had changed the imagery of daily life, said Frederica. Had changed the form of advertisements, which had gone through being conscious attempts to play on unconscious sexual metaphors and were now blatantly ironic about them.

Gander looked a little baffled. The camera rested on Pinsky's blue lenses. Frederica wondered if he saw advertisements.

Pinsky said he felt that Freud's romantic description of the unconscious mind had detracted from various very useful practical explorations of its workings. For we must all be aware that we lived in a stream of thoughts and observations and stimuli, only a very few of which could be ordered or used at any one time. It was like travelling in the tail of a comet, which was made up of a battering turmoil of lumps of ice and stone and flares of gas. One of the great mysteries of the mind was the storage of memory. Things we have known, and lost, but know we can find again. A name, an event. Why do we remember one thing more than another. How? What is the mechanism?

Freud, Gander said, had been quite sure that all attempts to locate ideas and excitations in specific nerve-cells or brain locations would fail.

That was *then*, said Pinsky. But we might agree that both our disciplines study the ordering of this doubleness of thinking. It's had various names. We can call it rational and intuitive, logical and prelogical, realistic and autistic. To come back to the subject of our programme, it's been labelled 'constrained' against 'creative' – as though the creative was always irrational, on the side of chaos and multifariousness. In computer terms we call it *parallel* and *sequential* processing. It may correspond to what Freud called 'primary-process' as opposed to 'secondary processing'. And all of us notice when the primary process seems, so to speak, to *invade* the rational, to cause a blip, a Freudian slip, which might also be a 'creative' error or intuition. In the end we may be able to describe the mechanisms which make the ineluctable associations of memory and forgetting with the help of which Freud performed his analytic revelations. I should like to tell you a Freudian story.

Gander put inscrutable finger-tips to pursed lips and dropped his eyelids.

Here is the story Hodder Pinsky told, which is the story Freud told, which is in some sense the story Virgil told. It was also to play an odd part in other stories, including Frederica's. It is a story which carries an immediate, wholly satisfactory verbal pleasure in pattern, and reaches out into biology, and human history, like rings round a stone in a dark pool.

Freud met the young man in a train. He knew him already – he was Jewish, of an academic background. They fell into conversation (Freud says explicitly that he forgets *how*) about the social status 'of the race to which we both belonged'. The young man said his generation 'was doomed (as he expressed it) to atrophy, and could not develop its talents or satisfy its needs'.

He ended an impassioned speech with a misquotation from Virgil's Dido, committing her vengeance on Aeneas to posterity.

Exoriar(e) ex nostris ossibus ultor.

Freud, appealed to, supplied the missing. *Exoriar(e) ALIQUIS nostris ex ossibus ultor.* The young man challenged Freud to use his theory that nothing is forgotten for no reason, to explain the inaccessibility of an indefinite pronoun. It was psychoanalysis as a train-game. Freud instructed him to free-associate to the word ALIQUIS.

He divided it. A liquis.

He added. Reliquiem. Liquefying, fluidity, fluid.

Have you discovered anything so far?

No, said Freud, but go on.

The young man, who appears to have been given to scornful laughter and irritability, went on.

He remembered Simon of Trent, and the accusations of ritual blood-sacrifice brought against Jews. He remembered a thesis that the slaughtered were incarnations of the saviour to come. He remembered an article in an Italian newspaper. 'What St Augustine says about Women.'

Freud waited.

He remembered various other saints. Simon, Benedict. He remembered Origen.

He remembered St Januarius and the miracle of his annually liquefying blood.

Freud pointed out that January and August were to do with the calendar.

He remembered Garibaldi threatening the priests and saying he hoped the liquefaction-miracle would take place shortly.

He remembered, hesitantly, 'a lady from whom I might easily hear a piece of news that would be very awkward for both of us'.

'That her periods have stopped,' said Freud, putting together calendar, blood, origin, child-sacrifice, the avenger who would rise up . . .

Frederica said the compression, the condensation, the interconnectedness made it seem like a work of art.

Or made it seem, said Gander, that works of art arose from such driven, condensed associations.

Pinsky said that somewhere in the brain was a mechanism for retrieving associations that worked like Pandaemonium. That Freud was an unusually lucid computer.

They laughed.

And so they went on to the Picasso. The clay pot was curved, and full-bellied, standing on hens' claws, with a cockscomb over its delicate beaked spout, and the pointed breasts and pleated navel of a human woman. Its handle was a curved tail. It was made in white earthenware, dabbed with smoke and black paint; it had wicked staring eyes, and pretty nipples, and a flurry of wing-pinions. All three laughed when they saw it, as though laughter were the appropriate response. (Hodder Pinsky raised it close to his face and scanned it with his blue gaze.) Frederica read out a description by Picasso's son of how, in Vallauris, he would seize the potters' vases on the wheel.

'My father grabbed it, wrung its neck, pinched it round the belly, pressed it down on the table, bending the neck. A pigeon. A hen. The hands had worked so fast that I hadn't noticed the head had been shaped. A pencil picked up, a few dashes gouged the surface – eyes, texture of feathers. How swift and sure the hands were.'

Frederica said it was a solid, tangible metaphor. Hen-in-woman. Woman-in-hen. Gander said we loved polymorphs for sexual reasons of childhood sensuality and for religious reasons to do with integration into the Cosmos – look at the human-animals in cave paintings. Pinsky said the cock-hen-woman-vase was, as the programme designer had cleverly known, an analogon of the Carrollian slithy toves and mome raths. A cross between badgers, lizards and corkscrews, he said, was a nice parody of the Lascaux stag-men, the jungle owl-men. Rendered comic and innocuous by the mechanism of the corkscrew.

It was all under the aegis of Humpty-Dumpty, said Frederica. Who introduced the idea of portmanteau words to the language, and to the dictionaries. Who thought words should do as he said, and behave themselves. There was some sort of intense pleasure she didn't understand in the inventiveness of compression. Hen/woman, From-home = mome.

Humpty-Dumpty, said Pinsky, believed that he was the master of language. He was either a grammarian or an anti-grammarian.

Gander grinned wickedly. 'Look where he ended up, the master of language. In a shattered heap of egg shells, that no amount of creativity can put together again.'

Overconscious, H. Dumpty. Overweening.

Frederica had grown more confident about addressing the camera. She smiled foxily at it, and told the invisible watchers that she hoped they'd enjoyed the various ideas of creativity they had looked at, which had ranged from raids on the underworld to a humming pandemonium of sequencing wires, from the compression of metaphor to the expansion of the chaotic comet-tail across the heavens, from the sphinx-like face of Freud to the creative fingers of Picasso and the tragic verbal over-confidence of Humpty-Dumpty. She was herself no more certain why we cared so much about metaphor, or mental connections, or great works of art, than she had been to start with. But she had many more metaphors and stories to think with, her world was richer. She remembered, she said, as their faces faded and the screen filled with midnight blue-black, in which little points of light appeared, the creation myth in which everything had sprung from the Mundane Egg laid by Night in the lap of primeval chaos.

The Hospitality Room was underground, a somewhat aimless place full of stale smoke and magnetised dust-particles. In those opulent days there was a trolley full of bottles – whisky, gin, vodka, red and white wines. There were sofas with bright blue and tomato covers round low tables. Frederica went to sit near Hodder Pinsky, partly so that he should be able to see her, and partly to avoid Elvet Gander. Pinsky took a large gin and tonic, full of ice. Frederica said she hoped he had enjoyed the programme.

'I assure you,' he said, 'that it is unusual to be able to utter consecutive sentences on the screen. I predict it will not last. For two reasons. Human beings will become used to thinking in rapid bytes. Sound-bites. And advertising will cut our thoughts to ribbons.'

He opened and shut his amiable mouth. His teeth were white and even.

Frederica hesitated.

'We play visual games. We have wandering cartoon creatures, and transparent screens. Chickens and eggs and Humpty-Dumpty himself.'

'And you are wondering if I can see them?'

He ran his finger-tips over the contours of the Picasso jar, which had come with them.

'I am still a visual animal. I place the *gestalt* of this creature – flesh and feathers – on geometrical planes. I have to teach myself to think with my fingers. Here – the little breasts – it is smooth, here the clay is roughened. You get a different surprise at the junctures – where a human curve slips into an avian one – with your fingers. But I think with my eyes.'

Elvet Gander had moved purposefully and silently across the carpet and sat down on Frederica's other side.

Hodder Pinsky said suddenly

'Do you want to see what I see?'

He handed his heavy glasses to Frederica.

'I suggest you look at the gin and tonic.'

She looked first at his eyes. They were very pale blue, the pupils huge, the balls rounded out. He smiled.

She put on the glasses, warm from his skin.

The gin and tonic was cobalt caverns, was vertiginous staircases, was drowning in blue Arctic seas, was ink and water. It swayed her stomach and made her breathless.

'You don't see what he sees,' said Elvet Gander. 'You have normal eyes.'

Frederica took off the glasses and handed them back to the psychologist.

'It was like being under the ice-cap.'

'That's why I suggested the gin and tonic.'

Wilkie came over. He said to Pinsky

'In the 50s, I repeated the experiment of the reversing lenses for a week. The rehabituation was more *nauseating* than I could have believed. Then I did a series of experiments with coloured lenses. Saturation viewing. Ten days per colour.'

'I read about it.'

'Have you ever thought of trying different colours?'

'I like blue. Blue is prescribed.'

Elvet Gander took hold of Frederica's elbow in the lift.

'I have a word or two to say to you.'

'I must go home to my son.'

'I know you don't want to hear my words. A few words won't hurt you.'

'You know better than that.'

He grinned. They walked towards the way out, round the television centre's apparently endless circular passages. They stood in its courtyard in the dusk, and Gander gestured up at it.

'It always appears to me to be a defensive fortification. Walled round, to keep the world at bay. Both Broadcasting House and this new cylinder seem to me to be like the towers in Tolkien – full of internal passages, with red blinking eyes on top. Childe Roland to the Dark Tower came. This is an inward-looking domain. All the glass walls face inwards.'

'It talks to the whole world.'

'It emits thought-rays and disembodied voices, and phantom faces, very true, very true. Many of my patients are made profoundly uneasy by that. Madmen knew about radio waves long before Edison and Marconi. You do not allow me to speak of the Heavenly Twins, Frederica.'

'My private life is my own business.'

'Ah, but no twin has a private life. And Zag's private life is my business.'

Frederica turned to face him in the growing dark, in the red light of the sodium lamps on the navy blue White City sky.

'Please. Leave me alone. I don't like – all the religious things Paul – Zag – the twins – are caught up in. It isn't my kind of thing. I don't like it.'

'Listen to yourself, woman. How can a human being use such *flaccid* language about spiritual powers? Something extraordinary is brewing – a huge change in human vision, a whole new access of spiritual power – and you think you can turn it away with "I don't like it" and "not my kind of thing".' He mimicked her, not inaccurately, still smiling. His bald crown had red and golden lights on the greyish flesh.

'Maybe feeble little ordinary words are the best way,' said Frederica. She shivered. Her body felt flimsy. Gander had that kind of electrical field the charismatic do have. He bristled with significance and magnetism at once attractive and repellent. Not a wizard, she thought, a gnome. A Rumpelstiltskin gnome.

'I know you mean well –'

'No, you don't. You don't even *think* I mean well. You do think I may be right.'

'No, I don't. I don't want to think about it at all. All right? I want to go home to my son.'

'You will have to think about it. You will need friends and allies.'

'I shall try to look after myself.'

'So small, so alone, so unaware,' said Gander.

A black taxi drew up. Frederica got in.

'May I come with you?'

'I am very sure you aren't headed towards my bit of south London.' Frederica slammed the door. He stood there, smiling, the little mirrors on his shirt glinting in the headlights, which illuminated his moon-head, swept on, and left it darkling.

XI

Jacqueline's working-space was in a cubicle in the Physiology laboratories in the Evolution Tower. Her very small, cellular window looked out on to the inner curve of the spiral, too high to see grass, too low to see sky. Lyon Bowman liked silence and privacy for his own work, so she was boxed-in with egg-box baffling partitions, which further reduced her ration of daylight. Her work was beginning to show results. She had various preparations of the suboesophageal ganglion of *Helix aspersa*, exposing the giant neurones, into which, through delicate micro-pipettes, she was injecting, alternately, potassium chloride and salt solution. There were problems with the chloride blocking the pipette. She had constructed a primitive version of a voltage clamp, and was measuring the resistance of the membranes of the cell by passing brief electrical currents through them. There had been many failures in the dissection of the cells, which were covered with layer upon layer of connective tissue, all of which had to be stripped away, since the membrane could not otherwise be penetrated without breaking the pipette or bursting the cell.

The fragments of living matter responded with rhythmic spikes of electrical activity. Hodgkin and Huxley, in the early 1950s, had suspected the existence of ion channels in the surface of cells. Through these holes in the membrane – which was more a thick glutinous, tensile oil than a film – they suggested, the chemical messengers permeated the cells, conducting the electricity, which was life, which, Jacqueline believed, was thought. Her pinned-down brains were communicating messages to severed feelers and feet. Somewhere here was the place where mind and matter were one thing.

She had had the idea that it might be possible to locate the electro-chemical moment of a memory if she could train her snails to learn, in a Pavlovian way, to avoid certain stimuli and seek out others. There might be changes in cells which had learned pleasure or pain, greed or avoidance. So besides the spread ghost-snails of the 'preparations' she had boxes of live snails in various experimental living-quarters. She had wondered, at first, whether the creatures could be trained to respond to a bright light. She had tried shining a very bright light into their boxes, and accompanying this with an electrical shock. This had not worked very well, partly because of the difficulty of controlling the snails' excursions outside their shells. She was interested anyway in whether the creatures responded differently at times of year when they would normally have been hibernating, and at times of year when they would have been vigorously mating and foraging.

She decided it would be better to work with aversion-training in foodstuffs. She had various groups of snails who were encouraged to feed on carrot, and then given potato, some with an unpleasant taste added, some without. She had begun with mild doses of snail poison in the experimental group, which had frothed and convulsed and died. She had now started with a kind of cyanogenic glucoside, naturally found in plants they fed on, but in increased concentrations. This seemed to be working better. She had several circular plastic dishes with perforated floors, with a two-centimetre footbridge in the middle. 'Trained' snails (slightly poisoned snails) avoided the half-dish containing potato. Untrained snails crawled everywhere. In principle. Sometimes they sat inside their shells, motionless but not dead.

The idea was to be able to check the chemical messengers carrying the memory of poisoned potato, from neurone to ganglion to rasping lip. And this would be one tiny piece in the jigsaw which might show how what is not there, or its representations, inhabit the neurones and the synapses, the flow of currents and molecules round the brain and the body. Carrots, potatoes, the smell of a lover's skin, or a child's hair, the second law of thermodynamics, the howl of King Lear.

Lyon Bowman came in from time to time, to see how Jacqueline was getting on. He admired her voltage clamp, and expressed an interest in the aversion-training.

'There's that man, Ungar,' he said, 'who trains rats to avoid darkness, with electric shocks. He thinks he's on to a memory molecule he calls scotophobin. Fear of the dark. He thinks he can extract it, inject it into other rats, and get the same reaction. It's a bit like the planaria, in my view. Dicey observations, dicey science. But in the end, you'll have to look into mammal synapses.'

'I know. I still have an intuition that Hebb was right. Learning strengthens connections. Or makes new ones. It *feels* right.'

'You're a bit in the dark here,' said Bowman, considering the gloom of Jacqueline's box as though it was new to him. He always said that.

'I know. And I'm scotophobic. I'm one of those people who slow down horribly in the winter months – I'm like my snails, I'm a born hibernator.'

'Well, you can't afford to indulge yourself in that sort of sensitivity in the competitive world we live in.'

He was standing quite deliberately very close to her, crowding her against her bench.

'You need time off. You need a change. I'm off to a conference on the visual cortex in Turin. Do you want to come along? The Department can support you. Meet a few new scientists. Get a little more sun, even in winter.'

He put an arm briefly about her shoulder. Jacqueline had heard about Lyon Bowman's conference invitations to women graduates. Like a cockerel in a farmyard, one woman had said, crossly, having locked her bedroom door and failed to advance her career. Jacqueline said 'If I can get my experiments to a state where I can leave them.'

'Good,' said Lyon Bowman. 'You'll like my new paper, it's elegant. You can help with the slides. You don't make mistakes.'

In the aeroplane, he said very little. He sat beside her, and made calculations with his slide-rule. Galton could remember the whole slide-rule, Jacqueline said. He could call it up in his mind, and operate it. How can that work?

Bowman laughed, pleasantly.

She thought, for the first day of the conference, that she had been mistaken about his intentions. He had taken her along as an assistant, as he had said. They were in the same hotel, but not on the same floor. He introduced her to Italians, Americans, Germans. He praised her research to them. She drank a few glasses of Chianti, said good-night, and went to bed.

An hour later, the door-handle turned. She thought of doing nothing, stood up, and opened it.

'Here I am,' he said. He was in shirt and trousers. He smiled. 'I hope you want me. I hope you're expecting me.'

'I don't know.'

'Come on, at least let me in so we can discuss the matter in civilised privacy.'

Jacqueline stepped aside. She sensed his impatience. The preliminaries bored him. Possibly, she thought, because he had gone through them so often. In which case, it was no big deal. For either of them. Was it?

'I brought a bottle,' he said, with the same faintly detectable weariness at having to say anything.

Jacqueline tried to think clearly. She was sleepy, and had eaten and drunk well, and what her mind said to her was, after all, why not? It was probably the quickest way of getting a good night's sleep, her body said. The line of least resistance, her brain mocked. She sat down, on the edge of her bed.

Bowman sat down beside her, took a swig from his bottle, and handed it to her.

'I've been looking at you,' he said. 'You don't sell yourself. You don't –' he sketched the exaggerated shape of a woman in the air of the hotel bedroom, with a hand which he then put on her breast. 'You don't dress to kill.'

'No,' said Jacqueline.

'You've got a sort of *comfortable* look. At ease with yourself. It's very attractive, in a subtle way.'

'Good,' said Jacqueline. 'Good.'

'You don't say much.'

'I don't know what to say.'

'No. Do you know what you want to do? If you want me to go away, you've only got to speak. Contrary to what you've no doubt been told, I never force myself on the unwilling.'

Jacqueline's cheeks were hot and the skin of her neck was flaring. Lyon Bowman had a disconcerting skin-smell, partly acrid, partly hot, which she found at once repellent and irresistible. She moved her legs a little closer together, which had the unfortunate effect of making her feel a distinct tug and twitch of desire. She was damp. She put her hand over his on her breast. She thought in her head, OK, I'll have this, I will have this, but he's got to stop talking to me or I won't be able to.

She turned her face towards his, and moved her hand under his shirt. His skin was electric, also both repellent and attractive.

'Magnetism,' she murmured.

'What?' he said into her hair. He was stripping her nightshirt.

'Magnetism. Sex as well as memory.'

He laughed, and revealed her nakedness.

'Very nice,' he said, staring brightly. 'You got a lucky set of genes. Lovely firm muscles. What a beauty.'

He stood up, still staring, and took off his own clothes. Jacqueline looked away. His mouth was red, the tip of his erection was redder. She closed her eyes.

He was not in a hurry, and he knew exactly what he was doing. He remarked in a practical voice that she was 'tight' and added 'Surely this isn't your first time, however old are you?'

'I'm twenty-nine, and no it isn't.' She said 'Put the light out.'

'Very few women,' said Lyon Bowman, 'like doing it in the light. Even little brown scotophobes like you.'

It was the nearest he came to an endearment. Jacqueline recognised this for what it was, a sort of honesty.

He touched Jacqueline's body into a whiplash of tension and pleasure. He turned her world on the tip of his finger on her clitoris, and she arched, and gasped, and waited for what *must* come. He said

'I suppose you *are* on the Pill. They all are, these days.'

'No,' she managed to say. 'I'm not.'

'*Shit.* You should have said. Now, have I. Did I?'

He whipped himself out of her, and she trembled, and her body ached and opened. She could hear and feel him fumbling in his pockets. 'Have I, did I?'

She heard the sound of the rubber being opened, the twang of its appliance.

'You should have said,' he said. He added 'I suppose you don't need to be on the Pill.'

Jacqueline did not rise to this. Her body most desperately needed him to finish what he had interrupted.

'Never so good with these things,' the professional voice muttered in her ear. 'Now, where were we? Back to where we were . . .'

It took time to retrieve the rhythm, and it was to his credit, Jacqueline thought, as her orgasm racked her and his followed, that he could do it at all.

As he came to his climax he cried out, in a kind of groan, 'Ah, good *girl*, you good *girl*.'

Like a rider encouraging a horse, she thought.

The phrase was to haunt her.

The 'Non-Maths' Group met every fortnight to study maths. It was one of Wijnnobel's institutions, and he himself was a regular attender. 'Non-Maths' was short for 'Mathematics for non-mathematicians'. The group met in a classroom in the Maths Tower (a pyramid on a cylinder on a cube) and adjourned often enough to a pub. The idea was to have a forum where the mathematical problems of non-mathematicians could be aired and solved. Marcus Potter was always there, sometimes accompanied by Jacob Scrope the professor in the computing department, and, more recently, by John Ottokar, who wrote the programmes which churned slowly through the great machines.

Both Jacqueline and Luk Lysgaard-Peacock depended on Marcus and John Ottokar for the number-crunching, the conversion into equations, of the traced electrical spikes of action potential in Jacqueline's case, and for the complicated and elegant models of variables in population genetics in Luk's. Luk Lysgaard-Peacock was a competent mathematician, though not a brilliant one. He liked to submit his ideas to Marcus in the pub and watch the long pale fingers sketch diagrams, connecting webs, to represent his own intuitions. Jacqueline was not a competent mathematician. Marcus had had to give her a crash course in differential equations. John Ottokar was teaching her to write her own programmes in FORTRAN. In later years, when computer screens glimmered and ticked on every student desk, it was hard to remember these heroic years of the huge humming machines, full of transistors, emitting monstrous empilings of print-out, and fed by punched cards. To get their sums done, both Luk and Jacqueline had to wait – for hours, or days – for their turn on the computer, which could be wasted if a mistake had been made in the programming, in the recording of the data, in the way the problem was put.

Another regular visitor to the Non-Maths Group was Vincent

Hodgkiss, the philosopher, who was writing a study of Ludwig Wittgenstein's dislike of the mathematical logic he had himself excelled in. Hodgkiss was a quiet man, whose appearance people found they misremembered, as though he was not quite embodied, a ghost in a machine. He was certainly short, and certainly balding, his remaining hair wispy, of an indeterminate colour. He sometimes wore spectacles, and sometimes didn't. His voice, when he spoke, was unexpectedly plummy, full of Oxford vowels. He liked to sit under the window, with his back to it and his face in shadow. An observant man.

Jacqueline continued to be irritated by Lyon Bowman's phrasing. 'Good *girl*.' She heard in her mind, over and over, 'Good *girl*.' He had reminded her that at twenty-nine she was hardly any longer a girl, was indeed a woman who was heading beyond the natural age for easy child-bearing. He had created in her a kind of angry hunger for sex, when she had intended him to be a neat, snipped-off episode. He had judged her, her Pill-less life, her solitude in which she worked. He looked at her in the lab as though it was only a matter of time, until he chose to suggest, or expect . . .

She strode into the Non-Maths Group with, as Vincent Hodgkiss put it to himself, 'a few cautious flags flying'. More careful make-up. A new jacket, in a chocolate-coloured suede, and a new golden jumper. Hodgkiss had been secretly amused for some time by the dynamics of attraction and repulsion between Marcus, Luk, and Jacqueline. If Jacqueline moved closer to Marcus, he shrank into himself. If she looked away, Marcus addressed his remarks to her as though she was the obvious person to understand them. The ease of childhood friends, and beyond that, unease. He watched Luk, too, watching Jacqueline with a proprietary look which was also discouraged and vulnerable. He was interested to see that the faintly flaming new Jacqueline looked at Marcus, almost shrugged, and went to sit near Luk. To whom she spoke animatedly, about her research, about aversion-training in slugs and snails. And the Dane lit up, as though he was a house with lamps in the windows. So simple, thought Vincent Hodgkiss. So simple, so far. I wonder why? He did not expect to know why and his wondering was, in a sense, mild and academic. Lord what fools these mortals be! he liked to think, aligning himself with the soulless immortal watchers.

But he had troubles of his own, and knew it. He watched, to distract himself. Jacob Scrope was talking that evening about a new programme for mapping random stimuli, new safeguards to ensure that the 'randomness' his computer recorded was truly random. Hodgkiss watched Jacqueline bend her head over Luk's notebook so that Luk's nose was in her hair. Nothing random about that. He looked at Marcus, who was frowning. He had never been able to make Marcus out. That was, he liked the way Marcus's mind worked, the clarity, the questioning, the separateness. He did not know what Marcus *wanted*. He prided himself on knowing what people wanted. Marcus's thin face had finally taken on some definition, a bony beakiness on which his large glasses balanced like windows, only in very few lights revealing the mildly alarmed eyes behind them.

Luk Lysgaard-Peacock, much more immediately than the observant Hodgkiss, noticed Jacqueline's perturbation and her deliberate move towards himself. Someone, he thought, had upset her, and he glanced briefly at Marcus, whose unawareness could not have been more marked. He let his hand touch hers, under the desk. Hers moved, not away, but closer. He sensed a rigidity of will in this gesture. He could refuse to dance. He put his hand briefly over hers. Which trembled, and then took hold of him.

Afterwards, he drove her back to the house where she lodged. They sat in the car and Luk thought of saying 'I love you' and thought of taking her in his arms, and said

'Something's upset you.'

'Is it so obvious?'

'I'm not *stupid*, Jacqueline. And I love you. As you know.'

'I don't know where I'm going.' She shook her head wildly. She took hold of his hand — again, he sensed the effort of will — and a few tears ran down her face. 'I've always gone on so carefully, one step after another, doing my work, doing what I felt was right, and now — and now — I feel suddenly old, without ever having looked at myself.'

'You're not old.'

'I'm not a girl.'

'No, I know that very well.'

'Luk, I must be mad, I should have listened to you, I don't know how I got myself so cocooned in my *self*, I want to be able to do the things — people do — I want to live, not just to think.'

'It's all a bit abstract.'

'I know, I know, that's the problem. I've always had a nice abstract *plan* –'

'I thought you were following some sense of things that was far from abstract –'

'No, no, it was an idea. Now I want to live. I want to be – I want –'

She began to cry furiously, and flung her arms about his neck. 'I've messed you about so,' she said to him.

'That's OK,' he said. He was not sure it was. He held her to him, burying her face in his clothes, stroking her body, like a man calming a nervous animal, until she stopped weeping and flailing, and sat, quietly, pressed against him, her body relaxing into his.

'We could *try* –' she said.

'You sound unsure.'

'I'm not. I'm just a bit – muddled by myself, by my muddle. I'm not unsure. I want to try.'

Luk Lysgaard-Peacock had recently bought himself a small stone house, halfway up Gash Fell, in the shoulder of a hill looking down on the village of Fengbeck. Its name was Loderby. Above him were the moors, and in the next valley was Gungingap where the Dun Vale Hall snail populations had tucked themselves away for the winter in clusters between the stones in the walls. Gunner Nighby was recovering elsewhere from his wounds, and Lucy Nighby was still in Cedar Mount, as far as Luk knew. The Hall, like the snails, was shuttered and cold. The children were staying with a schoolteacher friend.

Luk had planned his house as a solitary retreat, a field station, an outpost. He had, like various other lecturers, rooms in Long Royston itself, a small bedroom, a study, a bathroom, based on Oxbridge colleges. There he was comfortable with a bright Finnish bedspread, a poster of the Matisse snail on the wall and a television. On Gash Fell he lived austerely, with scrubbed pine-topped tables, an old stone sink, a narrow bed, and no curtains. He liked the sun and the moon to shine in on him. He was not visible to neighbours or passers-by.

He had a large living-room, a low-ceilinged kitchen, two small bedrooms, a primitive bathroom, and a terrace that jutted out over the fell, with a thick stone ledge round it, and great flagstones underfoot. The walls were thick and the windows small, deeply embedded in stony cavities within and without. Everywhere was simply white-washed. He had also various dressers and benches where he had piled boxes and tanks of specimens.

Fengbeck was a tiny village, a few grey houses clustered around the bridge over the rapid beck that poured down from the moorside. There were also stepping-stones, liable to inundation. There was a little shop – no Post Office – which sold sliced bread, and milk, hunks of Wensleydale cheese, and fresh vegetables from the farms around. Also Kendal Mint Cake, and thick oiled socks, and leather polish. Between Luk and the village was a wood, giving way to stony fields before his house was reached. He decided to invite Jacqueline to the house for a weekend. Both of them were intelligent, forthright people, and both were rather awkwardly aware that Jacqueline had made a rational decision to re-open the question of their relations, rather than suffering an emotional *volte-face*. They knew each other too well, Luk thought, too well for the 'right' kind of tension and exploration to be there. They were old friends, which was a bad thing for new lovers.

He thought of ways of making a surprise. He drove up to his house, and thought it seemed sparse, unwelcoming. So, like a bower-bird – an analogy that amused him – he began to decorate. He started conventionally with the idea of flowers and went into a florist in Calverley where he contemplated some nasty begonias, some pre-Christmas poinsettias and an exotic camellia, which he decided against. He was rather taken by some Chinese silk artificial anemones, which in the end he bought, brilliant crimson and deep purple and white, thinking he need not deploy them, he could keep them in reserve. He also bought some blue glass plates and dishes, and some green glass mugs. He filled the back of his car with odd bits of his own collection of feathers and shells and stones, telling himself that he'd always meant to take them up there anyway. He bought plain white dishes, and satin-steel ones, to show them off in. He bought more oil-lamps, and, after much consideration, some flame-coloured sheets, two bottle-green blankets, and a flame-coloured quilt patterned with paisleys. A few bottles – old medicine bottles – blue, green, brown – out of a local junk shop, which he washed, and polished with a tea towel. Some bottles of wine, a leg of lamb, some good wholemeal bread, beans, baking potatoes. In the junk shop with the medicine bottles, at the very back, very dusty, was a tall black lacquer vase – probably Chinese – full of peacock feathers.

He liked his odd name, which had come about because an intransigent English ancestress – a great-grandmother – a York-shirewoman – had made it a condition of moving to Copenhagen that her name be joined to her husband's. They had been intensely religious people, the Lysgaard-Peacocks, followers of Grundtvig, Protestants and educational reformers. He remembered his childhood excitement when he discovered that 'pea-cock' meant *påfogl*, the brilliant, unearthly bird.

Luk, when he thought of the name now, thought mostly of the image of the eye, the exotic, non-seeing, brilliant eye that stared from the wing of the peacock butterfly. He thought less often of the bird, slowly raising the ludicrous, brilliant, glittering, shot-silk eyes of its heavy train into a quivering, creaking fan. But he did not, suddenly, want to leave the moulted feathers to wilt in the dusty shop. So he bought them, too, and carried them up the fell, and spent some time preening them with his careful fingers, catching the tiny hooks back together into the textured surface along the plumes, so that the eyes glittered again in their green and blue and gold, bedizened and extraordinary.

He was amused by his own activities, and at the same time more and more anxiously obsessed. He arranged his trophies in carefully casual drifts and heaps, inside the window alcoves, along the benches. A group of shells, *Cepaea hortensis, Cepaea nemoralis*, some tiny flat ramshorns, a few giant white *Helix pomatia*. An interesting collection of *Vertigo*. A scalariform monstrosity. The silk anemones on the dresser in a plain jamjar. The empty medicine bottles on a carefully washed shelf in the bathroom, where he had put up a new mirror, framed in pale wood. Heaps of seaside pebbles, rows of ancient stones side by side, like families of strange lumpen creatures, or those rows of elephants brought back from the ex-colonies. Some dried fern leaves. Three skulls – fox, badger, shrew.

He put his oil-lamps – big ones with chimneys and mantles, little ones, Kelly lamps, with their glass spouts and heavy bases, so that their thick gold light fell and shone on what caught it – wrinkled silk and sheen of feather, gleam of stone and lacquer of shell, ribbed glass and white bone. In his garden – in a small patch behind the house, sheltered from the weather by a high wall, containing an apple-tree, a gooseberry patch, a herb-garden, some loganberries and one flowerbed, he found a whole clump of the plant he knew in Danish as *Judaspenge* and in English as Honesty. Perennial honesty, *Lunaria rediviva*, was fragrant; this was the biennial, *L. biennis*, a garden fugitive. The membrane inside the seed-cases, polished and exposed, was like transparent oculi of parchment, or abalone shell. He spent some time rubbing off the seeds, and creating wands of fragile, translucent windows. The French called them *monnaie des papes*. He mixed them with the peacock feathers in the black lacquer vase. The eyes and the monocle-windows looked, he thought, strikingly beautiful together. He stood his vase on the turn of the stair going up to the bedroom, and stood a Kelly lamp above it, on a stone shelf.

Jacqueline did not drive. He met her off the bus, on the Friday evening. In the car, she was tense. She was wearing the new brown jacket, had her hands crossed in her lap, and stared out at the mounting road, the dark woods, the night sky above the long edge of the moorland. There was a cold wind; the trees rustled. An owl hooted. A conversation about owls sparked brightly, and sputtered out. The lighted windows of the cottage, darkly golden, came into view.

He said 'I won't carry you over the threshold.' But he took her hand, as they went in, and held it, as she looked round, admiring the lamp-light. He sat her down in a high-backed chair at the end of the table, whilst he saw to the last stages of the cooking. She sat quietly and watched him. He had the sense he always had, that she looked *right*. She wore browns. A golden-brown turtleneck sweater, under the chocolate-brown suede jacket. A straight donkey-brown skirt – she never wore skirts on their field-work, always trousers – and warm dark brown tights, knitted with a cable twist. She had very long legs, very visible. Her hair shone in the soft light, black treacle, molasses, horse-chestnuts. Quietly shining. He put on an apron and hummed to himself. Her dark eyes followed him; her head was on one side, like a watchful bird.

The table was laid with woven Finnish mats, blue and green, and new tumblers, in seagreen glass full of bubbles. There were candles in dishes, and a bottle of claret. His apron was a butcher's apron, blue and white striped. He brandished prongs, spikes and ladles – the baked potatoes were impaled on metal tripods, the leg of lamb was spitting and hissing in its dish. He lifted it on to its warm serving-plate. Gravy ran in crimson runnels down the sweating fat, where his fork had pierced. He poured off the rest, and busied himself scraping the burned fragments into a whirl of wine, boiling, stirring. There was a warm, powerful smell of cooked meat, laced with garlic and rosemary. He strained his brussels sprouts – cooked to perfection – and put his dishes on the table with a flourish. Jacqueline, closed in by the arms of her throne, saw a neat bearded Viking, red-gold and bristling, wearing a garment somewhere between housewife and slaughterhouse, brandishing slicing knife and steel. He swished the blade through the air, across the magnet and across.

'You have to align the molecules,' he said. 'You must always stroke steel one way –'

'I didn't know,' said Jacqueline, 'that you did all this cooking. So well.'

'I thought I'd show you something you didn't know.'

He carved.

'I thought I'd show you I had many domestic virtues. I don't need a housekeeper. I am housetrained –'

'Ah, Luk –'

'A joke, a joke.'

The blade hit the flesh. The mutton fell away in pink-brown, perfect slices, the pale blood matting the surface of the fibres with liquid.

He waved his knife.

'My lady is served.'

He arranged the slices, neatly overlapping, on her plate. He hurried to and fro, along his kitchen table, bearing redcurrant jelly and peppermill, green spheres of sprouts mixed with chestnuts, the baked potatoes in an earthenware pot.

'Good *girl*,' said Jacqueline's mind. And 'My lady is served.'

'There's far too much there, far too much for me,' said Jacqueline. 'I eat like a bird.'

Luk grinned. 'You forget. I've spent days and days on the moors with you. With thick sandwiches.'

'It smells *wonderful*. It looks *delicious*.'

'Remains taste –' said Luk. He sat down. He had put on a festive sweater, in dark slate oiled wool, but he forgot to take off his apron. By some instinct of stage-management he had set them at opposite ends of the table, regally staring at each other. They stared. Jacqueline asked a few questions about the buying of Loderby; their banality appeared to puzzle Luk, who answered politely, briefly and distractedly, as though these were not real words, but must be ruffled through, for form's sake.

He then asked her about her research, and she spoke with bright intensity for some minutes about the comparative advantages of making slugs and snails artificially averse to carrots or potatoes, and the best ways to induce a measurable aversion.

He then asked her about Lyon Bowman. Was he treating her well.

'Very well.' The dark head was down. She cut small squares off the meat, and chewed them. 'He takes an interest,' she said, meaning in the snails, and hearing the doubleness too late. 'In the snails,' she added unfortunately, making clear what had not been. There was a silence. They ate. Luk offered more food, but Jacqueline's plate was still half-full. Or half-empty. Depending. Luk tried to remember what they had talked about when he felt so comfortably close to her, and could not.

He said that he was happy to know that Eichenbaum had accepted Wijnnobel's invitation to the Conference next summer. He will redefine 'instinct', Luk told Jacqueline. He has done some beautiful work on nesting responses. What vaguely egg-shaped object – and what colour – does and doesn't trigger nesting behaviour in seagulls, in sparrows, in the domestic hen. Will they try to brood a scarlet egg? How big does an egg have to be to be not-an-egg? Plovers appear to prefer outsize eggs to normal ones. Herring gulls recognise their own chicks, but not their own eggs. They recognise their mates at large distances – 50 yards or more. He's working on what triggers egg-recognition and mate-recognition.

Later, Luk was to wish he had not introduced this apparently safe subject. He went round to offer Jacqueline more meat on the point of his stainless steel fork, and saw himself suddenly as a male gull, clattering his beak against the female, proffering a propitiatory fish. Jacqueline declined the meat. She had enough. She said it was delicious. Luk cleared away – he would not let her move – and replaced meat with cheese, and cheese with lemon tarts he had made himself. During this time they talked, neutrally and amiably, about Wijnnobel's conference and the increasing size of the Anti-University encampment.

Luk began to be tormented by a series of inner visions: male birds, strutting and bowing, with worms, with gobbets of flesh, with wriggling silvery fish and eels. Waving rumps, distended throat-balloons, perky crests. Flushed sticklebacks, and cuttlefish across whose sac-like bodies played lights of successive blushes in successive waves of crimson and rose, amber and cool blue. He saw the blue booby, a bird he had once observed for a time, descending from a wintry sky, rotating its only remarkable feature, huge, flat, bright, swimming-pool blue feet, and offering its desired mate a symbolic twig to make a nest on land where no nest could be made, and where eggs were balanced in inclinations in bare rock.

He offered Jacqueline a dish of apples, and thought of the bower-bird who specialised in feathers from a bird of paradise known as the King of Saxony. The feathers are rare (they don't grow before the bird is four years old) and brilliant blue, with square pennants on fine stems, several times longer than the bird, and sprouting from its brow. Male bower-birds fight for these rarities, which they weave into their paradise gardens of ferns and twigs. He began to see all his movements as ritualised gestures. He should have been able to share the joke with Jacqueline. But because she was now ritually defined as the audience for his mopping and mowing, he couldn't speak.

She refused the apples. She had had, she said, more than enough. It had been delicious.

He poured red wine, accompanied by the ghost of a solicitous albatross. She accepted the wine, with a neat little inclination of her head. She had made a rational decision that it would be a good idea to be a little drunk. She was aware that something was bothering Luk, but could not quite guess what, and again, felt that the pattern of their dance required her not to ask. She did notice that he had arranged things so that he was constantly in motion, along the table, round the kitchen. She wished his plan allowed her to move herself. She wished to be able to follow his lead. That was what this was about. She sipped wine, thinking of the alcohol gently fuddling her over-active head.

When Luk was at his far end of the table, he looked like the old, familiar, too familiar Luk. As he came dancing towards her, with his offerings, his bearded face passed from pool of light to pool of light, from candle-light to island of lamp-light. When these fiery lights were under his face he looked unfamiliar. He looked demonic.

Recent research, she remembered, had shown that children raised together on the Kibbutzim to be good husbands and wives for each other had seemed somehow to share the primitive incest tabu, although they were quite unrelated. They had turned outwards for husbands and wives. She thought about arranged marriages. The quite different fears, and hopes, and excitements there must be when the chosen mate was the Unknown.

She was trying to arrange her own marriage, on rational grounds. These thoughts too, she could not communicate to Luk.

Bed-time came. Luk said

'Shall we go upstairs?'

Jacqueline nodded.

'This is just a weekend,' said Luk. 'I don't expect it – necessarily – to lead to anything. I hope, of course. But I want to take it step by step.'

Jacqueline nodded.

Luk held out his hand, and led her from the chair to the staircase. Beside him a ghostly grebe whirled on water, wreathing its neck. Rose and plum and azure baboon genitals flashed across his inner eye.

She stopped on the corner of the stairs and saw the peacock feathers and the honesty, gleaming under the Kelly lamp.

She said, before she could stop herself

'I was always told it was unlucky to have peacock feathers in the house.'

Luk's voice was light. 'Something maybe to do with the evil eye? Superstitious nonsense.'

'Of course.'

The little bedroom was cold. There were stars and scudding clouds across the little window. The paisley quilt, the flaming sheets, looked warm. They shivered as they undressed, without ceremony, and dived into them. He had imagined her nakedness in detail as they worked together, but scarcely saw it as she hurried it under the blankets. He could feel it however. He ran his hands all over it, collarbone and spine, breasts and navel, flanks and buttocks, and the unseen bush of dark hair. Timidly, trembling, she touched him in return. This was what he had waited for. He was careful. He was very careful. He could not speak for emotion, but he kissed the vein in her neck, he buried his rough beard in her soft hair. He was visited by an unsolicited and unwelcome memory – in ludicrously complete detail – of Szymanski's careful experiments, in 1913, on the long and complicated system of mutual stimulation in the giant Roman snail, *Helix pomatia*, which cumulated – since the creatures were of course, hermaphrodite – in the mutual release of the horny love-shaft, subsequently absorbed, for the calcium it contained, by the now inseminated pair. He touched the inner lip of Jacqueline's cunt and saw in his mind's eye the rearing, twisting mantle and the wavering horns of the creatures. It was like being a mediaeval monk tormented by diabolically induced visions. He might have told the old companionable Jacqueline the joke, and exorcised the demons with laughter. But this new, uncertainly responsive, reticent woman was another person, another problem.

As for Jacqueline, she heard in her mind's ear 'good *girl*' and her body bucked with retrospective irritation. Luk put his arms round her, held her tight, began to pump with his own rhythm, asking, in a whisper, 'Is it all right', which effectively disturbed her own weak response, before matters were out of his control altogether. Jacqueline squirmed, and twisted her body against his, both desiring and rejecting her own climax, and achieved a small shiver, like a single minor sneeze. Luk gathered her to him, and stroked her along the length of her body, over and over. In his mind, mercifully released from snail-slime and love-darts, he saw his own fingers, repairing the hook and eyes of the bedraggled peacock feathers. And then the blade of the carving-knife on the steel, smoothing the molecules all one way. 'My love?' he tried saying, and his love buried her hot, unhappy face in his shoulder, and kissed it, and he felt hot tears.

So much had hung on that inconclusive embrace. Luk knew that rhythms needed to be learned, and he was not sure Jacqueline was going to give either of them any more time to learn them in.

They should have been unable to keep their hands off each other, and were sitting politely apart, at breakfast, in the car. He thought of saying 'Next weekend?' and thought of not saying it. When he did say it, Jacqueline said 'I need time to think,' and this cool sentence sounded like doom.

Jacqueline felt desperate. She was behaving badly. She was trashing generous gifts, she was capriciously stirring mud in the river of Luk's life. She was trying to make sensible decisions about her own life − it was *the whole of her own life* she was disposing of − and appeared to be unable to make them either rationally or impulsively.

Over the next few weeks, her work slowed. Bowman noticed it. He came and stood behind her at her bench, touched her shoulder, and then her breast, briefly, and said

'Everything OK? You look a bit pale.'

'I'm a winter depressive. I don't like dark.'

'You're heavy-eyed. Take a few days off.'

'How can I? The experiments need watching.'

She had missed a period. The time came when she could say she had missed two, except that it was always the same one she had missed. She went more and more frequently in and out of the lavatory, looking for signs, a streak, a drop, of brown, or red, on knicker or paper. Everything remained pristine white. She had been here before, and knew that obsessive expectation delayed the desired flow. She went on long walks, and then rushed again into the lavatory, feeling, she hoped, the hoped-for bar of pain across the base of her belly, the twinge. Nothing. And the next day, nothing. Like a watchman on a high tower, looking for relief across a plain of snow, and seeing no movement, no change, day after day.

During this time, she dined occasionally with Luk, and talked brightly, alternating 'I' and 'we' in her descriptions of her future. He took away an image of wilful irresolution.

She went, in the end, to the university health service. A woman doctor inserted fingers, and cupped her cervix.

'Oh yes, I think so,' she said. 'I think so. I hope you're happy about this. We'll do a test, just to be sure.'

Jacqueline went back to the Evolution Tower and took out a heap of books on embryology. She stared at images of dividing cells, of curved seahorse-like chains of cells with huge bland eyes, of limb-buds and vanishing tails, and transparent frog-fingers and ghost-mouths forming busily out of formlessness, as the messages sped from cell to cell, and the division and building increased and increased. She felt a kind of pain – an imaginary pain – where the knot of new cells was, the invader, clinging to the very inside of her solitary self, using her blood, her food, her DNA. A creature. Not a missed period. A new creature.

She knew that that made everything easier. She had kept her hopes and fears to herself, but the knowledge needed to be shared. She put on her jacket – it was about eight in the evening – and went round to find Luk Lysgaard-Peacock. She did not want to think – let alone to feel – too much. She must now do what had to be done.

It was a long time since she had simply turned up in his Long Royston rooms. She had hurried across dark lawns and courtyards, and his little room was bright and lively. He was sitting at his desk, correcting papers. She came in, and stood with her back against the door she had just closed, somehow still clothed with the wintry evening. She held the collar of her jacket to her chin.

'I appear to be pregnant,' said Jacqueline, baldly, to Luk.

He stood up. She looked both wild and shrunk. He did not touch her.

'I'm very pleased. If you are,' he said.

'It's a shock.'

Luk's imagination danced. He saw a small boy with brown hair, a red-headed girl, their two faces mixed to make a new face. He said

'Pleased is a daft word, a ludicrous word, as long as you –'

She stood there.

'Jacqueline, you *do* want –?'

'I think so. I – I wouldn't do anything else. It's a shock.'

'What I want – what *I* want – is that we should get married, as soon as we can, and I will look after you – and – the child – and your work, because I know how good you are going to be, you are the real thing, a scientist –'

She began to cry, her shoulders sagging slightly, whether from relief or despair he could not tell.

'Will you? If you say you will –'

'Oh yes. I think this decides everything. I will. I do want to marry you. I do want –'

He said 'I feel like turning cartwheels, I feel like flinging open the window and screaming into the night – she will, she will, and there will be a *child* – I can't tell you how *wonderful* such a child will be, is –'

He said 'Look, you'd better sit down on the bed, and have a sip of brandy. Oh, Jacqueline, I do want you to be happy.'

'And I do want you to be.'

'I know. And we can both make – him or her – happy –'

No image of skin or hair or smile crossed Jacqueline's mind. Busy cells. Jelly fingers. Bulging eye-sockets.

Jacqueline said to Marcus, sitting next to him at the Non-Maths Group, 'I think I am going to marry Luk.'

Vincent Hodgkiss, sitting behind them, his nose in a book, looked up with interest.

'Wonderful,' said Marcus. 'It's what everyone always hoped would happen.'

'Is it?'

'Well, you know, people talked . . .'

'They talked?'

'People do talk,' Marcus said vaguely. Hodgkiss thought, no one can be as innocent as Marcus Potter looks. She wanted badly to know what *he* thinks. And he chooses a nice common noun, very vague, 'people', 'everyone'. And stares over her shoulder. He watched Jacqueline give herself a little shake, like a dog in the rain. He watched her, at the end of the session, which was on computer programming, walk away with Luk himself. Luk's arm was over her shoulder. A first. Hodgkiss said to Marcus 'Do you know anything about Alan Turing's ideas about what mathematical logic *was*?'

'I know about his early machines. Why?'

'I'm writing on Wittgenstein's lectures on mathematical logic in 1939. Turing attended a large number. They developed into arguments between the two. So much that Wittgenstein once refused to teach at all because Turing wasn't there. Odd. Two opposed kinds of genius.'

'What was Wittgenstein saying?'
'I'll tell you. Coffee?'

Luk and Jacqueline began to discuss arrangements. They sat in
Luk's tiny cheerful room, and discussed whether to buy a house,
or rent a university apartment, when to marry, when to tell
Jacqueline's family. Luk described his parents. His father was a
Lutheran pastor, with whom he had quarrelled because of his own
lack of religious beliefs.

'He would want me to be married in church.'
'I have always gone to church. Then I stopped.'
'You don't want a church wedding? I don't think I could bring
myself to go through one of those. Even if I told myself over and
over that meaningless words hurt no one.'
'I always thought I wanted – I ought to want – I did want – a
proper wedding-day. But it'd be a bit ludicrous anyway, given –'
She touched her belly.
'So, no church wedding. Do we ask anyone, or no one, have a
party, or be very private, present them all with a *fait accompli?*'
'My mother would mind that *horribly.*'
'I should meet her, perhaps –' said Luk.
Marriage involved strings of unknown, unrelated persons, who
were nevertheless related to the splitting and multiplying cells, to
him, or to her.

Jacqueline said
'Could we watch the television? There's this new programme
with Marcus's sister, Frederica Potter. The last one was really
good. They mix cartoon creatures with real ideas. They talked
about mirrors . . .'
It was in this way that Frederica's uneasy ribaldry about Free
Women, the mock kitchen, the gynaecological *batterie de cuisine,*
the hen-party, the *kaffee-klatsch,* the brightly intimate discussion of
the Pill, of abortion, of males, of the monthly wait for the drops of
blood on white cloth invaded Luk and Jacqueline's life. Jacqueline
laughed sardonically, from time to time. Luk felt her relax, as she
had not been relaxed during their discussion of their wedding. She
laughed a great deal – too much – at Julia Corbett's dismissal of
the floating veiling. A kind of ancient prudery – a heritage from
his rejected father – came over Luk. He looked at Jacqueline's

smiles and was overcome with an irrational hatred for that bouncing and insensitive person, Frederica Potter. Her face filled the screen, her painted eyes, her falsely innocent hair-band, her knowing, conniving grin. He stood up, instinctively, to turn her off. To repel the invader.

'Don't,' said Jacqueline. 'It's witty. It hasn't been done before. Don't you like it?'

'No. I think it's nasty and cheap and vulgar.'

'That's because you're a man watching women talking the way women talk.'

The three women were solemnly passing the Tupperware bowls from hand to hand.

'It's hysterical,' said Jacqueline. 'I've never seen anything like it.'

'Self-satisfied bitch,' said Luk.

'What?'

'I don't like her. I don't know why.'

'Lots of people don't,' said Jacqueline. 'I should think by now hundreds of thousands of people don't. She puts people's hackles up. They like to dislike her. She'll be a success.'

'What a fate,' said Luk, missing the right note of mock-scorn.

Jacqueline did not tell Bowman she was thinking of getting married. He came to her with a job advertisement for a post in Edinburgh, and asked if she would be interested in applying. She bent her head over her bench, and thanked him, and said she would think about it.

'The voltage clamp works?'

'It does now. I had to tinker and fiddle. It does now.'

'You're tenacious.'

'I told you.'

'Keep at it, girl. Keep at it.'

There had been some trouble with the pregnancy test. One had been inconclusive, and a second specimen had been collected, and sent away. The second test result came to the University Health Service, who sent it through to Jacqueline in an inter-departmental envelope that she managed to rescue from the Departmental Secretary.

It was positive. She was quite certainly pregnant.

She felt an immediate urge to go to the lavatory. Her pelvis hurt, her bladder hurt, her body was in turmoil.

Her knickers had a very faint, ruddy brown streak.

And then the blood came. A small, manageable, series of gouts, and – she looked to see – a kind of jelly bundle, with threads, which could have been a plug, or womb-lining. She could not see any sign of the hooked creature which had held on briefly, and let go. Another gout, another. She sat in the lavatory, and wept. She sat for a long time, and wept a great deal. Blood and tears poured out of her. She was appalled by her body, which shook, and trembled, by the sense that emotion was a bodily, unnameable, unmanageable *thing*. She could not call it grief. Or mourning, or anger, or fear.

When she came out, she told the Departmental Secretary that she felt ill and was going home for the rest of the day.

'You look dreadful.'

Bowman, passing, took a look at her puffed, flushed face and said he could confirm that, she looked dreadful.

'Anything I can do?'

'No. Well. If you – if someone – could measure how much tampered carrot the snails in the second row of boxes have or haven't eaten – and the potato – it should be done at 5.00. More or less.'

'I'll see to it. Don't cry, sweetie. It almost certainly isn't worth it.'

Jacqueline went to the remote floor of the Evolution Tower where Luk had his office. He was with a student, whom he dismissed immediately on seeing Jacqueline's desperate face.

'Come in, my love. Sit down. What can have happened?'

She stood with her back to the door. Her nails bit into her clenched hands. Her eyes were screwed up, behind her glasses, and looked mean.

'I've come to say. It was all a mistake. There isn't. I wasn't. I'm *not*, anyway, pregnant. Not any more, if I ever was.'

'Please sit down. It needn't change anything. We can still get married, and . . .'

'No. I came to say, I can't. I don't want to get married. I can't. I want to want to get married, but I don't. *It was all a mistake.*'

Tears ran down her face. Her mouth worked.

'You're upset. You must wait – you must calm down –'

He tried to put his arms round the rigid, hunched shoulders. She twisted violently, and pushed him away.

'No, no. We've always understood each other. You know I mean what I say. You must let me know what I want – and I do know.'

'Why?'

'There doesn't have to be a reason. As long as I know. And I know.'

He tried again to touch her, and she whirled round, and ran, hard, down the corridor, into the lift. The blood was hot, and wet. She went home, and went to bed.

XII

Electric waves travel through space and disperse human faces through the atmosphere, concentrating the image, you might almost say the engram, again, in boxes, through tubes, glimmering and shimmering in the grey out of nowhere, as though the disembodied lurk in waiting in every cupboard, over every rooftop, perched on forked aerials, driving in the wind, eddying in breezes cutting through clouds, in sunlight, and moonlight, and starlight. So Luk Lysgaard-Peacock, sitting down in his rooms in Long Royston to consider the wreckage of his hopes, pressed an idle button and saw Frederica Potter's bony face speed towards him out of a spinning point. She smiled knowingly at him, and he glowered back at her. He told himself he was not immediately turning her off again because he was interested in Hodder Pinsky, who was coming to Wijnnobel's Conference. In fact, he found her a useful focus for his fury.

Like all television watchers, he saw the faces first and the ideas as functions of the faces. An *aggressive* female, an insistent voice, too long a neck, a mistaken coquettish tilt to the chin. The cartoons included an image of Alice as bird-serpent, peering into the birdsnest. Pinsky's glasses made him look shifty and furtive.

Luk didn't like the subject of the discussion, either. He didn't like, and never used, the word 'creativity' himself. He considered the mental operations discussed by psychologists under that heading as hopelessly imprecise. The poetic evocations of Gander struck him as hopelessly vapid and pretentious. 'None of you are really talking about *anything*,' he told them, scornfully, enjoying disliking them.

The Picasso cock-hen-woman he thought was a monstrosity. And then Pinsky embarked on the story of Freud and the young man who was waiting anxiously to hear that his girl-friend was bleeding, and Luk shivered with disgust at the coincidence, and distaste for the subject matter. He thought of his non-child, for whom he was oddly in mourning, and felt that it was very vulgar of Frederica Potter to keep on harping on menstruation, and pregnancy, in this technical way in public. He was simply repelled by the idea that *Through the Looking-Glass* appeared to be connected in an arcane way to his own life. He did not like Jungian ideas of synchronicity, or ethereal messaging. He was a rational man. He was a fanatically rational man.

His dislike of the word 'creative' as applied to human beings had in fact religious roots. He had been thinking of his parents over the last few days, because of his approaching marriage, because of the need to organise a wedding. He had been thinking of them also as a geneticist, because the child he had so clearly imagined would have had their genes, which would have been combined with those of Jacqueline's pleasant parents to make someone quite new. They were about to be ancestors and now were not.

He had been remembering his religious upbringing in Langeland. His father had told him as a child that God had created the world, and that God would, in his own good time, destroy the world. Tøger Lysgaard was a follower of Grundtvig, bard, theologian, and world historian. Grundtvig's Christianity was intricately woven into his resuscitation of Norse mythology. 'Highest Odin, White Christ,' Grundtvig wrote.

He had asked his father, once, as a little boy 'Why is there something, and not nothing?'

His father had replied that the question showed that the boy had a truly religious soul. The answer was, that there was something because the Lord had created it, and had seen that His work was good. And that the Lord maintained it, at every moment, through His loving care, upholding it.

As a boy, Luk had been reasonably devout. Jesus Christ had been his friend, a better friend than any human one. He had tried to be good, and had not been prevented from being curious. As an adolescent he had come to find keeping up his belief strenuous and somehow 'thin'. One day, walking amongst trees in a wood, in sunlight, he had had an intense flash of vision, which because of his education he compared to the Pauline flash on the road to Damascus. Except that what he saw – what was revealed by the brilliance of the ordinary light – was that the stories they had told him were stories and were not true. And when he saw that, suddenly everything was differently real, shining with clarity, with particularity, and with a mystery which was to be a calling. He saw flies and worms, leaves and roots transfigured because they were not transfigured, they were what they were. He thought of his religious faith as a horny lens over his eyes which were now washed clean.

His experience was not unusual. But one thing it had in common with the religious conversion of which it was mirror-twin was a tendency to dogmatism, to extremes. His new world was washed clean of human stories. With human stories went other sets of mind, not necessarily connected. He particularly loathed — with a religious intensity — scientific ideas about the 'anthropic principle' which claimed that the Universe somehow spread out from the infinitely large to the infinitely small on a scale of which the human body and brain just happened to be the centre. He also did not like, very much, most works of art and most non-religious human stories. He read neither novels nor histories. His time-scale was evolutionary, the forms of his imagination were elastic but always factual. He noted, scientifically, that biologists shared his fiercely defended pragmatic agnosticism. Physicists, for some reason, found it easier to construct or retain beliefs.

He found Frederica's Picasso vase-cock-hen, with its painted eye on its dead clay spout, both ludicrous and faintly obscene. It was an artefact, a form of the non-existent, of nothing. Forms of what was real were always more interesting. He found Frederica ludicrous, too. She was wasting her life. He enjoyed the intensity of his dislike of her. It relieved his grief, and was energising. He was a man who appeared gentler and kinder than he was. Jacqueline's rejection had cast him into some other compartment of himself, where he found a sardonic cynic.

Anger gave him restless energy. He packed a bag, and got out his car, and drove in the dark out into the moorland, back to Gash Fell. He drove through dark pinewoods, and out on to the mountainside where his small house sat, cold and dark. He went in, lit an oil-lamp, and took a torch. His own shadow loomed at him, a bearded demon reaching over white walls and ceiling. He lit stoves, and considered his bower-decorations. He thought he would sweep them all away, in a rite of renunciation, pile them together, skull and shell, burn them and stamp on them.

Then he thought that the objects were objects, and had done nothing. They were what they had been before, and would continue to be. So he disturbed his aesthetic arrangements, piled everything together differently, heaped anyhow. He took the lacquered vase of peacock feathers and honesty out on to the terrace. He had a foolish and satisfying image of himself ripping them apart, the iridescent eyes, the glimmering moony windows, unhooking the hooks and eyes he had so lovingly joined. And throwing them out into the cold wind that was starting up, to whisk around the mountainside, green and gold and pearly, the shreds of his hopes. What was it Jacqueline had said? 'I was always told it was unlucky to have peacock feathers in the house.' Nonsense, superstition, rubbish. The feathers had disgusted Darwin and were lovely. They were male excess, and had been rejected. There was still no clear explanation of *why* the bird indulged in such fantastic, costly display.

He thought of the quadrilateral of dividing cells in a sexually engendered embryo, and thought, not for the first time, that the whole business of sex could be argued to be expensive and wasteful. Anything that reproduced itself parthenogenetically could produce twice as many direct descendants for half the energy cost of meiosis and sexual division. The maths was more complicated than that. He thought of his slug experiments, on *Arion ater* and *Arion rufus* which seemed to be proving that populations above a certain altitude reproduced themselves parthenogenetically, were genetically identical, and lived harmoniously. Whereas those who lived in warmer – possibly more disparate – environments, were both male and female, and fought to the death, or consumed each other cannibalistically. Maybe the advantages of sex were to do with environmental variety, or difficulty? To do with dispersal? It came to him that he would write his paper for Wijnnobel's conference on something like '*The Cost of Sex and the Redundant Male*'. It would amuse him, and be interesting, and could encompass various thoughts he'd been having about kin selection, selfishness, and altruism. Male and female created he them, he thought with self-induced irony, firing himself. Two by two. There are all sorts of other ways of doing it. Microscopic parasitic males, buds, hermaphrodites. He looked at the honesty. *Judaspenge*, Judas money. A window on nothing. An empty seed-pod. Contaminated with grandiose human stories. An empty seed-pod is an empty seed-pod. Sex is sex. Is dispersal, is aggression, is (almost) endlessly diverse and interesting.

He stood in the dark, on his cold terrace, with his jacket-collar up against the wind. He listened to the silence, and the small sounds in the silence, branches, rustlings, hurrying feet, a faint cry of a creature cut off. He had a sense of his house sailing like an ark on a waste of dark water, out into space. The sky was full of stars.

XIII

From Kieran Quarrell to Elvet Gander

Thank you for your last, and for your mediation with the Spirit's Tigers. I shall personally drive my two 'patients' to Four Pence, to hand them into your care, and that of the community. As I said, the problems of Lucy Nighby's future are becoming acute. Her husband, Gunner, is largely recovered from his wounds, and asserts vociferously that she attacked both him and their three children. One of the children is still quite sick and disturbed. Of the other two, one asserts that Lucy attacked Gunner and the children and the other that Gunner attacked Lucy and the children. There are witnesses to the finding of Gunner in the hen-house (at some distance from the farm. What was he doing there?) who met Lucy, covered in blood and apparently in a state of shock. They say she was 'going through the motions' of egg-collecting. No one – that is to say, the police, and the social and medical experts – really believes Lucy instigated the violence. Gunner has a long history of heavy drinking and wife-beating (much of it hearsay, of course, and he was not drunk at the time of the attack). The courts cannot really move – either to prosecute anyone for assault, or to decide the future of the children – whilst Lucy remains mute. Gunner of course asserts that her silence is 'her usual cunning'. My own view is that it is quite genuine. She *cannot speak*. It has been decided to try the experiment of bringing her to the more humane atmosphere of Four Pence, in the hope that a little TLC and openness will unlock her.

I am also bringing Josh Lamb. Not for the same reasons. But the protracted stay in Cedar Mount is killing something in him – he is a trapped animal with human eyes. He has a right to an exorcism of his terrible history, and here again the more relaxed, warmer, more 'spiritual' atmosphere of the Tigers may be what he needs. I think he will intrigue you. I do not want to sound, old friend, as though I am an entomologist offering you a choice specimen. On the contrary – if the creature is a winged creature, it is a caged eagle, or trapped angel. He is not quite a human being – but he is institutionalised, wary, and battered. I should like to see what he is in freedom.

It will be v. good to see you. I too can do with an excursion outside these asylum walls. Institutions affect *all* their inmates, not only the 'certified'. You can make mistakes with tongue, and facial expression, and lapses of attention, just as much as with hypodermics and electric shocks. I need a rest. An injection of *life*. You have always provided that, usually in surprising forms.

Yours ever,
Kieran

Dear Avram,

I enclose three cassettes, for safe-keeping. Please put them away somewhere safe, so that you are not tempted to festoon the bushes with them, or wind them round your head when you are happily spaced-out. (I remember very clearly what happened to my unique record of the interview-candidate's conversation in Woolworth's.) If you have facilities in your Anti-University for getting things copied – without danger to the material – I should be doubly grateful, and will reimburse you.

You will notice, if you try to listen to the tapes, that they contain longish periods of silence. This is not because the tapes are defective. It is because they are covert recordings of Quaker 'Meetings', which alternate silences with extempore interventions. (The degree to which these interventions are genuinely extempore appears to vary. Some appear to be as well-prepared as the normal sermon. I shall have to work on the indications from which I formed this conclusion.)

I am not sure whether I am observing a therapeutic group, or a religious community. Various elements from various recognised organisations are present here, in official and unofficial capacities. There are the Quakers, several of whom double their functions as medical, or social workers. There are at least three Church of England clergymen, one of whom is definitely the 'leader' of a group, which in this instance is a group-within-a-group, that is, *both* an 'inner group' of the Church of England, called the Children of Joy, and also a 'group-within' the Spirit's Tigers, though there is some conflict as to which – Tigers or Children – will, so to speak, 'swallow' the other, and indeed, whether it is 'better,' in this instance, to be a 'swallowed' 'inner' group, or a more loosely-formed, proactive 'outer' group. There must be sociological studies of splinter groups which I wish I could consult. But I am constrained by my role here as a 'member', though it is not quite clear, since the boundaries keep shifting, what I am a 'member' of.

You wrote a very interesting letter about the degree to which you were conflicted in writing ethnomethodologically about 'teaching' ethnomethodology in an anti-methodological environment such as an anti-university. I think you are fortunate in that, in the context in which you find yourself, *you are at least doing what you appear ostensibly to be doing.* You present yourself as an ethnomethodologist. You are part of the Anti-University. If you are observing and analysing it, this is only to be expected by all concerned. Whereas here, I am to some extent, to a great extent, playing apart, presenting myself as what I am not, at least by default. I present myself as a person desiring to participate in a group, indeed, to be a *member* of that group. I do *not* present myself as a sociologist studying the methodology by which the group defines itself, pursues its aims, achieves its coherence etc. etc. If I did so, I would change the dynamics of the group so that it was not what I was observing, or what I wished to observe. However, it could be argued that my very presence as a group member is not neutral. I am a visible woman, not an invisible 'bug' on the wall of the jury-room. As such, I am faced continually with little conflicts of interest. For instance, it is perfectly clear to me that the 'leader' of the Children of Joy, Gideon Farrar, rules, or leads, the majority of his flock or circle by a system (conscious, half-conscious or unconscious) of sexual manipulation – promises, threats and inducements. He makes people feel 'special' by giving them the thrill of his attention. In some cases I am sure this goes quite as far as intercourse, certainly with the women, and I believe I have observed him to be in the process of extending his charisma to the men. You will hear various remarks of his on the tapes about love 'without limits, without conventions, without exceptions'. When he says 'love' he always includes the idea of 'sex' as a sub-set, or maybe the other way round.

Here his vocabulary interestingly tangles with that of the psychoanalyst, Elvet Gander. Both are of course sexually interesting because they are professionally forbidden to offer sexual contact with patients or congregation. Both *use* this prohibition to induce desire. My question is, what effect do I have on the dynamics of the group(s) whose ethnomethodology I am observing, if I adhere to a strict scientific distance and objectivity when I am myself (as a female group member) the object of the charismatic seducers' attentions? This has, of course, happened, this is not a hypothetical question only. Gideon Farrar has stroked my buttocks repeatedly, and once accused me in a confessional session of being 'numb' and 'dumb'. Elvet Gander has stared 'mesmerically' into my eyes and told me I am 'an enigma'. This is tiresome, as I don't want to draw attention to myself. You see my dilemma, Avram, which is not without its methodological interest. I have always held as my ideal the exemplary behaviour of the two psychologists who got themselves admitted to hospital and *then behaved perfectly normally* declaring themselves to be sane, and even stating that they were psychologists – which is, of course, a frequent delusion amongst the insane. You know the case? They had all the difficulty in the world in getting out of the hospital, since no one believed them, and the structure of the institution did not permit the idea of a mis-diagnosis, or a fraud. But I cannot, perhaps, behave perfectly normally, as an undercover observer of a therapeutic group/religious community. I have to ask myself whether, if I was 'for real' I would have to either a) repel the advances of priest and doctor or b) give in to them, on the assumption that the dynamics of the group life would carry me along in that direction. If I was 'for real' and was *repelled by* them, it is likely that I would leave the group, and be no longer in a position to observe it.

If I *were* to succumb, for my own research purposes, I should be dramatically shifting and deflecting the group dynamic. Anyway, I don't know if I could bring myself to. I have to record – as part of the total situation – that I personally find Gideon Farrar's 'charm' and 'vitality' and 'spontaneity' somewhat manufactured – I must analyse how I came to that conclusion – and don't respond to it. I prefer Dr Gander – but he thinks of himself as a wild force, an individual, and I don't think it matters to him so much if one doesn't respond. I'm more afraid of him 'unmasking' me.

There is a man here – one of the other clergymen – who works with the Listeners (a telephone confessional) and seems to me to have the essence of the charismatic in him, if he wanted to use it. Only he turns it off. Quite deliberately. Like a tap. That isn't a scientific observation, it's simply a human observation. His name's Daniel Orton. Sometimes I think he's already unmasked me, and is simply watching to see what happens next. He's a watcher. He's a better watcher than I am. I don't know what he's watching *for*. He notices people's feelings, in the abstract, so to speak, if that isn't a contradiction in terms. He stops quarrels. Just because he knows how to do it, not because it adds glory to him. (Vide Farrar and Gander.) He appears to have no sexual atmosphere round him at all. He's fat, you might say ugly. I'd settle for him if we all had to have partners. I don't believe that absence of desire is 'sexy'. But perhaps absence of anxiety is. He's not an anxious man. I was going to say, he's sad, dreadfully sad, but I have no evidence for that. It may be a projection of my own.

Now, Avram, please treat my tapes responsibly. Please. I *have* to rely on you. Please let me know what you think about my interesting procedural problem.

Till we meet again! Brenda.

From Elvet Gander to Kieran Quarrell

It was good to see you, old friend. I felt briefly we formed a group-within-a-group, of anxious analytic minds, to whom it was both a credit, and yet a regret, that we cannot 'let go' and abandon ourselves to prayer, or loss of self (consciousness). I am reporting, as we agreed, on the comportment and presumed comfort, of your two additions to our company.

Neither of them has stirred very much. The analogy is peering into the reptile tank in the Zoo, watching coiled snakes for movement. I surprise myself – and may annoy you – with this image, but it sprang forcibly into my mind and it seems wrong to repress it. Everyone is of course *watching* them, waiting for them to make a move, and ostensibly looking the other way, in case he or she might be thought to be rude or intrusive. Lucy sits – always on a hardbacked chair, she eschews sinking into the pretty *fauteuils*, and always in a far corner. She presses her knees together, and she presses her lips together, and she clasps her hands together over her knees. One of the Quaker ladies brought her a little posy of flowers, and laid them in her lap, but this was not a great success. She gave them a nervous glance, but did not pick them up, and seemed to forget them. They fell to the ground when she stood up.

Josh Lamb, on the other hand, speaks when he is spoken to. Minimally, with a somewhat *vulpine* polite smile. Much of what he says, I have noticed, simply returns the observation made to him, slightly recast, as though he was playing a language-game.

'It's a fine day.'
'Certainly the weather is excellent.'

'We are working towards spiritual renewal.'
'There is indeed a sense of imminent change in the air.'

'The end of the world is nigh.'
'It appears that the world may come to an end fairly soon.'

I invented the last one. But he does look as though that is what he would say.

He did become more forthcoming – even vehement – oddly on the subject of television. There's been a lot of debate – polite, and heatedly *less* polite – in the group, about whether a television should be allowed in the farmhouse at all.

There are in fact, *two* at the moment, one in the Common Room, where we, in principle, relax together, and one in what is known as the 'study room' where special groups meet irregularly on special topics. I don't know if you got as far as that on your flying visit. Many of the Quakers feel that the box is an unnecessary distraction in the contemplative life. They use the words 'trivial', 'commercial' and even 'worldly' about it. This is not the view of Frank and Milly Fisher, the owners of Four Pence, who believe that religious people should be in the world, but not of the world, and that they will do better, more caring social work for being alerted to the 'mental pap' their 'clients' subsist on. Richmond Bly, the Blake man, goes into paroxysms of disgust at the *'crass'* level of discussion, and general vulgarity of the 'satirical' programmes. I have to declare an interest – which I did most forthrightly in their debates – since I am to appear on a new sort of programme called 'Through the Looking-Glass'. I am to discuss the concept of Creativity with Hodder Pinsky and the young woman who moderates these discussions. Her name is Frederica Potter, and she turns out to be the Freda or Francesca to whom John Ottokar, the twin brother of my Zag, is apparently attached. *My* programme is the third, and I am nervous and narcissistic enough to want to watch the earlier ones, which do take place at times when I am resident here at Four Pence. Zag too is pro the Box. He hopes to be able to sing and dance on it with his syzygy/ziggy Zy-goats, of course. It is possible that he envisages it as the medium for a global dionysiac orgy. Gideon Farrar is largely opposed. He says the Joyful Companions should be sufficient unto themselves, and find in each other's eyes and speech all they need to engage their hearts and minds. They must work out their own salvation, which means avoiding distractions and snares etc. etc. I think Gideon was, at least to start with, in favour of a ceremonial unplugging of both Boxes and ritual shattering of both screens. (Ray tubes? Do you understand the mechanics of the thing?)

Anyway, a heated democratic meeting was held to discuss the problem. Lucy came, and sat in her usual posture in her usual corner. Lamb came, with his look of grave concern. Some imp prompted me to ask his opinion, though I supposed he would not be an ally. I wanted to hear him speak.

He said, as near as I can recall – I wish I had a tape-recorder:

'This device does indeed make seen the unseen, and transport eidolons of bodies from one place to another. Its sendings pass through walls and join minds to minds. It is not a trivial thing, though trivial people choke it with trivial chatter, and meaningless material concerns. It is not trivial, but terrible. It will change the nature of our consciousness, that of the wise, as much as that of the ignorant and foolish. It will show our world to us. When our world ends we shall watch with it the towering advance of the last tidal wave, or the red roar of the final fire, until its eyes drown, or melt, with the rest of us. We cannot and should not ignore it. We may even, in time, be able to use it for good. It is a neutral, electrical thing. We should learn what it is and does, not shun it. This is what I think.'

Such a speech, written down, is on a knife-edge between the ludicrous and the impressive. I can assure you – after the logic-chopping, and little stabs at reasonable, or tolerant positions – he spoke like a knife to the heart. Everyone looked at him, and Gideon murmured thoughtfully that it was indeed a power that could be used for good or evil. I could see him seeing himself preaching on the box, extending his congregation through the English-speaking world. So the boxes are to stay, and Mr Lamb – who has returned to his normal courteous silence – is being looked at like an unexploded bomb that might go off. What will he say next? What is he preaching? (He sounds like a preacher.)

★

Josh Lamb, Joshua Ramsden watched the first *Through the Looking-Glass* in the attic lecture-room, with a group consisting of Elvet Gander, Canon Holly, Richmond Bly, Daniel Orton, Ellie and Paul-Zag. The Joyful Companions watched, as they did everything, companionably in the relaxation room. They included Brenda Pincher, and all the Quakers. It was dark and sparsely furnished in the lecture-room. The ceiling sloped, and a new moon was visible through the uncurtained skylight.

No two people step in the same river, and no two people watch the same television programme. Richmond Bly kept making comments about the cleverness of the graphics, and of those of his students who had helped to draw them. Canon Holly leaned back and smoked his yellow cigarettes. Ellie remarked that *Alice* had always frightened her as a little girl. Elvet Gander leaned forward, intently studious, noting the styles of conversation. Paul-Zag jigged and jerked to unseen, unheard music, occasionally stabbing a painted fingernail at the screen (each finger had a different circular mandala) and saying 'Ha!' with more and more excitement. 'That's *her*,' he said at one point to Gander. 'Her very self. Butter wouldn't melt. You'd think butter wouldn't melt. Well I can tell you it *creams* and *froths*.'

The mirror-images, the discussion of twins, Tweedle and Tweedle, over-excited him. He said again to Gander, stabbing him in the ribs with a sharp forefinger 'Hey, there's a lyric in that. Tweedle dark and Tweedle light, on the one hand sweet, on the other hand sour, two is one and one are two . . .'

Josh Lamb turned his dark eyes to him and put his own finger to his lips.

Paul–Zag fell silent.

Daniel felt concern for Frederica. Was she about to embarrass herself again? When he saw that his concern was misplaced, that she was bright and shining between the clever men and the mirrors, he allowed his thoughts to drift, leaned back, stared up into the dark. He did not say: that is my dead wife's sister. They did not need to know.

Josh Lamb's mind engaged slowly with the concrete world, and found it hard to take in fast-moving objects or rapid speech. In this case, the concrete world itself, the brown plastic box and grey screen were full of humming electric currents which perturbed, and darted between, the electric threadings in his brain. He found it hard to seize the exploding and vanishing creatures that infested the inner glass box. He saw worms and lizards and did not know if they were emanations from himself, or from in there. He saw, as he was used to seeing, drops and sheets of blood. The hand-mirror with the silver fruit that Frederica brandished was brimming with blood *before* Richard Gregory described Aristotle's connection between the vision of menstruating women and mirrors.

Later, others were to say they had seen these things.

Unsurprised, he heard Richard Gregory mention that the Manichees used mirrors. Of course, that would have been so, and would be so. Unsurprised, he heard Jonathan Miller describe Lewis Carroll's games of Syzygies, unaware in the mundane world of the message he was transmitting to its true hearer. He began to see wild flashes and his head began to buzz dangerously. With an effort, he kept still. The screen was emitting a great gold cloud of light, in whose brilliance the monstrous fleshy nature of the humans beside him was painful. Holly's stained teeth and spittle, Daniel's belly, Gander's lurid cranium, Ellie's cotton-wool foaminess, Richmond Bly's inanely drooping grin, above all perhaps the painted fish-eyes, the glittering claws, the oily blond hair of Paul-Zag, showed up in the luminescence as caricature and distortion, failure and sin.

When the transmission was over, he made an excuse to stay there, with the box. This was made easier because Elvet Gander was distracted by the over-excitement of Paul-Zag. When they were all gone, he sat down again, in the thick fug of Gander's pipe-smoke and Holly's more acrid cloud, and turned the thing on again. It was late. There was nothing but silver snow, fragments of the world of light spinning in chaos, coming in and out of being like arrowheads.

He went close. So close, his breath made the thing fizz, and he felt its power run into his finger-tips and hair follicles. His white hair stood up. His many-coloured beard fanned. He saw his ghost-face over the light-splinters, and then he saw the Other, speeding towards him. The Other burst the surface of the storm in the screen like a diver in reverse, plunging up from the deep.

He stood on the carpet in the attic. His naked white feet were beautiful. His face was Ramsden's face, but also made beautiful. He wore a garment of light that was all colours and no colour, white.

'It will begin, now,' he told Ramsden. 'Here, now, is where it will begin.'

'I am afraid.'

'Of course. It is a hard thing. Take it and hold it.'

He held out his arms, expecting the dark or the bright globus. What he was given was small. It was small, and spherical, and lay in his palm intensely cold and intensely heavy.

It looked as though it should have been warm. It looked like an eyeball of flesh, covered with a living, pulsing web of bloody threads of veining. Looked at, it throbbed. To the touch, it was freezing and still.

He was told that when the eye of the flesh was clean, the eye of the spirit would see clearly.

When the flesh of the people was clean, they would appear

light, and symmetrical, and ugliness would flake away from them like scales.

'You will tell them the messages. You will clean them. You will separate the light from the dark.'

He had a vision of what he was to lose, or had lost. It went back to the last 'normal' day of the eleven-year-old with the pitiful fat thighs, eating normal food, laughing normal laughter.

He was told that those things were not real things, were seen wrongly, were lumps, and disgusting.

He was shown his own face, crowned with a huge crown of woven bones, or thorns, of light. He stared up at the fingernail of moon, and the slivers of light danced out of the transmission, *through him*, into it so that sky and thick atmosphere were all glittering with it, like a shoal of fishes.

'You *will tell them*,' said the syzygos, as it mixed its substance into the light, and he fell, frothing and jerking like a puppet.

Daniel came back, and found him there, and fetched help, and got him to his room, and into his bed.

Daniel didn't know why he went back. It simply occurred to him to do so. He knew about clearing air-passages, holding down tongues.

Later, he thought he might have saved his life, but was not given to interpreting things in terms of special providences.

From Brenda Pincher to Avram Snitkin

I do wish you would acknowledge receipt of my tapes. There is so much irretrievable good material in them. I would keep them here, but it would be extremely embarrassing if they were discovered, and it would, of course, put a stop to this project. I imagine you for some reason lying on your back in your caravan seeing indescribable visions on the ceiling. Please use a bit of imagination and send me some reassuring message. Please, Avram, bestir yourself. I have to confess I should also like to hear a sociological voice. I feel a bit lonely and beleaguered here. Keeping up appearances, so to speak, is very tiring and can even become disorientating.

The material is so *rich*, that is part of the problem. I can't resist the temptation to give you an unscientific picture of what is going on – including a few hypotheses, untested until I've meticulously analysed the data on the tapes I hope you are keeping safe for me. Part of the richness is the different uses everyone makes of what I think of as a disintegrating, *in*coherent set of religious terms and references. Most of this of course is to do with Gideon Farrar. Canon Holly is what is called a Death of God theologian. I do not understand his language well enough to know *what* it means. If anything, I sometimes tartly think to myself. There are no images in my mind to correspond to the Creation of Nothing, or the Genesis of Absence. I'm too pragmatic. I suppose.

Farrar, however, I do have a grip on. Yesterday's Meeting for Worship, of which I enclose the tapes, is typical Farrar. Whereas the Quakers (whom I like) know how to confine their spiritual and ethical Messages to manageable lengths, which respect others, Farrar has not really learned not to deliver sermons. I shall need to do some serious scientific analysis of my data, but I do think I am getting an intuitive grasp of what he is *up to*, and intuitive perceptions have to be a part of ethnomethodological fieldwork.

The strange shufflings and snufflings you will hear at the beginning of the tape are the touching-feeling greetings which have been instituted as the *required* opening to each meeting. That is, you don't have the option of not touching everybody. Farrar's clothes, which I can't record, become more and more resplendent, and less and less C. of E., as time goes by. At the Meeting on this recording he wore a kind of white woollen robe/shirt, open at the neck, and somehow *billowing*. It was embroidered with Aztec or Peruvian motifs in very brilliant colours – a lot of puce, a lot of turquoise, bitty bits of black and yellow. Under that he wore ordinary blue jeans. He wears them (I should think) slightly too tight for comfort. Indeed, Avram – and this is significant – the zip of his fly is under strain, and various stitches are bursting. He has amplish buttocks. He wears quite a few chains round his neck now – well, bronze chains, and leather thongs – from which dangle various symbols, of which the cross – that kind with a twist at the top – is only one. Suns, and moons, and male and female ($♀♂$) and what I think are astrological signs too, round his wrists. Fishes and twins and arrows and pitchers and so on. (OK. I'll make a precise *list*. But I don't like getting near him, and they're all tangled up in his hair and beard and so on.)

The touching and feeling was complicated (almost amusingly) by our new members. Neither of them are at all at ease with it. The man, Josh Lamb, had an epileptic fit a week or two ago. He deals with Farrar's 'greeting' by laying his fingers against the side of your (well, anyone's, my, Farrar's) cheek. The woman, Lucy Nighby, is mute. I'll come back to her. Bits of her story filter through in gossip. There's a history of domestic violence, and she's apparently been mute since her children and husband were seriously injured. They are trying to make her speak in order to resolve the case. She looks dreadfully meek, as though she couldn't hurt a fly. She *really can't bear* to be touched. On the whole, the group respects that. It keeps its distance. She shudders if anyone gets in three feet of her. Gideon Farrar strokes her hair, like a horse-wrangler taming a mare. She doesn't stroke back.

I think Farrar sees Lamb as a rival. This isn't a scientific observation, but it *is* an observation. He watches the effects of his words on him, and he's got more flamboyant since Lamb came.

On the tapes – after one of the Quakers talking about Blake and tigers and lambs, and another talking of desirable quietness, you get a long, typical Gideon Farrar exhortation. I've decided one of his favourite words is *fellowship*. Another is *welcome*. Another is *boundless*. He's always talking about breaking down boundaries.

I've had the thought that a lot of these modern religious movements, zealously breaking down boundaries between the religious institution, and the 'normal' everyday world, are throwing out the baby with the bathwater. Religion thrives on mystery and distance and ceremony. Farrar was once the robed untouchable beyond the altar rails – which he's now symbolically torn down, with the rood-screen, and burned. He used to hold a symbolic wafer up before a sacred altar. Now, because he's demystified and demythologised the rails and the table and the bread and wine and himself he has to work a lot harder for his effects and his flock's enthusiasm. He talks a lot – you'll hear it on the tape (*please* make a copy, *please* acknowledge receipt, I do feel jittery) about the old monasteries, and how they kept open house, and fed all comers abundantly, and provided a constant *open door* between the spiritual world and the everyday. His love-feasts consist of great crusty sandwiches made from bread he slices with a flourish, and boiled ham he carves with a flourish. (Query. Did he choose ham because he's deliberately breaking the Jewish tabu on unclean pig-meat?) He is a kind of Mine Host. He does tend to *identify* with his own God, such as that is. He likes to quote 'Come unto me all ye who are heavy laden and I will give you rest,' and it's not at all clear who the 'me' is, Jesus Christ or Gideon Farrar. He also talks a lot about *openness*. 'Lay yourself open' he says, and I see his fly straining. (OK, that's *naughty*.) And 'The truth will make you free.' His idea of 'the truth' is that everybody should make a full public confession of their sins – well, he pussyfoots round the word 'sin' as you'll hear, and uses locutions like 'grievous faults', 'errors', 'mistakes' and even 'misfortunes'. Fellowship will heal. 'I will make your burden light,' 'I will cast out fear and shadow and you shall live in the clear.' (That *is* a direct quotation.)

Anyway, today he overstepped someone's boundary. His sermon went well, one or two people were sniffling and one or two more were smiling beatifically. So he decided – I think – to try for a miracle. He talked in a roundabout way about 'one of our dear fellows' who perhaps had very grievous matters heavy in her heart, whose strings she could not loosen. No matter what you have done, no matter what has been done to you, he said, sharing it will start up the healing process, confession will set you free. Jesus cast out devils, he said, and I say, you can be free of your torment, with the help of our fellowship. And he went up to Lucy Nighby, and laid both his great hands heavily on her shoulders.

It was not a success. To put it mildly. She jerked about as though a devil had got *into* her, rather than coming *out of* her. If anyone there didn't believe she was mute, I think they'd have had to concede defeat, for I don't think she could have put on that horrible face and choking noise of *silent screaming*. He went on holding her for some minutes, and her writhing got worse. I think he thought she really *was* wrestling with whatever possessed her. My own view was that he was torturing her. When he let go, I think he thought she would collapse. He began to say 'The process is working, the painful birthing of . . .' (This again is an exact quote. Check tape. I *daren't* play it back, in case anyone overhears.) But she didn't collapse. She stood up, and shook herself, like a dog shaking off mud or water, and simply turned her back and walked out. He said something (the twister) about 'hiding tears', but there weren't any. She was just *very cross*.

Elvet Gander went after her, and came back in a minute, and sat down without saying anything.

We watched a TV programme in the evening. It was 'hosted' (is that the word?) by that girl Frederica Potter who was a witness in the *Babbletower* trial you so brilliantly taped. We saw the first – they're called *Through the Looking-Glass* – the night Josh Lamb had his epileptic fit. This one was called 'Free Women.' It was a clever idea; she was trying to get a group of women to talk about being women the way they do when no one is likely to overhear them. This very public chatter will make an interesting contrast with my *Hen Party* tapes, when I publish them. (She's on one of those too, in the VC's ladies' loo.) Staged hen parties and covertly recorded hen parties. They talked about female blood, wch I'd have thought was tabu on the TV. They used a Tupperware bowl as a kind of ceremonial kitchen object. Anything looks different if you set it up as *an object to be discussed*. It gives it back a bit of that sacred mystique that Gideon Farrar's trying to eliminate. I can't do much about my Hen Parties here. There aren't enough hens, and they don't talk much amongst themselves. Quite apart from mute Lucy, that is. They could tell a tale or two about glamorous Gideon, I suspect, but I don't think they do. Or if they do, they don't do it when I'm in range. I may not be assimilated enough. But I *won't* let him fuck me for the cause of ethnomethodology, Avram, there are limits. His paws are hot. He reeks of over-confidence and anxiety in equal proportions. I'll stop, before I get even less objective and even more indiscreet. *Please acknowledge my tapes.*

From Elvet Gander to Kieran Quarrell

Well, my TV appearance in Full Technicolour went off well, I think. Certainly the Four Pence residents were impressed. Even your Josh Lamb, who is over his epileptic fit, and back amongst us. There have been changes – violent changes even – in the dynamics of this Group, which I need to report to you, both professionally and personally. As you might imagine, they involve your two protégés.

Yesterday, in the full Meeting for Worship, he made his move – there is no other way of putting it. Gideon Farrar the Good Shepherd spoke at length last week about sweetness and light, openness and contact. Our man rose up today to answer – and to confute – him, without mentioning him. It is hard to record the substance of his speech. The manner was gentle, quietly certain, as though he was speaking intimately and directly to each member of the group. What he was saying was something you'd already touched on in your letters about his interventions in your groups. He was saying that we underestimate the forces of evil and darkness. He praised the Quakers for their intuition that we all carry an Inner Light within us, but called them to task for their sweet reasonableness in not acknowledging the horrors, the terror, of the outer darkness. We tell ourselves stories, he said, about a good and omnipotent creator, who shares our suffering and will heal all our wounds. That is a *human story* told as a bulwark against the real fear we should feel of the terror of the dark. He said the Quaker Inner Light was like putting on a table-lamp and closing the curtains in a nuclear winter. He said the Creator didn't make the earth as a pretty walled garden for humans to inhabit. It was forged out of chaotic matter, and the light it imprisoned was dimmed and in pain. He repeated once or twice, we tell ourselves the wrong story. He said, a better story was the Book of Job, where the biblical God joined with Satan to torment Job. There was an intuition, he said, of the battle, the even battle, the poised battle, between dark matter and the threatened light. We are not little lambs who skip and play among the daisies. We are bloody scapegoats and poleaxed cattle, fed to the holocaust desired by the Lord of this World. (I paraphrase badly. The man is a theologian. I am not.

Anyway, he said all this, in this still small voice, almost sweetly, and suddenly sat down.

And Gideon Farrar stood up and said this was a Manichaean vision, and we were Christians, and knew better than that. He sounded petulant, not the utterer of a clarion call. I saw immediately that Lamb had *tempted him into* saying just that. He rose again, and said that the Prophet Mani had intuited the truth – had indeed, had the truth revealed to him by his syzygos, his heavenly twin in the world of Light. And had been flayed alive for his pains, and mocked by being exposed, stuffed with straw, on the city wall of Bēt-Lāphāt. He had known that the truth could *go down*, that suffering might not automatically redeem, that evil might win. His Way had survived, his secret Way, it had been carried along the Silk Road and had flourished amongst the Buddhists in China. It was a way of difficulty, a way of ascesis. The good is *unnatural*. The natural world – according to Mani's story – was made by evil dark beings who absorbed and ingested and distorted the Light. He had devised ways to free it. Lamb was ready to concede that Mani's story was a myth. Jesus Christ's life was a myth which had become a truth, both in history, and in the lives of his followers. Mani's myth was also a truth, but a truth which had suffered defeat and humiliation. In these days when even the atoms of matter were split to provide hideous destructive energy, and clouds of invisible sickness which ate into flesh and bone, mountain and tree, Mani's message and Mani's method might be worth contemplating again. For extreme remedies are needed.

I wonder very much if this – without the music of his voice, without the charm of his grave face, without the lurking threat in his idea of things, his *real fear* – sounds to *you* like a rigmarole, or a – a – vision of the Truth? *A* Truth? The Quakers – et al. – were all stirred up, like water with a wind on it, like a cornfield in a tempest. I forgot to say, he mentioned his own story, in riddles. I know, he said, I have survived the smothering, I have survived the knife, I have been evacuated into darkness and seen the light shining in it. I shall tell you, he said, at the right time, what these things mean. Stories are useful at times, including our own stories, and pernicious at others, when we should see clear light, uncluttered by the *personal*. You can free yourselves of your personal lives, he said. And live in the light. But it is hard.

I kept thinking of what Kent says to old, mad Lear, that he has that in his countenance he would fain call master. And Lear asks 'what' and Kent answers 'authority'. That's what Lamb has – and Gideon doesn't. I ought to be able to give a good psychoanalytic explanation of this *authority* – which I feel the attraction of. I ought to be able to say, he represents the Good Father, the figure from our childhood, the Good Mother, even. But he doesn't, you know. He has about him a real *noli me tangere* quality. He is, God help us, a man come back from the dead, and untouchable because he's *other*. When he touches you – touches me – during Gideon's little bodily-encountering charades, his long palm is cold on your cheek, like ice. It burns a bit, like ice. It feels transparent, like ice. It isn't clammy. It's dry and cold. Weightless. You want to feel it again, because there is absolute calm in it, in the midst of the tempest.

I've let myself run on, because you have to know what kind of boiling he's churned up in the cauldron. (Dry ice.) Last week Gideon botched an attempt to open up Lucy. When Lamb had finished, he didn't sit down, but stood looking round, like a triumphant athlete at the end of a hard race. He looked straight at her. And she stood up, very composedly and walked across to him. She knelt down in front of him, and held up her two hands to him – open hands – and spoke. She said only three words' 'All my life,' and then repeated them. 'All my life. All my life.' It wasn't clear whether she was telling him she'd been waiting for him all her life, or was offering him all her life. Her voice began faint and frightened, and then strengthened.

The next thing was the clincher. Clemency Farrar, Gideon's endlessly patient helpmate, stood up with a jerk, and went to join Lucy. She's a handsome woman, the worse for wear, and wears a lot of black – long black drapy skirt, a long black jumper with dangly things round the neck – turquoise and silver – a kind of knotted scarf (black) round and round her head. She walked like a sleepwalker, with her hands out, and trembling. I really don't think it was a performance, but I'm not 100% sure. Anyway, she arrived next to Lucy, and knelt beside her, and copied her gesture and her words. 'All my life. All my life,' she said, and a strangled utterance became a ritual declaration. Upon which my little Ellie – trailing a few white bandages from her wrists, her little stick-legs in white cotton socks – jumped up too, and went to make a third. 'All my life,' she said. 'All my life.'

And there he was the untouchable, with his three women. And then there were others. Not me, I should say. But enough. All saying, 'All my life' as though they knew what it meant.

He said, 'Today I take my true name, which is not Lamb, but Ramsden. I am Joshua Ramsden.' One or two of them repeated this name.

Very gracefully, not touching them, he made an ambiguous circling movement of his hands over their bent heads, blessing and dismissing them. A wonderfully tactful combination of modesty and power.

The *practical end* of all this is that Lucy has asked Lamb to ask me to tell you she's ready to come back and speak up in court, to answer Gunner's accusations, and to bear witness. Lamb says she needs to do this, because she knows now that she must make a completely new beginning, and clear the past, in order to enter the future. She follows him everywhere with her eyes, if not her body. Another *Noli me tangere*. But in this case, I think of Sir Thos Wyatt on Anne Boleyn. *Noli me tangere*, for Caesar's I am – And wyld for to hold, though I seem tame. They are a wild pair.

I've been thinking again, after – partially at least – *going through* this communal experience of – of what? Charisma? Otherworldly vision? Spiritual power and energy, let's say. I've been thinking about Jung and Freud. What is borne in upon you, when you see this kind of spiritual turmoil, is that Jung ventured into those worlds, without fear of the ridicule that often goes with the aesthetically repulsive vocabularies that usually go with spiritual journeys – auras and visions, journeys to the underworld and so on. Jung fought it out, with the demons and the creatures of the night, and said we should all go down to the Underworld, to the Mothers, the Dead, in order to hear them speak, before we could constitute ourselves, whole, healthy and sane. He claimed he might be destroyed by the collective dark and its images (stories) archetypes – a word I've always loathed, but it *fits* the things Lamb is trying to make us see, it fits the secret dark places he's been in. There *are* odd coincidences. He says he saw mirrors of blood on *Through the Looking-Glass*, and claims that the mention of twins and syzygies in the discussion of L. Carroll was a Sign. It was certainly *odd*. The world is odd. Our dear tough old Sigmund kept his head, and his biology, intact in the fusty drawing-rooms of bourgeois Vienna. But he did try to diminish – to rationalise in a painfully inadequate way – the sheer difference and strangeness of spiritual experience.

Zag and I have been experimenting with the psychedelic effects of lysergic acid. I have seen some beautiful Creatures, some visionary spaces – and some horrors, and monsters – which are not thought of in Sigmund's philosophy. Angels and ministers of grace, dead flesh and humping foul things. I can't agree with Timothy Leary that this is a short-cut to seeing infinity in every grain of sand, for everyone. I agree, I think, with Josh Lamb that an *ascesis* is needed, a discipline, inside which to conduct our journey into these worlds.

OK, Kieran, I wept too, when he spoke of the smothering, the knife, the evacuation. But I *knew*. They didn't. Yet. He is revealing himself to them, piece by piece.

From Brenda Pincher to Avram Snitkin

Have you received any of my tapes? I have a dreadful feeling this latest one – *much the most important yet* – is a defective recording. There seems to be a lot of interference, a lot of crackling. It's a recording of an *electrical* speech by J. Lamb but I refuse to believe that he cd have the same effect on my machine as he definitely had on the gathered assembly. Strong stuff about flayed men and demons. Listen, Avram, you must get this copied on to a decent tape. You must get in touch – tell me how much is there. I can't write it all down, it just looks weird. *Please get in touch.* My sanity is beginning to depend on it.

From Kieran Quarrell to Elvet Gander

Well, the Lucy question is in some sense resolved. She appeared in Court this morning. They wanted to get the matter sorted out before the Christmas recess – surprisingly kindly of them, considering the Law's delays in this part of the world. Ramsden (shall we call him Ramsden?) was allowed to go along with her for moral support, and because it's by no means clear she won't just clam up again if he's not there. The magistrate had talked to two of the three children, who persist in their varying evidence. They are called Carla and Ellis, aged nine and six. Carla says Lucy took the rake and went for Gunner 'because he was going on about dirt in the house'. Ellis says Gunner hit Lucy, and Lucy bit Gunner, and Gunner took up the rake and Lucy 'got it away from him and poked him and he ran away'. Nobody mentioned what effect, if any, the children's communications with each other might have had on their evidence in all these months. They weren't in court. It was feared that the little one, Annie, could lose an eye. I told you that. *Someone* laid about themselves with insane fury. On the evidence they had, especially from Gunner, they had to charge Lucy.

Gunner was the first witness and spoke up for himself. He's a burly slow cross-looking creature, walking now slightly hooked to one side to show he's wounded (his muscles probably *have* knit awkwardly or painfully, but he looks incompetently histrionic). He said he knew he hadn't been a perfect husband but he hadn't done all this stuff. He didn't bash children. Lucy had just gone berserk, that was what it was, she'd just begun to scream, and started laying about her with the rake. She'd hit his face with it. (He does bear those scars, too.) When asked why, if the children were in danger, he'd run away to the hen-house, he said he kept his motor bike out there and meant to go and get the police. He said the kids were fine when he left. He said he didn't think she'd hurt the kids, she never had before. When asked how all this had started, he said it was because he'd pointed out that the kitchen was filthy, which was no more than the truth, Lucy was a slut, and he'd told her so. But he'd just *told* her, not hit her. 'You didn't find no marks on her,' he said. Which was unfortunately true.

The people who found them gave evidence. Two scientists – snail students, a man and a woman, and a mathematician, who had found Lucy, and raised the alarm. They said Gunner *did* know that the children were hurt. He had been 'grumbling about how they were hurt', the woman, Jacqueline Winwar, said. When pressed, she said he had not been wholly coherent, as he had lost a lot of blood. But he had certainly said the children were hurt. She was asked about the tone of voice in which he'd given this information. Had he suggested who had hurt them? I am fascinated by the *unnatural* ability of lawyers to ask questions about violent emotions and indeed violent events in an artificially 'objective' and 'neutral' manner. Miss Winwar, a model witness, precise and unemotional, said he certainly hadn't made any suggestion that he had hurt them himself. His predominant tone was one of *indignation*, she said. About everything. No, she said, he hadn't actually said Lucy had hurt the children. He was more interested in himself. That was perhaps natural, given the circumstances. He was very clear that Lucy had 'murdered' him. He was indignant about that, too, she said. Being murdered by a small woman was an indignity. He was indignant because it was his own trowel. She created, very economically, a sense that Gunner was completely unreasonable. But she didn't say he had said he had hurt the children.

When it came to Lucy's turn, everyone was very gentle. She spoke from the dock and a social worker sat near her. I sat across the courtroom with Ramsden. She looked steadily at him, all the time she was talking. Her voice was small and husky, as though she didn't know for certain it would be there.

She said Gunner had attacked her with the rake. She said he often attacked her, especially when he had been drinking. No, he had not been drinking on that occasion. Yes, she had followed him to the hen-house and stabbed him with the trowel. She had done that in the middle of a further violent argument, yes, to defend herself. He had been going to hit her with something heavy. Possibly a spanner, yes. She hadn't been seeing straight. She was crying. Yes, she was afraid. Yes, she was afraid for her life.

Why had she left the children? She looked at Ramsden for help with this question. She said, she didn't know, she remembered nothing clearly.

Who had hurt the children? She looked at Ramsden again, and answered, Gunner had hurt them. She added 'He hurts people easily without thinking.'

She had not hurt the children herself?

No, she said.

Had she ever hurt them?

She began to shake her head from side to side. 'Why do you ask that? Why? I wouldn't. I don't. They are my children.'

'They are Gunner's children.'

'He doesn't *think*, when he's in that mood.'

So why had she followed Gunner to the hen-house and left the children, who were in need of help?

She stared quite desperately at Ramsden.

'I don't know why. It was all over, I knew it was all over. People don't always do the best thing, the sensible thing.'

'What do you mean, it was all over?'

'Well, it was. It was all finished. Everything was.'

Her little round face was a mask of misery. Pity rose in everyone, including me. She was convicted of actual bodily harm, and placed under a probation order, on condition she attend a psychiatric hospital. You can see that the police, and the Social Services, and the court, had a presumption in favour of Lucy. The police, too, have had several run-ins with Gunner, pub-fights, dangerous motor-biking. Gunner said he was shaking the soil of the place from off his feet and stomped away. The house and land were Lucy's not his, and it was always assumed he married her for them. Now it turns out they were not in fact married because he had a wife in Iceland all the time. He was a seaman, not a farmer, before they 'married'.

All the same, Elvet, for the first time I wondered. *Who* hurt the children? What exactly happened? We ask our careful, neutral, probing questions and come up with muddle and mystery. I don't know if anybody any more knows what happened, that day, or will, now.

But I need most urgently to see you yourself, to talk to you. For Lucy proposes to give Dun Vale Hall to the Spirit's Tigers, to found a religious (therapeutic) community. That is, really, she proposes to give it to Joshua Ramsden. And whilst, on balance, if the good Quakers come, I think this will do good, not harm – it could indeed do *much good* to many people – the potential for harm is also there, and not inconsiderable. I need to see you, to discuss Ramsden's state of mind – 'state of health' seems presumptuous – to discuss Lucy – to discuss the legalities of letting them both go, and the definition of the new group.

Ramsden is walking tall. He says 'This is our chance to make a good thing in this world.' We do have to take risks, sometimes. Don't we?

XIV

At the end of the autumn term, the Non-Maths Group was reduced to a rump, which met in the Argus Eye, in Blesford, and consisted essentially of four people, Vincent Hodgkiss, Luk Lysgaard-Peacock, Marcus Potter and John Ottokar. Marcus had been made convenor by Professor Calder-Fluss, and John Ottokar represented the university's computer.

The Vice-Chancellor was absent, Hodgkiss explained, because of administrative problems. The Anti-University grew, he said, like the Hosts of Midian. Plastic tents sprouted like mushrooms. Caravans and camping-cars came and went. The students of the UNY streamed steadily into the Anti-University's courses. Jonty Surtees's semi-situationists now had regular meetings with Nick Tewfell, the Students' Union president. There were now formal protests against the unique four-year course, with its required maths and languages. 'They want "theory and praxis of living situations",' said Hodgkiss in his high-pitched Oxford-drawl, leaning back in the wooden settle.

Luk asked what was taught at the Anti-University. Hodgkiss said there had been a 13-hour-long discussion, led by, that was, initiated by, Avram Snitkin, on whether anything at all should, or could, be discussed in artificially constructed forums of the kind they might at that moment find themselves in. There had also been an enthusiastically attended teach-in against exams, and a course on 'de-sanctification of oppressive structures'. And a 36-hour-long television-watching orgy, 'against passive consumerism' at the end of which the television had been hammered to bits and burned to ashes.

There were also Lady Wijnnobel's courses, which drew crowds, from inside and outside UNY. She gave lectures – orations – on Mystic Identity, Visionary Astrology, the Secret Wisdom of the Ancient World. She also gave 'interactive sessions' on things like chiromancy, oneiromancy, geomancy, and horo-scope-casting.

Luk said Gerard Wijnnobel was either a fool or a saint.

Hodgkiss said he was certainly not a fool. It was possible that he was a saint. He was a born liberal who took the line that self-expression was a right, and that in the end the students would be amenable to a judicious mixture of eloquence and reason.

'Reason is oppression,' said Marcus. 'I quote a sticker on the wall of the Maths Tower.'

Hodgkiss said that, as Dean of Students, he was himself, so to speak, the secular arm, and should perhaps do something. Something authoritarian, or something machiavellian. 'Both not in my nature. I prefer to sit here reading Wittgenstein and drinking beer. I do not think scholars are good at authority. As for Wijnnobel's wife, she is not his chattel. She has signed no vow of silence.'

Luk said he thought the Vice-Chancellor carried altruism to absurd lengths. Hodgkiss murmured that the iron seemed to have entered Luk's soul, to which Luk did not respond. No one had remarked on Jacqueline's absence. John Ottokar was still strug-gling with the complicated programmes needed to analyse her action potential spikes, but he said nothing to or about her as far as the Non-Maths Group went. He was also helping Luk with the equally difficult maths of his paper about sex and altruism. Luk had been very interested in John Maynard Smith's searching questions about the greater cost for a species (in energy used up) by sexual reproduction than by parthenogenesis. Why do creatures not simply bud, or clone. He had established that the northern black slug, *Arion alter*, was self-fertilising, and its populations were a dispersed clone. The southern slug, *Arion rufus* the red slug, was, in the usual hermaphrodite way, a sexual being, aggressively manoeuvring for sexual advantage, and, moreover, cannibalistic. If you carried home a bucketful of the gentle clones, they would huddle together companionably. Whereas a bucketful of *rufus* would tear each other into a soup, with one or two self-selected, fit survivors. If you put them in huts in hot dry conditions, the black slugs would lovingly offer each other a shared damp slime, whereas the red ones would swelter and shrivel in justified mistrust.

Hodgkiss remarked that biologists did something disconcerting to the word altruism. Which was used to describe human social care for others, even love. A man giving his life for his friend. The exquisite courtesy of Gerard Wijnnobel (if that was what it was). Not simply the preservation of the germ-line.

'We all grew up,' said John Ottokar the Quaker, 'with the image of the mother-skylark, pretending to drag a wounded wing to draw away the hunter. We were told, this showed that love, and altruism, were part of the natural world –'

'According to the maths of all this,' said Luk, 'which you understand better than I do – this is simply a case of the odds on protecting more of her genes by self-sacrifice. According to this statistical view of love, of course, perfect love wouldn't be mother-love. It would be – it could only be – monozygotic twins. Clones, like my black slugs.'

'A monozygote,' said John Ottokar slowly, 'is its twin's mother and sibling. Parthenogenesis after sexual propagation.'

Luk was about to embark on a complicated exegesis of kin-theory when he realised that for John, the problem of monozygotes was personal. He said

'Bill Hamilton has been working on the mathematics of spite. Looking for examples in the non-human world of successful malice, or malevolence. Spite as opposed to selfishness. Ethics sit uneasily with biology. I don't think the red slugs are spiteful. I think it's like overcrowded hens in batteries tearing each other's flesh. They pick on the weakest.'

'Scapegoats,' said Hodgkiss.

'That's a religious idea,' said Luk. 'Religion is a construction to explain things. Not an examination of cause and effect.'

'Humans are spiteful,' said John Ottokar. 'Humans enjoy executions. Humans get together in gangs and torment the odd and the weak. They pull wings off flies and burn cats.'

'Humans invented self-sacrifice and simple *kindness*,' said Hodgkiss. 'Respect for other selves. The unit of ethics is the biped in its skin. Not the molecule in the helix.'

'They have always needed religion to keep them to that,' said John.

'No one can defend truth with lies,' said Luk. Hodgkiss's slightly prissy mouth pursed with a mixture of glee and pugnacity over this wild statement. How the discussion would have gone on was never known, for it was interrupted.

A woman and a child appeared in the door of the bar, hand in hand, with flaming hair. It was Frederica and Leo, up North for the Christmas holidays, come to look for Marcus, at Winifred's request. She strode towards the maths table, pleased to see them. They were not pleased to see her. She broke the circle.

Leo said enthusiastically, 'John O – John O –' and, since John looked somehow dangerous and frowning, said more doubtfully – 'it *is* John? It isn't – Paul, is it? I *know* it's John, it is, isn't it?'

'Does it matter?' said John, heavily.

'Mummy wondered –' said Frederica to Marcus. She looked round. 'How nice you're all here. Where's Jacqueline? I suppose the snails are in hibernation. It's very cold. I wanted to talk to you, Luk, I wanted to ask you, whether you'd be interested in being on an odd television programme . . .'

Luk stood up.

'No,' he said. 'I wouldn't. I've got to go.'

'Perhaps I could come and talk to you . . .'

'I shouldn't bother. I see no point in trying to say complex things in simple phrases in very short sentences with joky distractions. No point. I've got to go.'

He went. Frederica stared after him. The barman came over and pointed out that Leo was a little boy, and was not allowed to be in there. John Ottokar said 'Come on, Leo, I'll take you out.'

Frederica, crestfallen, gave her mother's message to Marcus. Vincent Hodgkiss, leaning back in his settle, looked at brother and sister and thought to himself that the theory of kin selection broke down a little, here. The woman resembled the angry biologist – also red-headed, also bristling with energy – more than the delicate, reticent mathematician, owl-eyes downcast. He did not know – then – that Marcus was also thinking how little tie there was between him and Frederica. When Stephanie had been alive, Marcus thought, they had all three been connected. He then remembered her death, as he tried not to do. He had not been required to sacrifice himself. Only to show enough presence of mind to throw an electric switch. Which he had failed to do. He stared gloomily at the beer-rings, and said he was coming soon, he'd call his mother, he had things . . .

'We're having dinner,' said Hodgkiss. 'We have things to discuss.'

Marcus looked up, and then down. Hodgkiss thought, he's not

interested in people, and it's never occurred to him – until this moment – that I'm interested in him.

Frederica stood, having destroyed a harmonious group completely involuntarily. Then she turned, and went out to her son, and her lover, about whom she had no idea what to do.

Blesford's only restaurant was a cramped pseudo-Trattoria. Hodgkiss drove Marcus out into the moor, to a hotel, the Rose of York. The dining-room was formal with a large wood fire. There were three other hushed couples in the carpeted quiet. There were candles in silver candlesticks on white damask tablecloths, and a very bright central chandelier. Hodgkiss asked if this could be dimmed. There were green curtains with a design of white roses and briars. Hodgkiss ordered a bottle of white burgundy, a bowl of spinach soup, and a grilled sole. Marcus ordered the same.

'Don't look troubled. This is coerced altruism. I need your help with a problem. And you looked hungry.'

'Did I?'

'You did.'

Marcus stirred his soup. Hodgkiss thought, he never looks *at* people. He's a monad. Shall I tell him so? Better not. He watched Marcus stir his soup the other way, take a cautious sip, wipe his mouth. I shall never tempt him with the delights of the flesh, thought Hodgkiss, offering a bread roll. He said

'I thought you might be able to make me understand Cantor's mathematics of infinite sets.'

Marcus put down his spoon and took a mouthful of wine.

'Wittgenstein gave a course of lectures in 1939 on the Foundations of Mathematics. He attacked Cantor's Diagonal Proof. With extraordinary vehemence.'

Marcus looked up.

'Why?'

'Can you describe it to me, so that I can understand it? So that I can have enough of an idea to think about it?'

'Oh yes,' said Marcus. He smiled. His smile was gentle and tentative and opened his mild face.

He explained. The Diagonal Proof is a way – which can be visualised as geometry – of relating finite sets to infinite sets. Two infinite sets are equal if they can be put into a one-to-one

216

correspondence with each other. They are said to have the same 'cardinality'. Like, for instance, the set of all even numbers, or the set of all 'natural' numbers. 1, 2, 3, 4 and so on. They can be represented with a set of branching diagonals. He fumbled in his jacket pocket, found an envelope, and drew a rough, forking grid. Hodgkiss produced a leather-bound notebook. They bent over it, heads together. Marcus's hair smelled young, and his skin smelled faintly of witch-hazel in baby-soap. His fine fingers multiplied lines, through the soup and the sole, moving surely across the paper. When his pencil broke, Hodgkiss gave him his own pen, and watched him adjust his grip, test the slant of the nib and the flow of the ink. It was a stubby, mottled pen, black and midnight-blue. It produced, in Marcus's grip, a string of spider-webs, of ghosts of branches, of shapes like the graduated spines on the fish skeletons.

'And then you can arrange all the rational fractions systematically and beautifully – like this . . .'

Hodgkiss watched the confident fingers weaving and felt – quite agreeably – like a heavy schoolboy watching a light agile boy swinging and dancing, far above his head in the gymnasium, on ropes he couldn't even begin to mount.

'I see. I almost see. I see while you're talking. Does this relate to Gödel's ideas about incompleteness?'

'Oh yes.'

Marcus drew more lines, and drank two glasses of wine. He explained the Continuum Hypothesis, and said that Cantor had gone mad, and it was believed to be the Hypothesis which had caused him to do so. A shadow came over his face. He put down Hodgkiss's pen.

'I can understand that,' he said.

'Going mad with maths?' Hodgkiss asked lightly. Marcus looked up from the bony remnants, boiled white eye and gaping flatfish-mouth on his plate, and met Hodgkiss's eye.

'Why did Wittgenstein hate the Diagonal Proof?'

'Here you come up against my incapacity to understand what it *is* – which means I don't understand his objections to it. He treated it almost as though it was demonic. He spoke of it as a kind of glamour, like witchcraft, cast over mathematicians, who were led to believe that because it was mathematically and logically coherent it was somehow true and incontrovertible. Hilbert the mathematician said "No one is going to turn us out of the paradise which Cantor has created." Wittgenstein used to tell his classes he wouldn't *dream* of trying to drive them out of this paradise. He would simply demonstrate that it was no paradise. It was a swamp, a quagmire full of philosophical will-of-the-wisps and mess – and delusional metaphysics. When they saw it clearly, he said, they would leave of their own accord. Wittgenstein said they would leave. I take it you would prefer to stay?'

'It is very beautiful,' Marcus said slowly.

'And real?'

'To me, yes. I, I *feel* it is infinitely more real than the everyday world.' He looked around. 'More real than this soup, the candle, the spoon, the flame. Though number is in all those.'

He glimpsed the dissolution of the liquids and solids and gases, the shining silver, the vegetable fibre, into spinning forms of molecules, made of movements of particles. He looked up, and met Hodgkiss's enquiring eyes.

'As I understand it,' said the philosopher, 'there are mathematicians who believe that finite numbers are real *things* you can discover – intuit – in the real world. But they don't all believe that completed infinite sets are real in the same way. Mental phantoms, perhaps. Fictions? You tell me.'

'It's hard. It's hard to describe.' Marcus was ill-at-ease with language. 'You can move real numbers around on paper, or by doing experiments in your head. I don't believe in the infinites in the same way. They may only be flashes in the brain – which we need to think about numbers at all.'

It was a long time since he had talked to anyone about the nature of things. He became very vaguely aware of Hodgkiss's physical presence. Hodgkiss watched him draw circles on the white damask with his fingers, and made an instinctive effort to appear even more mild and unthreatening.

Marcus said hesitantly that it was true that Cantor's proof – and infinite sets – were in a way like a religion. He approached the word with a fastidious distress. The finite numbers, he said, were the visible universe. They were *there* even if our human descriptions of them and their nature were wrong – certainly they were incomplete. The infinities were like angels. Forms of forms.

'Did Wittgenstein hate angels? Did he think they were all really demons? Oddly, I feel the infinities with the whole of my body, not only my mind – they don't feel cerebral. I feel as though I'm *in* them, I *am* them – as opposed to observing them. It's possible I can't so to speak get out of them because human beings made them up.'

He smiled at Hodgkiss, who thought his rare smile, both innocent and beautiful, transfigured him.

'Do you understand that at all?'

'By analogy. I have to substitute other things – things I do understand – for the infinities I don't. But I know about thinking with the whole body, and observing with the mind. The connection between the two, as well the difference.'

Marcus gave a little sigh.

'Angels were fanciful. The burning angel with a sword at the gate of Paradise. I'll tell you something I don't tell people. When I was a little boy, I used to be able to do mathematical problems by visualising a garden. Visualising isn't the right word. *Seeing* a garden. And the mathematical forms were in the garden, branching things, hills and stones, a fountain. Angelic trees and hills and stones. They were different colours, or no colours, transparent things. I used to *release the problem* into the garden and – if you can understand – see the answer.'

'I don't really understand,' said Hodgkiss, truthfully. He was trained to be truthful. 'I imagine a kind of lifesize pinball machine, which can't be what you mean. Is it like unheard music? The score of a symphony, perfect and unplayed?'

'Pinballs isn't bad. Those machines remind me of that. It didn't keep still. There were spiralling paths round the fountain and spiralling branches round the trees. The branching things were animal and mineral too, I think – things like the dendrites and the bronchi, things like branching forms in shattered crystals or snow.'

'Can you still – so to speak – visit it?'

Marcus shivered a very little and hunched his shoulders.

'I got ill, when I was a teenager. Bad things happened. It was scary. I lost it then.'

'Closed out of Paradise. A pity.'

'I did think I was going mad.'

He was no longer looking at the philosopher. Hodgkiss told him lightly and conversationally that Francis Galton had collected a large number of accounts written by people who visualised landscapes or colour-plans or staircases, in order to do maths. They were mostly surprised to find they were not alone. Galton himself worked that way.

'He could visualise a slide-rule, and read it,' Marcus contributed.

'And you are working on thinking machines, on the brain as a computer.'

'I'm trying to. I'm getting nowhere. It's all to do with concept-forming and decision-making. I like the idea of machines that recognise patterns – but artificial intelligence is all to do with throwing switches and discrete modules. Number-crunching. A primitive automat that mimics a limited number of operations in the brain. Whereas what I *want to do* –' he hesitated – 'what I *want to do* – is –'

He was not accustomed to thinking in terms of what he wanted, and was struck dumb by the novelty of saying what it was.

'What do you want to do?'

'I want – to look at how numbers – *do* – inhere in things. I want to understand why certain things grow in the Fibonacci spiral. Twigs round branches, branches round the stem of trees. Daisy flowers and sunflowers. Some snails and pine-cones. You'd need a combination of maths, and physics, and cell biology, and . . . I want to solve phyllotaxis.'

'Alan Turing's obsession,' said Hodgkiss. 'As I understand it, his imaginary thinking-machine is behind Calder-Fluss's work and your bit of that. Wittgenstein said the whole system of mathematical logic was just what he called a "language-game" with human rules. Turing said that if there was a contradiction in your calculus, the bridge you built using it would fall down.'

Marcus had a brief vision of an imaginary bridge, stemming piles, curved arches, suspended arcs, and its disintegration into flying particles.

'It isn't just a game,' he contributed.

'Turing went around with his pockets full of pine-cones to demonstrate the mystery of phyllotaxis. He hoped to be able to improve his machines – real and imaginary – to solve things like that. Things like the growth of embryos, and the spread of regular patterns on zebra-skins and in moths and feathers –'

'I didn't know that. We need real machines that work faster and better. But I think it can be done . . .'

'Then you should be working on that, shouldn't you? Life's short.'

'I don't know the physics. I don't know the cell biology. It's horribly hard. *Horribly* hard.'

There was a light in his eyes.

'You should talk to Wijnnobel. He worked on Fibonacci at one point. He believes in stepping over demarcation lines. He'd like to think of you doing physics and cell biology and algorithms . . .'

Hodgkiss ordered a chocolate soufflé described in the menu as 'wickedly dark'. Marcus, at ease again, even animated, remarked that the maths of the expansion of egg-foam was also interesting. Hodgkiss turned the hot liquid and the brittle crust on his tongue.

'You are interested in everything except other people.'

'I'm not much good at people.'

'Jacqueline likes you?'

'She makes all the effort. She's got a lot of energy. She's had a bad time.'

'She appeared to be settling for Lysgaard-Peacock?'

'Something went wrong. She's unhappy.'

'Nothing to do with you?'

Marcus twisted in his seat.

'No, no, not to do with me.'

Hodgkiss saw that if he were to continue this delicate almost-intimacy he would have to eschew the pleasures of gossip. He felt carried away, his own blood humming, into some other world of extremes, transparent trees, infinite ranks of angels on sharp shining pinheads, long colourless lashes over troubled, liquid, evasive eyes. He was fishing in a glassy sea with a fine hook. The sensation was as pleasurable as the bitterness of the chocolate, as the white-gold-sap-green colour of the swaying wine in Marcus's glass. Language and Love, he had told Marcus, were his way to infinite sets. Marcus responded to neither. At that moment that made his delight keener, though in the end he might be pursuing, not an angel, but a demonic wildfire in an infinite swamp.

XV

From Brenda Pincher to Avram Snitkin

Well, here we all are in Dun Vale Hall. We call ourselves a Therapeutic Community, but there's an obvious sense (to a sociologist at least) in which we are an embryonic religious cult. I feel I'm in on something very exciting, and at the same time, I have to confess I'm a little scared. This kind of group enthusiasm, not to say passion, is unknown territory. I will try to go on making recordings, and to keep a scientific record. I wish you could ever bring yourself to answer any of my letters. It's going to be much harder to send them from inside this rather remote place. I think we can't now be too far from where you are, if you are where I think you are, or were. For God's sake Avram, *answer this letter*. Though come to think of it, how can you, now I'm a full-time inmate? How will the post work; what will be our communications with the outside world? I am hoping to be able to get this letter posted when someone goes shopping. I shall try to worm my way into the shopping detachment, which there will have to be.

People are already talking about self-sufficiency in food, and tilling our land ourselves. This is complicated by two things. One is that winter is coming. We're about, indeed, to celebrate the Solstice, and tilling anything is an idealistic dream (which some of us are rather relieved about). The second is that the Manichees didn't till things. They believed in not torturing the earth or harming its creatures. Joshua Ramsden gives talks – sermons – on the 'gentle Manichees' on certain evenings. They were divided into the Elect and the Hearers. The Elect never tortured the earth, or any trees, or creatures, and ate only food provided by the Hearers. The Hearers accrued merit by feeding the Elect. Joshua rather charmingly said that he felt that all of us were Hearers, and none of us were, or should behave as if we were, Elect. He went on to say that the Manichees had believed that eating, like sex, continued the entrapment of Light in Matter, and that eating animals, who were more complicated organisms, 'degenerated' more light. He said that

223

the Manichees ate only vegetables. This appealed to the Quakers, many of whom are Vegans anyway. Again, he didn't prescribe what anyone *had* to do. He just made it clear what he meant to do.

Two of the activities that weld groups into communities (cults) are well under way. One is hard work. The other is ceremonies.

The hard work is simple. Or was, to start with. The house used to belong to Lucy Nighby whom I've mentioned. *Does* belong to her, legally, I suppose, though she speaks of it as a 'gift'. It had been shut up, since her fracas with her husband. What is happening now is a ferocious stripping and destruction of everything that was in the building 'before the Hearers'. Not exactly (yet) the kitchen range, which is built-in and antique, but all the bedroom furniture, chairs etc. We all carry things out to huge bonfires near the midden (I'm not really sure what a midden is, but a mucky bit of the farmyard). We have burned a lot of chairs and tables and bedding. Including the children's nursery furniture and cot. One or two of the Quakers made the reasonable point that it would be better to give these perfectly decent bits and chattels to the needy. But Lucy and Joshua (backed up by Gideon, Clemency and Canon Holly) said that these were corrupt household gods, contaminated with lust and rage, and their destruction was a precursor of a new world. We smashed a lot of perfectly good plates and cups and saucers. They are being replaced with white bog-standard earthenware and grey blankets. There is talk in the end of making our own pots and garments. I don't know how this squares with avoiding the destruction of Light in Matter. I don't know what the Manichees would have made of synthetic fibres – or what Joshua Ramsden will say they would have made. He treads a fine line between the actual (smashing things, vegetarianism) and explaining that things are symbolic (modern scientific theories of light in matter, the vegetable origins of coal, photosynthesis and so on).

There is a lot of talk, in the *actual* world of the Hearers, about sex. (Surprise, surprise.) A lot of our vigorous and exhausting physical activity is the stripping of the servants' attics of this place (a seventeenth-century manor with additions all over). There will be no wallpaper, no colour, white walls, mirrors, but placed too high for people to see themselves in. Mirrors to reflect the Light and the night sky. A nice touch. Ramsden is determined that the sexes shall sleep separately. He is feeling his way – he needs the support of the married couples here – but I think he wants a landing of female dorms and cells and a landing of male ditto. I don't think he wants there to be *any* children. But he is very tactful with those who have them. Lucy Nighby has three, but they have not yet taken up residence again. It will be interesting to see what eventuates. At the moment it has to be said, we are squatting. I have an old hospital bed in a kind of cubby-hole. I keep a torch to write to you by the light of. I wish I ever got an answer, it is lonely, being a fraud and hypocrite in the midst of so much real live enthusiasm and – and what – oh *uplift* with no sarcasm meant.

Yesterday there was a kind of ceremony – the Freeing of the Beasts of the Field. Many of the animals attached to this farm are moorland sheep, which hardly need freeing anyway.

There is a resident sheep called Tobias, who thinks he is a dog, Lucy says. He follows her everywhere. She wept over him when she came back, and said he was scrawny and she had supposed he would have been killed, or forgotten her. He sleeps by the range and smells like a damp rug.

We went and released all the hens from the battery sheds. There were two kinds of chicken-house. One with several layers of wire cages for egg-laying birds. They sit three in a cage on sloping wire floors – the eggs roll out to be collected. They have pulled all the feathers off each other's necks and breasts, and look disgusting. The other is a big shed where a great flock of young broilers is kept in a kind of dark red twilight. They get music played to them to calm them down but they have pulled each other's feathers off, too. They are fed from holes in the outside wall, and they stand on a kind of grid with their droppings underneath. Apparently they get cleaned out once a year when they're all slaughtered. Lucy got rather twittery when we opened them up, and said she didn't believe in de-beaking chickens, but Gunner did. These do have beaks, so I imagine they may be able to scratch about in the frosty mud.

The ceremony veered between the ridiculous and the tear-jerking. We walked along the rows of wire cages and opened the gates and lifted the hens out. Clemency Farrar started a kind of ritual pronouncement amongst all the cackling and scolding and screeching. 'Go free, bless you.' So we all said that to all the hens, who shat and staggered and backed away from us, but were all firmly carried out to the yard and put on the ground. This took so long that we decided to do the releasing in stages, day by day. The farmworker has left. He didn't like our 'goings-on' so we feed the hens ourselves, those in, and those out. Those out flocked together and then did begin to do hen-like things, clucking and peering about and scratching. Quite a lot went straight back into the hen-house, but it was agreed that they should be allowed to do this – with an open door – as it was all the world they knew. The next day we threw open the big door to the broiler-house and turned out the red light. We scattered a lot of food — corn and such stuff — outside. The poor creatures backed away from the light, cowering.

Clemency Farrar, again, took a sensible step, walking carefully through the flock and saying firmly from the *back* of the broiler-house, 'Go free, bless you.' And she made shooing motions with her arms, and an apron she was wearing. And they moved forwards in a sort of undifferentiated mass, moaning and clucking and splattering, and Clemency became covered in white flying feathers (these are all leghorns) like a totem or snowman. But some did venture over the threshold, blinking, and then more did, and the first ones couldn't dash back because of the mass behind them, so they milled round and round. I have to say, there are hens everywhere now. They do prefer freedom, observably. They are learning to scratch. Their poor feet are swollen. I'm not a hen sociologist or psychologist but it's a pity we don't have one here, as it would be interesting to know which instinctual behaviours these denatured creatures can retrieve and which they can't. Hens are a very alien life form, I find. Not sympathetic. Human beings in general don't like hens. Their eyes don't have expressions I can relate to. Their noises make me anxious. They are *designed to make you anxious*, I think. There's a lot of them now, everywhere. They are slowly spreading.

Like most farms (so I am told) this one had its 'own' hen-house for 'real' eggs for family consumption. Those crème de la crème, pampered (i.e. allowed to scavenge and strut) hens are very cross and territorial about the arrival of all the other worried hens, and fly at them aggressively. Battles ensue. Ramsden says it is better not to interfere. There have been deaths. There have been arguments about whether to eat or bury dead chickens. They are part of our self-subsistence, according to some.

The ducks weren't really a problem. They had a duck-house and a pen, by the stream. We opened the pen door. We are one duck short, whether because of a fox or a bid for freedom we don't know.

Tomorrow we release the turkeys. There are about 100 in a kind of prison compound, gobbling away, and fattened for Christmas. I don't know where they will go or what they will do when the gates are opened. It will be interesting to see. They are a mixture of iridescent turkeys and boring white ones.

There are feathers everywhere.

I might get this letter into the post when the truck goes down for more hen food. How shall we afford hen food if we don't sell eggs? (Though we are still collecting quite a lot, both from hen-houses and from patches of nettles, etc.)

There has been talk of closing out the outside world. Only talk. At the moment a lot of people come and go. Elvet Gander, for one. One or two of the Quakers. Canon Holly. They come up for weekends, or 'retreats', to help with the building and demolishing. What will happen eventually, I don't want to predict. It is a god-given opportunity to watch the dynamics of a self-constituted group, from the inception. I shouldn't really say 'god-given', should I?

I wonder if you could see your way to coming up here in case we *do* close our gates, before we do? I've got things I need to give you, and things I need to tell you, in case. In case. The idea is (in some quarters) that we should encourage visitors, and learners, and gifts. In others, that we are an austere, contemplative, closed community. At the moment, there is a huge feeling of generosity from both sides to each other. Such emotions, it is quite safe to predict, don't last. I wish (no sarcasm) they did. I only wish they did.

Avram Snitkin, you bastard, *why don't you write*? I am in a professional position very few sociologists have been in, bang in the middle of the dynamic of the formation of a new religion or cult. I can test Weber's and Durkheim's theories of charisma and the collective against each other. I can look into group psychology. But I'm compromised and contaminated by being part of the group I'm studying. I do really need another pair (a pair) of objective eyes. I sit here at night and imagine all sorts of things, starting with ritual sex with Joshua Ramsden (not an entirely unattractive idea, if I'm scrupulously honest, and what does *that* prove? He is very very handsome with his leanness, and white hair, and dark dark eyes. He will have to watch the other women getting jealous of Lucy. That *isn't* the sort of thing he thinks about, but others do, such as Clemency Farrar, who watches him constantly. I can't read her expression, and my view of her expression isn't evidence.).

The thing is, Avram, I'm scared. I do what I do because I'm an onlooker not a do-er and that suits me fine. I understand that ethnomethodology requires observation *in situ*, and on the spot, and I'm on the spot. But if a group of people are boiling like a cauldron, my useless friend, it's hard to stay cool. Foxes are taking the hens. What will happen if my cover gets blown? Now, or later.

I do need a human hand and a bit of honesty. I was going to write, for God's sake, but I'm getting superstitious – for *Talcott Parsons's* sake Avram, *answer my letters*, or better, put on yr walking boots and come up here.

Here, my cautious friend, is my unofficial report on The Hearers of Dun Vale (the Vale of Darkness, of Tears) to accompany my official reports of the health and progress of Josh Lamb *sive* Joshua Ramsden, and Lucy Nighby, or it appears, Santa Lucia, the Maiden of Light. All shall be made clear in the fullness of time. Selah!

We've just celebrated the Winter Solstice. Since I wrote that sentence, I have sat and watched sand sift through the hourglass timelessly, uncounted times. The dark clouds whip across the firmament, edged with gilded lace and scattering showers of silver sparkles. Zag and I celebrated the Winter Solstice privately with a little lysergic acid. Half of me now wishes I had not done so for how can I give you a true record of what floats in and out of form accompanied by harmonious twanging and flashing glories? But I must try, my dear, I must try. It is also possible, even probable, that the acid droplet gave me a vision of the true nature of events wch I'd have only glimpsed, unaided.

I saw also what lurks on the rim of the hills, at the rim of the skull-pan, outside the dancing circle. I saw it.

There are more things in heaven and earth.

To our muttons. There were a lot of muttons, but We are Vegetarians.

Sorry, Kieran, I skitter. Pull myself together.

We had a ceremony of the Solstice, which was also a ceremony of the inauguration of the Hearers. So that you'll know the *import* of the ceremony, I need to tell you the tale of the formation of the cosmos according to Mani. Selah. We have a nightly gathering for tale-telling and talk – by fire-light and candle-light, in the old hall of this place. Gideon wanted to make the tale-telling into a personal confessional, but Josh Ramsden has hijacked it and tells tales of the Manichees and tales of the cosmos. He tells them well, with a note of scholarly scepticism and a poetic passion and a kind of entrancing hypnotism. It's all fiendishly complicated (*literally*, my friend, *fiendishly*) but I'll have a stab at the telling.

In the beginning were two Realms, the Dark and the Light, and they were quite, quite separate. The Kingdom of Light was in the East, West, and North, and the Father of Greatness reigned in it. The Tree of Life grew there (grows there) crowned with flowers, unvarying in its beauty. The Kingdom of Light is made of Five

Things – Air, Wind, Light, Water and Fire. The Father of Greatness is surrounded by Aeons – twelve by twelve, made of light. They dwell in the 'unbegotten air' in 'the unbegotten land'.

The Kingdom of Darkness is the Kingdom of Light in a glass darkly, id est, reversed. It lies in the South, and the Tree of Death grows there, which is Matter as opposed to Light, Death as opposed to life, 'as unlike the Tree of Life as a king and a pig'. Ramsden read out a passage in which Mani describes the king in his palace in his airy chambers, and the pig wallowing in filth, eating foul things, creeping round 'like a snake'. The Kingdom of Darkness is boggy, full of pits, fens, gulfs and dark pools. It is smothered by Smoke, the 'poison of death'. There are five worlds also in the Kingdom of Darkness – Smoke, Fire, Wind, Water and Darkness, inhabited by foul beasts or demons – bipeds, quadrupeds, flying things, swimming things and reptiles respectively. The Prince of Darkness is called Pentamorphos for he combines all these foul devilish shapes in one arch-Dragon. The Tree of Death is full of maggots which prey on the fruits of the tree, which oppress the branches of the tree, for all is disharmony.

The principle of the Kingdom of Darkness, *nota bene* O Kieran, is the random motion of aimless and excessive Libido or Desire. Ramsden smiled directly at me when he used this word, his sweet, sad smile of distant complicity, which is lovable in him. Selah.

Slopping randomly about in the dark and the smoke and the stench of the pit, some of the bipedal demons came to glimpse the Light, and lusted after it.

So they churned and stirred and boiled up, and invaded the Kingdom of Light.

And Light didn't begin to know what to do, because It was used to unvarying calm and peace.

So it divided itself into emanations. It made a female Mother of the Living, and they made (but did not engender) a Primal Man, who armed himself with the Five Elements – Air, Wind, Light, Water and Fire, which together make up the Life of the Father, which is also known as the Maiden of Light. The Primal Man wore the Elemental Maiden as armour, and went out to do battle with the Dark.

Which defeated him, and laid him out. And the infernal powers sucked in, ingested, the Light Elements of the armour.

Which acted like a baited hook, or a honey-trap, to make the Dark dependent on the Light.

Then a lot of subdivided deities were sent out to rescue the Primal Man, which they did. They all have very abstracted names, and are all part of the One.

Then the imprisoned Light had to be rescued. This gets complicated and I shall skip many of the operations. The Demiurge made the earth out of the defeated demons, and the sky from their flayed skins. The mountains are their bones. Matter is Darkness, is the message.

Pure light sits in the sky, in the form of the unchanging sun, and the changing moon, and the (slightly defiled) stars and planets.

Then it gets sexy. (Ramsden didn't. He remained serious-looking and gently expository.)

The Demiurge evoked the Maiden of Light who was also Twelve Maidens (the twelve signs of the Zodiac). Then the Demiurge and the Maiden revealed themselves naked in the sun and the moon to the female and male Demons. This over-excited the demons who ejaculated the Light they had swallowed which became seed and fell on the earth. It was mixed with the sludge of Sin in the dark beings, which worked in them like yeast in dough. From the sin came five trees, and from them all vegetable life.

The female demons were already pregnant but miscarried when they saw the Demiurge's beauty. Their foetuses fell to earth and survived, eating the buds of light from the trees, and becoming the animal kingdom.

So the Light is still bound in plants, and even (though less) in animals.

The first man, Adam, was the child of two demons, as was Eve. Their birth was engineered by the Prince of Darkness. Adam was a replication of the cosmos, containing Light in Matter − like an elephant engraved on a ring in miniature, according to the Chinese, the human world replicates the cosmic one, without addition or subtraction.

Adam knew nothing of his dark origins, or his infernal flesh.

Jesus of Light came to him as a messenger and revealed his true existence to him, eat and be eaten, shit and be shat, fuck and be fucked, stink and inhale the stench. Jesus of Light gave Adam to eat of the Tree of Life, and Adam uttered a cry, which Ramsden says is at the centre of the understanding of the Manichaean Universe. He howled like a maddened lion, 'Woe, woe, to the maker of my flesh! Woe to him who has imprisoned my soul in it, and woe to the lawless whose actions led to my enslavement.'

According to Mani − who felt sex and food were the roots of evil − Eve's first two children, Cain and Abel, were sons of demons, not of Adam. His only child, conceived in a moment of human weakness, was Seth, who is the ancestor of all of us in whom the Light particles are still imprisoned. Our world, according to Mani, according to Ramsden, is a Smudge, and evil in it is not caused by our Sin but by demons of darkness, whom we aid and abet. We must release the Light, but the only ways to do this are both painful and self-destructive. Still, we must do what we can. So Ramsden says. He has instituted two ceremonies – the grip of the right hand, on meeting, which he says the Manichees took from the grip of the hand of the Demiurge or Living Spirit when he released the Primal Man from sleep, and the touching of the Three Seals – mouth, hands and breast. The sealed Mouth eats no meat, drinks no wine (!), the sealed Hands will hurt no creature containing Light Particles, the sealed Breast is a reference to elective chastity and abstention from procreation. These rather graceful rituals remove some of Gideon's more touchy-feely explorations from our daily encounters, and give relief to some, and suppressed irritation to others. I have to say that Gideon appears to be carried away on a general wing of enthusiasm and renovation and *vision* – shared *vision* – and when I say shared, I do include myself, and of course, Zag. Aided or not by acid.

We celebrated the Solstice yesterday. It was decided to have a fire at midnight – the midnight of the longest night. Canon Holly – a predictable enthusiast for the Golden Bough view of interchangeable rites – came up with the idea of incorporating a dead Tree into our fire as a symbol of renewal. He also came up with the Savonarola-like idea of a bonfire of vanities – everyone should cast *something* into the flames. So we built our fire round a suitably gnarled and withered old apple-tree, which hasn't produced fruit for years. It's on the edge of the orchard, and there were moments when I thought the whole thing would go up, and flames would sweep the plums and pears and crab-apples. Did I tell you that the Manichees believe Jesus wasn't crucified at all – that the account of the Crucifixion is a symbolic account of the crucifixion of Suffering Jesus on the Light-Cross (*crux luminis*), which is all trees and all vines and all plants where the light is imprisoned in the flesh of fruit and flowers – and further imprisoned of course, for longer, every time we eat an apple. Anyway, we built our fire well, using old furniture and bits of hen-houses. Did I tell you we have released all the birds – the broiler-house was like some demonic hideout from Tolkien, with great red lights like eyes, and all the white feathered beasties huddled together, crying, in the bloody light. They're all over now, but their feet suffer.

On the Night, there was a procession to light the Fire – Lucy was given the honour of pushing the burning brand into the mound. Then we all threw in a treasured possession. Lucy began with her wedding-ring. Clemency Farrar immediately added hers. So then Gideon added his. They did not look at each other. Clemency provided roast chestnuts and baked potatoes and toasted cheese throughout the evening, and mugs of apple-juice, cider, cocoa, spring water. Zag put in a teddy-bear. He said anyone could see he loved it, looking at how worn it was. It was most unpleasant watching it shrivel. Various women brought garments – a pretty dress, a sweater – or rings and bracelets. And I, you will ask? I decided I had to play fair (and I *was* under an influence, which is now wearing off). So I cast into the flames my much-loved copy of *The Interpretation of Dreams*, with all my layers of notes, and interleaved commentary. It was a true sacrifice, for there was no one there to know what it meant to me – and indeed, I should be interested to know, professionally, what it means to *you*.

So there we were. The flames went up into the black, and you could see, I thought, the Particles of Light returning to air at the edge of the burning sheet which surrounded the pyre. Zag brought out some warm coats – Afghan I think – sewed with gold stitching, suns and moons and flowers – on blond leather, and lined with shaggy fleece. He put them on Ramsden and Gideon and himself, and finished them off with Tibetan goatskin kind of hats, with dangling ears and a tassel. We are at a stage where everybody accepts everything gracefully. No one said fleece wasn't vegetarian. They did *look* like priests.

The tree went up in great cackling shoots, most satisfactorily. We danced a bit, in a circle. Canon Holly quoted St Lucies' Day, by Donne. ''Tis the year's midnight, and it is the day's.'

> He ruined me, and I am rebegot
> Of absence, darkness, death; things which are not.

He made an impromptu little sermon. There were many of those, during the long night, listened to with more or less rapt attention. I shall spare you the rest, including my own, which I don't remember too well, owing to the acid. I do remember Holly's. He twisted Donne's brilliant black extravaganza of erotic despair into a prayer to the Deus Absconditus, the Dead God, to be reborn in the Particles of Light in all of us. Religious men always twist. Or maybe they see the truth, or a truth, we mostly miss.

It would be so very easy to mock our doings. The English *style* is fatally mocking – we can only have the Sublime, it seems, if we include the grotesque as a safeguard. So yes, we were absurd, a lot of predominantly middle-aged English people, some dressed-up, some not, shuffling and very occasionally prancing, round a bonfire, chanting hymns we didn't know the words to, tumtitty, tumtitty, waving our arms in spontaneous gestures. Canon Holly pointed out that Lucy was Lucy's name, and she was Lux, Lucis, the Maiden of Light, and was blessed amongst women for providing the Hall for the Hearers. It was half after-dinner speech, half pagan paean. I saw his horrible teeth glitter in the fire-light and I didn't smile. Clemency (her first error?) said Lucy wasn't a Maiden, and Ramsden (who hadn't said anything, just stood in his robe with the red light on the white wool of his head) said that from now, she was, for all was new at the moment of the turning of the Solstice – which, by a *half* accident happened exactly as he spoke. So there she stood in her fiery fleece, an appley little woman, with a lamb pressing against her legs (she has a tame one called Tobias) and greying hair coming out of its hairpins, and tears running all over her little round face.

The world is turning into the Light, said Ramsden. Hens were chooking all round us, stirred up by the light and heat and disturbance. A fox coughed, not far away. I heard an owl. The sky was full of sparks, and stars beyond the sparks. I felt. I felt – *why not?* Why can't we have back the tyger burning bright, and the burning lamb, and the Tree of Life and the Tree of Death (fire streamed from the dead fingers of the convulsed apple-tree). Why can't there be singing and ritual and meaning and a grand purpose, as men once thought there was? I didn't feel mocking, I felt like a Son of God.

At the end, at dawn, it was decided to take a brand from the burning and light a fire in the hearth of the hall in the Hall. Zag said he would take the brand. He said he liked lighting fires. No one quarrelled with his self-election – indeed, it was as though he had spoken with the common voice. So we followed him in, and (with the help of a cigarette-lighter, I have to confess) he started the home-fire.

And we all went to bed in the morning.

XVI

The family dressed the tree for Christmas. It was a bushy spruce, with a few cones, smelling still of wet resin and the life of sap. They hung it, as they now always did, with the golden wire hexagons and polyhedrons Marcus had made for Stephanie. The gathering was grown – Bill and Winifred were there, with Stephanie's children, Will and Mary, Frederica and Leo, and Daniel, who had just arrived. Agatha and Saskia were also there, staying this year in Freyasgarth. Marcus had made new decorations to add to the traditional ones, after his conversation with Vincent Hodgkiss. He had made gold and silver spirals and abstract lapped cones, Fibonacci angels. He wound a great snaking spiral around the form of the tree, measuring the intervals. Will hung the pin-points of light – red, blue, green, white – at random amongst Marcus's order. He was singing, loudly 'Lucy in the Sky with Diamonds'. Frederica said to Agatha that she would never have believed, never, that her father would live in a house with pop music singing from the attic, round and round, over and over, on and on. Agatha said she had heard Bill himself humming 'Eleanor Rigby'. 'It's a good poem,' said Agatha. 'Yes, but you wouldn't expect him to notice,' said Frederica.

Will was fourteen, and was singing in order not to have to speak. He was heavy like his father, and dark like his father. Mary, who was twelve, was singing solo in the Carol Service in the church. It was the first day of her first period, which she had learned from girls at school to call The Curse. She retired often to stare with a kind of awe at the red spots of blood on the soft white space of the towel. She had bought the towels herself, and had said nothing to Winifred, who as only a grandmother, however loving, was outside this female thing, was withered. She had said nothing to her schoolfriends, either, although the event was much

234

discussed in the abstract. It was private, and strange, and satisfying. She needed a confidante, and thought of Frederica, and rejected her. She wasn't a sympathetic person, she wouldn't listen. She thought she would tell Agatha Mond, who was quiet and kind, and also a private and secret person. In her mind, darkly, she thought of the wet red traces in terms of the tale of Snow White, whose mother had seen three drops of blood on the snow, had borne her daughter, red as blood, black as ebony, white as snow, and had died. Her own mother had carelessly let herself be killed by an ice-machine, and Mary punished her, by never thinking of her. She was singing Christina Rossetti's 'In the Bleak Midwinter'. She was singing of white things, snow on snow, a breast full of milk, a lamb. She had the beginnings of breasts herself, and was not invulnerable. She would speak to Agatha. There was a grave conversation about what to do, what to look out for, that was proper to have.

Later, Agatha told Frederica that Mary had confided in her. 'She's one of the lucky ones,' said Agatha. 'She looks lovely, she doesn't have spots, she hasn't got cramps, and feels she ought to have, she's just slipped into it.'

'Are you sure? She doesn't look old enough.'

'Of course I'm sure. She's a most practical young woman.'

'I'm a dreadful failure, Agatha. If I was a real human being – she should have told *me*. Not you. If not my mother, me.'

The dead are very present at Christmas. Sweet and terrible, Stephanie flickered in Frederica's body.

Agatha said, not quite truthfully, that the Curse was a rite of passage, that *non*-family was the right choice. She also knew Frederica wasn't who you would tell.

Frederica started to say to Agatha that the whole gathering was a gathering of non, or not-quite family, incomplete units like two sides of a square, or one of Richard Gregory's illusory hanging wire cubes, which turned out to have quite different properties. But she did not say it to Agatha, because remarking on that to Agatha brought up the never-mentioned subject of Saskia's absent, unnamed, unknown father. Saskia did appear, more than any other human child Frederica knew, to be the product of parthenogenesis.

Bill Potter had spent the whole of Frederica's childhood inveighing against the Virgin Birth. What are we to think, he would shout, of a squeamish set of monks who can't bear the thought of normal human bodies and have to invent all this farrago of an untouched, intact girl – with a lovely pure odourless inside, and a benign cuckold of a husband-to-be – producing the Incarnation, so to speak, at half-cock. The Word became Flesh, he would roar, but only *nice* girlish flesh, not real rough-and-tumble *affectionate* flesh. They had disgusting imaginations, those monks. Frederica had wished he would shut up, and had accepted his arguments. Hearing his voice raised again as she went in to high tea on Christmas Eve, before the carols, she assumed he was making his annual protest. But he was not. He had been testing the assembled children – Leo and Saskia, William and Mary – on their knowledge of the biblical narrative and had found them wanting. They knew about the ox and the ass, but were ignorant of the Slaughter of the Innocents. They knew about angels singing to shepherds, but had not been told about Lucifer and his fall. He sang the prophecies of Isaiah from the *Messiah* and they looked blank. He recited

> *The wolf also shall dwell with the lamb, and the leopard shall lie down with the kid; and the calf and the young lion and the fatling together; and a little child shall lead them.*
>
> *And the cow and the bear shall feed; their young ones shall lie down together: and the lion shall eat straw like the ox.*
>
> *And the sucking child shall play on the hole of the asp, and the weaned child shall put his hand on the cockatrice' den.*
>
> *They shall not hurt nor destroy in all my holy mountain: for the earth shall be full of the knowledge of the Lord, as the waters cover the sea.*

The children looked blank. Bill said 'No one knows the Bible any more.'

'I shouldn't have thought that should bother you,' said Daniel.

'How can they read Milton, and Lawrence, and Dickens, and Eliot without knowing their Bibles?'

'It wasn't written for that purpose. If it's not needed, it will all have to be rethought. Scripture isn't a *literary* matter. If Canon

Holly is right, and God is dead, and we must dismantle the mythology, all your stuff goes with it, I'd have thought.'

He looked both pugnacious and amused, Bill thought. He said 'You can't just *take everything away* – at once –'

'Why not? It's what the Revolution is supposed to do.'

'What Revolution?'

'The one the students want. The New World. We can't imagine it, they say, because we're stuck in the dead past. You and me both,' said Daniel, grinning blackly at his father-in-law. Bill's once-red hair was ash-silver, and his temper was damped. He grinned back, ruefully.

When they set out for Church, in the dark, for the midnight carols, Bill put on his fleece-lined jacket.

It was Frederica who said, astounded 'You *don't* – you never come. You never come.'

'Are you ordering me not to?'

'I'm commenting. You can't expect us not to comment.'

'I thought I would go to hear my granddaughter sing a poem by Christina Rossetti. Since the old order is about to pass away, according to Daniel.'

'I wasn't prophesying. Only commenting.'

'Are you going to tell us what you *do* think is happening?'

'No,' said Daniel. He had put on his dog-collar for the evening as a symbolic gesture, he was not sure of what. 'I'm not. I'm only one man. One priest.'

'But you have to say you're glad I'm joining your flock,' said Bill.

'I don't. I'm not sure I am. You're subversion incarnate. But I am glad we shall hear Mary sing together.'

The Potter family filed into St Cuthbert's Church. Frederica held Leo's hand, going up the path, although he was almost too old. They were another unfinished family, like Agatha and Saskia. Leo had received a very large parcel from his father, which he had brought, unopened, and put under the tree. Will was walking, not with his father, but with Winifred. Bill and Daniel were together. Mary was in the vestry with the choir. The church was hung with holly and ivy, with boughs of fir and pine, with golden baubles and silver starbursts. There was the old, good smell of leaves, and candlesmoke, and stone very faintly warmed.

The congregation was large. It was augmented this year by a contingent from Dun Vale Hall, the Anglican members of the Hearers. Gideon had come with Clemency, and Canon Holly in a long black shaggy overcoat, and Ruth shepherding a group of children – Lucy Nighby's three children, in knitted hats, the little one wearing a pink eye-patch, and three others. There were one or two more children. Gideon and Clemency's four, now in their twenties, were absent, though only Daniel knew them well enough to notice this. Gideon and Canon Holly also wore their dog-collars. Gideon wore the embroidered coat Zag had given him at the Solstice, gold sun and flowers on hide and wool. Clemency wore a swooping maxi-coat in black velvet, which made her look, Frederica thought, like the Wicked Queen, at least from the back. She had a black velvet cap with a long scarlet silk tassel. The congregation stole surreptitious glances. They were curious about the Hall.

Jacqueline Winwar came in late. Last year she had been part of the Potter grouping. This year, she was solitary, and looked ill. She bent her head – hatless – in prayer, looked up, and saw Ruth, who smiled freely and brilliantly at her old friend, transfiguring her own rather waxily serious little face.

The choir filed in. The organ struck up. Saskia observed audibly that they looked like angels, and so they did, in their white starched tents, fluted and floating. They all carried candles, which they then placed in glass holders before them. They were all ages, from mothers and aunts through retired churchmen and youths with acne to children, and almost not-children, like Mary. They had – she had – scarlet ribbons round their white frilled necks. Frederica thought of the guillotine, and Daniel thought of sacrificial lambs, and was overcome with grief for his daughter, her grave round face, her red-gold hair, her quiet, easy, precise movements, until he saw that the grief was for Stephanie, whose form moved like a ghost in and round her daughter's. There was the cast of her eyelid, there was the curve of her neck and the pulse in it, there was the golden cheek in the light of the flame. He shook himself. Mary was Mary and alive. He was Daniel, and was mostly alive. He saw her tongue moisten her lips as she prepared to sing.

They sang 'The Holly and the Ivy.'

> *The holly bears a blossom*
> *As white as lily-flower*
> *And Mary bore sweet Jesus Christ*
> *To be our sweet Saviour.*
>
> *The holly bears a berry*
> *As red as any blood*
> *And Mary bore sweet Jesus Christ*
> *To do poor sinners good.*

Mary sang descant. Her young voice rose to the stone and moved over it and descended again, air in a stone chamber. The candle flames flickered and leaped. Mary's shadow moved like a ghost on the stone; she was still, but the flame was not. They sang 'We Three Kings'. Daniel hummed the verse about myrrh.

> *Sorrowing, sighing,*
> *Bleeding, dying,*
> *Sealed in the stone-cold tomb:*
> *O – Oh –*
> *Star of wonder, star of night . . .*

The Vicar, who looked like a farmer, asked Miss Godden, the headmistress of the Freyasgarth school, to read the Epistle, which was Hebrews 1.1. She read well, respecting Cranmer's rhythms, trenchant and matter-of-fact about mystery, infinity, and the divine Man who was co-eternal with it. As angels are not, St Paul insists.

> *God who at sundry times and in divers manners spake in time past*
> *unto the fathers by the prophets, hath in these last days spoken unto*
> *us by his Son, whom he hath appointed heir of all things, by whom*
> *also he made the worlds; who being the brightness of his glory, and*
> *the express image of his person, and upholding all things by the word*

*of his power, when he had by himself purged our sins, sat down on
the right hand of the Majesty on high; being made so much better
than the angels, as he hath by inheritance obtained a more excellent
name than they. For unto which of the angels said he at any time,
Thou art my Son, this day have I begotten thee . . . And again,
when he bringeth in the first-begotten into the world, he saith, And
let all the angels of God worship him. And of the angels he saith,
Who maketh his angels spirits, and his ministers a flame of fire . . .*

Frederica was always moved by angels. She looked up into the
roof of the church, and small, stony, solid ones stared down at her,
between stony feathers. Great impossible sailing beings, half-
human, half-bird, creatures of a threshold. She looked at Agatha,
who had invented the terrible Whistlers of *Flight North*, and
thought that her mind naturally inhabited the world of living
metaphor which was myth and fable, whereas she, Frederica, was
confined to stitching and patching the solid, and you could still see
the joins.

Miss Godden read serenely on.

*And thou, Lord, in the beginning hast laid the foundation of the
earth; and the heavens are the work of thine hands: they shall perish,
but thou remainest; and they all shall wax old as doth a garment;
and as a vesture shalt thou fold them up, and they shall be changed;
but thou art the same, and thy years shall not fail.*

> *Hark the Herald Angels sing . . .*
> *Veil'd in flesh the Godhead see*
> *Hail the Incarnate Deity . . .*

Daniel sang for the pleasure of the sound, and behind him heard
Gideon's golden voice, louder and clearer, and beside him a small
creaking, unaccustomed throaty voice, Bill Potter, singing Charles
Wesley's hymn, in Freyasgarth Church.

The Vicar announced that they had the great good fortune to
have in their midst the well-known − indeed, he dared to say,
famous Canon Adelbert Holly, one of the most lively and up-to-
date of our new dispensation of theologians. Canon Holly had

agreed to say a few words to mark this joyous occasion. He would speak on the meaning of the Incarnation in a time of doubt and trouble. He would speak of things that changed, in order to remain steadfast, and not to fail.

Canon Holly creaked past Daniel's pew end, to take the pulpit. Daniel smelled his smell, years, months, weeks, days and hours of stale smoke and exhaled tobacco. Canon Holly, like Daniel, and also like Gideon, had put on his dog-collar. His white hair was very long, hippy and patriarchal, even angelic. He began, rather importantly, by saying that he knew he was famous for his elucidation of, indeed his enthusiastic *embrace* of, the new Death of God theology. The term was a paradox, but then theology, words about God, a theory, a discourse, a human *logos* about God, was in itself a paradox.

He leaned over the edge of the pulpit, white head between black hunched shoulders, and said amiably

'I can see you all thinking, the old chap's going to drone on for *hours* and we shall never get to our mince-pies. Well, I'm not. But I do prefer to say something real, rather than a few nice platitudes, telling you to be good, turn round like stray sheep, pat you on the head and so on. This is God's house, it was built for God, to hold Faith and Hope, yes and Love inside its walls, to shelter their growth and aspiration.

'But where is God? Where do we meet Him, in daily life, at prayer, in the horrors of recent unredeemed history, where is He to be found?

'Theologians have marked a steady distancing of God from the earth. As the excellent lady read out to you, God once spoke directly to men, to Abraham and Moses, and later for a time He sent angels, who visited men, and prophets, through whom His Voice spoke like a trumpet of flame. But of late He has gone away. He is not present. When Nietzsche declared that He had died, he described a state of affairs people recognised, which was why people were so disturbed by Nietzsche.'

He smiled blithely upon them, the radiance of his good will mitigated by his stained teeth and his fluttering jowl, his very apparent mortality. He said that at the moment of the Incarnation the Eternal Unchanging God had *emptied himself out* – the word was Kenosis – had shrunk his infinity, which was timeless, and poured it into finite flesh. When God became Man, said Adelbert

Holly, the timeless entered history. The infinite became finite. The circular became a linear arrow. That which had no beginning and no end became a begun infant, with its umbilical cord full of blood and its blind mouth full of milk, and the blood and the milk were doomed in due course to find the end of everyman, sooner or later, to suffer and to die. Some believed that the message of Death of God theology was that it was incumbent upon all mortals to learn to live in this world, with no sense of heaven, and no fear of Hell, beyond hell on earth, of which we know something, each in our degree. But I say to you, said Canon Holly, that when God died as God and became Man, He entered History, and the joy of the mystery of His Birth is repeated daily in historical time, as is, of course, the sorrow of the mystery of His death, which has become infinitely finite.

He smiled beatifically. Frederica felt irritated. The remarks were *almost* meaningful, but not quite, they were in the end a game with language. But then, the Canon thought they meant something. What? She frowned.

They sang more carols. The candles flickered more wildly as they burned down in their glass cylinders. Finally, Mary stood up to sing 'In the Bleak Mid-winter', and as she did so, the choir took up their candles and extinguished them, so that the only light was the tall candles round the crèche at the crossing of the aisles. She sang high and clear. Frederica the unmusical heard the sound, and made sense of it because of the poet's words, could even see that the singing voice added a lightness, a soaring, to those words.

> *In the bleak mid-winter*
> *Frosty wind made moan,*
> *Earth stood hard as iron,*
> *Water like a stone;*
> *Snow had fallen, snow on snow,*
> *Sno-ow on snow,*
> *In the bleak mid-winter,*
> *Lo-o-ong ago.*

It was a good poem. It was an uncompromising description of elemental solids – snow, water, ice, iron, stone, with the adjective at work, bleak. And, Frederica thought, the wind moaned, which is a human sound, and there was the woman with the boy child. The earth moaning. And then, infinity.

> Our God, Heaven cannot hold Him
> Nor earth sustain;
> Heaven and earth shall flee away
> When He comes to reign . . .

Lovely, lovely, economical *words*, Frederica thought, fast, fast. Sustain is perfect. The earth can't either hold him up, or keep Him alive.

> Enough for Him whom cherubim
> Worship night and day,
> A breastful of milk
> And a mangerful of hay . . .

Mary's voice grew sweeter as she negotiated her way through angels, maiden kiss, shepherd and lamb, to the human heart. Her father saw her voice beat in the channel of her throat, in the movement of her lips, across the shimmer of her teeth, as she moved her lovely head with the rhythm, and the curtain of her thick red-gold hair swung in the light of her one remaining candle. Beside him, Bill Potter coughed unhappily, phlegm rising and suppressed in his dried channels. There was no life in Stephanie Potter, but life that had come from this cross old man had moved in her, had mixed with his own, which had come from his cross old mother and his unknown father, and there it was now, briefly alight in the shadows, singing of milk, and fleece, and snow.

Why had he called her Mary? It was a plain name, and a weight. He thought confusedly of Adelbert Holly's idea that God had emptied himself out of heaven. Bill coughed again, and Daniel thought that God had walked quietly out of this stone building, too, he was present in his absence only, and that was why the old man had felt able to cross the threshold, for the live force that had once held the stones together, which had once urged 'Put off thy shoes, for this is holy ground', had flickered and ceased to burn.

'*Gi-i-ive my heart*,' sang Mary. And bent her head over the glass before her, and blew out the candle, and stood, head bowed, in the spiral of waxy smoke.

Daniel heard his own heart. Thump, thump, in his ears. Pumping blood. It was all there was, and one day, it would stop.

Bill cleared his throat again.

'Like an angel,' he said.

'Hmn?' said Daniel, thickly.

'She sings like an angel, our Mary.'

'Aye,' said Daniel. 'She does.'

'She doesn't get it from *our* side. We're tone deaf.'

Afterwards they stood and ate mince-pies round the crèche. This crèche was white and gold. The figures were Italian, large white glazed china figures, descendants of della Robbia. The crèche itself, the stable, was made of real straw and wood. Inside, the figures were white and sleek. The Virgin, at one with her white veiling, the stolid ox, the shaggy ass, all blanched white, as was the infant, chubby in his stick-cradle. St Joseph stood, as he always stands, puzzled, redundant and slightly apart, his hands folded and set in their glaze, his beard snowy. There was a white lamb nestling by the cradle and white doves on the thatched roof. The other colour was gold. Gold angels hung suspended around the great gold tinsel star over the rafters. Golden apples, made of stuffed silk, gold-painted holly and ivy were heaped around the place where the footlights would have been if it was a stage. Night-lights in glasses surrounded the apples and leaves.

'Pretty,' said Saskia.

Mary joined them, disrobed and breathless. Gideon and Clemency hurried up and congratulated her. Will stood apart, with his grandfather, in the dark shadows. Gideon sipped hot punch, and talked of his sense of the new community at Dun Vale Hall, of the spirit moving like yeast, of the energy released like the hens and turkeys, into freedom.

'You should have seen them stretch and scurry. All those feathers being preened and shaken. It's the sort of gesture you dream of, and then find you're actually *making* –'

Ruth said 'Some of the down is actually growing back on their poor bare necks.'

Gideon stroked the long snake of her gold plait down her back, which she still wore, though she was no longer a girl.

'We all feel it. It's going to be like ancient monasteries, a religious house, where a core of contemplatives inhabit, and others come to rest and recuperate and escape the busy world, and still others come through, as it were, on the crossroads of their life, to catch a glimpse of how things *can be* . . . We mean to have open days for children, storytimes – Ruth will be in charge – days of prayer, days of singing and dancing . . .'

Jacqueline Winwar asked how Gideon and Clemency's own children were. Frederica, partly still exalted by Rossetti's hard absolute words and Mary's voice, partly anxious now to go home, looked distractedly at her. She was not sure she would have recognised Jacqueline. She had been a glossy nut-brown girl, and had become a sharp woman who looked somehow emptied out. She had become thin, her mouth was tighter, her bones more pronounced. It suited her. The removal of her comfortable persona made her real intelligence visible.

Gideon said all his children were fine, just fine, they were making their way in the world, finding their way, falling over and struggling up again, like everyone's children. 'Jeremy's away in India – he's on a spiritual pilgrimage – Tania's working with a wonderful group of creative people selling unusual clothes in Carnaby Street – Daisy's training to be a social worker – she feels a call, because she has a black skin, to work in black communities – Dominic's living in a squat, mixing with those who live on benefit and choosing to share their lot and their life-style. He's finding his way, he's finding his way. I sometimes wish it wouldn't take them so long to find a settled life-style, but that's only because I'm an old unregenerate bourgeois fuddy-duddy. Really, I admire their courage. You have to.'

Clemency Farrar looked at Daniel, and looked away. She knew that Daniel knew that Dominic had been arrested for receiving stolen goods, more than once. She did not know that Daniel knew that Tania was usually silly with an increasingly large mix of hemp and LSD. She knew Daniel did not know that they had not heard from Jeremy for two years, and did not know whether he was alive or dead. She had burned the letter Jeremy had sent, saying he hoped he would find a peace that would mean he need never come back and that it was necessary to him to cut all ties whilst he looked. She stared blankly at the white china Madonna with her plump white infant. She knew Daniel knew that Daisy, a black child with a white name, had repudiated her adoptive parents, had moved to a place where all her neighbours were black, and lied routinely about her origins and upbringing.

Gideon stroked the gold snake of Ruth's plait, and held out his arms to Jacqueline, who had been part of his Church Youth Group, when Daniel was his curate. He said

'You must *particularly* come and meet the Hearers, Jacquie, love. Ruthie would be so glad, so happy. We all should.'

Jacqueline evaded the embrace.

'Please,' said Ruth. She said 'You should hear Joshua Ramsden. He is the most marvellous man. The most . . . You can't imagine. You must see.'

Her face was white and ecstatic. There was an edge in her voice.

'I might,' Jacqueline said.

'And Daniel. And Marcus, you must all come, you must all come,' said Ruth. 'And see what we have done, how different everything is, how real, how *new*.'

Jacqueline said she had a complicated experiment she was looking after single-handed.

'And you come too,' said Ruth to Mary. 'We sing a lot. They would love your lovely voice there. Everyone would love it.'

She nestled against Gideon's shoulder, and smiled at them.

Later, they remembered this.

Under the Christmas tree the next morning, among the presents, were two identical books for Leo and Saskia, from Agatha. Saskia found hers, first. Leo was sitting amongst a heap of gilt paper considering his present from his father, which was an inordinately large mechanised tank, complete with guns which flashed, smoked, and ejected whining pellets. Saskia opened the book, peaceably. It was from Agatha, and was an advance copy of *Flight North*, which was out in the New Year. It had a dramatic dustjacket, largely in black and white, with flashes of crimson and scarlet. The lettering, in crimson, ran across a line of snowy turrets or mountain peaks, on top of which black cockerels crowed in silhouette against a red sky. The group of travellers stood in silhouette by a thorn-bush, bottom left, and in the centre the Whistlers hovered on extended white wings, with bird-necks, female faces and human hair. Saskia gave a little cry, and clutched the book to her chest. Agatha said 'Look at the dedication.'

Saskia read it. 'For Saskia and Leo, who listened to this story. With love.'

Leo looked up from his tank.

'You've got one,' said Saskia, busily. 'You've got one, too. It's dedicated to *us*.'

Leo crawled across the floor amongst the wrappings, and found his neat package. He undid the ribbon, and folded the paper. He studied the cover, and looked at the dedication. Saskia hugged her mother. 'I didn't know, I didn't know,' she said.

'It was hard enough keeping the secret.' Agatha was equable. She was good at secrets.

'It looks quite different, quite, in real printing,' said Saskia. She opened the book and read, at random

> *'All your book-learning will be of no use in the wilderness,' said the page-boy to the Prince.*
>
> *'We shall see, as to that,' said Artegall. 'Books describe the world, and are useful. It is only that I have never been permitted to go outside my study. That will change now.'*
>
> *'We must all go together,' said Dol Throstle. 'And we must pretend, if we are found, to be one family, so we shall be harder to find. You must pretend to be brothers.'*
>
> *'That is a good idea,' said Artegall.*
>
> *'You won't find it easy,' said Mark.*
>
> *'Wait and see,' said Artegall.*

Everyone congratulated her on her reading. Leo opened his book, and held it close to his face.

> *'No one has seen the Whistlers and lived,' said the thrush. 'Indeed even to hear them is fatal. They glide or fly like grey shadows and make a high whistling sound at the edge of what other creatures can hear . . .'*

He closed the book with a snap. He went and kissed Agatha. 'Thank you,' he said. 'For the dedication.'

His face was hot, shining with the reflected colours of the lights on the tree. He went quickly out of the room, shutting the door carefully behind him. Frederica's straining ears heard him creep up the stairs. Daniel and Winifred congratulated Agatha, and Saskia's book was examined and exclaimed over.

Bill said to Frederica 'He wasn't reading, was he? He had it by heart.'

Frederica found tears in her eyes.

'He won't admit he doesn't read. I don't know what to do. He has your – our – temper. He's proud.'

'You have to do something *now*, or it's too late. Better someone else, not you, at least at first. Can I talk to him? Can I talk to Margaret Godden at the Freyasgarth school? She always had all her first class reading before they went up. Then she got a directive, saying they shouldn't be driven, they should learn in their own good time, when they were ready. It doesn't work.'

Frederica stared at him. The tears brimmed.

'You can't teach him and cry over him. Let me try. Can't do much in a short holiday. Can make a start. I've become a reformed character. Patience itself. And anyway, I was always a good teacher. And he reminds me of myself, Frederica. I had trouble starting –'

'*You* did?'

'I used to play that trick. Reciting from memory. I recognised the look.'

Frederica never knew what her father said to her son. She overheard the beginning of the conversation, the sound of Bill's voice, reasonable, quiet, adult, man-to-man, and she crept away. Later she saw the two walking together into the village, two stocky, wiry creatures, one flaming, one faded. They called on Margaret Godden, the Freyasgarth headmistress, who later came to see Frederica, with a professional diagnosis of Leo's reading. Leo came back skipping. He and Bill vanished again into Bill's study. She heard her son's voice making primitive sounds. a. b. c. (s) d. s.n.a.(ay)k.(silent e). The s.n.a.k.e. ate (ay-t silent e) the a.p.p.l. (silent e). U.n.d.e.r. the tree. ee. I saw a d.r.a.g.o.n. The m.a.n. and the w.o.m.a.n. are under the tree in the g.ar.d.e.n. The snake is in the tree. The apple is on the tree. The snake smiles. He g.i.v.es the apple to the w.o.m.a.n.

In this case, said Miss Godden, in the beginning must be

phonics. Your son is not severely dyslexic – he reverses his writing, but his memory retains letters and forms in a normal way. He is a boy who needed to be taught to analyse the sounds of letters, and he appears to have been given the 'freedom' to find his own way with 'Look and Say'. I suspect he was under some strain at the moment when he was being required to recognise 'aeroplane' and 'house' and 'machine'. He is a boy who needs – as most of us need – precise forms of thought into which to stitch or slot his discoveries and inventions. Most of us are enabled by knowing the alphabet by heart, without thinking about it, and the possible sounds of the letters. As most of us are enabled by knowing the patterns of the multiplication tables, both visually and aurally. It is not helpful to expect children, as many modern teachers do, to discover multiplication and division for themselves, or to organise their own idiosyncratic alphabet. Rote learning is not a form of torture or inhibition. It is a tool. Also a pleasure. In the case of a child like your son, whose memory is organised in his particular way, it is a necessity. No one should make a means into an end. You don't learn the alphabet in order to know it, but in order to *use* it. But knowing is a human pleasure. Like perspective drawing, or staying afloat in water.

Miss Godden was tall, with a mass of hair like white wool. She wore a straight-down fir-green woollen dress, and had a face at once severe and kind. She had brought with her a box of hand-made reading cards she had made for children like Leo, cards where the words were interesting, where there were rhymes and tales of adventure, not only washing-up and going out to a shop in a car. Later cards had sound-games. 'Though I peer through the boughs I shall hear no sound.' She left the box with Bill. The man and the boy closed themselves into the study and chanted together. Frederica heard Leo singing on the stairs. 'The single silly starling stands and sings in the stinging rain. The rain hisses. The rain sings. The wind blows the rain.'

Bill told Frederica that Leo was making giant strides. It was all coming together. Frederica burst into tears.

'What's all this about? Margaret Godden says he'll be fine. He'll learn. He'll catch up.'

'We shall be back in London in ten days. He'll be back at that school.'

Bill said 'You wouldn't consider leaving him here for a while? He'd be happy at the Freyasgarth school. It'd suit him. We've got Will and Mary –'

'I can't.'

'Think about it. Not forever. Just a term would make all the difference. Little boys go away to school at his age.'

Frederica wept as though she herself was the small child, facing separation. After a moment, Bill put an awkward hand on her heaving shoulder.

'You're *my* child. I care about you, too. You must do what you want.'

'What *ought* I to want?' asked Frederica, wildly. Leo came in, and stared. His mother never wept. He squared his shoulders and looked enquiringly at Bill. He said 'What's wrong?'

Bill said 'Nothing much. Honest. I'll look after her. You run along. I don't mean, go away, run along or anything. I mean, it's *really* OK, I'll look after her.'

They exchanged a shrewd, measuring glance. Leo went away. Frederica wiped her eyes and sniffed. Bill said

'He's as sharp as a needle. As quick as a fox. And wise for his years.'

'He's had to be.'

'Don't start crying again. We'll sort it out.'

John Ottokar came back from Christmas with his parents in Welwyn Garden City. Paul-Zag had stayed behind, with the Hearers. Leo greeted him at the door with a leap into his arms, crying John O, John O, John O, is back. Bill and Winifred welcomed him. Agatha and Saskia were away, visiting professional acquaintances of Agatha's on the UNY campus. After tea, Bill took Leo off to do reading-exercises. Leo said to John 'I'm reading a document which Grandpa and Miss Godden have specially constructed for me . . .' He said 'It's to do with Agatha's story. It's printed, you have to see it, I'm reading it –'

'*He's* happy,' said John to Frederica, when they were alone. He held her in his arms, and kissed the top of her head. He touched her spine. It shivered with its own pleasure. 'Are *you* happy? Did you have a good Christmas?'

Frederica said that it had been an odd Christmas. She told him most, but not all, of her thoughts about their odd incomplete family groupings, the single mothers, the grandparents-and-grand-children, lone Daniel. She laughed drily over the idea of St Joseph with the child who wasn't his, and the angels and the ox and the ass. She told him about the surprising alignment of Miss Godden, Bill Potter, Leo and the reading-scheme. She did not mention Stephanie. She said that Bill had suggested – she didn't know if he was serious – leaving Leo there for a term. She said it made sense. She said she didn't know what to do. She said she was responsible for Leo's odd life. John Ottokar's intelligent fingers massaged the nape of her neck, which prickled with grateful warmth. She asked, had John had a good Christmas.

John said, not really. He had been a token. His parents were worried about Paul. They thought Paul was taking drugs. They didn't know what sort of life he'd got into. I was a reflection of his absence, said John Ottokar. As usual. I was there, but I wasn't, because I was only me, myself. One child to them is half a child.

'Are you *sure*?'

'Oh yes, I'm sure.'

He turned the conversation back to Leo's reading-progress. Frederica said Leo said his mind was a maze of mirrors, he saw mirror writing, or his hands traced it. He would be happy here, she told John Ottokar. Inner cities aren't good for strung-up children. Her tenacious mind had a grip on that idea, and others were peripheral.

John said

'It all seems to lead one way, to my mind. I think we should get married, and you should find work here – in the University perhaps – and Leo could go to the school – and we should be a family, a man and a woman and a boy – at least one boy –' he said, and smiled a nervous, empty, anxious smile. Frederica bristled.

'That disposes of me very simply.'

'No, love, listen, *think*. You don't like him being in the city. I'm here, we're right together, there's the moors and the fresh air, and the university's humming with life.'

'And my life?'

'I'm not saying Leo and I are your life. I *am* saying, I think you can do something, anything, *anywhere* – you're a great teacher, teaching is *here* – I am asking, because you're the best thing I've got, have ever had, I have to *try* –'

He was gentle, and anxious, and something in him expected defeat. That expectation filled Frederica with self-distaste and a brief desire to hurt.

'And Paul?' she said.

'Paul's in there with the Hearers. I have to have my own life.'

'And I'm to be that life.'

'Yes.'

His arms were round her. Her body warmed to his. Her mind was cold and clear and unhappy.

'Is it important to be a television personality?' John asked, with false innocence.

Frederica snapped. 'No. It's work. It's fun.'

Fun is a foolish, weak word. John stroked her flanks. She could feel her guts pull, and the empty space in her head. She had a vision of a man and a woman and a boy, walking over the moors, hand in hand. She remembered Nigel and his fierceness. She had married Nigel because she had listened to her body. And she did not have nothing to show for it, she had Leo. Could she do it again, for gentleness? What did she want? She didn't like herself.

At this point the doorbell rang. It was Jacqueline Winwar, who had come to propose to Daniel and Marcus – and John, since they found him there, and anyone else – a visit to the Hearers at Dun Vale Hall. To see how Ruth was. She said it would be easier to go in a body. Daniel, who had known she was coming, appeared from his room, and said he was ready. He went to look for Marcus. He thought Marcus would be disinclined to come, but Marcus said he was ready. Jacqueline asked John if he wanted to join the party. John looked at Frederica.

'I'm not coming. I don't like religion. I don't like groups. As you know,' she said to John.

'I might just go and see if Paul's OK. I promised the parents I'd go and see. Jacqueline's right, there's safety in numbers.'

'They don't bite, do they?' said Frederica.

'They might,' said Daniel. 'Anything might happen. We shall look in on them.'

Frederica found herself briefly alone with Jacqueline. She asked politely how the other woman's work was going, and got a surprisingly detailed answer about neurotransmitters, axons, calcium ions, and the difficulty of the equations, which made Marcus's help absolutely necessary. She did not listen precisely to this answer, but did respond to the tone of enthusiasm in the sharpened voice, the sense of urgency in the expression of the newly-narrowed face. Jacqueline had always looked nice, and placid, and now she looked driven, and edgy, and unwell.

'You've been ill?' said Frederica, when Jacqueline came to a break in her explanation.

Jacqueline understood that Frederica had not understood what she had been saying. Her flicker of light went out. She said

'I've had problems. I'm fine now. I just need to get some clear results . . .' She said politely 'I saw you in the Box. It's all very witty. Must be great fun to do.'

'It's a way of earning a living. I have to earn a living.'

They stared guardedly at each other. Both had a sense of a cold space in their own heads, which they needed to protect, and yet were afraid of. Jacqueline thought briefly of describing to Frederica the muddle and horror of the miscarriage, and decided to keep quiet. Frederica was not a woman with whom you could be woman-to-woman, even if you were both trying to be something else as well. Frederica had an uncomfortable apprehension that Jacqueline knew what she wanted, knew what she was doing, much better than she herself did, and this was not a pleasant feeling, for she was used to being at least probably the cleverest person in the room, and was also used to Jacqueline being just a nice girl, a friend of Marcus. She could have said, how hard do you find it, being an obsessed intellectual, and a woman too, does your own biology bother you? But she didn't. She said brightly, distantly

'You ought to come on the Programme and tell everyone about neurotransmitters and all those things.'

Jacqueline said it was probably incomprehensible. Frederica registered a very small barb.

The others came back, in anoraks and woollen caps, ready to go to Dun Vale Hall. Will had added himself to the party. Daniel had tried to dissuade him, telling him clumsily it would bore him – Daniel never knew how to speak to Will. Will said he was fond of

Ruth, and didn't see why he shouldn't go to see the community. Ruth had, he said, *particularly* asked him, himself to come.

The journey to Dun Vale Hall needed half an hour in a country bus, and another half-hour's walk. Marcus sat down next to Will – Jacqueline thought he might be avoiding her, not out of hostility but simply because he was embarrassed by the explosion of emotion in the Non-Maths Group. John Ottokar went and sat alone, staring out of the window at the frosty moor, with old snow in its hollows, and a steel sky beyond the rim of the horizon. The first part of the bus journey ran along a ridge, with moor on each side, and valleys falling into dales beyond. Jacqueline found herself sitting with Daniel. For a time they didn't speak. Then they discussed the events that had led to the formation of the Hearers. Jacqueline said that Ruth sounded ecstatic. She asked if Daniel had been interested in joining. He said no, he didn't like groups, and was not over-fond of leaders. As she knew.

'You belong to the Church.'

'Barely. The stones hold together just about, when I go into the building. I dream of ruins. I work in a bomb-site, in a ruin, listening to voices without faces. I seem to fit in better, there.'

'You care about people,' said Jacqueline. 'It's beginning to look to me as though I don't.'

Daniel sat quietly for a moment as the bus rumbled on. He said into the machine-noise

'You don't look well. You do look different. Alerted.'

'My work's going well. I keep finding things. Things about the chemistry of memory – that might change the way we look at brains. It's agonising when it goes wrong, and when it falls into place, it's beautiful.'

She added, with a dry little laugh, 'My mother said at Christmas, it was taking too much out of me. I ought to relax, she said, look around me, get married and so on. She said time was running out. She can't listen to two consecutive sentences about cell-structure without her mind switching back to cleaning the oven, and planning the next hols. She said I was eating myself up, and no man would look at me. Really, she said all that. I was put out. I don't know why I'm telling you all that.'

'It's my job, listening. She was saying what she wanted from you. It's her right. But I'd say, you know where you're going, and you must go there.'

'I was going to marry Luk. I said yes, and then I said no. It was a dreadful mess, he's furious. And unhappy. I didn't tell my Mum all that.'

'Why did you say no?' He asked easily, with no preconceptions of the answer. She replied truthfully

'Because I didn't want to. Because — because I want to concentrate on what I'm doing. Because I don't want to be split. I didn't know I was like that. I always assumed everything would fall into place, work and life and sex and so on. It won't.'

Daniel sat silent, and did not offer soothing sounds, such as the banal remark that this could all change, or the banal reinforcement, that what she wanted must be fine for her. He listened with his large body to the beating of her heart and the whirring of her head, and took in her fingers on her knees, clasping and unclasping. After a moment she said, as though answering what he wasn't saying

'I thought I was pregnant, actually. I thought I was, and it seemed right to go on with it, and marry. And I wasn't. And then I couldn't. The whole thing was just *wilful* from start to finish, I wanted to be human, and I'm — not.'

'I see.'

'And I've messed up Luk.'

'He seems tough, to me.'

'He's writing a paper on the problems of meiosis and the redundant male.'

Daniel laughed. Jacqueline's face turned to his with a new smile, a wary, thinking smile.

'You can laugh,' she said. 'It was appalling. It's appalling to find out you're not quite human. I always thought I was interested in people . . .'

'There are very many ways of taking an interest in people.'

'Well, you do.'

Daniel looked out of the window at the earth and the air and the frozen grass and bracken. He said, not looking at Jacqueline

'If you are to go on — looking at people like watches with broken springs — you end up as precise and detached as a scientist staring down a microscope and watching bacteria swarming. You get diagnostic. It gets steely. It's not like ordinary love.' His heavy head turned to stare at the back of his son's head, and Jacqueline,

255

who was in fact a quick observer, saw his cheek-muscles tighten. 'It might incapacitate you for ordinary love.'

'I don't think I've ever heard you talk about yourself.'

'It does no good, in my profession. You probably haven't.'

They sat in silence, as the bus rumbled on. Their thoughts ran in the same direction. Jacqueline said

'Gideon is interested in Gideon and ordinary love.'

'He is. He has a lot of it to spare.'

'I worry about Ruthie.'

'I know. You always have.'

'Gideon doesn't.'

'We don't know. I think he doesn't.'

'This new man, Daniel. What's he like? This Joshua Ramsden?'

Daniel waited, as the bus bumped on a stone.

'He's a religious man. He loves the Light. He wants to love God. He is sick – physically, he has fits – he knows extremes. He's –'

'He's?'

'Oh, I was going to say, he's dangerous. But I've no right. I'm just going on the pattern of how it always is, the vision, the intensity, the excess, the – the violence. Maybe it'll be contained, this time. You can feel it crackling. He means well. Indeed, he means the best –'

Jacqueline had a sudden vision of the beautiful zigzag of intensifying spikes produced by her oscilloscope, its beauty and its meaning. The electric charge of matter, running through a single giant neurone. Connecting. She laughed. Daniel asked why. She told him how his words had produced her image. He said, there you are. The best in your case is clear enough. Get on with it, girl. He felt her shoulder-blades unhunch.

The bus left them on the top of a ridge. They walked down and down, into the valley. They could see Mimmer's Tarn glimmering in the cold bright air, at the other end of the valley. Jacqueline and Marcus knew where they were, because it was where they had so often come, to count the snails. It felt different, now. Jacqueline looked at Marcus, whose hands were deep in his pockets, whose head was down. She asked if he was worried about Ruth. He shrugged.

'It was Ruth you really fancied,' said Jacqueline.

'Was it?'

'I think she thought so. But you didn't say anything.'

'What was the point? She had other ideas. *These* ideas.'

Marcus needed to see Ruth, because he was afraid of Vincent Hodgkiss. The philosopher had put his sense of himself, always fragile, in doubt. He had sat there in the flickering candle-light and had entranced Marcus's mind, where it lay coiled and hidden inside Marcus. He had stared at Marcus's mind with glittering eyes, and spoken to it with serpent-tongue, and it had crept out and revealed itself. And then Marcus had noticed that the flames of attention were playing roughly over his body, which felt both transparent and incandescent. Anyway, hot. He did not like this heat. He wished to retreat, and felt himself to have been warmed into molten glass.

He needed to remember what it had felt like to want to touch Ruth, with her heavy gold twined hair, with her clean soft whiteness.

He did not go so far, in his wishes, as to hope that Ruth could be persuaded to leave the Hearers. He just wanted to see her and want her, to restore his sense of his own direction. His own nature. He said silently to the rimy moorland, I need a sign, a little sign, that's all.

He thought that it would be interesting one of these days, to talk out Fibonacci with Jacqueline. She appeared to be getting satisfactorily over whatever had been the problem.

When they came to Dun Vale Hall they were expected; the telephone, at this point, still connected the community to the outside world. The door was opened by Clemency Farrar in an enveloping white apron, smiling very brightly. When she opened the door, they smelled the wonderful smell of baking bread, and baking biscuits or cakes, sugary and brown. Other Hearers were gathered on the flagstones of the entrance hall, under the balcony where Luk Lysgaard-Peacock had watched with the wounded children. It was warm and bright in the dark wood and stone space. There were candles and bowls of floating night-lights. There were wreaths of evergreens, holly and yew and ivy. Paul-Zag skipped out and embraced his brother, Canon Holly shook Daniel's hand in a Manichaean shake, Ruth in a white dress and white stockings put up a warm cheek for Jacqueline to kiss, and smiled brightly at Marcus. Gideon Farrar gave everyone a bear-hug and a slap on the back. He was wearing his embroidered sheepskin and his red-gold hair was flowing on his shoulders. Canon Holly wore a sheepskin too, a little awkwardly. It was cold in the Hall, although there was so much light, and such a good smell of warm work in the ovens.

They went into the dining-hall, where a meal awaited them. There was one long table, holding about thirty or thirty-five people, pushed fairly close together, on folding chairs. The table was spread with large white cloths, and heaped with food – warm loaves, plates of buns and biscuits, bowls of eggs, wooden bowls of various fruits, apples and pears, plums and boiled prunes and crab-apples and blackberries, fruits of the country around. They all sat down in an amiable huddle, though certain people clearly had places reserved for them. At the head of the table Lucy Nighby (also in a large white apron) and Clemency Farrar flanked the seat where presumably Joshua Ramsden would sit. Daniel sat down at the other end, not at the foot itself, which was occupied by Canon Holly, but next to him. Gideon sat in the centre of the long side, flanked by Ruth and Ellie, with a little group of Quakers opposite him, and the children, Lucy's three, and three others, clustered round them. Jacqueline sat next to Daniel. Marcus thought of sitting next to Ruth, but could not, for she was occupied with various children near her. Elvet Gander went up to John Ottokar and invited him to take the seat next to him. John declined, and went to sit with the Quakers. Gander followed him, leaning over his shoulder.

'We have music during meals, as we have readings of poetry and religious texts. Zag plays and sings for us. We should be honoured if you would play with him.'

'I don't have my clarinet.'

'We have one; chance, or fate, or in this case Milly Fisher provides. A little seasonal music? "The Lord of the Dance?"'

Paul put the clarinet, assembled, with a new reed and oiled wood, into his brother's hand.

Clemency Farrar and Lucy Nighby went out to the kitchens and returned with two dark cauldrons of steaming soup, which they placed on the side-table where the serving-ladles were.

The woman on the other side of Jacqueline said

'We made it ourselves, out of what we've got. It's a concoction of potatoes and leeks and sprouts and nettles and broccoli tops and carrots and cows' milk and goats' milk and a dash of Marmite. And some herbs. It's pretty good. It's vegetable. Are you a vegetarian?'

'No,' said Jacqueline.

'Are you a Quaker, or C. of E. or something else?'

'I'm a scientist.'

'In your view, does that preclude religious belief?'

'I don't know if it need. In my case it does.'

'Why are you here?'

'To see an old friend.'

'Is it easy, being a woman scientist? Do you face problems?'

Jacqueline was irritated by the small brown woman's persistent questioning. She said

'Your turn. Why are *you* here? What is *your* profession?'

'Oh,' said Brenda Pincher, rearranging her cutlery. 'I'm a seeker, a researcher, a looker-on.'

'Do you live here, or are you visiting?'

'I live here. I'm part of the original Group. Daniel knows me.'

Daniel said vaguely that he did. He had forgotten, if he had ever known, her profession. She deflected Jacqueline's attention by leaning across her and asking Daniel a series of questions, how was he, what did he think of residential communities, what were his views of Manichaeism . . .

Joshua Ramsden came in. He stood and looked gravely down the table at the assembly, letting his glance rest on each face. His eyes, they all thought, searched their minds, noted tangles, combed knots. Marcus saw Ruth blush and smile, although her hand was next to Gideon's hand spread on the table. The man, Jacqueline thought, was a beautiful man. There was a draught in the room, which, like the entrance hall, was cold, apart from the heat of their contiguous bodies, and the steam of the vegetable pottage. Gideon sat majestically, taking up more than one man's space, on the long side of the table, like Leonardo's Christ at his Last Supper. Ramsden stood like a pillar, carved and still, making them all still. He said 'Let us eat, no more than is needful, for our bodies are only temporary means for our spirits, we live in husks, and it is right that they should fall away. Take the goodness of the fruits of the earth in sorrow and in gratitude, and think of a time when there shall be no bodily needs, but only pure light. Think of the Light, as you eat those living things in which it is captured.'

As he spoke, Marcus felt a latecomer slide plumply into the empty space beside him. A voice he knew said 'Very fine, very fine, but it will be a delicious soup, I saw it in the making.'

Marcus knew the very smell, unchanged, of the body next to him, a fat smell with an acid edge of anxiety. He knew the comfortable chuckle with the note of stress under it. He knew, even, the pressure of that soft buttock. He did not look up. He ceased almost to breathe.

Lucas Simmonds, whose attentions, both religious and religiously amorous, had led to Marcus's earlier collapse into terror and incoherence, noticed who his meal-companion was. He began to babble.

'It's you. I've prayed and prayed for this moment. It's you. Are you here? Are you staying? I have suffered so long over where you were and how you were living, and how you thought of me, how you judged me, whether you had a place in your heart and mind . . .

'This is a good place. This is my resting-place after my trials and tribulations. Here there is a Man who sees into the heart of things, Marcus. Do say you are staying, that you too –'

'No,' said Marcus. He looked up, desperately, and saw that Joshua Ramsden, from far away, had seen him. It was as though the man could feel his terror, his disgust, his concern, his paralysed soul.

Ramsden stood up.

'We will have music,' he said. 'We will eat in silence, and hear Zag and his brother, who will lift our minds to the Light. We will forget ourselves.'

Joshua Ramsden surveyed his people from his distant seat. He noted harmony and disharmony, heat and cold, fear and elation, greed and moderation in eating, belief and scepticism. When his eyes rested on one or another, that one or another inevitably raised his or her head and his eyes held their eyes for a long look, of searching, of trust. He saw, as it were, spiritual forms of matter around faces and figures. Young Marcus, whom he did not know, was surrounded by a brittle cage of icicles. Full of light, but icicles, meltable. The man next to him who had just come was covered in sweat like a roasting carcass: it fell in great gouts, soaking his curly head and his woolly clothing. Brenda Pincher was always an eyeless ball of fur, which quivered. He came, staring onwards, having dealt with Gideon's flowing milk and honey, to Daniel Orton.

There it was again, the running sheet of blood he had no choice but to see. It welled fantastically out of Daniel's dark hair and ran in glistening sheets and runnels over his thick brows and heavy cheeks, catching on the corners of his mouth as he drank the green soup, pouring down the stalwart neck muscles, collecting in the sweater-neck, brimming up and over and sliding down over shoulders and cable-stitching, breast and belly under wool. The vision was always precisely detailed: he saw little splashing drops from beard-stubble to neckline, he saw a steady drip from the thick hair-root. He saw, he did not imagine, red, gushing, shining, coagulating. It was sent, and must not be spoken of. He had the idea of Daniel as a kind of dark volcano of matter, gushing blood like hot lava. He thought briefly that maybe this was a sign that he was a demon, the demon. He rejected this. The man was fat, and he did not like fat men, they repelled him, and the repulsion was unworthy, to be fought against. The blood, he thought, was his own demon, it was blood he poured over Daniel, not Daniel's blood in a visionary fountain. Daniel ate. He raised his spoon, the green soup went into the disgusting dark cave of his mouth, between the paling of thick ivory teeth, over the carpet of slimy tongue. Daniel broke bread, and turned with a smile to Jacqueline, saying how good warm brown bread was, putting a thick smear of golden fat butter on the bread, masticating, masticating. Joshua Ramsden put down his own spoon, leaving his soup untouched. The fountain of blood dried up abruptly. Daniel's shining surfaces became again dusty, drab, and matt. Ramsden drank a little water from a clay goblet made by Clemency Farrar. Lucy asked him if he was not hungry, and he said no, his needs were small, he had had enough.

The music played on. They played 'The Lord of the Dance', and they played 'The Holly and the Ivy', improvising, the clarinet playing the voice parts, the guitar running round and over and under, catching, losing, strumming. The two bodies moved together, gold heads nodding to each other, toes tapping, fingers leaping, stopping, rippling. Only Zag's mouth was smiling widely, ecstatically, and John's was tight round his reed. Two angels, said one Quaker lady to another. Oh the rising of the sun, and the running of the deer . . .

After the meal, they gathered to say good-bye to their guests, who had to reach the road in time for the last bus, as the winter evening closed in. Marcus managed to make his way to Ruth, who was helping to clear the table. Lucas Simmonds hovered behind him. Daniel tapped Lucas on the shoulder, and turned him, asking how he was, leading him firmly away.

'Hi, Ruthie.'

'It's good to see you here. It's good to see everyone here.'

'Are you happy?'

Her guileless eyes met his, her hands fluttered up and crossed on her breast like an angel in a painting.

'Isn't it obvious? Isn't this wonderful? To have a glimpse was something, but this is more than a glimpse, this is steady, and real . . .'

He put out a wavering hand, and touched her. She shrugged. He said

'I'm glad if you're happy.'

'Well *look* glad. Better, come back often. Best, join us. You only live once, I think. You have one chance.'

She was plumper than she had been, as a graceful girl. He felt nothing. He felt nothing. He felt the damp heat under Lucas Simmonds's bundling sweater and flannels, across half the room.

'Well, go safely,' said Ruth, turning away.

'We'll keep an eye on you,' said Marcus.

'Don't say that —' said Ruth. 'That sounds menacing. I'm happy. I'll pray for you.'

She turned away, with a load of dishes, and her plait swung behind her with its own life.

On the doorstep, Joshua Ramsden spoke to Daniel.

'You haven't felt the call to join the Hearers?'

'I haven't.'

262

'Those who know you better – the Canon, Gideon – they value you.'

'The Canon is much missed in the crypt. The calls don't diminish.'

'Like Mary, he has chosen the better part.'

'Well, Mr Ramsden, I'm a Martha, as you know. Of the earth, earthy.'

'The poor earth.'

'I go about in it,' said Daniel, and grinned. Will was standing, for once, next to him, his gaze fixed on Ramsden.

'Your son?' said Ramsden. 'You can see it, in his look –'

Daniel was afraid. The fear came from nowhere and was wild. He said

'We must be off. We've a bus to catch.'

The silver head nodded, dismissing them.

They climbed up again, to the road on the ridge. In the metal sky, white doves and pearly pigeons were flying back to Dun Vale Hall, to roost. As they walked, they scattered whole flocks of wandering half-wild hens, chirring anxiously, scurrying on yellow scaly legs. One or two plump overweight turkeys lumbered alongside, gobbling. In the distance, a sheep coughed, and a dog howled.

'You didn't like him,' said Will, addressing his father, as he rarely did.

'I don't say that. He means good. He means to be a good man.'

'You weren't respectful to him.'

'What do you mean, respectful?'

'He was trying to – to – be friendly to you. You pushed him off.'

'I didn't mean to. I think what's going on is dangerous.'

'*I* think it's exciting. New. Not boring.'

'Ah well, if your only criterion is not to be *boring* –'

'You never listen to what I say.'

'You never say anything.'

'Well, I was saying something. And you weren't listening.'

They went on up, amongst more creatures, some sheep, a young pig, a flock of black pullets, all making their way down.

XVII

In January Bowers & Eden published both *Flight North* and *Laminations*. *Flight North* received little attention. It was reviewed amiably in certain fantasy-science-fiction roundups, and amongst Books for Older Children – but most of the reviewing in this area had been before Christmas. *Laminations*, on the other hand, was widely reviewed. There were headings like 'Only Disconnect', 'A Scissors-and-Paste World', or 'I Ching for Intelligent Chicks'. There were also articles on Frederica, describing her as 'a new mini-personality', 'the fausse-naïve face through the Looking-Glass', or 'the Intelligent Woman's Guide to doing your own Writing in your Spare Time'. Both the reviewers who liked *Laminations* and those who didn't referred to it as 'clever'. The hostile ones added 'facile' and qualified clever – 'merely clever', 'irritatingly clever'. The friendly ones compared the cut-up technique to Burroughs and Jeff Nuttall, but said that the woman writer lacked the lunge for the jugular or the absolutely subversive intention of these models. They asked if the whole added up to more than the sum of its snipped-off torn-up parts and concluded that on the whole, it probably didn't, it was just very clever.

Frederica had her photograph taken for the *Evening Standard*, leaning on the railing by her basement, wearing high boots and a maxi-coat, with a Russian-style fur hat, faintly Anna Karenina. Hamelin Square residents peered out of windows, or crowded behind the photographer with bikes and footballs. Frederica was also photographed for *Nova* magazine, on the set of *Through the Looking-Glass*, in colour, her face reflected and refracted in the various mirrors, screens and transparent partitions of the set. She was wearing a tight-sleeved, tight-waisted bottle green dress in wool crêpe, with a very demure white collar. It was a good photograph, full of slivers of geometrical overlay, bones and edges, repeated wary eyes, ripples of red hair. 'These fragments I have shored against my ruin', began the article that went with the image. This line had haunted Frederica, who had rejected it as an epigraph to her book only because it was such a cliché, a line everyone quoted in every context. She had always had an image in her mind of a boat on a beach surrounded – like a kind of cubist painting – with a defensive wall or buttress of broken stones and pebbles and pieces of carved angels and ancient Greek winged victories or the breasts of Diana of Ephesus. She knew really there was no beach, no shore, no boat. Only the Prince d'Aquitaine in the abolished tower, temporarily shored up. With quotations.

She had not told her parents that she had written the book. She felt about her father as most of her generation felt about Dr Leavis, that anything she could conceivably produce must fall short of his high requirements. Her writing was clandestine notes, out of his gaze. She had not even thought of advancing a writing career as a reason for not moving to the North, because she did not think of herself as a writer, or of her writing as a career. She was not now either writing or planning anything other than more of the same, more laminations, more discontinuous jottings, and anyone, really, could do that. She felt a writerly distaste for her own product, now it was out in the open. Once she saw a student reading it on a bus, which pleased her – it was another cliché – but she never opened it herself. It had a nice enough cover, made of Escher-shapes, scissors where the gaps made Chad faces. She didn't even send Bill and Winifred one. If they had noticed its existence, they didn't mention it.

Most beginning writers intend to impress, placate or shock imaginary parents. Real ones are a different matter.

Large envelopes began to arrive from Freyasgarth. They were addressed not to Frederica, but to Leo. They contained reading exercises, carefully constructed with phonics, and vowels, and exercises on the ambiguous and the counter-intuitive, from Agatha Mond's *Flight North*. They were scenes Leo would know, and sentences he would have heard, but arranged by plan, readable by a halting reader. They contained instructions for Leo and Frederica. *This is to practise c, ck, s, qu. This is long vowels.* Mother and son sat down and read. Leo was obsessed. He had a day of spelling everything with ph. Phish, phunny, phood, elephant, pheasant, cornphlakes. Frederica laughed, and Leo laughed uproariously. Frederica showed him 'laugh'. He said '*It is too much.*' He laughed. He tried out lauph.

He said 'Thano says his mum says you make her laugh on the telly. Are you *meant* to be funny?'

He was worried.

'Well, witty anyway. Yes, funny, I think. People are meant to laugh.'

'That's OK then. She says you talk too fast.'

'Everyone talks too fast, on telly.'

Leo was reassured.

Through the Looking-Glass became a regular programme on the new BBC2. Wilkie tried to cast his net wide, and to choose topics that were neither predictable nor related to each other. During the first quarter of 1969, the programme included:

Benjamin Lodge, who had produced Alexander Wedderburn's plays, *Astraea* and *The Yellow Chair*, and who had a new Theatre of Cruelty-based production of *The Cenci*, opening at the Dolphin Theatre. He was talking, in the first flush of excitement, about the abolition of the Lord Chamberlain's powers of theatrical censorship. He discussed it with Jude Mason, author of the novel *Babbletower*, which had survived a trial for obscenity (on appeal), and was selling steadily. The subject for discussion was censorship, the historical person discussed was D.H. Lawrence. The *object* lay before Frederica in a round box tied with a crimson ribbon. When she produced it, it turned out to be an enormous, springing tangle of dark curly hair – whether real or fake was not clear, on the screen. Lodge and Jude discussed, wittily, the current musical *Hair*, the fashion for long hair amongst hippies and students, Kenneth Tynan's *Oh, Calcutta!* and the public display of pubic hair, and, more darkly, Sacher-Masoch and fur, fetishism and androgyny. Jude Mason, who had been made to cut his long, greasy, grey hair for the trial, had grown it again, and peered out fishily from amongst its locks, looking like a hobgoblin. Frederica's own hair was demurely held back under a – crimson – Alice band. The set was decorated with images of the Queen of Hearts crying 'Off with his head'.

The programme subsequently discussed sleep, undergrounds (playing knowing games with the Underground, the Tube, and the Lost Boys in Peter Pan, as well as Alice's Rabbit-hole), war heroes (opposing an articulate general and a bemedalled pop star). Who are the Germans? (with a Beuys lump of fat, a German film director and an American actor who played German generals in war films). Also *The Outsider*, with Colin Wilson and an articulate and dangerous-looking James Baldwin.

There was also an interesting programme on babies and infants, with a Natural Childbirth expert and a child psychologist, discussing Bowlby's theories of maternal bonding and the effect on his own generation of having been left to scream for regulated periods. The person discussed was William Blake – 'Sooner murder an infant in its cradle than nurse unacted desires' and 'Infant Joy'. The object was a rather sinister bone teething-ring, with a silver jester, dangling little bells, attached. Tenniel's version of Lewis Carroll's baby-into-pig careered from time to time across the screen. There was a good discussion of the shift in sensibility which led to the Flower Children and the valuing of the infant spontaneity which the Age of Reason had suppressed.

Wilkie suddenly had a wild idea for a programme on ball games, and spent some time trying to find articulate snooker, tennis, football, golf players, declaring that the rules and the geometrical and physical constraints of all the different games were fascinating. In the end he staged a splendid conversation between a physicist interested in dynamics and trajectories, and a syllabic poet who was also an Oxford don and a fiendish croquet player. The object was a mediaeval ball-and-cup game from a museum. Frederica had always despised sport, most especially team games. She suddenly had a brief vision of all kinds of human ingenuity to which she had paid no attention.

She could not bear to be caught out, asking an ignorant question, making a foolish observation. She learned to skim, to recognise pitfalls, to skip from essential to essential, to recognise the skeletons of ideas and activities she could neither articulate nor understand. She was training some kind of provisional, short-term or half-term memory. It was exciting, and not wholly satisfying.

She began to be recognised, in streets, in shops, picking up Leo and Saskia from school. Also at parties. People thought they knew her, when they did not, and thought they knew what she would say before she said it. She had always supposed that it would be exciting to have a face that flashed into public consciousness.

Charisma, the papers said, mini-charisma, in a mini-personality. She found, rather grimly, that being a personality thinned her sense of being a person. She had a face which was a mask, a film, a projection, something which stood between the people she met and her ability to listen to them, watch them, or speak directly to them, since they had this idea of her, from somewhere, to which they addressed their remarks. She dreamed, predictably perhaps, after the programme on the Virgin Queen, of Elizabeth's mask in old age, painted an inch thick, with the black eyes trapped behind it. She dreamed she was walking across Hamelin Square carrying this white mask on a pole in front of her. Behind the pasteboard the real woman (she was and was not inside her body; she was also a pitying, anxious watcher) was wearing a bra and an open shirt and nothing else at all. The street-children gathered and laughed at the thin naked buttocks and the cold toes.

Charisma in the extra-mural class was another matter. She went on lecturing to her disparate group of grown-ups, and what took fire, from time to time, were ideas. She lectured on Dostoevsky's *Idiot*. This phantasmagoric tale appears to have an ineluctable shape. It is one of the few novels where the end is as great and as satisfying as all that has gone before, leaves no sense of let-down, or half-measure, or thinness, or turning-away of imaginative intensity. Was this, Frederica asked the class, because of, or in spite of, the fact that Dostoevsky *did not know* from serial episode to serial episode, what would happen, or even if his characters were good or evil, innocent or guilty? His notes existed – the whole phantasmagoria was *in flux* for the whole length of the writing. Frederica felt complete, and passionate, and unselfconscious, considering this narrative miracle. It contained Western myth – the innocent sick Prince Myshkin was a figure of Christ, and his innocence, his goodwill, moved Frederica as the New Testament did not.

In the same way, teaching *The Great Gatsby*, she read out the scene in which the murderer comes through the yellowing trees to find Gatsby in the pool

> . . . *he must have felt that he had lost the old warm world, paid a high price for living too long with a single dream. He must have looked up at an unfamiliar sky through frightening leaves and*

shivered as he found what a grotesque thing a rose is and how raw
the sunlight was upon the scarcely created grass. A new world,
material without being real, where poor ghosts, breathing dreams like
air, drifted fortuitously about . . . like that ashen, fantastic figure
gliding toward him through the amorphous trees.

Frederica admired this passage, and had made tidy notes on it, as
the culmination of her lecture. Note, she had said, the implications for *American* literature, of the phrase about the 'new world',
'material without being real'. Note, she had written, that Gatsby
has created his whole world out of his Platonic idea of himself, his
romantic dream, and it is disintegrating.

But as she read it out, she caught the full force of the achieved
simplicity of every word in that perfectly created paragraph about
destruction, that perfectly, easily coherent paragraph about disintegration. She felt something she had always supposed was mythical,
the fine hairs on the back of her neck rising and pricking in a
primitive response to a civilised perfection, body recognising
mind.

She stopped in mid-sentence, and began again, urgently. Look,
she told them, I've just *really seen* how good this paragraph is.
Think about the adjectives, how simple they look, how right
every single one is, out of all the adjectives that could have been
chosen. Look at 'unfamiliar' and think about a man who had made
up his own heaven and earth, who *was* his own family. Look at
'frightening leaves' which are flatly bald and menacing, but lightly
so. 'What a grotesque thing a rose is.' The idea of intricate natural
perfection undone in one atmospheric and one psychological
adjective — which is also an ancient *aesthetic* adjective.

And then, 'raw' describing sunlight — where did he find that?
Raw is cold, not heated, raw is bare and open, raw is unripe and
with 'scarcely created' it suggests a virgin world either at the
shivering beginning or the end of time, when it doesn't hold
together. And from these sensuous adjectives — grotesque, raw —
we move to mental ones — new, material, not real — and the solid
creation disintegrates into phantasmagoria, fantasms, ghosts,
dreams — *like* air, not even really air, and then finally, the
wonderful rendering of shapelessness, the 'amorphous' trees.

And if you use the negative Greek word, amorphous, you carry
with it all the positive Greek words for shape, and form,

metamorphosis, morphology, Morpheus the God of Sleep. What Fitzgerald has done, quickly, briefly, and *clearly*, is to *undo* what art and literature have done over and over again, the image of the human mind at home in the beauty of the created garden, with the forms of trees and the colour of the sky and the grass, and the intricate natural beauty of the rose.

Frederica stared almost wildly at the class, which stared back at her, and then smiled, a common smile of pleasure and understanding. For the rest of her life, she came back and back to this moment, the change in the air, the pricking of the hairs, of *really reading* every word of something she had believed she 'knew'. And at that moment, she knew what she should do was teach, for what she understood – the thing she was both by accident and by inheritance constructed to understand – was the setting of words in order, to make worlds, to make ideas. Smiling at cameras was tawdry, compared to this real skill, which revealed things.

And yet, and yet. The Golgi-stained slide, the flashing movements of the snooker balls, the new-born child sliding out in its bloody caul, the killing of the countryside (her next *Looking-Glass* project) – these existed, outside the classroom, outside the book-covers. These were real. These were also real.

XVIII

The detailed planning of the Body and Mind Conference was on
the agenda of the General Purposes Committee of the UNY
which met at the beginning of the Spring Term. The Committee
included the Vice-Chancellor, Hodgkiss the Dean of Students,
various Heads of Department from all the faculties, and two
student representatives, Nicholas Tewfell, the President of the
Students' Union, and Maggie Cringle. The activities of the Anti-
University were also on the agenda.

The Meeting was in the Council Room, which was at the top
of the octagonal Administration Tower, and contained an
octagonal table covered in blood-red leather, a number of throne-
like chairs, and some lonely-looking Chinese vases on octagonal
pedestals. Vincent Hodgkiss chaired the meeting. Over coffee,
before they began, he said quietly to Wijnnobel 'I've got a rather
disturbing letter here from Hodder Pinsky. I think you should see
it, but I think it would be inadvisable to discuss it on this
occasion.'

'He is still planning to come?'

'Oh, I think so. I think so. He has a moral problem. I think you
should cast your eye over this.'

Nick Tewfell, who was within earshot, and talking to no one,
overheard this remark. He had come with concerns of his own –
of those he represented – about Pinsky. It had been suggested to
him by Jonty Surtees, who had it authoritatively through several
international student sources, that Hodder Pinsky's work on
thought processes, memory and memory loss was secretly funded
by the CIA and had possible applications in techniques of
interrogation and brainwashing.

'Table a question, do it lightly, see what they say, don't make
an issue of principle out of it just yet,' said Surtees. 'We don't

know yet whether we want to protest his coming at all, or let hell loose when he does. If he does. Find out. Worry them a bit.'

Nick Tewfell did not like the way in which Jonty Surtees spoke to him. Surtees threw back his great red mane, and laughed, and issued orders, like a leader of men, like an aristocrat, Tewfell thought sharply, an anarchist with the carelessness of the 'well-bred'. At the same time, he saw that Surtees had the quality he admired above all others, the capacity to get things done. The sprawling caravanserai of the Anti-University was something that was clearly working, if by working you meant swelling and spreading and attracting students and always having some new Happening from fireworks to group sex, from three-hour lectures on Kropotkin to psychological experiments in sense-deprivation or sense-overwhelming, buckets of sewage and buckets of hyacinths, strobe lights and pinhole shadows, touchy-feely crawls through damp fleshy tunnels with occasional pinpricks.

Nick Tewfell was the son of artisans and socialists. His father worked in a power station, his mother took in dress alterations. He believed in a world where there should be no social distinctions, where everyone would live in more or less the same size of house with the same reasonable garden, and be educated with their next-door neighbours as a matter of course. He believed in unionism and had lost any real hope for anything from the Soviet Union after the tanks rolled into Prague. He had what would loosely have been described as an '*instinctive*' dislike for the exaggerated Oxford bleat of voices like that of Vincent Hodgkiss, and this bristling reaction of his was to have its effect on the events to come.

His belief in getting things done had led to the great library sit-in at NYU. The library was still in the process of construction. Some rare books were held in the original library at Long Royston, an elegant place to which access was restricted. The new library was in the Ziggurat Tower, with underground storage and, at that time, a smallish reading-room area with a limited number of tables and chairs. Librarians do not like readers, and the library had (as Sir Gerard Wijnnobel ruefully acknowledged) been designed on the recommendations of librarians. Deputations of students went repeatedly to tell the Vice-Chancellor that there were not enough chairs, or tables, and for that matter – since the University was a new foundation on a remote site not near any major city library – not enough books. Books would come, in due course, the authorities said. A student had not time to wait for books to come in due course, Tewfell said. He himself was so busy with Union matters that he rarely sat down with a book, but he meant to, and those he represented did. In the days before the Anti-University, Tewfell organised a sit-in in the library Tower when every available stair and patch of floor space was occupied. They sat for ten days. They were peaceful and clean. The University then found it possible to buy up various libraries at sales, to replan the issue-desk and cataloguing areas, and to double the reading-space for readers. Both Wijnnobel and Tewfell learned from this episode. Wijnnobel learned that Tewfell was reasonable and determined. Tewfell learned that it was no good talking, you had to act. He was pleased, but wary, when the students were put on committees. That was talking. He needed to see where it led to. Then action might be necessary.

It was also true, and this was also part of subsequent events, that group feelings are infectious and change thoughts. Nick Tewfell was middle-of-the-road English Left, canny, suspicious, pragmatic. But the drum-beat rhetoric of the Anti-University, the idea that Revolution might be possible, might be possible *now*, this year, this month, the idea that all authority was bad (was evil, Jonty Surtees said) and must be brought down, that teaching itself was an inordinate exercise of power by one human being over equally valuable, equally endowed others, stirred in his blood. At that time, most of the young felt guilty over most compromises. And Nick felt that the grudging, sparring respect he felt for the Vice-Chancellor was a compromise, and suspect. He was glad he hated Hodgkiss's bleat. He was very interested in what was in Hodgkiss's letter from Pinsky which Hodgkiss did not propose to share with the Committee.

Arrangements for the conference, Hodgkiss said, were advancing in an encouraging way. He asked the Vice-Chancellor to speak to the list of proposed papers and speakers, both those now definite and those still provisional. A xeroxed sheet was distributed.

Body and Mind

Hodder Pinsky, University of California at La Jolla.	Forms of thought. Gestalt, schemata, how does the brain organise the mind?
Theobald Eichenbaum, Grünewald Research Centre.	Instinct and learning, in wild and domesticated animals
Lyon Bowman.	The neurochemistry of memory
Jacob Scrope.	Can machines think?
Luk Lysgaard-Peacock.	Sex and slugs: the biological disadvantage of sexual reproduction
Christopher Cobb (director of the UNY Research Institute in Animal Behaviour).	Learning to sing: variations in behaviour in orphaned and family songbirds
Griselda Bragge (Professor of Music from Lincoln).	How 'natural' are musical intervals?
Edmund Wilkie.	Vermeer and Picasso: the representation of the act of perception
Canon Adelbert Holly.	Changing interpretations of the Incarnation
Professor Sir Brendan Cleaver, FRCS.	Animal or vegetable: consciousness in the 'persistent vegetative state'
Vincent Hodgkiss.	What is philosophy? Wittgenstein, maths and language-games
Sir Gerard Wijnnobel.	Deep structure and surface fluency. Ideas of a universal language?

There was general approval of the list – Tewfell kept quiet about his doubts about Pinsky – and discussion ranged on, as it must, to what was missing. The Professor of English Literature, Colin Rennie, pointed out that literature was conspicuously absent from the idea of human nature presented in the list. Vincent Hodgkiss said he had just heard from the distinguished scholar, Dr Raphael Faber, who was prepared to speak on Proust and memory, biological and cultural. Colin Rennie said that was good news, but he felt that English literature should not be absent. D.H. Lawrence, said Lyon Bowman, was always going on about blood and semen. Was there something there? Nick Tewfell could never tell, from Bowman's engaging, fleshly smile, how far he was trouble-making, and how far he was serious. Colin Rennie said there was a distinguished Lawrence expert in Edinburgh who had written, precisely, on Lawrence and blood-consciousness. It was agreed that this person should be approached. Bowman made a light remark about fascism, and dangerous theories of superior and inferior bloods. Hodgkiss asked quickly what other areas were not covered. The only woman present, Minna Lascelles, Reader in Anthropology, said you could hardly hold such a conference without including an anthropologist. She proposed herself – she would like to speak on body-ornament and body-language in different cultures. Including decorative mutilation and modern hairstyles, she said. She added that there should also surely be psychologists, not to speak of psychoanalysts. Someone should speak on Piaget's ideas about child-development. Wijnnobel said there had been an excellent man on the Steerforth Inquiry into language-teaching, whom he would approach.

'And psychoanalysis?' said Bowman. 'Very *à la mode*. Why don't you get Elvet Gander? He draws audiences. Like a snake-charmer.'

Hodgkiss said, with a trace of discomfort, that Gander had indeed been approached, and had offered what sounded a stimulating paper on 'The fairground mirror: Schizophrenics' perception of their own body-parts'. But he was now spending much of his time with 'those encamped around us' lecturing on expanded consciousness. Hodgkiss's voice was a little more fluting than usual. Nick Tewfell said he didn't see that that mattered. Lots of people were giving interesting talks in the Anti-University. Encouraged by the crisp sound of his own voice, he added that history and politics were conspicuously absent. He proposed that someone should give a paper on the history of the factory-metaphors for human beings – 'hands, heads, mouths to feed'. Wijnnobel raised his head and smiled at Tewfell. That, he said, was an excellent idea. Would Mr Tewfell even consider speaking himself – as a university representative. Nick said hurriedly that he wouldn't have time, he wasn't ready, he had his work and his degree, his exams. His own voice suddenly annoyed him. He stopped, redly. Bowman said

'And thinking of the Anti-University which surrounds us and interpenetrates us, should we not have a talk on astral and etheric bodies, to complete our sphere –'

There was a rustle, a tension. Nick Tewfell was really annoyed by his own incapacity to work out where Bowman was coming from. Bowman smiled a small smile to himself. Wijnnobel said

'As many of you may know, my wife is putting a great deal of energy to talking on just those topics to – to the alternative audiences. Everyone has a right to their own beliefs, and to free speech. I'm afraid I cannot bring myself to think that a talk on those topics will enhance our conference.' He frowned a little. 'Everything has its interest, of course –'

Hodgkiss watched the Vice-Chancellor silently thinking out, with frightening justice, ways in which lectures on astral and etheric bodies might indeed be of interest to the assembled academics. It could be done. One of the reasons for his great respect for the Vice-Chancellor was the judicious way in which Wijnnobel found everything interesting. He himself had a clear vision of Lady Wijnnobel in her black and purple velvet cloak, radiantly surveying the assembled grandees.

'I think the consensus is, that it is outside our purview –' he said. 'It looks very good as it is. Let us agree to leave it there and adjourn for coffee.'

The coffee-room was one floor lower than the Council Room. Everyone trooped into the lift. Nick Tewfell lingered. Hodgkiss had left his papers on the table. He wondered if he could risk looking at the 'rather disturbing' letter from Hodder Pinsky. He listened for the end of the lift machinery whirr, and then flicked rapidly through Hodgkiss's papers. He was partly impelled by his failure to ask the difficult question recommended by Jonty Surtees.

Dear Vincent,

I am happy, as I have said, to speak at what promises to be a rich and exciting conference. There is however, a problem, to which, after much deliberation, I think I should draw your attention. It concerns Theobald Eichenbaum. I do not know whether or not you are aware that, like other scholars who retained their posts in Germany and Austria during the last war, he has been accused of having what is referred to as a 'brown past'. This has not been much discussed, in his particular case, but there is evidence waiting to explode, in my opinion. I enclose a paper he wrote in 1940 on herd mentality and innate slavishness, and the desirability of breeding improved individuals, which I personally find distasteful because of its uncritical social-darwinism and eugenicist near-fervour. As you will see – it was published only in German, and only in periodical form – the vocabulary echoes from time to time certain terms of exhortation and approbation which form part of the National Socialists' detestable vocabulary. It could be argued very plausibly that it was designed to obtain favors. It is certain that Eichenbaum's work was uninterrupted by the Party, whereas Tinbergen, for instance, was incarcerated in a Dutch concentration camp for protesting the dismissal of Jewish professors.

I am not saying that I refuse to appear on a platform with this man, whom I have never met. He has done good work, and has never been asked to speak in his own defense. I am also not saying – *cave canem* – that I shall not confront him with his own words, if that seems necessary.

What I am mostly concerned with is the volatile student reaction to many kinds of speaker at the present time. In my country, they believe it right to deny a hearing to right-wing politicians, believers in differences in inherited intelligence, military historians, and others. I hear that your own students are becoming more vociferous and more active. I believe first of all in free speech. They often do not. I think you should read Eichenbaum's paper, and reflect on all these things. It would be most improper for me to pre-empt any decision you might then make.

Cordially,
Hodder

Nick Tewfell did not read German. He looked at the photocopied pages of Eichenbaum's *Helder und Herde*. He had the idea of stealing the whole document, or attempting to descend in the lift and find a xerox machine. This seemed too dangerous. He took out his diary and copied out the German title, the name and date of the periodical, read the letter twice again, noted the phrase 'National Socialists' detestable vocabulary' and went down to coffee, which was almost over.

After coffee, the Vice-Chancellor said that he felt that real progress had been made. The Conference would show the new University to be what it had been designed to be – a paradigm, a web, a microcosm of interconnecting studies and ideas. Hodgkiss, looking at Wijnnobel with exasperated affection, knew what he was imagining. New intricate relations between the flow of the blood, the history of the genes, theological certainties and uncertainties, languages of men and beasts, flesh, bone, brain, thought and feeling. Wijnnobel was a polymath who had a very unusual recall of detail in very many contexts simultaneously. This passion for detail extended to the planning of the university community. He was interested in the design of chairs and walkways, and the meanings of those for the life of his small world. He was interested in microscopes and telescopes, computers and aesthetic theories. He was, Hodgkiss often thought, an innocent idealist who did not understand that the brute powers that really controlled the universe were not interested in – were alarmed by – his sphere of knowledge and understanding. He was not as aware as most Vice-Chancellors would have been that most of his colleagues saw the Conference in terms of the advancement or the overlooking of their own areas of expertise and political power. He noticed these things when they were brought to his attention.

Nick Tewfell said he thought he should say there was considerable unrest amongst the student body about the stresses placed on them by the four-year multi-subject course. They did not enjoy – many of them – being required to do maths and a language. It was hard on them.

Hodgkiss said that he was always ready to discuss this with them.

The Anti-University was discussed. It was growing. There were two fields now of caravans and tents. There was a lot of persistent noise – music, drumming. The NYU students were sampling classes on sex and astrology and anarchy, despite not having time to learn maths and languages.

'They are not breaking the law,' said Wijnnobel.

'Technically, they are,' said Hodgkiss. 'The original cottages they set up in are on land belonging to the University. I don't know where we stand as far as all the bill-sticking and paint goes.'

'You ought to know,' said Lyon Bowman.

Hodgkiss wanted to say that provoking universities into calling in the police was a recognised aggressive tactic. He then decided not to. It was probably up to him, as Dean, to have been more vigilant about things, both on the University land and on the adjacent farmland, which might be thought of as nuisances, or health hazards, which might spontaneously, without any action from the University, attract the interest of the police. He said 'I should probably pay them a courtesy visit.'

'That,' said Bowman, 'might be acknowledging that they have squatters' rights. Depending on what you say.'

'They probably do have squatters' rights,' said Tewfell.

'They think they do, do they?' said Bowman.

Tewfell didn't answer. Bowman asked what the adjacent landowner thought.

'The land belongs to a Mr and Mrs Gunner Nighby,' said Hodgkiss. 'Mr Nighby has left the country after some problems with the law. Mrs Nighby was, until recently, in hospital. She is now in a therapeutic community in her own house – Dun Vale Hall. Various letters have been written to her about the use of the land, but no replies have been received, that I know of. The land was never in use, although sheep did graze from time to time, both from her farm and from others.'

'I think watchfulness is all that is called for,' said Wijnnobel. 'At present.'

'If we bore them enough with inaction,' said Hodgkiss, with a pursed smile, 'they may strike camp and move on.'

Tewfell, who had been staring baffled at Wijnnobel, felt restored to healthy animosity by the high little laugh with which Hodgkiss accompanied this observation.

Striking camp was by now an accurate metaphor for any potential dismantling of the anti-institution. Someone had procured – whether by theft or by loan was not quite clear – two large marquees, of the kind normally on hire for wedding receptions or flower shows. One of these had been painted blood-red, and hung with streaming banners of hammers, sickles and little brass bells. It had a placard at the door saying Mao-Marx Marquee. There was a poster with a picture of Che Guevara. Inside the space had been divided into one large speaking area ('Bring your own chair, stool, cushion, carpet etc.') and several small spaces for discussion groups. The other had been painted in gaudy psychedelic jungle and hothouse floral patterns, pink, mauve, lime, banana, sky blue, orange. Over the door hung a board painted lovingly by Deborah Ritter, announcing that this was 'The Teach-Inn of Cosmic Empathetic Wisdom'. This work of art (decorated though it was with lotus-flowers and huge blankly calm eyes), was covered with graffiti denying the meaning of these words all and severally.

Noteachcan'tbetaught. WisdomisNothing. Cosmosisgrainsofsand. And oddly 'Empathyisinvasion'.

Inside the Teach-Inn, there were moveable canvas walls and painted paper screens. There was a space covered with mattresses, velvet cushions and Indian bedspreads, there was a circular dais for musicians and a pile of cushions for listeners, there were spaces resembling fairground booths which offered information on biotic diet and brown rice, a disc exchange and a henna expert who coloured hands, hair, and other body-parts. Everywhere was lit by floating candles in bowls and buckets, by dangling lamps with red glass and brass. Both tents were heated with rickety paraffin stoves, and smelled of paraffin and incense, curry and an underlying taint of sewage (a smell which was indeed everywhere on the anti-campus).

Lectures were advertised daily on notice-boards posted at the doors of the marquees and the door of the cottage occupied by the Core People (they did not want to use the word Administration and half of them disliked the word Committee). Lectures that were advertised did not happen, at least as often as they did happen, and they could last anything from a minute − 'If you think I think I can tell you anything useful you can think again −' to lectures that went on for four or five hours, to audiences varying from sixty to two or three.

Often also − it was winter, and raining or snowing − the schedules of gatherings were washed into trickles of weeping ink, or blown into trees and bushes (from which nobody thought they need be collected). The trees and bushes were also hung with shreds and streamers of ripped and rippling plastic, moving like perched ghosts or faded knightly pennants. Some of the more mystical Anti-Universitarians thought these bleaching strips resembled Tibetan prayer-rags. Others thought they were not nice and represented the last vestige of capitalist conspicuous waste. No one fetched a ladder to take them down.

Tewfell and Maggie Cringle picked their way through rain, across sucking mud, between the big and little tents, benders and scout tents, wooden huts and bits of sacking. Maggie Cringle was wearing a strawberry-coloured mini-skirt, a tight blue jumper with silver and puce stars sewn on to it and a transparent hooded raincoat, also mini, that skimmed her strawberry buttocks, above an expanse of plum-dark, violet-blue, goose-pimpled fleshy thighs, above a jaunty and very muddy pair of tight white plastic boots. Under the hood her hair was a mass of Medusa-coils. Tewfell, walking behind her, thought, in words, 'Mini-skirts only work on thin women.' Maggie Cringle, a second-year student reading English, had been elected because the Vice-Chancellor had said that two student reps would be better than one – for the students – they could feel freer to speak and would have someone to discuss projects and debates with. Tewfell found Cringle's presence largely hampering. He was more worried about her judging him than whether she supported him. She never said anything, ever, in the university committees, but sat picking at bits of her body and crossing and uncrossing her legs. Her face was heavily made up, with careful eyeliner and dark brownish blusher. Underneath there was a small, nicely symmetrical face with intelligent grey eyes, which he had never really seen, because of the fake eyelashes and the descending hair. But he had noticed that she could not stop looking at Jonty Surtees. She turned into 'one of those pointing dogs' he said to himself, when they entered the Cottages.

Outside the cottage, a hand-written schedule promised

'Mao-Tse-Tung-thought – the astonishing genius, philosopher and general poet and statesman'
'Correct theory is fact because it is correct theory.'
'Ongoing analysis of bourgeois ideology. Criticism of British philosophy and economics.'
'And I saw a new heaven and a new earth. Where shall the young, disgusted with their parents' materialism and narrowminded-ness, look for reality? We can change minds – literally. And minds change matter. They do. Come and hear.'
'The signs of the Zodiac and their esoteric natures.
This week we shall speak of SCORPIO.
Private consultations also given on Tarot,
Clairvoyance and avoiding malign influences.'

Maggie Cringle was intrigued by this last. She stopped to read it, and Tewfell stopped to wait for her. She said she might look in on the talk on Scorpio. 'I am a Scorpio,' she said. Tewfell said non-committally that it might be interesting. He was curious about Eva Wijnnobel.

The atmosphere inside the Griffin Street Cottages was at once heady with loose energy, and soporific with smoke of various kinds, lounging bodies, and streams of speech. There were heaps of paper everywhere now, yellow and purple, posters and pamphlets, typescript and hand-written documents. There was a scattering of enamelled Polish dishes, scarlet and ink-blue, full of half-eaten curry and fruit-skins, amongst the papers. There were two paraffin stoves, a sullen fire in the grate, which belched smoke as Nick and Maggie came in, and a mixture of fug and icy draughts of air. A typewriter clicked; it was Greg Tod, writing an article on the hidden ideology of British historical writings. A ladle clattered. It was Deborah Ritter making soup in a preserving pan. The soup had a strong, pleasant scent of apricots and cumin. Tod wore a tartan blanket like a cloak, and a crimson knitted hat. Waltraut Ross was arguing with Jonty Surtees. Phrases purred through the air like sexual provocations, which perhaps they were. Greg Tod looked up uneasily from time to time and clacked louder. 'A culture whose dogmata presume that self-organisation has to be hateful and derogatory', 'The hypostasisation of a static concept of freedom defined as freedom from neurosis', '*Curing* the individual means accepting rebellion or martyrdom . . .', 'false consciousness', 'illusory centre of self' . . .

'Ah, Tewfell,' said Jonty Surtees, stopping Deborah in mid-sentence. 'Come to report?'

Nick Tewfell's hackles wriggled. He knew very well that Surtees regarded him as his delegated and manipulated organiser within the target institution; he had read the handbooks for revolutionaries; the idea was to keep him happy by showing a specious interest in his own immediate aims (getting rid of maths and language, relaxing exams, improving the library) so that he would be led to help with a far more radical overturning of order. Surtees saw him as a minion reporting to a general. That was OK, as long as he himself knew he was not. Two could use people for their own ends. The presence of the antis could (couldn't it?) help liberate students from hampering regulations and structures?

That wasn't why he was here, he knew. It was the whiff of the possibility of unimaginable violent change, that drew him like a magnet crackling with power. He didn't know *what* might happen. He didn't want to back off. He sat down without being asked and offered Surtees his delicious information. Pinsky thought Eichenbaum was a Nazi. He had the references to the offending article. He recited what he could remember of Pinsky's letter. 'The vocabulary echoes the National Socialists' detestable vocabulary', 'The desirability of breeding improved individuals', 'social-darwinism', 'eugenicist'.

'That's disgusting,' said Waltraut Ross. 'He has to be stopped.'

'We don't want Pinsky, either. He's CIA-funded.'

'We don't know that,' said Greg.

'That's worse,' said Waltraut. 'If it isn't open, if it's covert, that's even worse.'

Deborah Ritter laid aside her ladle and joined them.

'We should organise a march.'

'I support that,' said Nick Tewfell.

'Wait a little, wait a little,' said Jonty Surtees. 'The time is not ripe.' He turned to Nick Tewfell. 'You must get a copy of the whole Eichenbaum article, and a translation.'

'Get it yourselves. You have contacts in Germany. I'm just a student with an inadequate library. We don't have old German periodicals.'

'Microfilm,' said Surtees, his eyes glinting with argumentative pleasure.

'OK. I order microfilm. *If* I can. And they see we are interested. Very clever.'

'He's right,' said Greg Tod. 'Ask the Germans.'

'Then we can march,' said Waltraut.

'Wait a little, wait a little. Let them come, and then confront them. Lie low, and when they are here, throw everything at them. Stick to *constant criticism* as Che said, and then, when the enemy is assembled, move to de-stabilise. De-sanctify the institutions. Expose the kind of corrupt power-structure they are. Make Sir G's Round Table into a Witches' Sabbath.'

'With what ultimate aim?' Nick Tewfell asked.

Surtees smiled. He had the most pleasured, the most animated smile Tewfell had ever seen.

'Anarchy, initially. Followed by a free restructuring. A new Heaven and a new Earth, so to speak.'

Maggie Cringle smiled in response to his smile. Tewfell drew himself together. He said tightly that his own aims were not as extensive as that. He really didn't want to countenance people like

Pinsky and Eichenbaum, who supported, or were supported by, evil entities.

'Evil, you say,' said Jonty Surtees. 'You say evil, you don't say incorrect. Evil is out of my vocabulary. Recognising Evil leads to trying to establish a new Heaven and a new Earth, when the things of this world have been burned away.' ·

Tewfell realised, with an edge of distaste, that Surtees was off on some trip, had expanded his consciousness chemically in one way or another. Tewfell himself was a cautious man. He liked control too much to experiment. And yet, and yet, the thread of sulphurous smoke, the crackle of hidden flames, attracted him. *What if* you didn't compromise, *what if* you broke up the whole rotten structure, *what if* you pulled down the self-important mighty? He thought of what eugenicists had done in Auschwitz; he thought of what the CIA was doing in Vietnam; he thought of the crowding police horses in Grosvenor Square, where he had not been.

'We can't let them come,' said Greg Tod. 'We have to take a stand.'

'We *must* let them come,' said Surtees. 'We must be quiet, and secret, and plan our campaign, and blow all this apart when it happens, we must get the police to descend in force, and the Press to expose both of these men – these bad men – and with them the complicity of the Establishment . . .'

Nick Tewfell said that the television would be there, as the whole conference was to be filmed by Edmund Wilkie.

'We could hijack the film crew,' said Deborah Ritter. 'Tell the world how it is.'

A smell of burning molasses was adding itself to the apricot smell. She went back to her cooking. Surtees grinned mightily at Nick Tewfell.

'This is a great day,' he said. 'Well spotted, well spied, Nick Tewfell. Keep your beady eye on developments. Keep us posted in our encampment. Will you stop for soup?'

Nick was feeling suffocated, and it was no meal time he recognised. He said no, he must leave, and took Maggie Cringle with him.

Maggie said she just wanted to bob in to the Talk-Inn and see if there was any astrology going on. Astrology was so fascinating.

'Astrology is nonsense,' said Nick Tewfell.

'No more than most things,' said Maggie. 'And it's old, and it seems to work, and it's *fascinating* –'

Nick reflected that it might be expedient to see Lady W. in action. She was, she must be, the weak spot in the Vice-Chancellor's armour. It might prove very useful to know what she was up to.

The astrological booth in the Teach-Inn was full of a gloomy hay-coloured light from the canvas roof, spotted by patches of crimson light from two ornamental silver lamps with glass shades which had been arranged provisionally on cast-iron tripods. To the left of the space was a small cast-iron table with Egyptian-looking legs in the form of sharp-breasted sphinxes, painted gilt. On it were terrestrial and celestial globes, an astrolabe, a few peacock feathers in a silvery vase, and some small Egyptian-looking figurines of cats, scarabs, coiled snakes, ankhs, winged messengers, and a hippopotamus. The hippopotamus was painted with an overall design of flowers and leaves, on a bright blue-green ground. There were also various leather-bound books, and some dusty papers. The speaker herself stood behind a brass lectern in the form of an eagle with spread wings. The stem of the lectern was a scaly dragon, whose claw-feet clutched a sphere which was the counterweight to the eagle. The dragon appeared to have no head and the whole impressive object appeared to have been cobbled together from at least two sources. Behind the speaker, flapping on the canvas wall of the tent, was a map of the heavens with the signs of the Zodiac picked out in gold on black, the sidling Crab, the twisting Fish, the majestic Ram, the stolid Bull, the Twins in each other's arms, two-in-one. It was home-made, but not unimpressive. From the lectern dangled a lively home-made Scorpion in black cardboard, gilt paint, and crimson bead-work, its tail poised to strike, its claws open. On each side of the speaker crouched the fat border collies, Odin and Frigg, their noses on their paws, their tails in the dust, their eyes bored somnolent slits. There was a water-dish with DOG in black on gold under the table. The dog-smell mingled with the incense-smell from various candles and incense sticks in glass pots around the space.

The talk on Scorpio had already begun when Nick Tewfell and Maggie Cringle arrived. The audience was small but rapt – several young women with flowing hair and mystic head-bands, some long-haired men in Indian shirts, two with strings of bells round their necks, and some indefinable people in overcoats, hunched against the outside weather, though the tent was full of currents of hot, doggy, incense-laden air cycled by the paraffin stoves behind the speaker. Some of the audience were sitting on oriental kilim cushions and rugs. Near the entrance to the booth, on a campstool he had brought himself, sat Avram Snitkin, the ethnomethodologist, a heap of curly pelt, his own long, uncombed hair flowing into his beard and the unkempt fleece of his Afghan jacket and his fleece-lined felted boots. He was taking notes – to distract attention from the whirr of the recording-machine concealed in his bulky garments. His lips were spread in a perpetual benign smile. He was engaged on one of his many projects – a study of the definition of 'charisma' by those who considered themselves 'charismatic' and also by those who received, or responded to, or were exposed to, or created, the charisma (if it existed, which was still unproven).

Eva Wijnnobel at least had presence. She wore long, black, voluminous robes, under a black and purple velvet cloak with a huge, Hollywoodish hood. Her very straight black hair was cut with an Egyptian fringe and shone with oils, either natural or applied. Her lips were sculpted with blood-dark lipstick, and her large, black-brown eyes stared from under gilded lids and thick black brows and lashes. Her skin was uniformly whitish, and a little dead-looking. She had a heavily-sculpted gilded breast-plate hanging from gold chains about her neck, dangling tiny bells and charms from its periphery. When she saw Maggie Cringle and Nick Tewfell hesitating in the mouth of the booth, she lifted her arms like a bat, or a great bird, and made a circling movement to draw them in.

'The most terrible, the least attractive, perhaps the most potent and poetic of all the Signs . . .

'Welcome, welcome to our midst, please take a cushion. We are discussing a difficult subject, the Sign of Scorpio, which is of all the signs the one a man or a woman would – you might think – least choose to be born under, if we had free-will, which *of course we have not.*

'The Scorpion is a dry, terrible creature, a creature with a scaly, exogenous skeleton, which hides under stones and inhabits deserts, and bears at its tail-tip a terrible secret sting. The time of year allotted to the dominance of this creature by ancient wisdom is the time of the autumnal withdrawal of the sun from the earth, the time of decomposition and disintegration, of analysis not synthesis, of the reduction of living cells to dead excretory products.

'The sign of Scorpio is a Water sign, but it represents not the flowing Spring waters of Pisces, the rising tides, the source of life, nor yet the sun-kissed ocean of Cancer, full of mid-year light, but the dark depths, where the light scarcely penetrates, and matter decays and becomes mud and silt. Scorpions avoid light – they are creatures of darkness. Because of this association with the Dark Forces, the Scorpion has always been viewed as a special entry-point for the forces of evil in the cosmos. It paralyses its prey with liquid poison, it flees the harmony of the creatures and tries to hold what it has greedily to itself. The Scorpio character in human beings is capable of great malice and pleasure-in-suffering. This is so, it has been noted again and again. You may think, we should ask, how may those who are born under this dark Sign mitigate the dangers and restrictions of their destiny?

'I will tell you. For I too was born under Scorpio and suffered for many years from the sense that my path was dark and my ways low and close to the dust. But there are esoteric doctrines which give a different aspect of the Sign. Not completely different, but they change the way this semi-divine Insect plays its part in our personality and our life-pattern.

'Madame Blavatsky, in her Secret Doctrine, describes an ancient time in which *it is said* that ten signs only were known to the Ancients. This was true of the Profane only. The initiates always knew of twelve. For from the time long ago, when mankind was first separated into two sexes, the sign of Scorpio was separated into two, the Scorpion and the Virgin, which are, in the secret doctrine, ineluctably linked, the dark and light images of each other. You will say that this bifurcation still makes only eleven signs. But there is another, wholly secret sign, which represented for the Profane by a sign added by the latecome Greeks, Libra, the Scales, the only man-made, unliving thing in the Zodiac. I shall not tell you the secret name. I shall say, however, that there is hope for us dark Scorpios in our twinning with the pure light of the Virgin. We are bound as Yin and Yang are bound, and the one gives constant rise to the other.

'In ancient Egypt there was a great ruler named Selek, the Scorpion, and the female form, Selket, is the name of the patron goddess of the white witches, the healing sorcerers, in that civilisation. It is no accident that I myself was born in Egypt under the family name of Selkett. I was twice chosen by the Scorpion goddess. We Scorpions are the interpreters – our sign is the one most closely linked to mysticism, intuition and the occult – the domain of powerful female intelligences. It is true that Scorpio has also always been linked to the destructive aspects of male sexuality. The shape of the creature, the venomous liquid projected from its tail, are sufficient reminder of this. But in mythology it may often represent destructiveness subordinated to female wisdom and power.

'The virgin goddess Artemis sent a Scorpion to kill the hunter Orion who invaded her secret and inviolate Grove. Then she turned them into constellations, and the Scorpion forever pursues the Hunter across the heavenly plains. The goddess Isis had seven scorpions for companions when she fled from Set the destroyer, after he had slaughtered and dismembered Osiris . . . St John the Divine refers to dangerous sects as scorpions, but he failed to understand the esoteric significances . . .'

Nick Tewfell was distracted by wondering if he should tell the Vice-Chancellor's wife that a scorpion was not an insect, but an arachnid. He suggested *sotto voce* to Maggie Cringle that they should go home. Maggie demurred. She said she wanted a horoscope. So they waited until the end of the discourse, when the lady walked over and sat behind her table. There was a certain reluctance in the audience either to approach her or to leave the space. Maggie went up to the desk. She asked for a horoscope. Lady Wijnnobel said she must come back privately for that – she would need to take down many many details of precise dates and even hours. 'You, of course, are a Pisces,' she told her, with an attacking certainty.

'I am –' said Maggie. 'How did you know?'

'A fluid, labile quality in your bearing. A spring-of-the-year hopefulness in your outlook. A softness. A responsiveness. Your transparent garment is a natural choice for a Pisces.'

'And me?' said Nick. He was irritated by now, he wanted to get out of the odours and closeness. 'What am I?'

'You ask brusquely, you look keenly. You are a Sagittarian.'

'Wrong,' said Nick. 'I'm like you, I'm a Scorpio.'

'I do not think I can be wrong. What is your birth date?'

'November 23rd. Scorpio.'

'On the contrary. By a hairline, a Sagittarian. Strongly *under the influence* of Scorpio of course, since you are on the cusp. Your horoscope should hold great interest. You have the lumbering animal nature of a horse, docile and amenable, and you have the head and hands of a hunter-warrior, which strike a dreadful dart – the more dreadful, the more furtive, from its contiguity with Scorpio, and Scorpio's subtler sting. A dangerous combination, animal passion and human ingenious *aims*, I think you know already.'

Nick had always pictured his reluctant followers in the Students' Union as the cartoonist Lowe's Trades Union horse, heavy and difficult to manoeuvre. He smiled wryly. He said 'Will I succeed in my aims?'

'I am not a *fortune teller*. And I do not know – because I think you do not know – what your aims are. When you do, you will be formidable. I read characters. I do not foretell events.' There was a kind of portentous flirtatiousness on the heavy pale face. Nick thought, she has seen me visiting the Vice-Chancellor, she is playing with me. He felt suddenly threatened.

'Good-bye, then,' said Lady Wijnnobel, before he had moved more than a mouth-muscle.

A little whirr recorded the end of Avram Snitkin's tape. He coughed mildly to cover it. Nick retreated, taking Maggie with him.

XIX

Like the student leader, the Dean of Students felt a need, moral and political, to observe what was going on in the anti-institution. For quite different reasons, most of them to do with his loyalty to, and affection for, Gerard Wijnnobel, he knew he should keep an eye on what Eva Wijnnobel was doing and promulgating. He knew that he himself was inadequate to the tasks of infiltration or confrontation. His instincts were profoundly liberal and *laissez-faire*. He had accepted the post as Dean partly because everyone was obliged to have a turn at exercising authority as opposed to simply thinking, and partly because he wanted to make things easier and more open for students. He was better at dealing with nervous instinctive acts on his own side – restrictions, repressions, exclusions – than he was at dealing with doctrinaire opposition for the sake of opposing, which he recognised, but failed entirely to understand. When he came to look back on the events of the first half of 1969 he wondered if they would have been any different if he himself had not fallen uncharacteristically and violently in love. He had noticed, and named, his emotion about Marcus Potter, in the Non-Maths Group, wryly acknowledging its unlikeliness. He had been quite unprepared for its subsequent obsessive ferocity.

He had known since his school-days that he fell in love with males, not females. As a schoolboy he had had various experimental experiences, both of romantic longing and of brief and ingenious bodily experiments. Since then, without too much repining, he had lived largely in his mind. It had been easy, as a Cambridge don, to be part of a homosexual world that talked continuously about buggery, created and dissolved relationships and affairs. He was reasonably at ease in the company of such men without ever exactly joining in either the intrigues or the promiscuous buggery. He trod a fine line, instinctively and with a certain pride. He was verbally quick – he could make the right jokes and references, he could be seen to share gossip and forms of words. But he was also, he discovered, both a natural ascetic and not beautiful. He thought he ought to mind not being beautiful more than he did, and wrote a paper on beautiful and ugly philosophers which amused his group.

Vincent Hodgkiss thought, being a man of weak desires and not brave, that he might have been driven to be an anachronistic bachelor in any case. He also held a very English aesthetico-moral belief that asceticism should be unostentatious and unremarkable. He would not wear simple worker's clothes, drink tap water exclusively, take hard exercise in walking holidays, or furnish his rooms like Wittgenstein with deck-chairs and card-tables as a symbol of his transitory presence. He believed in protective colouring – a row of fine editions, elegant pale linen curtains, modern glass crafted decanters with good wine in them, Florentine ties and hand-made shoes. He made jokes, but tried to see that they were never malicious. When he was alone in his room – which was much more of the time than he allowed anyone to know – he tried to behave as if no one was there, no personality, simply an observing, self-correcting intelligence. Disembodied, he could almost have said, but he paid fastidious attention to his body, keeping it clean and pleasant, from toenails to teeth, for no one. He liked to encourage a mild amount of speculation as to whom he loved, what he did, with whom. He had a gnomic, prissy look for these occasions, which his friends mocked, affectionately. He wondered if the intense pleasure he felt, alone in his room, as his mind moved into action, was sexual or not. He thought it was, and tried to ensure it was neither narcissistic nor onanistic. That interested him too. He wondered fleetingly if being a thinking woman felt differently, but he knew none, and had nothing to go on.

He was in some sense prepared for falling in love with Marcus Potter, because he had previously, for two years altogether, been hopelessly and occasionally painfully in love with Raphael Faber. He had meant Raphael not to notice this. Raphael himself was an ascetic on principle, with a fastidious hypersensitivity partly owed to his family's wartime experiences in prison camps and invaded cities. But Raphael was a man who used his apparent asceticism to charm and to tempt. He was delicately greedy. He liked to be loved, by both men and women, though he returned love only fitfully, and with cruel intermissions and endings. He liked the dance of flirtation, retreat, advance, turn back, turn face, retreat, advance. If Hodgkiss had wanted to play this game – which he did not – he would only have lumbered ludicrously. He used his intelligence to keep his distance, which prolonged the situation, since the distance aroused Raphael's sexual curiosity, piqued him, led him on. Hodgkiss was tormented by Raphael's carved lips, by the fall of his lovely hair. He wanted to have Raphael to himself, and noted an inconvenient tendency to see everyone as rivals, which Raphael, elegantly and secretly, encouraged.

All this dance went on without a word being spoken. The two men were friends, as they had been before, and were to be again after. It was primitive and civilised. When Hodgkiss – partly to break this spell – decided to move to North Yorkshire – Raphael exhibited an uncharacteristic agitation. He touched his friend, on meeting and parting, as he had not done. He visited late at night – with a serious question about Wittgenstein and silence – and stayed to say 'He did sleep with his young men, didn't he? You would know.'

'He didn't see why he shouldn't. He thought it was natural. If he thought he shouldn't, it was for their sakes, not to confuse them.'

'What do you think? Yourself?'

'I hope never to have disciples.'

'You are a good man, Vincent. Would you sleep with me?'

'I should hardly sleep,' said Hodgkiss evasively. Raphael's lips were parted, like a bird about to strike or sing.

'Have you thought about it?'

'You know I have.'

'We could try. Too much thinking and no action is bad for a man.' Vincent was sitting, he remembered, by his fire. His whole body hardened. He tried not to move a visible muscle, and looked, reasonably quizzically, at his friend.

'And what do you think would be the outcome?'

'I don't know. That's why I'm interested, I suppose.'

'We all know,' said the philosopher, 'that satisfied desire is the end of desire.'

'*Omne animal post coitum triste* and all that. Don't you die for a bit of post-coital peace?'

'On those terms,' said Vincent, half-angry, half-laughing. 'Anything for a bit of peaceful post-coital sadness.'

Raphael should then have taken the lead, and did not. Vincent, over-eager, clumsy, hot with embarrassment and obscure anger and simple desire, initiated a quick and clumsy love-making that he still remembered with anxiety and shame. Afterwards he held Raphael's fine body in his arms in the firelight, kissed his collar-bone, and said 'That should never have happened.'

Raphael's sharp lips brushed his bald patch, which was the part of his body he most disliked, and Raphael's fingers explored the protrusion of his belly, which was his other place of shame.

'I know. It was an aberration. Let's never speak of it again, shall we?'

'I could murder you, Raphael Faber.'

'No, no. You'll be grateful, you'll see you'll be grateful.'

He was. He was restored to himself, he covered his nakedness. Desire, satisfactorily, failed.

So what was it about Marcus Potter? Hodgkiss was a good teacher. He was proud of his capacity to detect an unexpected range of intelligence in a half-articulate student, as he was proud of his capacity to hand back a half-formed idea, rephrased, added to, so that the student could develop what was still his own idea, recognise where it might lead. He was not a showy teacher, as Socrates must have been, as Wittgenstein, driven, inexorable, certainly was, for all his self-abnegation. He was a watcher. He was at his happiest watching others learning to think clearly. Unlike Wittgenstein also he did not love – particularly – the innocent or the biddable. He loved the thwarted, the secretive, even the lost. He sat in the Non-Maths Group and observed, as nobody else appeared to observe, the marginal and wayward intelligence of Marcus Potter. He observed his mathematical quickness and his sense of the forms of thought, the occasional excited movement of his pale, almost transparent, ineffectual hands, the glimmer of light and life coming and going behind the moony rounds of his glasses.

He began to notice Marcus's body as an expression of Marcus's mind. A disconsolate, disconnected series of gestures, a pale impermanence, as though the inhabitant of the body was not himself quite sure that it had real mass, inhabiting real space. He came to know the hunch of the thin shoulders, the long, gawky line of the hips under the twist of unflattering trousers, the gesture with which the long fingers ran through the fine, nondescript hair, the line of the untouched-looking cheek, averted in embarrassment or modesty, the flicker of the pale lashes over those light and empty eyes. He wanted to make him move easily – his awkwardness now appeared to Vincent to be a fine form of grace, but it was not free, he wanted him to be *easy*, happy in his skin, as the French said. He wanted him not to shrink. He wondered when he had begun shrinking, and why.

The only thing Vincent Hodgkiss knew about Marcus Potter's family was that he was the brother of pushy Frederica, which had genuinely shocked him when he discovered it. He did not like Frederica, whom he considered brash, unsubtle, and conceited. She thought her bony, gingery energy was sexy, whereas her brother's vanishing fineness was infinitely more appealing. Vincent Hodgkiss told himself a Freudian story about the two of them, how Frederica had always demanded the place in the sun, the warmth of attention, had defined herself as the clever one, and her interests as the important ones. The parents must have colluded. He did not know about the dead Stephanie, and thus left her out of his fairy tale. He did not know about Marcus's part in her death.

What he did know – half through intuition, half through intelligent extrapolation from Marcus's flurried remarks – was that someone, a man, had once made terrifying and unwanted advances. Were they unwanted because Marcus was not queer and was repelled? Or because he was, and was afraid? How did this affect his beloved's feelings about himself? What should he do? He was unskilled in campaigns of seduction, or declarations of love. He felt he should do what he did best – teach, listen, give his whole attention – and see what happened.

Among the floating scraps of paper in the air between the Ziggurat and the Evolution Tower was one which singled out the Dean himself, flying over a puddle and up, with a dark streak of mud, to plaster itself across his breast. It advertised a Plural Talk by Greg Tod and Waltraut Ross. 'British Culture Is Inert. Why? The Hidden Implications of Ordinary Language Philosophers, esp. Wittgenstein. Why Have We No Sociologists? A Radical Critique . . .' It was printed in scarlet on dull flesh pink. Hodgkiss decided it was time to go and listen. He invited Marcus Potter to come with him. He thought he must make some other offering than rich food. Marcus looked startled. Hodgkiss explained that he needed Marcus for cover. He wanted to blend into the audience. Marcus replied that he couldn't blend. Into anything. And that he was ignorant of British Culture, inert or not.

'I need moral support,' said the Dean.

'I'm not support. I always run away from trouble – of any kind.'

'Precisely. You look entirely harmless. Cover, as I said.'

He had the impression that no one had ever discussed Marcus with Marcus before he had taken to doing so. Successive expressions of anxiety, and limited pleasure, flitted across the pale face.

They set out for the Teach-Inn, both wearing duffle coats with the hoods pulled forward. Hodgkiss, silly with love and mildly elated, thought of them as hobbits disguised in elven-cloaks, and then, as they passed successive booths in the thick canvas light, with its pools of candle-flame and pervasive tinkle of bells and spasmodic breathy flutings, he thought of them as Christian and Faithful, making their way through Vanity Fair.

They passed Eva Wijnnobel's booth. Her voice purred darkly in the incense. 'Aries the Ram is a warlike Sign. He has triumphant energy and bounding confidence in the youth of the year. A ram touches the earth but he leaps for the heavens. He is unlike the massive Bull, who stands square on his heavy hooves in mire and humus. The Ram is fiery and hot and sprinkles light from his golden fleece . . .'

Over another booth was written: *The Birth of Tragedy from the Spirit of Music*. Inside a group of musicians played a skein of music, part-oriental, part-jazz. They wore gilded masks. In the centre sat Paul-Zag, in a tunic covered with sequinned flames and silver-scaled trousers. His blond hair swung. He wore a half-mask, with goat-horns, also gilded.

A small child ran across their path, bead-bedecked, crumple-headed. Round a corner was a booth with paper apple-trees and paper geese, and a wicket-gate. *Mother Goose's Orchard. Stories for Children and Child-like Perennial, Second-Childhood, World-weary, Fools and Wisemen, No Ending without a new*

Beginning. Inside, Deborah Ritter, sitting in a rocking-chair, read aloud.

> *And Artegall heard the voices of hidden things. The thrush continued to speak, full of itself, scolding. Beyond its clarity, Artegall heard the whisper of beetles chewing dead wood to sawdust, of spiders hissing as they spun their fine traps, of giddy flies murmuring as they blundered past the silk threads. He heard the slow cold speech of the worms, pushing sinuous and blind between compacted layers of leafmould. He heard the glutinous uncoiling of snails in the sunlight, and the infinitesimal cry of hungry larvae in the ants' nest . . .*

Marcus observed that there was a pervasive sewery smell. Hodgkiss said, keeping his head down, in a mutter, that he himself should probably be doing something about that. Though some of the land belonged to Dun Vale Hall.

Marcus stiffened.

Hodgkiss asked if he knew what was going on there.

Marcus said, unforthcoming, that it was very intense and religious. He remembered Lucas Simmonds and told his companion that he had a friend there, a girl called Ruth. He said, not quite convincingly

'I worry about her.'

Lucas Simmonds's face, red and smiling like the sun, rose over the rim of his mind's eye, and was beaten down. He sighed. Hodgkiss made no comment.

In the Marx-Mao Marquee the Plural Talk had attracted an audience of about thirty-five people, several, if not most, of whom were Hodgkiss's own students. Avram Snitkin was on his stool in a corner, smiling mildly. There were some school benches. Hodgkiss and Marcus sat together, at one end, at the back. Marcus folded his shoulders inwards and pushed his thin arms down between his legs, like a roosting bat. Vincent Hodgkiss had a vision of his skeleton, like transparent ivory.

Tod and Ross spoke in practised counterpoint. Their verbal javelins, Hodgkiss decided, had points. Tod accused the British of mistaking a passive inertia for an empiricist scepticism. The British evaded concepts, and thus evaded thinking. History, Ross said, taking up the argument, had kept the British padded and insulated from the idea of Revolution. There had been no disturbance since the Civil War in the seventeenth century. Capitalists, bourgeois, and the remaining aristocrats, colluded to persuade the working class that change was impossible and undesirable. Modern French philosophy was all about the conditions for making new concepts. The British denied the need and the possibility.

Tod took over. Look, he said, at modern British philosophy. Wittgenstein's pupil, Wisdom, thought it was clever to point out that philosophy begins and ends in platitude. Clever-clever Austin praised common language, common sense as the repository of evolved wisdom. Quite apart from *whose* common language, this was complacent endorsement of all actually existing *status quos*. Wittgenstein had fled Europe and its turmoils to sit in a rich British university playing *language-games* which worked because they supposed that there was an unchanging body of ideas and an unalterable pattern of social context governing them.

In Britain, said Waltraut Ross, 'ordinary language' masks a fuggy determination to restrict problems to arm-chairs, tennis and tiddly-winks, hypothetical rhinoceroses and whether there are *apples* or *some apples*. Outside, people suffer, they live in strait-jackets of mechanical repetition and/or hunger or boredom. They do not believe change is possible, because they don't know language is a *weapon*, to be used to make a revolution – to prepare for a total overturning of the system –

Several of Hodgkiss's students applauded vigorously. One said he had come to study philosophy to understand good and evil, love and meaning, and he was stuck with the semantics of cricket and how to cook fish. Greg Tod applauded him. He looked across at Hodgkiss, who saw that Tod had known from the beginning who he was.

'You,' said Greg Tod. 'What do *you* think?'

Several of the students turned round and noticed Hodgkiss.

'There is something in what you say,' said Hodgkiss.

'There is something in what you say,' cried Waltraut Ross, in a gross parody of Hodgkiss's Oxford bleat. 'English fairness is *so* appealing.'

Hodgkiss met her cold grey eyes, and saw that what she felt for him was hatred. Impersonal hatred, becoming personal as she stared.

'We don't want you here,' said Waltraut Ross. 'Get out.'

'It's a free country,' said Hodgkiss, smiling involuntarily.

'That's precisely the point,' said Greg Tod. 'It isn't a free country. It isn't a free country, or a just country. Those who are not with us, are against us.'

'A good debate,' said Hodgkiss, 'is a model of being both with and against, without actual bodily harm.'

'We aren't interested in debating you,' said Greg Tod. 'We have other, urgent, matters to attend to.'

A kind of sullen murmur began among the students. Hodgkiss was suddenly aware of Marcus's emotion beside him. It was intense embarrassment. He thought, I can only make myself look silly. He stood up, said to Marcus, 'Come on,' and left the marquee. Behind him he heard the rising cry of Waltraut Ross:

'The Establishment always talks about Free Speech. Free Speech is a reification, a mystified absolute value. They use it to suppress questioning, to make all beliefs vapid and identikit, when in fact there are real and urgent − and *rightful* − causes and projects. Freedom is not the freedom to witter on instead of acting. Freedom means change, and change means action . . .'

They avoided the Teach-Inn's veggie-sandwich bar, and went back to Blesford, where they sat in the Non-Maths Group corner of the Argus Eye and ordered sausage and mash. Hodgkiss was nervously excited. He wondered if he should do anything, and if so what, about the revolutionaries. They had only been rude, and rudeness, in his liberal canon, was not a sin, only a behaviour. Also, he was not thinking clearly because of Marcus. Marcus drank shandy, and said nothing.

'Of course, they are wrong about Wittgenstein's life,' said Hodgkiss. 'He couldn't bear the Cambridge life-style any more than they could, and for some of the same reasons. He was an ascetic and an extremist. He worked as a hospital porter in the last war, and then as a lab assistant. He actually contributed considerably to a project studying the effects of wound shock in the Blitz. His first contribution was ordinary language. He suggested they stop using the word "shock" which he said wasn't a diagnosis − didn't *mean* anything and masked the problems they should be looking at.'

Marcus said that Wittgenstein appeared to have been both

unusual and good. Hodgkiss recognised this as an attempt to talk to him about something he himself was interested in.

'He was good – in an almost saintly way – and impossible. Impossible. He fell in love with young men – characteristically very very clever young men, who understood what he was saying – but also, characteristically, rather innocent young men, biddable young men, natural disciples. Then he ran their lives like a moral tyrant, urging them to work in factories or garages because such work was pure and uncontaminated – morally –'

Marcus withdrew his hand from the fork he had been about to pick up. Hodgkiss, trembling slightly, found himself racing on.

'Odd, really, because Turing, who was the other genius in those sessions on mathematics we were talking of, Turing was the same way. He tried to change himself. He got engaged to a woman, a cryptologist, during the war. He used to show her pine-cones and talk about Fibonacci. But he broke it off. A young man he – so to speak – *befriended*, robbed his flat, and when he reported the matter to the police, it ended in them prosecuting him. For sex.'

Marcus was silent. Hodgkiss, feeling that he was destroying himself, filled the silence with his own grim and truthful thoughts.

'He was found guilty, of course. It was a choice between a prison sentence and voluntary submission to hormone treatment. To reduce his sexual drive. They filled him full of oestrogen. A female hormone, I'm sure you know. He grew fat, he grew breasts. He made jokes about being Tiresius, an androgyne, but my own view – I've known other cases – is that it crazed him. He couldn't think clearly.'

He was revisited by his own vision of the debonair boy disporting himself amongst high ropes in the roof.

'I think he experienced something like the stress women are said to feel before menstruation. Only perpetually. He killed himself. With an apple dipped in cyanide. In 1954.'

Marcus still said nothing.

'He had a hypothesis about the formation of regular patches – spots, stripes – in natural growths. Zebra skins, butterfly-eyes, peacock feathers, angelfish. What we were talking about the other day, as paradise-gardens. He thought that the forms were made by the physical interaction of two substances, one flowing or expanding, one – which he called a "poison" – chemically inhibiting it.'

'I've thought of something like that. The maths is very difficult.'

The voice was clear and colourless.

'It is not good to feel that your whole nature is unnatural. Or, if not unnatural, unacceptable.'

Marcus looked up, and met Hodgkiss's gaze. He opened his mouth, and closed it again. Wittgenstein would not have known how to describe the colour of his hair or eyes, they were no colour. Give me a sign, thought Vincent Hodgkiss, feeling beads of sweat form on his own collar-bone, in his own groin. A man must wish to poison a relation before it starts, to embark upon it with such a fatal tale.

'The law has changed,' said Marcus. He moved very slightly away from Hodgkiss.

'I'm sorry,' said Hodgkiss, the ordinary-language man.

'There's no need,' said Marcus, polite and quick. He said 'Think of the complexity of the patterning in feathers, what with iridescence, and hooks and eyes, and patterns that are only made by the overlapping of many single feathers on one birdtail . . .'

'More shandy?'

'I don't think so.'

★

It was a spring day. Not on the dark high moor, but visible in the pink haze of buds on the silver birches and a spice of green on the dark thorns, and the first white flowers on the blackthorn in the woodland lower in the valley. Watchers in the farmyard saw the striding figure on the ridge, black with a solid core, surrounded by flapping movement in the wind. The head was up, a black disc on a blue sky, and the arms were flung wide from time to time, like a scarecrow, one thought, like a priest greeting the sun, another thought. Black sliding shapes rushed out from the whirling skirts, circled, and were apparently reabsorbed. Black crows went over, flapping strongly. The figure whirled and waved at the head of the Dun Vale path, and then dipped into the path itself, and became invisible.

The woods, still sooty-bare for the most part, were full of dead leaves, dead bracken, through which new shoots pushed, Lords and Ladies, hoods tightly folded, grey bluebells, a few wind-flowers. The undergrowth was full of crashing and hissing. Creatures rattled and scattered. They were semi-wild hens, their plumage dusty, their necks, once pecked naked and bleeding in the batteries, now soft with resurgent down. If the creatures were descended from jungle fowl, the ancestral jungles must contain no natural enemies, for their scaly feet and their jumps of alarum or clumsiness, made a revealing racket. Indeed, there were bones and claws and scattered pluckings on the path, showing that many had been killed and – at least partly – eaten. They clucked and chuckled and peered with nervous yellow-rimmed eyes out of the brushwood. The two dogs made little snapping sallies at them, but were themselves fat and easily winded. 'Shoo, shoo,' cried Lady Wijnnobel, with contempt. She stomped through a flurry of golden chicks. Further into the thicket a turkey gobbled, and raised his blue-green shining tail. Odin and Frigg backed off. When they came to the end of the path they found their way barred by marching white geese, heads high, long coiling necks full of dangerous muscle, crowding and hissing. Lady Wijnnobel stopped, and said 'Shoo' with less conviction. Clemency Farrar and Paul-Zag appeared out of the house, and Clemency threw grain to the geese, placating them with murmurs.

'They are the traditional guardians.'

'You are vestals?' Lady Wijnnobel enquired, unsmiling.

'Not exactly. We are a community.'

'I know who you are. I have come.'

The sentence should have had an end. I have come to visit. I have come to learn. It stood truncated.

'Do you think you could – call the dogs, put them on a lead, they're upsetting the ducks and pigeons.'

'They don't require physical control. They respond to command. Odin, Frigg, do not worry the birds. Come here.'

They came, prostrating themselves, grinning their dog grins, their hairy bellies in the mud.

'Can I help you?' asked Clemency, in her vicarage manner.

'I am told you welcome all seekers. I am an astrologer.'

'A powerful one,' said Paul-Zag. 'I've seen you performing.'

'I do not perform. I communicate. I instruct.'

'I know. I said the wrong thing. *I* perform there. It's my *way*, performing.'

'I have seen you.'

'Tea,' said Clemency. 'Please come in, all are welcome, I'll make tea.'

Odin and Frigg scared a whole, shimmering flock of pigeons into the air, and a duck with dishevelled neck-feathers into the midden. Lady Wijnnobel's brows set together, and Clemency thought better of what she had been going to say. She bowed her head under the low door, and went into Dun Vale Hall.

XX

Many thanks for facilitating the release of Joshua Ramsden, alias Josh Lamb, and Lucy Nighby. Release seems the wrong word, since one is the owner, and the other the centre, of the extraordinary world in which I find myself. People in our profession do not expect things to go well, and do not always know what to do with – how shall I describe it? It isn't ecstasy, or bliss, though it has things in common with the acid experiences I have shared with Zag. It is a sense of hope, and well-being. And carries with it, since I am a cynical old soul-doctor from the unregenerate outer darkness, the fear that like all happiness, it is in its very nature brief. We have all prayed earnestly in our different ways to be transfigured, and now we are shimmering on the edge of transfiguration, it is frightening. For what does a transfigured soul do, in space and time? How do we pass our infinite days? We are not there yet, for which I am grateful, for I am not ready. My fingers still reek of tobacco, my arm-pits and my groin have their usual animal stink, I am not perfect. Indeed, I find myself praying like St Augustine, Lord make me good, but not yet. Not yet. I am afraid of the light I glimpse as a man may be afraid of spending his seed in an infinitely delayed orgasm. What then? What then? There was a poem by Donne I used to use with my so-called 'patients' (and patient many of them had to be, I see now, from this rim of the world). Do you know it? It is called 'A Lecture upon the Shadow.' (Yet another example of how
this resolute Freudian is being sucked inexorably into the world of C.G. Jung.) It describes a machinery of affective relations which mimics the orgasmic *mounting* I've just mentioned.

> *Love is a growing or full constant light*
> *And his first minute, after noon, is night.*

There are the Manichaean opposites. Light. Night. We are all moving towards the Light. But when we reach it, shall we be extinguished in a puff of smoke? It sometimes feels probable.

Maybe, on the other hand, we shall reach a state, or stage, where living in the full glare of enlightenment becomes tolerable and even necessary. It's hard to describe the early symptoms. One is a sense I think we all have – some intermittently, some all the time – that we are not separate creatures, but one Being. The Quakers were already prepared for that, with their Sense of the Meeting. We drop our walls, we extend beyond our skins, we move in beautiful synchrony, whether we work, or sing, or dance, or listen, or sit in lucid silence. I knew if I tried to put it into words I should strike a false note. *It is so.* The other symptom I've noticed – and many of us have remarked on – is that we experience ordinary things as transfigured. How can I tell you? I lay the breakfast table, when it is my turn, and the forms of the forks and spoons, the metal in the light, the bowls, the tines, strike me as subtle and perfect, as though I was a painter, maybe, taking apart the forms light makes of them and putting them together again – seen *in the light* – as infinitely surprising. I am shocked by the surface of a broken bread roll, the grains, the crevices, the softness, the way my tongue sees the satisfactory taste. Looking out of the window is an unbearable revelation. The loveliness of the uneven glass, a bubble, a streak of rainwater, the rushing of white birds in the farmyard, the dark line of the moor edge, the unbearable variety of the blues of the sky. I know the others feel like this, most of the time, if not all. We discuss it. Gideon Farrar and his wife make their ordinary feasts and all of us savour every mouthful as though we had been starving. Gideon, as is his nature, sees all the women transfigured, too. He speaks of the infinite beauty of the human form, and the ugly amongst us smile and carry their poor bodies more proudly.

And what, you will ask, as it is your duty to ask, about Joshua Ramsden? Charisma runs off him like a waterfall, it shines mildly from him like candle-light, it occasionally flares from him like sunlight. He walks about amongst us like a creature in a diving-bell of light under treacherous depths of murky water and forests of kelp. If you touch him – which he doesn't like you to do – you get, I swear it, a minute electric shock. A prickle, a flicker. If it's sex (which our Master would insist it *must be*) it's diverted and also transfigured. He is very genuinely *against* sexual activity of any kind, like the Cathar Perfects and the Manichees before him. He's an ascetic. He speaks often – in the talks he gives in the evenings – of withdrawal, of emptying out, of self-annihilation. Many religious leaders, I know, impose chastity on everyone else and are themselves the centre, the potent as opposed to the impotent, the begetter of all the children, the fulfilment of all desire. My old self says this untouchable quality he has is only a double turn of the screw – you want it more, to put it crudely, because you can't have it. I have no idea whether he is conscious or unconscious of this – *and I wouldn't dare ask*, which is interesting.

It doesn't really feel like that. It feels as though he's been somewhere – out there, over the rim of the world, beyond individuation – to an extreme place which is both entirely desirable and entirely appalling. He *knows* what we want to know and are afraid of knowing. He's our talisman, that's it, he's our talisman. He talks to us harshly and beautifully, and we listen to the voice of experience, beyond the inadequate words (in the sense in which words are always inadequate).

Anyway, to retreat from the ineffable to gossip, which persists.

We received an odd visit today. From the improbable Eva Wijnnobel, the Vice-Chancellor's wife, who holds sessions on astrology in the Anti-University. Gideon really wants this place to be like a mediaeval way-station, a religious House that succours travellers. His desire to invite everyone in – and to charm them with his attentiveness – borders on the pathological, I sometimes think nastily. (But we are, truly, almost never nasty, now, and he did look magnificent with his white-gold mane and beard and his religious symbols dangling over his loose white shirt. Ankhs, snakes, crosses, the ourobouros, a kind of plastic mermaid, he is eclectically weighted.) Anyway, he welcomed her in, and she stood blackly and hot and dark and absolutely *not* shining, even though her face was sweaty with the effort of walking, and her black hair does have a greasy sort of gloss. She came accompanied by two rather nasty, rump-waggling dogs. There's something rather disgusting about perverting a beast as beautiful in itself as a border collie into a fat subservient grinner.

They are called Odin and Frigg, but she inclines heavily towards the Egyptian, via anthroposophy, I'd guess. She's got an Egyptian haircut. And a kind of stagy black cloak over a priestess-like black garment with purple bindings here and there. And fingernails. Bloody fingernails, incongruous. Zag has rainbow-coloured fingernails, every one iridescent with fish-scales (I'm told), pearly blues and mauves and yellows and oranges. The really odd thing – I am jumping forward in my narrative, forgive me – the really *odd* thing is that Zag seems to have formed some sort of relationship with her, between their stints at the Anti-University. How to describe this. Complicity; yes, but that's too weak. She paws him. Very well, dear Kieran, writing like an analytic session in a kind of spiritual dustbin, I am tempted into words that reveal wicked feelings I trusted no longer to have.

I feel physical revulsion for this woman, and she paws Zag, and Zag pats her hand, and grins sexily at her, and hugged her when she departed. They sat next to each other at lunch and talked about Gemini, twinned unbounded Souls, and the alchemical Work (Jung again) where the Stone is the hermaphrodite who is manifested as Mercury, quicksilver in a bath of coloured light becoming white. She ate rather a lot of Clemency's vegetable shepherd's pie, and alternated between Holding Forth (rather as I imagine she must in her anti-u-chapel), and a kind of grim silence, like a volcano working itself up. One of our members, Lucas Simmonds, who is some sort of 'social worker' and has been a teacher, and has certainly been in institutions like yours, possibly Cedar Mount itself – Lucas S. also knows a lot about alchemy and hermaphrodite Mercury, and the *mysterium coniunctionis* and became excessively smiling and dog-like in his eagerness to partake. Canon Holly said it was easy to make a fantasy mish-mash out of this material and was almost spat at, or cursed.

The women don't like her. Ellie went and sat at the other end of the table. Clemency tried very hard, and was treated as a kind of superior house-servant. She took this in a Christian way, redoubling her hostess-ly attentions, but she was miffed, her light dimmed a bit. As for Lucy, who only really comes to life in Joshua Ramsden's presence, she was seriously upset by a nasty attack made by Odin and Frigg on her pet sheep, Tobias. Tobias is very much a member of the Hearers. He is vegetarian and woolly and entirely good-natured. We have children here – some are Quaker offspring, some come to classes in pottery and weaving and cookery and story-writing which Clemency – our total guarantee of sane respectability – has set up. The more nervous ones love to play with Tobias, who butts them very very gently, and lets them thread things in his fleece. He was driven into the chimney-corner with snarling and snapping, and stood at bay, looking confused. Eva W. ordered everyone to pay no attention. She said it was the dogs' nature, they were simply herding the sheep. Gideon said that the sheep believed himself to be a dog, and she said that that was inappropriate, and belled out 'Odin, Frigg,' which elicited no response.

Fortunately, perhaps, at that moment, Ramsden came in. He calmed them all down, with his new authority. She fell for him. I heard her telling Zag, over lunch, that his hair was white like wool. He sat frowning, himself, between Clemency and Lucy, with the sheep bundled under his chair. I sometimes think he comes in late because he doesn't eat, and doesn't want to be seen not eating. A man can be ill, in our old sense, our 'professional' sense, yet be a spiritual leader, that is what we have learned, in our time. The way is not round, but through, and I suppose that applies to that woman, too.

I hope she doesn't come again. I know she will, of course. She snuffed him out, she gravitated towards him, and she won't let go. He looks very calm, but not happy.

Maybe she's necessary to our new life in some way. You're the Group groupie. You know how groups have an irritant which causes them to coalesce – like the grit in the pearl? Or maybe she'll cause us all to fly apart, like a stink bomb. Or maybe – as we sail heavenwards in our silvery skin of sky-balloon, she'll be the heavy black ballast holding down our basket and its burners? I get tearful these days, what with the after-acid and the over-oxygenation of spiritual extremism. I am sitting here sniffing to myself, and giggling over my own cleverness in reducing that silly and dangerous woman to cheap metaphors. God forgive me. What has happened to charity? The new spirituality is not long on charity, Kieran. Ask Zag, who waits impatiently for a Dionysiac dismemberment and release. I wonder how the V-C has lived with her for so long? How he could bear those monumental limbs burning in the same bed? How could he sit by the hearth with those denatured dogs? Marriage is a mystery to me, *mysterium coniunctionis*, as the alchemists, and Eva W. and the blessed Carl Gustav would say.

Ramsden saw Eva and recognised an opponent. When she saw him, she walked straight up to him, and stood close, head down. Too close. He wanted to step back, or push her away, and did not. The two dogs bustled up behind her, and suddenly shot forward, in a whirling twist of fur, teeth, claws and feathery tails, as they perceived Tobias the sheep, who had come in, with Lucy, at Ramsden's heels. Tobias gave a high bleat of fear, and retreated into the great chimney-space. Odin and Frigg hurtled after him, pinning him against the wall.

'Stop that,' said Ramsden.

'It's their nature,' said Eva Wijnnobel. 'Down, my darlings. Come to mother. Come to mother.'

Odin and Frigg snarled and worried. Tobias shivered. Eva Wijnnobel went down on her knees in front of the silent, motionless audience, and pulled at rumps and waving plumes.

'Bad dogs. Bad dogs. Mother is very cross,' she said. Her voice was thick and not motherly. The dogs were finally pulled out, and

Lucy with a little cry knelt to comfort Tobias, whose ankle was bleeding. Eva Wijnnobel went back to Ramsden. There was a smudge of blood and wood-ash on her right cheek.

'It is only collie nips,' said Eva Wijnnobel. 'They are herding animals. I hope you will not send us away.'

Her breath was hot on his face. He could see into her dark mouth. He saw her exhale damp air, meat-juice, curdled milk. He wanted to step back and did not. Her black-rimmed eyes stared into his over the smudge on her skin.

'I think you may have, I think you may be, what I need, what I am seeking,' she said, in an urgent undertone. She was fawning on him, and at her feet, the dogs writhed in parallel subservience. She hissed in his ear

'Hair as white as wool, it is written. And I see the film of blood, oh yes, I see it, the sign of the master, the rosy sweat, the red tears, I see who you are.'

He wanted to send her away. His everyday self, an entity always tenuous and wraith-like, knew that she was 'a charlatan', an unreality that would eat up the work of the spirit. His spirit knew that she saw him, his hair white as wool, his body washed white in blood, for what he was being driven to become. He could not bear to be touched, and she was crowding him, breathing most literally down his neck. He feared his own anger, which he believed he had never allowed to break out or show itself. He knew the Hearers were afraid of his anger, which was right, yet indicated a secret sharing, for he had never showed anger to them, never, only patience, gentleness and understanding.

He looked at the woman, and saw the phantom blood he had watched since the day of the terror of the plump, pitiable boy, well out from among the thick black hair and run down her wide cheeks and thick neck. He thought, with a moment of illumination, that she was the Smudge into which dark matter would be gathered at the end of the process, when the light was separated out. She smiled, as though she heard his thoughts.

'I have studied the mysteries,' she said. 'I know things about how to bring the Work to completion. Do not reject me.' She said 'Everyone has a seed of the light in them, you know that.'

'Sit down,' he said. 'You are welcome to eat with us, as everyone is welcome. But the dogs must not touch the sheep.'

'Come with Mummy,' she said, taking her gaze off his face, cutting the electric current between them.

He sat at the table with them, but he didn't eat. He didn't eat at all, that day, and every day he ate less. He knew that they liked him to be with them when they ate their lovingly cooked feasts, and he sampled things to please them, flakes of oats, spoons of lentils, grains of wheat. Eating was necessary to life. But his body appeared not to need to eat. It appeared to him to be becoming transparent. Sometimes he spoke to them, whilst they ate. He told them about the Manichees' respect for the particles of light trapped in seeds and apples. He told them about the spirit, trapped in flesh, which could be released into light by disciplining and diminishing the flesh. He knew, when he began to speak, that the whole air in the room became still and heavy with the mass and energy of their attention, like the concentration of power around lightning-conductors, before thunder. He looked into their upturned faces, and their faces shone a mild light, a pale gold warmth on him. But also the dark holes of their eyes, and their open mouths, with the wet shine on their teeth, took him in and ingested him, consumed his body of light as the flame consumes the candle.

They were eating him, and he was a trained theologian and knew to what this thought related. Gideon still broke bread ceremonially at all these meals, bustling from seat to seat with his warm-smelling basket of crust and crumb. If he was eaten up, would he become light, or nothing, or be scattered and broken into dispersed specks of light-energy? He was not a god, he was a being, he did not understand his own nature, he only knew that it was not what he had been told it was. The syzygos knew what he was, but had not been seen for some time. And now this semi-Egyptian mummy was come. He saw blood on Gideon's bread. He had never told any of them about the blood. Like the whiff of the flame of his anger it needed to be hidden until it broke out and drowned everything.

They were emptying him out, the marrow of him, leaving the iceglass husk walking in the light.

He walked, too, when it was dark, most of the night. As he did not eat, so he did not sleep. He prayed, if it could be called prayer, his white head and his pale face turned up, as he strode across the dark pastures, to the pale stars and the white moon. He walked more, and faster, by full moon. He did not believe that light was flowing in brimming bucketsful to the well of the moon, for he knew a little, though not much, about the planetary system and the modern cosmos. He knew that the moon pulled the great mass of the oceans around the rocky sphere of the planet he stood on, with its molten centre, and he knew that the pale light pulled him, pulled the life out of him. He knew a body needed sleep, as it needed food, and he knew his own body was in revolt, was trying to dispense with both. His cold energy was coming from elsewhere. His inner flame was diminishing to a pinhead, like the stuttering bubble on the wick of an almost-empty lighter. He felt his own blood running like lighter-fuel, and knew enough to know that it was full of red corpuscles and white, and in his mind's-eye he saw his veins transparent, and the dangerous red turning white, the pale seeds of light extinguishing the blood-red which tried to ingest them, escaping, bubble by bubble, from bloodstream to innocent air. He cat-napped after walking. If he was exhausted in his body, he didn't dream, and he didn't like to dream.

He also instituted what he called 'Night Watches'. He liked to sit motionless, on the floor, in front of the empty television, which he liked to have on when it was transmitting nothing, full of whirling snowflakes of light. He had devised a spiritual exercise in which he poured the blood into the glass tank of the box, and the snowflakes soaked it up, and dispersed it, as though it had never been. He did not tell the others about the blood. He kept his most secret things in his heart. He was strong and very fragile. He permitted occasional privileged Hearers to watch with him in the dark hours. Lucy came and sat quietly. Lucas Simmonds was banished: he was told courteously that he perturbed the currents in the box. This remark was and was not a joke. Gideon – who did not often come – was twice asked to leave because Joshua could smell sex on his clothes. He did not give this reason. He said Gideon's spirit was disturbed, and Gideon accepted his judgement with a soft smile in his beard. Ruth came, now and then, and Canon Holly, who was forbidden to smoke, but stank of dead burning. Clemency came. Zag came, but could not keep still for long.

The night of the day of the coming of Eva Wijnnobel, he was perturbed. He went up to the Night Watch room, and turned away those who timidly, or meekly, tried to join him. I must be alone, he said, not wishing to be weak enough to ask for their understanding, and therefore speaking forbiddingly. Lucy nevertheless had the temerity to say 'I want to watch with you,' and because he had to say 'Not tonight' he had also to touch her hair, and her tremulous red cheek. She kissed his fingers, and withdrew. Then he was alone with his own disturbance.

He lit the box, but did not sit down in his usual meditative position. He walked restlessly, and became aware that the rectangle of glitter was reflected like a ghost of itself both in the dark window of the room, and in the skylight. He took off his shoes and stood in the place where the lines which joined the shadows to their origin crossed and recrossed, as he turned his head. He had a sense of power, and recognition, as though this bare room was a lovely place he had known, and been seeking, all his life. The face of the syzygos, unlined and smiling, appeared on the black windows and the bright box. The Other said, as he had said before, come out, come out in the moonlight, and Ramsden saw the full moon hanging in window and skylight, perfectly framed, hugely sailing, clouded, clear, clouded, clear, dizzying. He went out, purposeful and barefoot, slipping the back-door catch with confident stealth, striding silently across the farmyard, under the trees, which blackened the moon with turbulent spikes, and out on to the moor, where it sailed high, the shreds of cloud dropping away like dead skin, dead lashes, leaving the great silver eye staring blankly. The Other came to him barefoot, dressed in white, over the heather. His hair gave out white light, his smile was lightness. You have had the sign, the other told him. His voice was unbearably pleasant. You have been visited, now you are ready to make the descent. It will be hard and hurtful, but if you return, you will be able to save them. To save yourself, and all of them.

Will you come, with me, he asked the Other. The Other smiled more and more. I must come, he said. I am the executioner. I conduct the evacuation. I will be there. We will go down into the dark together.

Then he knew he was having a fit in the moonlight, and he was cast down on the heather. In foam and froth, bones and teeth jerking and jangling, flesh bruised and bleeding.

They went down together a long way, into a funnel of rock so deep that the orifice was smaller than the illusory moon, and then smaller than a pinhead, and then it was dark. His feet were cold, the uneven stairs were icy and slippery. He found his voice, and asked the Other, whom he could no longer see, if he was now dead. The Other replied cheerfully that he was not dead, no, but they were going among the dead, and when he had spoken to them, he would know death. I do know death, he told the other, death is what I know. The Other told him that he did not know that he had been excluded, evacuated, eliminated. The dead, the Other told him, hang on the underground roots of the Tree, and cannot leave them. They have their own moon, but it is only a makeshift, and you may not be able to see by it. It is a fake moon they made from stolen light. They make fake living-things in their heads, the dead, though they would do better to let go.

Then after a long, or a short, an immeasurable time, he began to be aware of the dead hanging like black fruit, or folded bats, or bundles of tubing, from the immense knot of violently-probing iron-hard roots he saw above him, moving through earth-crust like great blind worms, hung about with hairs that also thrust out, clung, thickened, entered cracks and crevices. The dead were fitfully restless. There was a smell of humus, and a sickly smell he remembered.

They went on, and on. He had been in that place long enough to know that simply being there, in that stultifying closeness, was worse than torture. He asked if the dead had faces. They make fake faces, he was told. With an effort of will, they make fake faces. You will see faces. He said he did not want to see faces, and was told brightly that it was not a question of want or not want. The syzygos' voice reminded him of something. His father's church voice, telling him what was good for his soul. He did not want to see his hanged father but his mouth would not form those words. To be helpless in dream, or vision, or dream-vision, is to be more helpless than anything living, with any semblance of will or thought, can comprehend.

Round a corner, they came upon the fake moon. It dangled from the root-roof by an insubstantial aluminium thread, and appeared to be a kind of lopsided silver-coated balloon shrinking and wrinkled where its inflation was failing, painted clumsily with grey-blue fake continents, craters and oceans. It gave off a miserable light, like inadequate fluorescent tubing in cheap canteens.

Sitting on heaps of rags were three people he recognised, though as he recognised two of them, one in a ghastly flesh-pink nightgown, one in mouldering pyjamas, he saw that the syzygos was right, they had faked their faces. They lifted their arms rather uselessly towards him, like rag dolls who could not hold a position. They had dirty feet which looked more successfully like flesh than their almost prosthetic cheeks and brows. The third figure was full of rude health. Her hair glistened, her eyes glittered, her mouth and nails were crimson. She sat at her ease, and stretched out strong arms towards him, as if to embrace him. All sorts of creatures ran in the damp sawdust around the ragheaps. Earwigs, slugs, blind white snails carrying their spiral houses. And scorpions. Fat and pink, black and busy, tawny and rusty, their energetic tails curved.

His mother began to speak to him. Her denture was still half out of her mouth, and she gagged and yammered and her words clacked on her false teeth. Eva said, I can interpret her speech. We, the Mothers, welcome you. We feed the sap as it rises, and we alone – we alone – help you . . . she doesn't say, what we help you to. But I know.

His mother clacked a little more. His sister managed to lift a limp finger to point out her bruises. Even when the dead speak, he saw, they do not breathe. He did not know speech without breath could be so obscene. Eva, alone of the three, breathed, long, slow, sleepy breaths, filling out her great breast, pumping air, in, out, in, out.

This place has a bad smell, he told the Syzygos. I do not like this woman, he said, in his mind, to his twin.

'It isn't a question of like or not like. She cannot be rejected. You will need her. She is what you need. She is not what you see here. Or there. She *is*. You must take in what you do not want, to finish the Work.'

Next, as he remembered only in snatches, the Syzygos, smiling whitely in the light of the fake moon, took out a knife and dismembered him. He felt no pain, indeed he saw the process – the expert flaying, the stripping of nerves, the coiling of living organs in a series of strangely coloured earthenware bowls and vases – more through the eyes of the Other, than through his own body, which felt no pain, only an increasing bewilderment and sense of scattering and loss of coherence, of which his fits had been a mild premonition. There came a point when he was a cleanly-scraped living skeleton, with red films clinging to living ivory, looking curiously out of the bone-box of his head. The Syzygos said that now he would also part the bones from each other, and build them into a cairn, from great to small. 'And if you can reassemble all these parts, and thread back the nerves, and hook up the muscles,' said the smiling Syzygos, 'you will find you are able to mount the tree, and go up as high into the heavens as you have come deep into the foundations. And then you will see in the sky how to prepare for the mystery that will be enacted and the consummation that will come.'

His own voice clacked out of his own bloody teeth.

'And if I cannot?'

'Why then, the flesh will decay and after a time the bones will roll apart, or be dispersed. But I think you can do this. You are ready.'

And he reassembled himself, trembling, hearing in his head the fat-thighed boy of long ago, singing, dem bones, dem bones, *connected* to . . . It was all precisely lived, the fingers at the end of the arms above the rib-cage collecting the pelvis, attaching the hips. He squatted under the roots, and spread his skin over the slippery bloody surfaces of his breast and buttocks. Then he found he could stand, and his strength was inordinate, and his senses were sharpened so that he heard worms, miles away, sifting loam, and the top point of the tree rattling in a light wind against the night sky. And he climbed, surefooted as an ape, agile as a tree-frog, bursting through the crust like a blind mole, who became a marmoset, a snake, a lizard. Up he went, and up, and the real moon beat about his head with floods of silver, and he stood on the very top of the tree and crowed and crowed at the dawn.

They found him out on the moor, wounded and unconscious, with bleeding mouth and broken nails in the peaty dust of the heather. They carried him back to Dun Vale Hall, which seemed to him for two days to be an unknown place, full of unknown people. On the third day, at dawn, he opened his eyes on a washed world, and saw Ruth, sitting beside him, watching. She was wearing a pallid garment, with a square yoke, and pleats falling like a gym-slip or perhaps a Greek garment, down and out. He liked Ruth, on ordinary days. He liked her fastidious face, her reluctance to speak. He moved his bruised tongue to tell her she was a maiden of light. She appeared not to hear, so he stirred himself, and said it again, more clearly. Her eyes were wet. She brushed them with the back of her hand. He told her not to cry, he was back. She nodded, and her tears ran more freely.

From Brenda Pincher to Avram Snitkin

Writing to you, Avram, is a real act of faith by now, quite as irrational as the increasing *fervour* in this place. It's all building up to something, and I've been racking my brains to remember what. I've got no access to any library. As I seem to remember, lots of more recent cults have been sort of cemented together by things like group sex, or the leader having the right to sleep with everyone and beget lots of children. Our situation is odd, because the leadership is sort of split. We've got the Ram who is genuinely ecstatic, and also genuinely ascetic, and then we've got good old Gideon, who likes to be cock in his own midden and I think doesn't always understand how he got to be involved in the Ram's thing.

It is *all to do with women*, of course, either way. Gideon is here because Clemency deserted, and Clemency's here because she's in love with the Ram, in the way all the women sort of are, including those Gideon fucks. I expect they lie there imagining Gideon is Himself, but the old fool is far too self-satisfied to imagine that, though he may have to, in the end. Some of the men are in love with the Ram, too. The Ram went away on a spiritual journey a week or two ago (time isn't real here) − i.e. he had a quite severe epileptic fit − and came back with all sorts of new instructions and prohibitions and practices. Most of these are to do with making things physically harder for ourselves. We now do an awful lot of digging and carting − we are building a bloody great fence to close us in from the contaminating dirty people out there. Also we get to eat less and less because there's a sort of competitive fasting instituted by the Ram, who says the body thrives on self-denial. Elvet Gander chipped in with the info that experiments on rats and anecdotal evidence from long-lived tribes in the steppes had proved that eating markedly less led to longevity. The not-eating bit has hurt Clemency F. since her great contribution to the community was buns and biscuits. But she's regathered herself and now makes exquisite little soups and vegetable platters containing almost no calories, which are ceremoniously and *very slowly* chewed. What with the digging and the not-eating, I've become very trim myself. You wouldn't recognise me, you old slob, and I'm enough of a Ram-groupie to feel a positive distaste for the idea of all those fatty folds of your overindulged belly – though sometimes I cry for you in the night, Avram, sometimes I'm scared, *why don't you write, you bugger?*

Because I've got trim, I do understand that you can get on a sexual high as well as a spiritual high with a lot of hard work and not-eating much. I lie awake thinking how blissful a good long fuck would be. I lie. I lie awake like all the others imagining the Ram has chosen *me* to so to speak break his fast on, that he's come into my bed-cupboard and is standing there smiling gently with his cock swinging up and I *hurt inside* with wanting him to touch me, my poor bloody vagina grips and grips on nothing (sometimes I help it, but it doesn't help). Listen, Avram Snitkin, you shit, I'm writing you porn to show I'm not part of all this even if I'm ethnomethodologically committed to observing it from *inside*, and also to punish you, because you never answer. If I didn't know you, I'd have given up long ago, because anyone *sane* would suppose they ought to take a hint and realise the letters weren't wanted. But I do know you, and I think you're just sitting there stoned and smiley, thinking how funny it is that I'm getting in such a state here. Well, it isn't, damn you, damn you, Avram Snitkin. It isn't funny, it's scary.

What happens to cults, and this isn't a therapeutic Group now, it's a full-blooded *cult* – is that they implode. They've got nowhere to go but up in smoke, the theory goes. They get more and more intolerant of deviants and more and more in synch. – including things like menstruation, wch I've tried to do a bit of research on, but so far failed. Everyone does wear more and more the same clothes. White sort of lineny shirts and dresses. There's a girl here called Ellie who was a 'patient' of Gander's – we're not allowed to speak of patients now, only spiritual explorers – and she's kind of invented a very new complicated technique of embroidering white on white. Suns and moons and grapes and daisies (day's-eyes, apparently) and other Manicheeish things. With all sorts of knottings and satin stitch (I bet you don't know what *that* is, I didn't) infinitely time-consuming. All the chairs and tables and beds are slowly getting covered with bits of white stuff with all this white stitching on. White with secret little bloodstains of course, the poor things *prick themselves*, it's classic. Over-determined. Then there are special ways of drinking water. And good old Canon Holly's poetry readings of seventeenth-century poems about seeds of light and things. He reads like a creaky hinge, but this place is at the moment awash with charity and everyone listens lovingly.

I've got my theory about how it will begin to implode. Gideon can't *rampage* as he does without it bearing fruit — to move from an animal to a *vegetable* metaphor. And then what? Since it isn't his wife he fucks. Then what? One of the real brain-teasers of this situation is that *the Ram doesn't appear to know what Gideon gets up to.* Maybe he sort of lets him do it for him by proxy so to speak, but that's an ethnomethodologically untenable theory, and I oughtn't to advance it without evidence, wch I don't have.

Another thing that I think *will happen* is that we shall get shut in. Right in. We're building this fence. I can foresee when the Ram ceremonially locks the gates, and the sheep stay in, and the goats are despatched into the outer moorland. At the moment there's still a lot of coming and going. That funny Blake man Richmond Bly comes and goes, he looks sweet and puzzled. The Vice-Chancellor's horrible wife pays sinister visits and reads people's palms (well, not really, she casts horoscopes). I think much depends on Elvet Gander. He's like me, so to speak, professionally *interested in it*. He goes away and gives talks and things, but less than he used to. I think he'd resist enclosure. But he's on a kind of high with it all — it's his way of stepping over some boundary, of going on his own spiritual journey, he might feel he had to want to see it through. He likes that Ziggy Zag, who is quite often stoned himself and in need of a helping hand. I think we could do without *him*, but his singalong evenings like Canon Holly's recitations, are part of our ceremonious normality. Some of the Quakers are quite good at all that — as though it came naturally to see everything with a ~~religious~~ contemplative eye. They still have little gatherings for outside youngsters, who come to hear stories and make things out of cardboard and such.

The thing is, if and when, we get shut in — with a fair possibility of starvation, for we are not feeding ourselves a subsistence diet — what do I do? The project is fucked if I miss the (I presume) final act. But it really is scary. It's like one of those boxes you see on

317

pylons, saying Danger High-Tension Wires. Keep Out. But I'm in. And I get my letters out to you, and you don't answer them, you bastard. Unless they're all secretly going nowhere, and being read and judged by a committee consisting of the Ram, Gideon and Gander. No, they aren't, that's sheer paranoia induced by group mentality. I've put almost all in post-boxes *myself*, haven't I? So why don't you write, you bastard, you bastard. What am I going to do?

XXI

There is nothing like hard work for restoring gloss to the plumage, glitter to the eye, a strut to the stride. Luk Lysgaard-Peacock began somewhat grimly to prepare his half-thought-out paper on the cost of meiosis, and found himself trying to stare through a shining swarm of relevant and irrelevant facts and figures. This was a time when some scientists were beginning to ask distinctly awkward questions about the adaptive benefit (if any) of sexual reproduction (as opposed to parthenogenesis, or budding) in the Darwinian scheme of things. The answers they were offering were profoundly unsatisfactory – and therefore intriguing, and maddening, and exciting.

Luk read studies of the dissemination of clouds of elm seeds and scattering of cod-eggs. He read about the life-cycle of the aphid, which produces parthenogenetic clones until its last days, when it produces males, and mates with them. He read about the slow distribution of strawberries and corals, about the habits of sessile beings like oysters, as well as elms, about competition for territory, crowding, and the frequency of death in its relation to the number of offspring of cod or starlings, minute marine beings or snails. He studied hermaphrodites and clones. He went into precise details of arcane research on generations of ants and cockchafers, and tried to come to grips with theoretical models of distribution, competition, statistical advantages, handing on of genes and chromosomes.

New intriguing paths opened up before him, new flocks and herds of relevant bodies flew and ranged and lumbered across his field of vision. He was only averagely good at mathematics. He needed help in formulating his questions, let alone in answering or amending them. He began to waylay and buttonhole John Ottokar, asking for more time on the great computer than was allotted, taking John out to drinks and persuading him to help turn questions of the reasons for life, death, reproduction and immortality into elegant equations and satisfactorily crunched numbers. He bombarded the patient – and largely silent – John with a great many more urgent sums than could ever conceivably be adumbrated in one paper in the Body–Mind Conference.

On his way to and from the computer, he met Jacqueline, from time to time, also carrying bundles of punched cards and sheaves of print-out. The air between them was still full of ice splinters. He asked if her work was going well. For a moment her face was transfigured by satisfaction. Yes, she said, yes, she was really getting results. There was a spring in her step. A month ago, he would have found this self-sufficient hurry personally wounding. Now, he transferred his attention back to rotifers and rotating winged seeds.

One evening, rather late, John Ottokar came to his flat to deliver a delayed heap of results. Luk, who had been talking agitatedly *at* John for weeks about Darwinian altruism and selfishness, ruthless self-propagation and the harmlessness of cloned slugs, noticed for the first time that Ottokar looked unwell. He had grown his shining blond hair to shoulder length. It was very clean, and he tended to hide his face behind its curtain. Luk said he was afraid he must have been overworking him, asked him in, and gave him a glass of whisky. He had been watching the television news, student protesters at the LSE, government wrangles over unofficial strikes. As John Ottokar took his glass, *Through the Looking-Glass* swam on to the screen, fireplace, glass box, Tweedledum and Tweedledee, Frederica Potter in coral and white silk. Luk remembered that Ottokar was, or appeared to be, in some way involved with Frederica. He had once referred to her as 'my girl-friend' which had struck Luk as a singularly inept way of describing this angular person. Because of this, he did not spring to his feet to turn her off. John Ottokar stretched out his legs, settled into the arm-chair, and stared impassively at the screen. His look was, Luk considered, morose.

Frederica's guests for the evening were Roy Strong and Lucinda Savage, a photo-journalist, who wore a business-like jumper and dark-rimmed glasses. The object for discussion was an Elizabethan miniature of an unknown lady, whose fine face, soft gold curls, beautifully gleaming pearl necklace and ear-rings, over blue velvet, against a background of evergreen leaves, briefly filled the whole screen. The person of course was Elizabeth I, the Virgin Queen, and the idea to be discussed was, Frederica announced, 'Resemblance and Reproduction'. This idea was Wilkie's, one of his more arcane ones.

The three talked well enough about Elizabeth's portraits as icons, the fact that most were copies of copies, not attempts to copy the Queen's face directly, the *mana* that attached to her portraits, which, Roy Strong pointed out gleefully, were objects both of veneration and witchcraft, as if she could be stuck to death with pins and needles. The photo-journalist, predictably, went on to discuss the reluctance of certain cultures to be 'taken' in snapshots or photos, the belief that each reproduction, each copy, took from, or thinned, the life of the original. Frederica said that this was so, there was something unexpectedly alarming about one's image being loose in the world. They talked about the iconic nature of the endlessly replicated face of Che Guevara, hanging in student rooms, in squats, in guerrilla tents.

Frederica tried, as Wilkie had wanted her to, to start a discussion about the different words. Likeness. Resemblance. Reproduction. Replication. We all have our own faces, she said, and yet we are all constructed by the endless replication of the family genes, so that we also have the family face. Luk's attention was caught by this, possibly not very meaningful, ploy, simply because it slotted into the jigsaw of his own thoughts about clones and diploid zygotes. Roy Strong spoke of the family resemblance between Elizabeth and her Tudor brother. The photographer mentioned Andy Warhol, who was making icons of repetition, Marilyn Monroe, Elizabeth Taylor, who were already mechanically reproduced icons. Marilyn flashed across the screen in silvery greens and oranges, grape-purples and shocking pinks. Roy Strong said he had chosen the miniature because it was so clearly a portrait of a singular person, with her own history and attitude to the world, none of which was so far discoverable, and yet, there she was, and, even though the painter's style conferred a kind of likeness on all his models, there she was, unique. Frederica said brightly that every day on the underground she looked at all the faces, and they were *all* unique, unrepeatable. She sounded, for her, almost saccharine. Luk however felt friendly towards her, because she had touched on his own problem. If human reproduction was not sexual, the persons on the underground would resemble each other like the black slugs *Arion ater*.

John Ottokar said 'Shit. How can she sit there between those two and go on like that?'

Luk assumed for a moment that 'those two' were Roy Strong and Lucinda Savage, and could not think why they were suddenly so objectionable. Ottokar could surely not be obsessed enough to be jealous? Then he realised that 'those two' were the cardboard cut-out figures of Lewis Carroll's Tweedledum and Tweedledee, who flanked Frederica. He had seen Paul-Zag wandering across the campus from time to time. His hair seemed to grow *pari passu* with his brother's. He had once, even, on a darkening evening, mistaken Paul for John, and watched blankness succeeded by a sly grin as the other observed his discomfiture. Lucinda Savage began to advance a theory that in the future we would all have moving narrative portraits of our loved ones on our walls, like television screens. Luk stood up and turned her off. He wanted to ask John a question, and couldn't think what it should be. He settled for

'When is Frederica coming north again?'

'I don't know. Easter hols, probably. Bringing Leo. Also, they are going to film your Conference. She says. I dunno when. So she'll be here.'

The words were ground out. Luk said

'You're not happy about it.'

'No.'

There was a long silence. John Ottokar drank whisky, and jerked his long limbs into various postures. He said

'Talking isn't what I do. Didn't really speak English until I was eleven. Spoke Jabberwocky and maths with my brother. Not easy. He makes things difficult.'

'He must,' said Luk, at a loss.

'I've been thinking. We're some kind of clone. Or some sort of virgin birth, one from the other, dunno which, dunno if scientists could find it out. All your stuff's been making me think. I never really did much biology, only maths and computers. I worked on where oil tankers ought to go. What you've worked out is an explanation of everything. From the point of view of cells and organisms. Makes all sorts of ideas meaningless. Kindness, love. God.'

'I don't think we need God.'

'I know you don't. You don't know what *I* think, however. God's always been there. As a reason for.'

He seemed unable to say as a reason for what.

Luk murmured something awkward about it being difficult perhaps, to be here, when Frederica was there . . . John Ottokar looked at him almost aggressively.

'I came up here so she'd make her mind up, one way or the other. And to get away from him, to be myself.'

'But he's here, not there.'

'I know that. The point is, he *wasn't*. Not when I came. I came on my own, to do my own thing. And then he comes. With God all round him. It's like a ghastly Fate. Those people could have gone anywhere else and they came here. There isn't really any Fate, of course, or any sort of – sort of – watching over us. There's just genes, as you keep saying. I'm really glad,' he said, with a useless attempt at irony, 'that you get so much pleasure from all these ideas. I don't. I see they're *right* but they just take away – the meaning. And they don't change the fact that he's my fate, because he's my genes. We're interchangeable and dispensable.'

'Have some more whisky,' said Luk, male and at a loss. He said 'I thought it might be – good – having another person like oneself.'

'Oh, it was. As long as that was the only person. Before we were in the world. Then it got complicated. He's got his group he plays with, of course. I've got the lab. But the group's better, the music's better, with me in, not out.'

'At least you've thought it out.'

'You can say that. You can say that. And where has it got me?'

He drained his whisky rather quickly and subsided into silence.

Frederica did come north for Easter, bringing Leo to spend his holidays with his grandparents and cousins. She was accompanied by Edmund Wilkie: they were making arrangements for filming parts of the Body–Mind Conference for the television. They went to a meeting with Gerard Wijnnobel, Vincent Hodgkiss, Abraham Calder-Fluss and Lyon Bowman to discuss what should be filmed, and how, whether the two 'stars', Pinsky and Eichenbaum, would consent to be interviewed on camera, how the University's unique architecture should be presented. Vincent Hodgkiss had had what he believed to be a politically astute idea, and had invited Elvet Gander to join them. This was because it had come to his attention that Gander was also speaking – on myth and psyche – at the Anti-University, and he believed he might give them some intelligence about the attitude, benign or otherwise, of the encamped counter-culture. Gander's own proposed paper, in the Human Sciences session of the Conference, on schizophrenic perception of body-parts, was scheduled next to a paper on autism, and a paper on concept formation in early life by a Reader in Education.

Hodgkiss had not invited Nick Tewfell that morning: this was not a meeting of an official university body. It took place in Gerard Wijnnobel's study, round a rosewood table in the window looking over his secluded lawn. It was a cold, bright spring day. The academics were in various kinds of corded trousers and shabby jackets. Wilkie looked natty, in a very tight dark blue silk roll-neck sweater under an iron-grey velvet suit. Gander and Frederica were both, by some odd accident, wearing long, loosely knitted black woollen cardigans. There the resemblance ended. Gander had a whitish flowing woollen shirt with a grandfather collar, unbuttoned, over baggy trousers. Frederica had a transparent black shirt, belted above a long black skirt, patterned with poppies and cornflowers. Hodgkiss considered her very visible black lace bra, and her almost visible pointed little breasts, with a socio-historical eye. Semi-nude women at Vice-Chancellorial meetings, purely matter-of-fact, were not something he would ever have thought he would see. He put Frederica into the plural in his mind, though there was only one of her. He thought about Marcus's analogous thinness. Despite this, he thought Frederica's breasts were too small.

Wilkie exclaimed over the Mondrians and the Rembrandt prints. How perfectly proportioned, he said, how *final*. Would the Vice-Chancellor be interviewed on camera in front of them? Wijnnobel said he had no particular wish to be interviewed. He wished to remain behind the scenes. He had heard from both Eichenbaum and Pinsky, who were both happy to be interviewed, although Pinsky had stipulated that he would not be interviewed with – or about – Eichenbaum. He waited patiently for the inevitable question. Wilkie asked it. Professor Pinsky, Wijnnobel said, had reservations about some of Professor Eichenbaum's opinions – old political opinions, nothing to do with the conference. Hodgkiss looked at Wilkie, whom he knew well, and waited for the terrier to fasten on to the rat. Wilkie, not catching Hodgkiss's eye, said smoothly that that was quite all right, he would fit in with any such wishes, he was glad of the chance of the interview. Hodgkiss felt uneasy. Gerard Wijnnobel moved on to his next point. He said the University was prepared to contribute to the making of as full a filmed record of the proceedings as possible. We know you must select and discard, he said. But televised film is the medium of the future, and when we are discussing the juncture of body and mind, it will be in every way enhancing to have a visual record of the bodies, expressing the minds, so to speak, of the speakers. For our archive. We shall be pioneers in this.

Wilkie, who had every television director's desire to work with luxuriating coils and heaps of overmatter, agreed happily. He said he hoped his programme – his eventual programme – would be true to the purpose of the gathering, which he respected enormously, enormously. Hodgkiss again felt uneasy.

The discussion moved on to the content of the various papers – the pure sciences, the applied sciences, the human sciences, the arts, the humanities, languages, maths, philosophy, even sport. Frederica looked distractedly out into the garden. The Barbara Hepworth wound its paradoxically weightless volute of weight around its captured air and silent strings. Frederica thought the easy, banal and invigorating thought, There's a woman who has *done* things. With heavy hammers and mallets and chisels, she imagined vaguely. Her attention was recaptured, as attention has statistically been observed to be, by a reference both to a person and to a subject she understood. Raphael Faber was coming to speak on Proust's metaphors for the activity of the mind. Wijnnobel announced this with enthusiasm, and Hodgkiss permitted himself a prim little ironic smile. He said he was sure the paper would be a high point among high points.

Frederica saw a ring of snow-capped mountains on a horizon where none were. She was reading *The Lord of the Rings* aloud to Leo, and found her mind taken over by Tolkien's absolute landscapes and battles. 'There shall be counsel taken,' her mind had been muttering irrelevantly all morning, 'stronger than Morgul spells.' What a shivered, splintered mess her own mind now was. She remembered a much younger Frederica, who had

had some idea of metaphor as the flicker of fiction and connection in a world of religious belief, in what she had thought were the last days of the power and certainty of religious belief, in the days of *Paradise Lost*. She remembered demanding – or abjectly begging? – to write a thesis on religious metaphor with Raphael Faber, who had turned her away with a glass screen, a division, he was a modernist, he worked in French. And why should a Mallarmé expert not understand *Paradise Lost*, Frederica thought angrily in the mist of her own past, and then grinned at herself. (The grin was observed and misinterpreted by Hodgkiss, who was thinking about naked Raphael with his own grin.)

Frederica looked at the assembled academics and wondered why her own mind began to move so swiftly, so surely, in places where people were discussing ideas which had nothing (little) to do with what she was thinking about. An idea of herself in a library with time to pursue the nature of metaphor until she had understood it – well, until her understanding was quite other than it was now – overwhelmed her with sadness. She had made a wrong choice. She sat about dressed as a clever metaphor, in an easy-to-grasp metaphorical glass box, like a mermaid in a raree show, and posed trivial superficial questions with trivial superficial brightness. She saw herself as a mayfly on water, and changed the metaphor to one of those copper-coloured dragonflies that dart and glitter. She looked at the assembled academics, and saw, not as Hodgkiss did, the windings and manœuvres of small territorial jealousies and large ambitions, but an angelic group of humans dedicated to thought, to thinking things *through*, thought Frederica, staring mistily through the Hepworth stone tunnel.

Gerard Wijnnobel was in fact talking about the artificial invisible barriers between disciplines. He said it was natural for the mind to erect them and to work within them – they were forms, philosophy, bio-chemistry, grammar – to which the Towers of the University gave a metaphorical solidity. But such forms were scaffolds, he said, such towers were lookouts, from which other forms could be seen, to which other forms could be linked. The world was infinitely multifarious and its elements were simple and could be seen from infinite viewpoints, in infinite rearrangements.

Frederica, not quite listening, though later she remembered every word, for half her attention was enough for memory, thought of John Ottokar, and his idea that she should work here, with these people, on these things –

Vincent Hodgkiss looked at Gerard Wijnnobel with love, and saw him as the Architect of Babel. An architect who, contrary to a quick imagining of such a person, was intent not upon chaos, but upon the discovery and communication of extraordinary order.

His love for the Vice-Chancellor had always included the rhythm of Browning's poem, 'A Grammarian's Funeral', in which a group of mediaeval disciples bear their dry-as-dust, detail-obsessed, time-defeated teacher to his last resting-place on the peak of a high mountain. 'Leave him, still loftier than the world suspects / Living, and dying.' Most people read that poem as a comic condemnation of a life drained of humanity by minute obsessions. And so it was, and yet it was not, because a fine excess was to be finely human, and grammar was *essentially* human, Hodgkiss thought. He thought Gerard Wijnnobel would not thank him for thinking of him in terms of funeral elegies, when he was concentrating on his work.

At this point in the discussion, silence fell, as Lady Wijnnobel, accompanied by Odin and Frigg, crossed in front of the window, resolute and angry-looking. For a moment she stood, her big face under a vaguely academic tricorned hat peering in at them. Then she swung away, and stomped off across the lawn, leaving a trail in the damp grass.

Elvet Gander said, when she had gone through the hedge, 'She is very diligent and very much appreciated in your, so-to-speak, shadow-entity.'

Wijnnobel said nothing. Wilkie asked Gander, what does she teach? Astrology, said Gander. He added that he himself had recently become very interested in astrology. He added that it was an ancient form of thought – of experience – *in* which, so to speak, generations had lived.

Hodgkiss saw his moment, and asked lightly if Gander had any idea how the Anti-University might propose to react to the Conference. Gander said he guessed many of them might attend, if permitted. He said, abstractedly, that he didn't suppose there'd be trouble from them, if that was the question. He thought they were humming along with their own affairs. Humming along.

Hodgkiss thought Gander looked unwell. He was thinner, and had aged. He seemed, somehow, perpetually distracted.

They stood and chatted over coffee. Wilkie and Gander considered the uncompromising reductive mystery of the Mondrians. Wilkie said it wasn't clear to him why human beings were driven to reduce their world to minimal elements. Horizontals and verticals, particles and pixels, it might be wired into the way the brain worked. Maybe a Mondrian was a map of a brain, Mondrian's brain, anyone's brain. Gander looked restlessly about him and fixed his gaze on the Rembrandt astrologer. He said he himself was becoming more and more involved in more elementary, that was, more elemental, forms of experience. The word 'primitive' was probably nonsense.

Freud began as a neurologist, said Gander. He made his map of the mind like a three-storeyed house, with the Id rampaging in the basement and the Superego frowning away under the eaves. It was all in the end *personal*, said Gander. Carl Gustav was an old charlatan, but old charlatans know things – about things – about the general consciousness – that tight-arsed ironists like the supremely rational Sigmund don't pay enough attention to. What things? said Wilkie. Gander's hooded eyes stared over his head. Gods and demons, said Gander. Forces of nature. Things you meet in the great dreams, not the nagging little personal ones. The things behind the forms people thought up for mystery, like alchemy and astrology. Those kids, he said, waving vaguely in the direction of the encampment beyond the garden, beyond the University, those kids in the counter-culture are playing with the things of the spirit as though they were clouds of coloured smoke, or – corn-dollies – or – or mugs with pretty crabs and scorpions and bulls and lambs painted on them for birthdays.

No harm in that, necessarily, said Wilkie.

I think there's harm, said Gander. Ideas are stronger than individuals, so are forms of the spiritual life, they twist, they pull. They mould.

Lyon Bowman came up and said he hoped Wilkie was going to televise his paper on chemical and electrical communication in neurones.

Wilkie said, oh yes. He was still considering the psychoanalyst. He had just had an interesting idea.

Frederica was surprised to be tapped on the shoulder by the Vice-Chancellor. He wanted to show her something, he said. His long, nutcracker face smiled down on her. 'It's a new project,' he said, leading her out of his study, and away into the antechamber of the Hall of Long Royston, with its minstrels' gallery. This space now contained several free-standing glass cases. 'We are building a collection to show the history of this house, and the history of the University,' he said. 'As you see, most of our space is still empty. But I have something here which is of interest to you, perhaps.'

The box contained Alexander Wedderburn's drawings for the costumes for *Astraea* in 1953. It contained also some of the costumes, and photographs of the actors and actresses. There were ribbons and embroideries, bum-rolls and ruffs, a fox-coloured cone of artificial curls, a necklace of fake pearls and false enamel. There was Marina Yeo, photographed in black and white, dying regally on a monstrous cushion. There was the glass-and-wire crown, the musical instruments, rebeck and lute, pipes and tambours. There was Wilkie, playing Sir Walter Raleigh, much thinner and wearing his own look of intelligent mischief. There was Alexander, holding hands with Frederica and Marina Yeo, in a photo-call of the entire pinheaded motley New Elizabethan cast. There was her old school-teacher, Felicity Wells, who had died on a school trip, quite suddenly, in front of the Bayeux tapestry, her finger raised to explain that here was the death of Harold, the last English King. Marina Yeo was not dead, but was crippled with arthritis, her hands twisted into claws, her legs bowed. She had been – to an extent – saved by the television, on which she played spiteful and super-sharp detecting ladies in serial thrillers, swathed in chiffon, holding herself up in arm-chairs.

And there was Frederica, running in her shift past the fountain with the naked putti, her red hair streaming, her thin legs visible through the streamers of her scissored skirts.

She stared at the uninhabited dresses and the lifeless faces in their airless space.

Time had not stopped there, oh no.

All the photographs were black and white (and grey, of course).

The silks and satins and nylons and rayons had faded – and were a little stained – but not much.

She smoothed her real hands over her real gaudy skirt, and felt the ground under her feet.

'Interesting,' said the Vice-Chancellor. 'I was wondering if you had kept – if you have any – mementos?'

Frederica said she didn't think she had. Certainly nothing significant.

They walked back to join the others in the study.

Wilkie said he had had a brilliant idea, he would tell her later. *Who is it that can tell me who I am?*

XXII

Luk Lysgaard-Peacock went to look for John Ottokar. He should not have needed to go and look for him, for it was working hours, and he should have been beside his machinery. Luk's calculations continued to burgeon. He walked across the increasingly inhabited campus, where buildings were still going up, and asked people if they had seen John Ottokar. He came on him – or rather, them – unexpectedly, in the grassy amphitheatre in front of the Henry Moore statue of the King and Queen.

They were sitting facing each other, astride a stone bench strategically placed for those who wished to sit and contemplate the statues, and the moorland behind them. They were both wearing jeans and the rainbow-coloured tabard-like sweaters, which were striking enough singly, and which John, recently, had seemed to have abandoned. They were leaning in towards each other, and apparently arguing – their long, pageboy hair swung along the sides of their heads, which they tossed first forwards, then sideways, in emphasis or denial. Their arms flung out, or gestured, in symmetrical reverse, left and right, right and left. He wondered if they were mirror-twins, as he had wondered before, and never asked. It seemed too personal a question, and unwanted. Their knees were touching. Luk had the thought, looking up at the King and Queen, that they were like a two-headed playing-card, the Knave of Hearts or of Diamonds. He had no idea which was which. He thought that it was curious that a duplicated reality appeared to be less, not more, real than a singularity.

When he came up to them, they both became still, and turned their same faces on him, with the same questioning look.

He saw which was which, because one had differently-glittering fingernails, blue, black, pink, green, as he pushed back his hair.

He said he had another problem, with his figures. Paul-Zag said 'We have problems, ourselves, too.' He smiled sweetly. John continued to stare, emptily. Luk said he was pretty desperate, in a matter-of-fact voice. 'Desperate's a relative term,' said Paul-Zag. 'There's desperate and desperate.'

Luk did not know what he would have done, if at this point Frederica Potter had not appeared, with her red-headed son, looking determined and anxious. Paul-Zag sat on his fingers. They stared their identical stare at the newcomers.

'Hi, John O,' said Leo, vaguely, to both.

'I was looking for you,' said Frederica to John.

'Nice of you,' said John. 'You didn't say you were coming.'

'I did, in general. I wasn't sure when, in particular. I'm here now.'

'So I see.'

The twins were taking up the whole of the stone seat. The others had to remain standing. Frederica asked Paul how the community was, with an effort of courtesy.

'Great things are happening,' said Paul. 'We're building a Pale. We're enclosing our own ground. We may become an enclosed order, so to speak.'

'Enclosed?'

'Not coming out. No one coming in,' said Paul-Zag. 'We aren't good enough at cultivating quite yet. We're working it out.'

Luk said 'Where does it go – where will it go – this Pale?'

'Round and round. Round all the land inside. To keep it from exploitation and destruction. To preserve it.'

All the land, asked Luk, who had been upon the moors and had seen a wandering group of diggers, and a small white van full of planks, at a distance.

Paul-Zag said *yes, all*. He said it was good for body and soul to work so hard. Then, he said to John, we shall all have to choose.

'You come in and out,' said Frederica. 'You come and play your music. In that tent, in the Anti-University. I know, because Will comes and listens. He thinks you're the greatest.'

Paul-Zag swayed back and forwards on the bench. He said that would come to an end, it would all come to an end. He said inanely that it was the birth of tragedy from the spirit of music, and winked knowingly at Frederica, who felt as though he had spat at her.

On the gravel road below them, the same small white van drew up, the one Luk had seen up on the moorland. It was being driven by Elvet Gander, who parked it, and came up into the King and Queen's amphitheatre. He nodded pleasantly at Frederica, acknowledged Luk, patted Leo on the head, and said to Paul he was glad he had found him, he would give him a lift back to the Hall. Paul stood up, looking down, his arms hanging. John moved his leg, so that he was now sitting rigidly on the bench, facing the others, almost in an imitation of the pose of the bronze figures. Gander said to him

'You want to come?'

John did not answer. 'Not yet?' said Gander pleasantly. He said to Paul 'Not yet.'

Luk said to Gander 'I'm told you're enclosing the land.'

'So it would appear. A symbolic reality of some importance. A space for contemplation, for concentration.'

'A concentration camp.'

Gander waved a dismissive hand. 'Not worthy of you, Mr Peacock. A *bad* joke. Be careful with words, they hurt.'

He led Paul away to the van, where he, though not Paul, turned back to wave amiably enough at John and the others. The van gave off a curious winking glitter as it drew away. It appeared to be full of mirrors, piled against each other, their planes distributing light.

Luk, worried now about his snail populations as well as his figures, turned to expostulate with John Ottokar.

John Ottokar said to Frederica 'Well, shall I? What do you think? Shall I go in there?'

'Don't be silly. You don't want to. It's all nonsense. It's all increasingly frightening *nonsense*. You know that.'

'I do, do I? And you know me, do you? You think you can do away with the god I grew up with, just because you choose to call Him nonsense?'

'*John –*' said Frederica.

'I'd better get on with this stuff of Luk's,' said John, snatching at Luk's folder of figures. Luk opened his mouth to explain his problem, and John strode away without waiting to listen.

Frederica and Luk sat together on the bench, beneath the

statues. Frederica wanted to cry, or to shout, but not in front of Lysgaard–Peacock, who had rebuffed her the last time they had met. She said, in a small voice

'It is all nonsense.'

'Of course it is. But not to him, apparently.'

'I can't understand how *anyone* can believe – can seriously believe –'

'Can't you? I can. I did myself, once. I don't now. Then it was clear to me – that there was – oh –' he was embarrassed – 'God. And now it's quite clear that there isn't, or anyway, nothing we can know or care about.'

They sat together in silence for a moment. Leo had wandered off to inspect the statues.

Frederica said 'I behaved badly. As usual.'

'Not particularly. He's been in an odd mood. I've been pushing him around, with figures.'

There was a silence, not uncompanionable. Luk said 'If they put their damned Pale round my snail populations . . .'

'Surely they can't. Surely they'll let you in.'

'Why? Why should they?'

Frederica subsided into silence. Luk said

'It can't be easy, there being two of them.'

'It isn't.' Frederica thought and then said 'It's hellish. I was so determined not to give in – that is, not to let it – them – *it* – get me down.'

'Hard to see how it will change,' said Luk, with the gloomy satisfaction of a man whose own life is going badly. 'Though if that one gets concentrated in a *camp* – this one –'

'He came up here to get away from him. And now he's back.'

'He's good at his job,' said Luk. 'Indispensable. I'm writing this paper for the conference. Snarled-up in maths. He's been very good.'

'He is good,' said Frederica. She thought they should stop talking about her own problems, and asked how Jacqueline was.

'As far as I know, absolutely fine.'

There is a whole narrative in the words 'As far as I know'. Frederica nodded quickly. She asked what Luk's paper was about.

'The disadvantages of sex for Darwinian adaptation. The cost of meiosis, if that means anything to you – the splitting of fertilised cells to form the zygote. Uses up a lot of energy compared to other methods.'

'Other methods?'

'Parthenogenesis. Clones. Budding.'

'I see. Well, I don't, but I'm interested. I shall listen to your paper.'

'Twins, of course, are a sort of clone. In some cases. Or one can be a bud of the other. We think. He doesn't like my research. He doesn't like the idea – from the *religious* point of view – that what we call altruism is a kind of machinery of self-propagative interest. And he doesn't like my views about the redundancy of the male.'

A small smile flickered over Luk's intent face, as he thought of the satisfactory lining-up of his evidence and his argument, however involved and difficult it was proving to be.

'What matters,' he said, 'is getting things as right as we can. Describing the world *as it is*.'

'Oh yes,' said Frederica. 'I wonder if I ought to go after him?'

'Do you want to?'

Frederica thought about it. 'I've got to sort it out.'

'You might let him take a run at my figures, first,' said Luk Lysgaard-Peacock.

Men, thought Frederica, as Leo came up and put his arms round her, neither bud nor clone, but himself. She smelled the hay and fur smell of his hair. Luk Lysgaard-Peacock moved along the bench, stood up, and walked away.

'See you,' he said.

'Sure,' said Frederica.

Will and Leo went into the Teach-Inn. Leo wrinkled his nose at the intense smell of sewage and incense mixed. Will had become a silent and solitary teenager, dark like his father, slighter in build, with his father's dark eyes and his mother's milder mouth, which in him, at this age, often looked sullen. He seemed to like Leo, and was happy enough to take him about, despite the five-year age-gap.

He said 'You've got to hear this mind-blowing music. If he's playing. He comes and goes.' Leo said 'OK,' amiably but without enthusiasm. Like his mother, he was impervious to the enchantment of music. He was explaining to Will, as they negotiated the earthy paths between the booths, that since he got his new family he didn't really see it any more. He said his new step-brother and sister were younger than him. He said that when he did go to visit his father, he couldn't go riding. Sooty was dead, and the new family, Robin and Emma, had got new little ponies that were much too small for anyone Leo's size. They were called Shellover and Petit Gris. Shelly and Petty for short, said Leo. I'd look ridiculous if I went on them, so I don't. Even if I was asked, which I'm not, actually. Shame, said Will, who was listening for sounds, which he heard. He's there, said Will. Now you'll hear something. Blow your mind. Leo said, had Will noticed the funny smell. Naturally, said Will. You get used to it.

Leo was surprised, on entering the singing-space, to see that the singer was John O's unnerving brother, though he realised at once that he went with the smell. He was sitting on a tallish three-legged stool, bent over his guitar, from which ribbons dangled, crimson, gold and silver. He was wearing his jester's jerkin and his fingernails were painted alternately black with white whorls and white with black whorls. He also had glittery eyelids. His audience was mixed, and rapt. A few hippies, a large number of boys and girls more or less Will's age, a group of student-looking people from the University. They were all sitting on a kind of oriental floor of patchwork cushions. It was quite dark. It was a dull day, and the light through the canvas roof was dimly ruddy. Leo opened his mouth to say that this was only Paul O, and Will hushed him, and pulled him down among the gathering on the cushions. Leo listened to the strumming. There was no microphone. Simply the flow of the music, and then, the clear singing voice.

Leo thought that if Tolkien had been describing this music he would have said that it was like the endless rippling and eddying of a brook, with rapids and whirlpools. There were quite a few Tolkienish people in the audience, people with silvery bands round their brows and those sort of flimsy shirts which flared out to pointy cuffs and dangled. Leo didn't like to see them. They looked sort of made-up and unreal, and in some way diminished the shining reality of the Tolkien-world in his head. He felt Will next to him settling into the cushions, and glanced at his face, which was smiling vaguely and gently.

The song wasn't really vague and gentle, though it twanged and rippled in an endless sort of way.

O the One and the Many, the Many and the One
The fire in the flame, the crystal in the cone,
The brain in the skull and the red thread in the bone
The air going by, and the shadow in the sun.

Flakes of flame in the flint, flakes of ice on the moon
Flakes of green in the leaf, we are many we are one
We are one, we are many, flakes of ash on your sleeve
We are eaten, we are whole, we return, we stay, we leave.

A bubble on the ocean, a flower on the loom
A worm in a loam-maze, a day's-eye in the gloom
We are one we are many, we are many we are one
We spin the thread and twist it, and cut it when it's done.

I am god I am maggot I am minstrel I am string
I am mind I am matter I am motion I am thing
I am gun I am bullet I am many I am one
I can kill and resurrect you I am god when you are gone.

O the feast and the firelight O the goat and the skin
O the horns and the knuckles and the dancing and the din
O the One and the Many, O the Many and the One
O the dancing and the dreaming, until the feast is done.
Until we have consumed ourselves and feast and fire are done.

Burn me up burn me up, make me fire make me light,
Eat my skull eat my heart, eat my bo-ones so-o white.
We are one, we are many, we are many, we are one.
We are god, we are lymph, we are god, we are gone.

Leo looked at Paul-Zag's face, in its swinging hair, in the
incense-smoke. He felt he didn't want him to notice him, and he
felt he didn't want to be there. So he wriggled away from Will,
who was nodding with closed eyes, with the music, and crawled
on his stomach to the edge of the booth, and went out. He took a
deep breath, forgetting the smell, and then told himself it was no
worse, really, than Sooty's stall when Sooty had just pissed in the
straw. There was no one to whom he could speak of the loss of
Sooty. He wandered along a branch of the internal pathway, and
came to the Mother Goose at the wicket-gate, and Deborah
Ritter reading to a smallish assembly of children. He thought he

was too big for such community tale-telling, which reminded him of school. And he didn't like the paper sunflowers, much, or the cardboard cabbages. But he heard a sentence he knew, and turned back to listen.

'Unlikely though it may seem,' said the Whistler to Dracosilex, 'there are things we have in common.'

Artegall thought there could be no two creatures less similar than the tall birdwoman, with her long neck and soft, soft overlapping feathers and down, and the flint-lizard, who moved little but his golden eyes, like slivers of light in soot. The wind ruffled all the Whistler's plumage, so that she looked light enough to blow away like a cloud, and vanish in an airstream. Whereas Dracosilex was squat and compact, even his strong claws only sketched on his rocky body, unless he needed to move. Little threads of fire flickered constantly along his black back.

'We are both neither one thing nor the other,' said the Whistler, mournfully. The Whistlers had many moods, of which mournfulness was only one. They could scream with joy in the wind, they could scold, they could sing in harmony. Dracosilex chuntered to himself quietly enough. He had two moods only. Stolidity, verging on inertia, and incandescence, which terrified everyone. At the moment, he was stolid.

'We are neither birds nor women,' said the Whistler. 'And you are neither snake nor stone. What runs in your veins is not blood, but stonelight, and what runs in ours is not human kindness, but veins of sorcery full of sky and air. We can never have mates, for we would have to choose, men or birds, and we will not give up our feathers.'

As for him, Dracosilex said, he and his kind appeared when certain so to speak knots formed in the silica. It makes eggs that make us, he said. There is never more than one of us, in any mountain range.

Leo stood and listened, just outside the gate. When Deborah Ritter had closed the book, she smiled amiably at Leo, and asked him if he liked the story.

'Oh yes. It's my story.'

'*Your* story?'

'I'll show you,' said Leo. He opened the gate, and went in.

'It's dedicated to me. For Leo and Saskia, it says. We were *told* this story.'

'How wonderful,' said Deborah Ritter, politely. She said 'So you know the writer of this book? She must have a lot of money.'

'Not really,' said Leo. 'We all live in a very *mean*, that is *ordinary* place. We are not really a family, but we are like a family. We are two women, and two children, and this story was told for us . . .'

He was happily settled, lecturing the assembled children, with some of his mother's arrogance, on life in Hamelin Square when Will caught up with him, and pulled him away. Will was embarrassed. And a little annoyed that a sense of responsibility had made him leave the singing. They walked home in a complex silence.

★

Gerard Wijnnobel looked at his wife across the breakfast table. She was eating fiercely, forkfuls of scrambled egg, great gleeful snatched bites of butterbright toast. He said

'Eva, I have tried not to restrict your freedom, or dictate your actions in any way. You must do me the justice of recognising this.'

Lady Wijnnobel chewed. She smiled through the chewing.

'Please listen to me. I do ask you *not to do this*.'

She swallowed, and smiled.

'You cannot prevent me.'

'No,' said Wijnnobel, patiently. 'I cannot. But I have never before asked you – myself – for a concession, a consideration. Please consider what is at stake. With the Conference so near. And the volatile situation with regard to the students.'

'Hmnf. All my life has been subordinated to your whims and your *importance*. Now, I am asked to speak for myself. And you try to prevent me. It is all of a piece.'

It is not, he told her in his mind. It is not so. Not quite or altogether so.

'Free speech,' said his wife, through more toast. 'You b'lieve in free speech.'

'Oh, yes.'

'And *I* am asked to speak – on the air, in person – about what I believe. And you try to prevent me.'

'It is a bad moment.'

'You mean, you don't like what I say. But you can't stop me saying it, Gerard, unless you restrain me. Bodily, so to speak. Bodily.'

He looked down at the table, and saw his own wooden face in the polished wood.

339

It came to him that since she would not listen, his speech had made things worse. God knew, he thought, what she would now do, if, for instance, he were to appeal over her head to Edmund Wilkie, who must in any case have thought of all these matters – his own problems – before making this – on the face of it – dangerous and absurd proposal.

As she often did, Eva appeared to read his mind.

'The young man came to hear one of my weekly lectures,' she said. 'To assess me, no doubt, to assess my presence of mind, and so forth. He said he was very impressed. He said there is a great deal of interest in astrology, these days.'

'So there is,' said Wijnnobel, truthfully.

'Well then,' said his wife. 'It is natural that I should be approached. And natural that I should accept. Please think no more of it.'

Gerard Wijnnobel, daunted, lowered his crest in defeat.

John Ottokar stood in the doorway of his university room, and tried to prevent Frederica from leaving. They had not been to bed together. Frederica had not felt able to be naked in front of this man who knew every inch of her skin, outer and inner. She wanted to be separate. She wanted to be gone. She was not thinking. John was both thinking and speaking, as though she might be able to hear him. His voice churned in her mind like water at the bottom of some deep pothole, vaguely audible. He said that he had come to her classes, all those years ago, to learn how to speak, and now he was speaking and she must listen. She must help him, she must save him, for he was being torn apart and destroyed. In the days before she had taught him to speak, he said, he had had maths and mutterings, mutterings with *him*, which no one understood. Except God, maybe, and Frederica did not like God. He had wanted to be – he said, his language faltering – an *individual* in an ordinary world – and she was the way, she must not let him go. He had tried to – to keep steady through work – but work was full of terrible things, it was soul-destroying. I work to prove the individual is nothing, said John Ottokar, eloquently. Frederica stood and waited, inside the door. I want you to marry me, said John Ottokar, and we will make a good home for Leo, and you can do whatever you want, whatever you want.

She had been attracted to his grace and self-assurance, and now these were gone. She had a terrible sense of a weight of responsibility and an even more violent urge to escape, to get out, to go away. Instinct had got her into this, and instinct was hoisting her out by the hairs, and reason and humanity were nowhere. She waited for him to finish speaking, which took a long time, for he had become good with words, and appeared to believe he was pleading for his life.

Then she said she had to go.

John Ottokar said she was a bitch.

Frederica said that was very true, she was, she saw she was.

She said, let me out.

He lowered his crest in defeat and she went out. She was leaving for London the next day.

She wept in bed, for what seemed like hours, a pillow over her head, out of consideration for Leo, in the next room, who must not hear a grief that was not his.

When she finally fell asleep, she dreamed that she was running between trees, naked among the ribbons of her cut dress. Someone was behind her, was gaining on her, had grabbed her from behind and hoisted her high, driving an anonymous cock in between her arrested legs. Someone was stroking her hair, and she twisted round to see who, for she hated lovemaking in dreams, she fought invasion and involuntary surrender. She was lifted up, and up, ridiculously high, always with the rigid thing between her legs. Her face saw a face between the leaves of the canopy, and her mind had a momentary memory of Alice's encounter with the angry bird. The face was the face of Luk Lysgaard-Peacock, and he was laughing.

★

The Vice-Chancellor watched *Through the Looking-Glass* alone in his drawing-room. The curtains were open, and the stars were scattered across a clear sky, interspersed with thin cloud, and the purposeful linear winking of man-made lights. The Alice-in-a-box-of-mirrors set was decorated with the vanishing grins of the Cheshire Cat, interspersed with fishbones and nursery stars. Frederica wore black, with a necklace of spherical green glass beads. Gander sat on her right hand, white-robed, perspiring in the white lights. Eva was on her left, arrayed in a velvet gown of dull purple, with a boat-shaped neck and a heavy gilded collar, with inset stones, almost certainly of symbolic significance. Someone had smoothed her thick hair into a sleek form, and had sprayed it into a crisped solidity, like meringue-crust, cinder-black.

He saw immediately that she was very nervous. Her nostrils were flaring, her breathing was laboured, she was dabbing at her red-red lips with a screwed-up tissue. Little spheres of sweat stood on her frowning forehead, above the huge, uncompromising eyebrows. The one thing he had not thought to worry about was whether she would be afraid, or made ill again by the experience. He was angry with himself: he had been concerned simply with what she might say, and how she might say it.

He watched Frederica Potter, who must by now be experienced in reading nervous states. She embarked on a series of banal, easy questions. Astrology wasn't anything so simple as fortune-telling columns in newspapers, was it? Astrology had always been there, hadn't it, it had been used to explain history and the human psyche and the movements of the heavenly bodies? Eva began to make her usual cumbersome, angry, faintly threatening assertions. Like a bull, he thought, no, a cow, hurling itself at a fluttered pink silk cloak. She felt better for getting her mouth open, as everyone did. She said that the moon pulled the seas, which was hard for common sense to credit, and small human lives were part of large cosmic movements. And over the ages, people, some people, had learned to read these movements and connections finely. Astronomy, put in Gander, was the child of astrology, as chemistry was the child of alchemy, and there were two ways of looking at ancient things, one of which was to understand that they were deeply human, deeply human, not just errors but clues to our own nature, as our genes and chromosomes also were. Also our dreams. All had their limitations. All their power.

They discussed Dr John Dee, who was the evening's personality, his occult knowledge, its human consequences. They discussed the fact that many contemporary cultures and communities still did nothing without consulting an astrologer. Gander said that the counter-cultural movement was aware of old spiritual forms, was deeply into their renewal, their so to speak *re-volution* into the Light once more . . .

342

They looked at the object, which was a Renaissance celestial globe, showing the creatures spread across the dark, crab and scorpion, bull and ram, goat and fishes. Frederica said that as a little girl she had always thought of these as the stuff of poetry, made-up things, that weren't there, and yet were there, because you said they were there. She couldn't get her mind round the celestial globe, she said, because it wasn't a real thing, what was out there was infinity, this was just an imaginary spherical skin, unlike a terrestrial globe.

Lady Wijnnobel said, with a toothy smile that wasn't really placatory, that Frederica must have been, must be, quite a *silly* little girl, since these forms were poetic truth, but also truth in a form that all those – she waved her arm dismissively, shaking the frame of the set – molecules and things – couldn't express, couldn't begin to express. Her voice took on its liquid, beating note. She spoke of how the Creator had wanted to make a world in which He had created ensouled creatures linked with every conceivable area of nature in the most profound sense. Every ensouled creature had its form, pincer and horn, fin and feeler, that connected it to the whole universe at one particular point. The old myths knew this. Modern man dissected everything with his senses and had made a new ignorance. 'Instinct is a deeper and wiser guide to the totality of nature, to the ultimate wisdom, than ordinary human understanding. True, we humans fly, we swim, but unnaturally, but awkwardly, at what a cost to earth, to water, to air. Now, the signs are the forms which head us *back* . . .'

The camera held her wide, urgent, stressful face. Gerard Wijnnobel stood up, as though embracing the glass box, or breaking it, could stop her flow. Frederica Potter said, conversationally, lightly,

'You know, it's hard on those of us who have the *human* signs. If you buy a pottery mug, or a place-mat, or something, with your own sign on it, you get a beautiful form if it's a crab or a scorpion or the fishes, and usually you get not bad goats and rams and bulls. Even Sagittarius is OK. But the Virgin and the Twins they always come out simpering and sentimental. They look like Disney's Snow White, or ghastly mass-made statuettes of the Virgin Mary, with sweet little doll-faces. I know, because I'm the Virgin.'

The camera had moved away from Eva, whose long sentences

trailed like underwater weeds amongst the beginning of Frederica's froth. Frederica's face smiled out at the Vice-Chancellor, modern, trivial, and reassuring.

Lady Wijnnobel could not resist the inevitable question. 'Virgo, are you?'

'Does that surprise you?'

'No, no. I knew you were Virgo.'

'And what is the Virgo character?'

'She is closed in herself. She is focused inwards, and shuts off the outside world. She is innocent and without dark wisdom. There is a price to pay for this dreaminess, in general.'

Gander joined in, and challenged Eva to diagnose his own position on the Zodiac. He was correctly – according to him – told he was Sagittarius, warhorse and archer, animal and semi-divinity, two beings in one. Lady Wijnnobel had lipstick on her teeth. The conversation trickled into the runnels of many, many, previous human conversations, and was duly brought to an end.

The Vice-Chancellor thought hopefully that it could have been much worse. Given that it had happened at all. Better not to count in his head how many millions was it of people would have seen her. It was of course possible, even probable, that what she said made more sense to them than anything he himself might ever say about the algorithms of the Universal Grammar. He thought with his usual pleasure of Noam Chomsky's example of a perfectly grammatical, perfectly meaningless sentence. 'Colourless green ideas sleep furiously.' He always associated it with Sir Charles Sherrington's more ornate, and not meaningless metaphor for thought. 'The brain is an enchanted loom where millions of flashing shuttles weave a dissolving pattern.' He thought he would include both in his opening remarks for the Conference. Poetry struck out of everything like sparks from flint. The forms of astrology were not privileged, were indeed worn, over-handled coinage. He smiled at the gallant banality of Frederica Potter and her multiplied simpering virgins on mugs. And their juxtaposition, oh yes, with the cats' teeth, and the fishbones, and the stars, and, he was afraid, his wife's teeth, and the jagged edges of her necklace-thing. In a glass box. A new metaphor.

Meanwhile, since his wife was in London, and not at his side, he could sit and read a book. He took up the one he was currently reading. As was everyone else, he had discovered.

Artegall said, 'Just because it is written in books, doesn't mean it isn't real. The books say take notice of every little detail, how every stone lies, how every twig is broken. They have drawings of how sand is disturbed, and how deep fast footprints differ from light springing ones.'

'They can't do smells,' said Mark. 'You can't describe a smell, so's anyone would recognise it, if they didn't know it.'

'You'd be surprised,' said Artegall. 'They've got lists of honeys that resemble each other — ones like wine, ones like roses, ones like heathers, ones like primroses . . . They've got lists of rotting fishes and which you can still eat and which you shouldn't . . .'

'You've got to begin by knowing a rose, or a rotten fish, though.'

'That's the point,' said Artegall. 'In the schoolroom, there was neither one nor the other. Only the words. I liked the words. But out here, there's the things, and of course they're different, but you've got to admit, the words have helped. Now and then.'

Mark had to admit grudgingly that Artegall's knowledge of tracking and fishing had in fact proved extremely useful.

The Vice-Chancellor read on. It was a good story. He could feel things looming, in the world outside. He read on.

XXIII

The Conference opened without problems on 15th June. Gerard Wijnnobel welcomed the guests in the University Theatre in the Central Tower, and made a brief speech on the Idea of a University. There was then a welcoming party in the great Hall of Long Royston, where the television people mingled with the assembled scholars. The students had finished their exams. Some had gone home, and some were attending the Conference. The assembled scholars smiled benignly at the little group of protesters organised by Nick Tewfell, with placards denouncing the unjust tyranny of exams. Inside, there were very acceptable Nordic open sandwiches, red and white wine, and a summery fruit punch. Hodder Pinsky and Theobald Eichenbaum were both there, and were not speaking to each other. Frederica was pleased that Pinsky recognised her. He was standing by a pillar, under the minstrels' gallery, himself a gleaming pillar, ice-blond head, blue glasses, ice-blue shirt, off-white linen jacket and trousers.

Wilkie pointed out Eichenbaum. He was short and very broad, standing close to the ground on thick legs. He was not fat, he was big-boned, and very muscular. His skin was tautly wrinkled all over, and tanned, no doubt because he spent most of his working life out of doors. He wore heavy owlish glasses, and had very thick white hair which pushed into a very thick, fanning white beard, surrounding full, complicated lips. He was a walking legend. His work on wolf-packs, domestic dogs, foxes and jackals contained a series of classic descriptions of the behaviour of beasts in the wild and under domestication. He had also worked on the learning patterns, parental and sexual behaviour, mating rituals and displacement activities of generations of domestic fowl and wild quail. He lived by a lake, in a German forest, and had a famous wood hut to which he retired to think, surrounded by animals who thought he was a kind of stag, or goose, or fox, or rabbit, or crow, or chicken, or wood-god. He could always think up a way of studying a behaviour pattern but did not bother with scientifically controlled experiments. He was unmarried, and kept his assistants, it was said, at a distance.

He was criticised more and more frequently for believing that human beings, like all other creatures, were full of an energy he called aggression, in English, and 'so-called Evil', *sogenannte Böse*, as Lorenz did, in German. It was said that he believed that this force was nature, and its suppression was damaging to animals, including the human animal. He had no time for those who believed in universal gentleness, or the possibility of teaching lions to lie down with lambs (unless the lions were denatured). And he preferred nature to nurture. As an explanation, and, it was said, as a state of being. There were photographs of him taken from a distance, wandering naked amongst his thickets and trees, his tanned hide blending with the bark, his brush of hair gleaming. Children were told stories about the man who spoke to the creatures. Social scientists told other tales, of intolerance and lack of understanding of human society or community.

Frederica saw Luk Lysgaard-Peacock, standing below the plaster frieze of the Death of Actaeon. He was talking to Jacqueline Winwar and Lyon Bowman: all wore cocktail smiles. Jacqueline was even thinner, and even more handsome. She was wearing a very plain nutmeg-brown mini-dress, which could only be worn by someone very confident of having a trim body, which she now had the right to be. She wore a soft scarlet buckled belt, resting on her hips. Frederica tried to guess the current relations between the three scientists, and couldn't. She walked up, anyway. She knew them all. She was pleased to see them.

Her arrival seemed to act as a signal for Bowman and Jacqueline to move away. This left Luk, who looked, and was, cross. He had had a difficult time, and was suffering from unexpected but intense stage-fright about his controversial paper. Shortly after Frederica's spring visit, John Ottokar had disappeared. He had not turned up to work one morning, had not turned up the next morning, and never turned up again. His room was found to be cleared of anything personal, such as clothes, razor and toothbrush – his books and slide-rule were still in their shelves. Luk prompted Abraham Calder-Fluss to ask Elvet Gander if the missing computer-scientist was in Dun Vale Hall. He had to do this, because Dun Vale Hall had ceremoniously closed its gates, when the Pale was completed, and had cut off the telephone. Gander appeared to be still coming in and out, as indeed was Canon Holly; they were both still scheduled to give papers at the Conference. But a resolutely dejected small group of members – mostly Quakers, crestfallen founders of the Spirit's Tigers, had shaken hands, it was told, and walked away from the locked gate towards the moorland. One or two more appeared, not saying much, during the next few weeks, and took trains back to the south. On the other hand, walkers were seen making their way with satchels and staves over the moorland, long-hairs and seekers, from Calverley and further afield. They were welcomed in. Some came out again. Elvet Gander told Abraham Calder-Fluss that there was no need to worry about John Ottokar. He was indeed inside, he was safely inside. Calder-Fluss asked whether he should consider he had resigned, or was on sick leave, or *what*? Gander said, he is certainly in need of help, that is my professional opinion. He will find himself in there, that is my personal opinion. You must do as you think fit about the salary.

Luk at the time was more concerned at the hiatus in his figures than at the possible spiritual fate of either or both Ottokars. He tried – with some success, but not enough – to persuade Marcus Potter to sort out some of the distributions and equations. Marcus was also helping Jacqueline, whose giant neurones were producing new bursts of action potential, and Christopher Cobb, who was giving a paper on learning in songbirds, especially chaffinches. Cobb, who ran the Centre for Field Studies in the moors, and was a world authority on ants, had branched out into birdsong, and had been working with some research students in the University's new animal behaviour centre. He was even less mathematical than Luk, and even more beleaguered by the approach of the Conference. He knew Eichenbaum slightly, and revered his work – with qualifications, and caveats, of a scientific nature. He was not a political animal. He did need computer help.

On top of that, the Hearers had enclosed what Luk was accustomed to think of as 'his' snail populations, although he knew very well that the land they were on belonged to Lucy Nighby, and the snails belonged, if to anyone, to themselves.

Luk marched up to the front gate of the drive leading to Dun Vale Hall. Two very thin young men, with very long lank hair, in white overshirts, were, so to speak, languidly guarding it. Luk explained about the snails. He explained about the length of his study. Geese gathered behind the guardians, spread their white wings experimentally, serpentined their sharp heads on their necks, and spoke like abrupt trumpets. The young men said he could not come in, and ceased to listen.

A letter to Gander, and a letter to Lucy Nighby, produced no reply. Luk reasoned that the perimeter could not all be always guarded. He made his snail observations at dawn. He did some prowling – his snail-infested wall was unfortunately *near* the place where Gunner had kept his motor bike, and the hen-battery had been. Luk reasoned that the buildings might still be in use, and tried to peer through knotholes in the fence. He heard hens running and bustling, and peewits, but no human movement. It was not a concentration camp. It would not have an armed guard and a watchtower. He came back before dawn with a saw and a shovel, and managed to remove a slightly split plank, making a hole he could slip through, replacing the plank behind him. He prospected. Farm-birds ran wildly out of his way. The buildings were dusty-windowed and their doors swung. Next day, he returned before dawn, with a back pack. He had to park some distance away, and had to carry his things over a hilltop, on rough ground. But no one had touched his entry point, and after a time, he felt it was safe to make regular dawn raids, to record snail movements, to put dabs of fresh blue, to count. All this filled him with a kind of irritated energy.

In some dark part of his soul, he put the absence of John Ottokar down to Frederica Potter, ignoring any part he himself, let alone Paul-Zag, might have played.

He had also seen the astrology episode of *Through the Looking-Glass*. His mood had veered back from cautious benignity to a semi-automatic hostility.

Frederica did not know whether to mention John Ottokar, whose absence was heavily present. She smiled her television smile at Luk, and said she was greatly looking forward to hearing his paper on sex. Luk glowered. Frederica said even more brightly that she hoped he would consider recording a personal interview. Sex was a topic that would be certain to interest the viewers. Luk said that he regretted the presence of the television, which trivialised things. And worse. Worse? said Frederica, behind her bright mask.

'Look what you did to the Vice-Chancellor. You should be ashamed. Letting that woman make a fool of herself – and him – in front of millions. Disseminating a package of dangerous lies.'

Frederica received an image of floating fungal spores over a pristine landscape. From one of those puffballs that exploded. She became combative, the more because she was, of course, disturbed about the Vice-Chancellor, who had been kind to her, in his way.

'Come on. There's nothing wrong with astrology. It's a sort of popular poetry. It lets people think in metaphors. Make lists and categories. People enjoy that. It's beautiful in its way.'

'No it isn't. It's fabrications, and untruths, and it does harm, because it prevents people from thinking. That woman's dangerous.'

'She's absurd. But I thought she – she stood up for herself.'

'It's like looking through a window covered with disgusting cobwebs and saying, that's what the sky's like,' said Luk.

'Well, you're the scientist. If the cobwebs're there, you have to be interested in them. You can't say they're not there. Been there for centuries.'

Luk was briefly baffled. He rallied.

'No, no, they're obscene, unreal forms of thought.'

'Our brains made them.'

'But they're *dead* forms. They're so much less interesting than – real things.'

'Reality's what you think it is.'

'No it isn't. It's what is. You're too clever to give me that one.'

'It wasn't my idea to put her on the programme. It was Wilkie's, he's got a streak of anarchic naughtiness. And he was right, we've had hundreds of letters, people are hungry for all these things, astrology and alchemy and spiritualism . . .'

'That's *why* –'

'Don't go on. I do know. I hate Elvet Gander, too. He's much more dangerous than she is, because he isn't obviously *mad*.'

The shadowy forms of John Ottokar and Paul-Zag shimmered between them.

Luk said 'I've had sleepless nights getting my paper together. It's too long. It's not wholly coherent.'

Frederica felt it would be presumptuous to try to console him, or to say anything anodyne, it'll be all right, or anything like that. She said well, she would be there to hear it. Unless the students disrupted everything.

'So far, there's only been placards, and a suspiciously docile little demo.'

Nick Tewfel, who had organised the demo, was visiting Deborah Ritter, Greg Tod, Waltraut Ross and Jonty Surtees. He knew that the demo was only the beginning, and he suspected uneasily that there were things about which he had not been told. The room in the cottage had changed: it was not that it had been swept for action, it was simply more cluttered. Three very large objects, like bedrolls, or stooks, stood against one wall, covered with old blankets. Greg Tod's working-table was covered with copies of a cyclostyled, stapled document. He and Waltraut Ross were bundling them together.

'We got them,' said Surtees. 'I was afraid they wouldn't be on time.'

They were translations of extracts from Theobald Eichenbaum's 'brown' paper of 1941, *Helder und Herde*, which was based on Francis Galton's chapter, in *Inquiries into Human Faculty* entitled 'Gregarious and Slavish Instincts'. Eichenbaum's paper was an exploration of the herding, flocking, and shoaling behaviour of creatures who found safety in masses. It observed the effects on predators of the massing and wheeling of the bodies of potential prey. It also, following Galton, took up both the comparison of the intelligence of wild and domesticated cattle and a comparison with civilised, or domesticated, human beings. Galton had argued that humans had inherited what he perhaps unfortunately called a 'slavish' attitude – a shrinking from responsibility, an incapacity to think independently – from some gregarious primeval ancestor. He believed that democracy, and careful breeding of intelligent men (eugenics), would increase responsibility. Galton believed that modern domesticated cattle were more independent than wild ones because the more aggressive and wilful had not been 'pruned' from the edge of the herd by lions and leopards, but had propagated themselves. Eichenbaum had subtly switched the emphasis – or anyway the language – and had used phrases derived from the vocabulary of National Socialism, to suggest that there were superior and inferior races of cattle (and men), some of whom were heroes, and some of whom were born to be the slavish herd, or to be eliminated.

Greg Tod had written an eloquent preface to the selective document, which was printed on what he called 'shit-brown' paper. The preface which began 'Has a man like this any "right" to be heard in a free society?', explained with rhetorical hammering every suspect term, and its political overtones. Sideswipes were taken at Galton and the evil of eugenics and selective breeding. Connections were drawn between Eichenbaum's admiration for the rituals of aggressive combat in wolf-packs, Prussian sabre-fights, and SS initiation rituals. The whole was illustrated with a cartoon image done by Ross of Eichenbaum with a slavering wolf-head on a puny poodle-rump (an allusion to the famous breeding experiment) surrounded by swastikas.

Nick Tewfell whistled. He asked if they were going to barricade the Theatre, or sit-in, or . . .

'We are going to make them sweat,' said Jonty Surtees, who was incandescent with enthusiasm. 'We are going to release these one by one, so they don't know where they're coming from, and go from a trickle to a flood . . .'

'They'll know they're coming from here.'

'No they won't, because they won't be. Don't ask. What you don't know, you can't tell anyone. We are going to begin with *little* things – minor irritations – so they keep thinking, is this it, is this *all*, and of course, it won't be. A good organiser makes his own troops feel they aren't going far enough fast enough . . . But it mustn't get out of hand. Yet.'

'And what are *these*?'

'These are for the Finale. You'll know in plenty of time.'

He swagged his mane, and smiled with huge cheerfulness. Nick Tewfell felt vaguely humiliated, and vaguely excited. He said

'We aren't going to let him speak?'

'Of course not. But we want to scare the shit out of him, first. And all the others. This is *it*. This is when we strike. This is when we were always going to strike. A blow towards the Revolution.'

He grinned again.

'We'll have some pretty fireworks and alarums and excursions before then –'

Hodder Pinsky gave the opening address. He stood in the theatre, in the centre of the circling blue velvet seats, his eyes invisible behind his flashing blue glasses, his white suit faintly gleaming over the sky-blue expanse of his shirt. His subject was 'Metaphors for the Matter of the Mind'.

He began with a compliment to Wijnnobel, who, he said, had tried to map the growth of the branching forms of language whose seeds, or germs, were, he was himself convinced, already in the developing human brain *in possibility*, before birth. And the branching diagrams of the hypothetical grammar resembled the Golgi-stains of dendrites and synapses for reasons both − so to speak − matter of fact, matter of physics and chemistry − and matter of metaphor. The word 'dendrite' derived from the Greek word for a tree, the name was an analogy. Human beings could not think without such metaphors and analogies, the action potential for an electrical jump of comparison must be born with the branchings of the grammatical forms in the embryonic brain to which he had just alluded. But what he intended to do, today, was to make opaque and visible and problematic, these facile and often beautiful metaphors with which human beings tried to think about thinking.

He himself was convinced that brain, nervous system, and mind were the *same thing*. There is, said Hodder Pinsky, no ghost in the machine, no external and invisible soul, no spirit, come from heaven, hell, or the pit of the stomach, that is not *in* and *of* that convoluted layered slab of white and grey matter and its branches and pulses. There was a time when psychoanalysts − Sigmund Freud himself − had been neurologists, had looked for things like the repeating compulsion in the closed-circuit firing of neurons. But now the human sciences had backed away from neurology. This was at least partly because they disliked the metaphors. It was very hard to make a philosophy of mind that was not simply a criticism of particular language.

He himself was interested in a science of mind that dealt with things that were only *approximately* objects of language, at all. We name them, but their names neither contain, nor confine them. We do not know what the largest part of them do, or are. In physics, it has been helpful to understand the nature of the atom by making an analogon, a metaphor, from the solar system, the planets moving around the sun. It had also been obstructive, and unhelpful, because electrons and positrons and neutrons are not, and do not really resemble, planets moving round the sun.

He talked for a time about mechanical images for the mind. He said that the founders of cybernetics had named their new science – that new metaphor – from the Greek, κυβερνητησ meaning a steersman, which gave rise in the mind to the idea of the brain as the intelligence guiding the beautifully designed vessel through the waves of chaos, or just possibly of the inventor of a system, a computing machine, as the political *governor* of another kind of system.

He spoke of the profound human resistance to the idea of mind as mechanism, or mechanisms in the mind. It came from many sources, often paradoxical. There was the old idea of God the watchmaker, and the human need to posit a designer for anything that was found to be working in a coherent and orderly way. There was the later, and quite different, fear of automatons, of man-made, non-vital, creatures or beings who could sing, or dance, or calculate, and might learn to replicate themselves. This fear of the machine had informed much of the anxiety caused by Galvani's discovery of bodily electricity, the mechanical jerking and twitching of dead frogs' legs attached to magnets.

There were also uses, and objections to uses, of metaphors from systems of human communication. Words like programme, code, information, transcription, encryption, message, translation, were not invented to describe either the operation of the neurones of the brain, or the physical mechanisms of computing-machines. They were derived from factual descriptions of writing and speaking, from human language, talking about itself.

He spoke of psychological metaphors – the idea of the 'entry' of a sense-impression into the brain, of the 'reproduction' of the outside world as a 'representation' inside the head. He spoke of the beautiful Renaissance idea, derived from all this, that the physical world, the vegetable world, the geological world, which had succeeded the creatures named by Adam in the Garden of Eden, was so to speak written by God in *signatures*, the names of things being inherent in the things, being, so to speak, their nature.

He spoke of mechanical metaphors drawn from the world of computing itself. To call certain patterns of behaviour, or reactions to stimuli, desires or aversions *hard-wired*, was to obscure as much as it illuminated about the physiology of mental processes, for there is no wiring, and the relation of permanent functions and memories to random or 'free' movements does not precisely resemble the decision-pattern of computing machines.

He spoke of the dangers of analogy in the comparison of the possibility, in the neurobiological world, of describing what went on in terms of simple electromagnetism and chemical reactions, to the simplifying descriptions of economics, the equating of all human activity to pounds, shillings and pence, stamped-out coinage, repeated, minted currency. The difference was *endlessly* more instructive than the analogy, said Hodder Pinsky. The analogy is made by the slipperiness of thought with words. We need linguistic philosophy to sort out the beautiful and fatal snarls we are fated – *not* designed, but fated as we are shaped into embryos – to entwine ourselves in, with words. But thought is not words, life is not words.

He ended with a simple, clear summary of what he said was the present knowledge of the activity of the brain. It was now known that the nervous system was activated by a chemical set of signals, as well as the other two forms of coding already known – a complex geometry of molecular connections and symmetries, and the temporal succession of electrical nerve impulses, what used to be known as negative energy, and became known as action potential.

He spoke about new work on chemical signals and codes, and their diffusion along long distances, in, for instance, the blood-stream. He became technical – and lost Frederica – about how chemical signals brought diversity to synaptic connections with a similar geometry.

She realised that though she had *understood what he had said*, which was lucid, and interesting, she was profoundly ignorant, blackly, thickly ignorant, of *what he was talking about*. She knew the words, neurone, synapse, dendrite, and she liked them because she could do their etymology. But the human world – including maybe some of her own forebears – had invented microscopes, and telescopes, and dissected tissues and identified cells, and if it all vanished tomorrow she *would not know where to start*, though she might be able to write down quite a lot of *Paradise Lost* by heart (whatever her heart was, and however it worked).

Electricity, chemical messengers, geometry.
The matter of the mind.

Someone pushed a brown packet under her feet. It said 'Bog-paper. Open it at your peril.' It had been shuffled along, from end to end of the row. She picked it up. It was found to contain the Eichenbaum pamphlet. The first batch was finding its way out.

On the evening of the first night, there was a dinner in the University. On the campus, there was a student rally, not very big, which dispersed peacefully. Hodgkiss acquired a copy of the Bog-paper pamphlet, and asked Wijnnobel if they should speak to Eichenbaum. They agreed to wait until the next day. The college staff did not know where the papers were coming from.

In the morning, the Henry Moore statues of the King and Queen were found to have been damaged. Someone in the night had been very thorough with crimson paint. Both figures had wide bloody bands around their necks, like the red ribbons worn defiantly by French aristocrats in the time of the guillotine, but dripping. The King's cloven crest or helmet had also been painted like a bloody cockscomb. The Queen's bronze lap was full of red paint, as though she had haemorrhaged – much of it was in wet puddles, tacky on top. And a hand had been painted on the stone seat, a white hand, the Isengard hand, with red fingernails. 'You have been warned,' someone had written, in Elvish letters.

Luk spent much of the night revising his paper. He always told his students not to do this. He deleted several of the equations which had so painfully gone to its making, without which it would not exist. He added, on the spur of the coming moment, some generalisations about human society he was usually far too cautious to make. He looked at himself in the mirror, and took a pair of scissors to his beard, making it sharper-pointed, more aggressive. In the morning, he put on a suit, and took it off again. He put on a ribbed black sweater, and black cords. He thought he looked trim, but like a danseur. Finally he rolled up a scarf in Liberty lawn, with their peacock feather design. The feathers were emerald and a rather good Prussian blue; the peacock eyes were white, with a tiny purple splash in the centre. The floating feather-fronds were on a background colour of deep crimson. Luk knotted all this brilliance about his neck, and set off for the Theatre. He knew it was all going to go wrong. He had put so much into it, and it was about to fail.

There was a full house, including Wijnnobel, Pinsky, Eichenbaum and the television team. Luk strode on to the stage, and said his subject was one that was puzzling honest population geneticists. How and why had sexual reproduction evolved, given that other methods of self-propagation, of passing on the genes which strict Darwinian theory supposed was the function of organisms, appeared to be less costly, biologically speaking. We are so used, he said, to the idea that sex produces more – that parents beget children – that we don't think about the fact that at the *cellular level* sex diminishes the number of cells; it is a process whereby *one* is made of *two* – one zygote. Why should a female not prefer to reproduce parthenogenetically – which would pass on more of her genes?

He argued his case, with elegant diagrams and slides of the extraordinary fecundity of aphids. He spoke of diffusion and territories, of flying seeds and creeping worms, of elm-trees and oysters, of aphids and rotifers, of sessile organisms like strawberries and coral. He was brisk, he was lucid. He was witty – he made jokes he had not intended to make. He spoke of the expense of being male and quoted Charles Darwin's letter to his son, in which he said 'The sight of a feather in a peacock's tail, whenever I gaze at it, makes me feel sick.' They laughed. He felt them held to him by threads of attention and laughter, like an electric spider-web which he was spinning. He described his slug research, on the ruddy *Arion rufus*, the black *Arion ater*, the ruddy ones in the south of the hills, the black ones in the north, the sexual ruddy ones intensely aggressive, the meek black ones a clone.

He was sharp, he was fierce, he made just enough reference to the unknowns, the not understood, that might dilute, or shift his argument. He said he didn't deny sex was there, it must be in some ways adaptive – but the case must be made.

He was witty at the expense of ideas of altruism which claimed that selection worked amongst groups, or that creatures could act 'for the benefit of the species'. He explained, patiently, reasonably, happily, that competition between organisms worked within small groups, and by mechanisms of immediate survival, which made nonsense of self-sacrifice for an idea. If you give up your life for another, he said, all your altruistic genes are annihilated with you, unless that other has as many of your genes as you do. We do not like these thoughts, for we have grown up with, we have inherited, beliefs in self-denial, in turning the other cheek, which some of us, in history, ascribed to imaginary Fathers beyond the grove or in the heavens.

You might say, said Luk Lysgaard-Peacock, thinking of Frederica and her inconvenient assertion that mental cobwebs were real things – you might say, that if an idea has survived for a very long time, it has its own adaptive fitness. You could argue that religions and moral instructions survive in the world because they are like larger organisms, struggling for existence. You could argue that Christianity spread to be a world religion because it had better survival characteristics than Manichaeism. There is a simple sense in which this might be true, in that strict Manichaeism forbids both eating and sexual reproduction, so it is in its essence designed to implode and self-destruct. But a faith is not an organism, and survival works at the level of the fitness of cells, through the adaptation of cells. I would like you to recall the admonitions made yesterday by Professor Pinsky, against thinking loosely with analogies and metaphors.

In a recent book on *The Life of Insects*, Professor Sir Vincent Wigglesworth wrote that insects do not live for themselves alone but *devote* their lives to their species, of which they are representatives. They do no such thing. There is no question of 'devotion' or 'representatives'. Please understand that this is quite a different idea from the one that in a nest of ants all the workers are sisters, daughters of the same mother, with the same genes. They have no noble idea of the species. The German philosopher, Feuerbach, tried to prove that the idea of God was simply a personification of 'the species', the big Man, as the Nest is the big queen-ant. These ideas, whether right or wrong, do not help with thinking about survival and fitness at the level of the dividing cell, and the inherited DNA. An idea is not a cell. Although we need cells to form ideas.

So where does it all come from. Our final speaker, Professor Eichenbaum has argued that domesticated species are degenerate, in that they are less capable of communicating with each other than their congeners in the wild. Except for man, in whom communication has burgeoned to an astonishing degree. We gabble, we babble, we sing, we chant, we paint, we draw, we carve, we use wires, and lights, and amplifiers from taut skins to knobs on radios. Professor Eichenbaum describes displacement activities in captive creatures. J.B.S. Haldane suggested that an ethologist could describe religion as a vacuum activity of communication – a displacement ritual – in which human beings communicate with non-existent Hearers.

In human society, Luk said, as in other niches where competition takes place, there are winners and losers. Females are the losers. They have to bear the nutritional cost of reproduction – the growth of the zygote – for both themselves and their mate. Human societies in general have made ethical and religious traditions out of the patterns of human sexual reproduction. Humans have so arranged matters that women are oppressed by men, and children by both. However, if you look at the working-out of lives, I would suggest the ultimate losers are the redundant males. You need only to begin by considering the sex differences in the statistics of illness in general, and of death at all ages.

Frederica watched Luk, amazed and delighted. He seemed like some sort of small golden fire-demon, with sparks coming out of the ends of his fingers (which he used a lot, as he paced the platform, very effectively). She had been infected by his stage-fright, and was now infected by his joyous contact with his audience, which had become one attentive creature. She thought, he's sweeping around like a great peacock, showing off, and laughed to herself that he was doing this to demonstrate the wastefulness and pointlessness of just such male display. She remembered her dream. It was odd to make love to someone in a dream. It was not his body, it was something she had called up, but it made her feel differently. Once, she would have asked herself, was she 'in love' with this person to whose shadow she had in her sleeping brain made love. He was very busy explaining that this was an unaskable question. He was taking everything apart – ethics, romantic love – with great good humour and controlled aggression. She wondered what Jacqueline had done to him.

Everyone gathered round, afterwards, to congratulate him.

Eichenbaum himself stumped up, and held out a hand. 'Du bist der Geist der stets verneint,' he said. 'It's not so simple. But it was *resplendently* argued.'

Luk glowed. As he was leaving the Theatre, someone pushed the bog-roll pamphlet into his hand.

The next two papers were about the biology of memory. The first was Christopher Cobb's paper on birdsong. He accompanied himself with both recorded birdsong and his own very musical renderings. He described the difference between chaffinches and canaries which need to hear singing to learn, but can learn in isolation to produce a well-structured song, whereas the chaffinch needs to hear both its own song, and those of other birds. A chaffinch deafened within the first three months of life will produce little more than a continuous screech. It cannot learn from a song-tutor which has pure notes and not a chaffinch-voice, but it can learn from recordings of chaffinches even if played backwards. A bird can be muted by destroying the left side of its nervous system, but – since birds are more plastic than humans – an aphasic canary will recover its song. Cobb looked like a woolly Pan, his hands cupped to his mouth, with the bubbling, inhuman music pouring out.

Someone in the audience – it was Waltraut Ross – cried out 'And it is worth imprisoning and mutilating these free creatures to find out this kind of thing?'

Christopher Cobb said mildly enough, 'Well, of course, you do always wonder.'

'Shame!' cried Waltraut Ross.

There was a moment of shouting and counter-shouting in the audience. Cobb mildly turned up his sound-system, and produced a choir of variegated nightingales. He went on to explain how they invented new songs, varying those they heard, learning the new sequences in groups. The audience subsided, and he was warmly applauded.

The final paper of that day was Lyon Bowman, and was about the debate between those who argued that particular neurones had very specific, precise functions, and the holists, or Gestalt thinkers, who believed in the plastic functioning of the complicated networks. He explained that in the cerebral cortex there are perhaps 600 million synapses in each cubic millimetre. In a human cerebral cortex there were somewhere between 10^{14}–10^{15} synapses. Imagining large numbers is something the human mind is generally bad at. If you counted 1,000 per second, he said, it would take you somewhere between 3,000 and 30,000 *years* to count them all. Let alone to disentangle the branches and stems of the axons and dendrites. Nevertheless work was being done on individual groups of neurones and in some cases – such as Alving's work on *Aplysia* pacemaker neurones, and work in his own laboratory on the giant neurones of *Helix aspersa* – on individual neurones. He spoke of the location in the anaesthetised brains of cats and macaque monkeys of particular sets of cells which appeared to react very precisely to fine angles and movements of light sources. He described the chemistry of the snail neurones. Deborah Ritter rose in the audience to denounce him. What he called a *preparation*, she said, was an impaled living creature. He had no *right* to indulge his reductive speculations at the expense of the helpless cat or monkey. Jacqueline Winwar sat there and heard her results described, and so to speak, claimed, without acknowledgement. It was her work – her months of trial and error, failure and triumph, smoothly taken over, as part of the Lab's generally excellent performance. Of Bowman's performance. She was a see-through implement, that was all.

Various other contentious voices were raised. Bowman smiled and finished his paper, speaking more loudly.

There was a cocktail party afterwards. Jacqueline stood at the edge of it, possessed by fury, and also by the knowledge that her academic future – the snails, the oscilloscope, the lab space – were in Bowman's plumply delicate fingers. Luk Lysgaard-Peacock appeared behind her.

'Pretty cool,' he said. 'Those were *your* figures. Very smooth.'

'As though I don't exist.'

'Good work, though. And the bit about the effects of injected calcium sounded surprising –'

'It doesn't do what you might think. You'd think it would increase membrane resistance – but it appears to increase permeability – I'm not sure yet –'

'You should be speaking yourself.'

'Your paper was very good.'

Luk grinned. 'The rage of the rejected. Good for the mind.'

Jacqueline smiled doubtfully. 'Then I'd better learn to use the rage of those whose work is appropriated –'

Bowman came up to them, leading Hodder Pinsky.

'This is the young researcher I was telling you about, Hodder. Jacqueline Winwar. Very promising. Professor Pinsky is founding a new – very broad-based – discussion group. I suggested he might ask you along.'

'*Filaments*,' said Pinsky. 'Cybernetics suggests hierarchies and central power. Filaments is a good – well, a goodish – pun. Neural networks, spider-threads, all that. But it's got files in it, to suggest memory, and *mens*, or almost. Karl Lashley uses *double-entendres* as an argument for some sort of residual mental representation in the cells of the brain. You have to connect the one to the other, arbitrarily, so to speak, to "get" the idea. Tell me about your research, Dr Winwar.'

Bowman smiled, like the Cheshire cat, and moved away, leaving the smile in the air. Jacqueline saw in her mind's eye her preparations of neurones, the wonderful steady bursts of action potential, the perturbations, the gaps.

'What I've been trying is –' she began. Pinsky listened.

Wijnnobel, Hodgkiss, Calder-Fluss and Wilkie met to discuss the opposition to Theobald Eichenbaum. Calder-Fluss was of the opinion that it might be a good plan to call in the police. With the vandalism, and the pamphlets, and now libellous posters about animal experiments, eugenics, and proto-Fascism. Wijnnobel said that if you called in the police, the matter became a criminal investigation, in their hands, not the University's. Hodgkiss said he was sure that what the core of the opposition wanted, was that the police should be called in. It didn't follow, unfortunately, that anyone could guarantee that Professor Eichenbaum could give his paper without some major disruptive act. Wilkie said why not ask Eichenbaum himself, and Hodgkiss said he would prefer not to perturb him. He had a right to speak freely, and was an invited guest. Wilkie said he must have been the object of a lot of this sort of thing already. Wijnnobel said no, he had not been. The offending 1941 paper had not been translated – or returned to life, so to speak – until Pinsky had sent it to him. He did not know how – or when – the Anti-University had got hold of it. Hodgkiss remembered its arrival. He remembered Pinsky's letter. He remembered, suddenly, the excited comportment of Nick Tewfell.

He saw no point in confronting Tewfell. That would be what Tewfell wanted. He saw no point in mentioning Tewfell to the Vice-Chancellor. He rather hoped the whole problem would go away. He must have known it would not, he thought much later, without being able to think of any very good course of action he might have taken. All they could do was to be vigilant, he said.

Wijnnobel said that he would take it upon himself to discuss the matter with Eichenbaum.

The penultimate day of the Conference was devoted to what are known as the Humanities – as though, Luk said crossly to Jacqueline – genetics or neurology or biochemistry were somehow *inhuman*. Jacqueline, a little rattled by the rash of posters and leaflets depicting Lyon Bowman and Christopher Cobb as torturers, said that it was a general perception that they were, precisely, inhuman.

Hodgkiss, looking nervously at the audience, for he did not think of himself as a brave man, gave his paper on Wittgenstein's ideas of colour – which did not include any discussion of the physics of wavelength, or the physiology of the retina, but did somehow describe the mind describing its own operations.

There were various literary and historical papers, including one on George Eliot's metaphors from anatomy, perception, tissue study and webs in *Middlemarch*. There were papers on Lawrence on blood and semen, and blood and brain in Shakespeare; Raphael Faber spoke on Proust's visual metaphors, and Canon Holly spoke excitedly about the idea of the Incarnation, that God was made flesh, and had blood and brain and bone – was confined in them, he said, quoting Marvell on the prison of the rib-cage and the nerves, on the walking corpse *impaled* on the spirit, which reached upwards. Frederica had expected to find these literary papers the most interesting. She had grown up in the narrow British educational system which divides like a branching tree, and predestines all thirteen-year-olds to be either illiterate or innumerate (if not both). She had grown up with the assumption that to be literary is to be quick, perceptive and subtle. Whereas scientists were dull, and also – in the nuclear age – quite possibly dangerous and destructive. She thought of F.R. Leavis's *Education and the University*, which she had studied, and which had said that the English Department was at the centre of any educational endeavour. This suddenly seemed, as she listened to Lawrence's dangerous nonsense abstracted from Lawrence's lively drama and held up for approval, to be nothing more than a Darwinian jockeying for advantage, a territorial snarl and dash.

What is important, she thought, is to defend reason against unreason.

XXIV

Jonty Surtees believed in the logic of history. He believed that the Revolution must come, and therefore could come, that the old order must be overthrown, and therefore would be overthrown, and that he must and would help it along. He believed, and often said, that Socrates and Jesus were political activists, who in their time asked awkward questions, taught the young to ask awkward questions, and were killed by the then Establishment. He had studied the logic of destabilising institutions, and knew that you used whatever forces were to hand – if they wanted to believe they were elves and wizards marching on the Dark Tower, that was fine by him – *at this stage* – as long as they marched. He didn't think the new forms of government desired by Greg Tod and Waltraut Ross, still less by Nick Tewfell, bore much relation to the true anarchy he felt was right for human life, but they weren't there yet, for the moment he needed to work them all up. He told them that now was the moment for the *Act* that followed talk. They sat around in a fug of scented smoke and stared through blurred vision, and felt the logic of his smile, his voice, his urgent body movements. Avram Snitkin kept falling asleep and had to be shaken awake. Nick Tewfell stared with a kind of horrified fascination at the three shrouded figures. Deborah Ritter gave Maggie Cringle some hashish fudge and stirred a nourishing pot of bean soup. We go tomorrow, said Surtees. We let him get into the building, and then we march on it.

'And – those?' said Nick Tewfell.

Surtees pulled the covers off, like a magician unveiling sawn women. They were horribly life-like effigies, squat Eichenbaum, pale Pinsky, and the unmistakeable long lined face and lanky figure of Gerard Wijnnobel. About one and a half times life size, with papier mâché masks.

'We shall burn them in front of the Maths Tower, the

Evolution Tower, and the Language Tower,' said Surtees. 'Since the students are having their demo against compulsory maths and languages.'

It was text-book revolution, a rallying point.

Tewfell said, he feared there were not enough protestors to make fires in three places.

Surtees said little did he know. There was an army of protestors, coming to join the cause, from Essex and the LSE and further-flung places. They were rolling up the A1 in buses and vans as he spoke. They would need signs to carry. There would be music.

'They will send for the police,' said Nick Tewfell.

'Precisely. And when the pigs come in, we have won. If we make them send for the pigs, and use *force*, they show themselves for what they are.'

He flared with conviction. Whatever in Nick Tewfell was reluctant felt shame and humiliation. All they did was talk. Now they would *act*. In the beginning was the *Act*. He looked at the lolling simulacra of authority, and felt loathing. His mind was full of threatening cold-voiced authorities and blundering lackeys. And pigs. Which were disgusting.

Deborah Ritter, handing out fudge, said 'Come on, we need a hand with the bloody paint.'

Gerard Wijnnobel gave Theobald Eichenbaum a glass of wine, in his study, and asked if he had seen the brown pamphlet. Eichenbaum put down the glass, and sat with his hands on his knees, block-like.

'Several people, most of them anonymous, have made it their business to see that I have seen it. So I have seen it.'

Wijnnobel waited.

'The original paper – the language of the original paper – was an error of judgement and a failure of imagination. For which I have been lucky enough not to have to pay. *This* version is a distortion, both of Galton's work and of my own. We both make it very clear that human crowds – herds – become mindless under domineering dictators. Galton gives some statistics of the prison population – of people suspected of speaking against the state – under Napoleon III. He liked statistics. They are not pretty figures. He also talks about fanatical priesthoods. They do not, of course, translate these passages. I could argue that what I wrote was a coded attack on our leaders. But it was not. It was simply unthinking folly. I did not then know – though I should have known – how a word or two can inflame exactly such a crowd as I loathed and loathe. I am a scientist. I had insufficient respect for the power of words.'

Wijnnobel said 'Niko Tinbergen was in a concentration camp in Holland.'

'I know. I am sorry. Efforts were made to get him released. He would not consider it. *He* would not.'

'I think there is going to be trouble, if you speak. I think there was always going to be trouble, and they are waiting for you.'

'I am going to speak about how we have weakened our courage, and denatured our children, under domestication. I cannot *not* speak because I once wrote wrongly. That would be compounding a wrong with a wrong.'

'I cannot guarantee that there won't be – trouble, greater or smaller.'

'Are you asking me not to speak?'

'No. How can I? I believe in the right to speak and be heard.' He laughed, briefly. 'I do say, I cannot guarantee how well you will be heard.'

The auditorium was packed. The visible breath above the ranked heads simmered. The notice on the door, announcing Theobald Eichenbaum's lecture 'Domestication and Dehumanisation, Instinct versus Culture, Ontogeny and Phylogeny', had been smeared all over with something brown. Nevertheless, the Vice-Chancellor and the ethologist appeared promptly on stage. Eichenbaum had chosen to dress in brown – a slightly dusty, crumpled brown suit, and an ill-fitting cream-coloured shirt, out of which his walnut-brown thick neck rose into the fan of his beard and the white bush of his hair, which glittered in the stage lighting.

Wijnnobel said very directly that he knew that Professor Eichenbaum's passionately-held views were controversial. They were also not simple. Those who disliked his stance in the nurture–nature argument must surely admire his stance against environmental poisons, about which his early warnings were proving to be accurate prophecies. A university was a place for discussion and debate, and he was glad so many people had gathered to hear someone who was both an independent thinker, a true experimental scientist, and an uninhibited polemicist.

When Wijnnobel sat down, they heard the drums. Eichenbaum stomped heavily to the rostrum and took the microphone in his hand.

'I am going to talk to you about packs, and groups, and shoals, and herds, and individuals —' he said.

This was in fact all, or almost all, that was heard of the final paper of the Conference as the hall erupted into howling and baying, and, outside, Jonty Surtees's marchers swarmed across the campus, singing, shouting, dancing and making music. They had been organised to come in waves, from all sides, from the encampment and up the road from the village. They wore all sorts of costumes — there were maenads and tin soldiers, masked executioners and carnival demons, elves and witches and wizards and huge *commedia dell'arte* cockerels. There were drumbeats and clashing cymbals, pan-pipes and guitars. There were banners — Down with SKOOL, Mao Thought is True Thought, Free the Grass, Feel the Rain, Free Speech is a Fetishism, Smash the Establishment, No more Grammar, No more Maths, No more Vivisection.

They sang

> *We are One We are Many, We are Many We are One.*
> *We are gun we are bullet, we are bullet we are gun.*
> *We can kill and resurrect you, we are god when you are gone*

They also sang

> *The metal men in coats of white*
> *In shuttered rooms with shuttered eyes*
> *Make metal death with metal claws*
> *Black out the sunshine from the skies*
>
> *The children dance in forests free*
> *They smell the sunshine and the rain . . .*

They also sang the war song of Tolkien's tree-men, the Ents.

> *Though Isengard be strong and hard, as cold as stone and bare as bone*

Theobald Eichenbaum settled on his feet, gripped the microphone, and raised his voice.

'Our culture,' he said 'has infantilised its young people, and set generation against generation as though they were different breeds –'

It was doubtful whether anyone heard him. Things had begun to be thrown. Eggs, good and bad, fruit, books, a few stones, and a strange floating series of bunched flower-charms, wreaths of bryony and nightshade, drooping grasses and bindweed, corn-cockles and wilted poppies.

The marchers burst into the auditorium. Jonty Surtees, businesslike in blue denim, and Paul-Zag, in silver, carrying his guitar with red and yellow streamers, stood high at the back. Paul strummed and sang 'We are one, we are many, we are many, we are one.'

Surtees stepped down between the rows of seats. He advanced on Eichenbaum, who briefly had the advantage of being above him and holding the microphone. The lighting had the auditorium in darkness, and a spotlight on Eichenbaum's mask of pure rage. He leaned over and growled at Surtees.

'I see what you are. Do you know what the nastiest kind of herd is? It is *rats*, it is *rats*, tame *rats* in an enclosure. Do you know who you are, Pied Piper with a crowd of denatured children draggling behind you –'

Jonty Surtees, limber, surefooted, vaulted up on to the platform and struggled with the Professor, who resisted for a moment, having the advantage of weight, and rootedness, but only for a moment. Surtees twisted the microphone out of his hand, and cried into it 'No one's going to listen to you, old man, no one wants to hear you.' He whirled round, raising the microphone above his head, in a trail of sparks. 'Freedom begins, *here*, and *now*,' he shouted, and felled Eichenbaum with an efficient blow from the microphone, which filled the hall with a shriek, and a groan, and gave up the ghost.

Wijnnobel in the front row said to Hodgkiss 'We must get the police.'

'We have to get out of here, first. We cannot get out, at the moment.'

Fighting had broken out, most of it merely the result of those outside trying to pour in, and those inside – at least those who did not suddenly feel combative – trying to get out. There was pushing, and trampling, and worse. Hodgkiss climbed up on to the stage, ignoring Surtees, and bent to check Eichenbaum's breathing. Surtees was smiling.

'*Why?*' said Hodgkiss, mopping Eichenbaum's face with a handkerchief.

'How stupid can you get?' said Surtees. He jumped down, and vanished into the crowd.

It was, the University ruefully recognised, very well organised. The gibbets were set up outside the Evolution Tower, the Language Tower, and the Maths Tower. By the time the authorities had fought or wriggled their way out of the Theatre, the effigies were burning brightly, amongst a stink of petrol and a lot of noise, musical and unmusical. Wijnnobel, hurrying to meet the police, who had been called, but had some distance to come, stood momentarily at the back of a dancing crowd that was watching him burn. His own long face looked down on him through greasy smoke and sullen flames. The University health-centre team hurried past him in the opposite direction, presumably to collect Eichenbaum, and were not opposed.

We come, we come, with horn and drum: ta rûna rûna rûna rom!

Small fires and battles were breaking out all over the campus.

Someone threw a petrol bomb through a window of the Language Tower.

Wijnnobel had managed to lock himself into the Dean's office and speak to the police, and the fire brigade, on the phone. The police asked if they would have trouble getting in, and the Vice-Chancellor said yes, they would, they should come prepared. There were a great many more protestors than the University alone could have provided.

It was Frederica Potter who noticed the flames in the windows of the old house, of Long Royston. Curtains were flaring, flames crawling up them, although there was no crowd encamped outside. It took a little time to find the Vice-Chancellor and a group of staff, who began to run across the lawns. Frederica ran too, followed by Wilkie. The front door was open. There were very small fires in the hall – slowly burning neat heaps of books, which Frederica recognised. Skoob. An art-form.

Someone had set fire to the bed-curtains in the Elizabethan bedrooms. The beds were burned, and the ceiling, with its painting of the Death of Hyacinth, had fallen in on the bed. People brought fire appliances, and succeeded in dousing the flames, though more damage was done to the ancient embroideries and carvings. People gathered, including Matthew Crowe, in a velvet dressing-gown and slippers.

'Has anyone seen my wife?' asked Wijnnobel.

Crowe said 'She was here, Gerard, she was here.'

Wilkie said 'She was seen – I'm sorry, Vice-Chancellor – she was seen – marching in with them. When they marched in. With one of the singing groups.'

Wijnnobel stood in the burned bedroom.

'She had better be found. I had better find her. Has anyone seen her *recently*?'

No one had. Frederica said, she knew who burned little heaps of books, like that. It was a habit of Paul Ottokar's. There was one at the foot of the bed. Lady Wijnnobel, she did not say, had been marching behind Paul-Zag. But she knew that the Vice-Chancellor knew.

'There are many, many things that need attention,' said Wijnnobel. 'Of which the whereabouts of my wife is only one, and not the most important. But I should be very glad to know if anyone can find her – and even more glad if they can persuade her to come – here – to come – back, home.'

On his way across Long Royston, conducting his own grim search for his wife, he heard noises in the antechamber with the museum exhibits. They were noises of breaking glass. He walked heavily towards the sounds, and came upon a group of his own students, breaking up the cases with the handles of placards. Several were drunk, including Maggie Cringle, who, dressed like a heroine of *Dr Who*, was jabbing not very effectively at the case which contained the relics of *Astraea* with a banner that said 'What do we want? Cultural Studies. An End to Rote-Learning.'

Nick Tewfell was gesticulating in the middle of the group. He was, in fact, being naturally lawful, attempting to get them to stop. He was waving his own placard, which said 'Break the Mind-Forged Manacles. No More Compulsory Grammar and Maths.'

Wijnnobel advanced on him. He said

'Stop that! You are an historian. You should know where book-burning leads.'

'This is a revolution,' said Nick Tewfell.

'Against *what*?' said Wijnnobel, advancing, the dark biting in his mind. Every choice he had made appeared to him to be wrong. He wished to hurt someone. He was not used to the feeling.

'Against *you*,' said Nick Tewfell, waving his placard.

The Vice-Chancellor waved his arms at the group, like a farmer scattering fowl.

'Get out. You have done enough damage. Get out.'

Most of the students turned and ran. Nick Tewfell turned, and looked back. He wished to hurt someone. He was not used to the feeling. He glared at the Vice-Chancellor, through one of the undamaged glass cases, which contained two pieces of Renaissance glass, donated by Matthew Crowe, a green German beaker made of Waldglas, or forest glass, so named because it derived its green colour from ferns, and an ornate French beaker, with a helical foot, showing the Expulsion from the Garden, with the inscription *En-la Sueur – de ton visage – tu mangeras – le payn.*

Nick saw the Vice-Chancellor reflected in the glass cube, and multiplied into an army of ghosts. He had two options, as Eichenbaum would have recognised, fight or flight. He chose the first, raised his placard, and brought it down on the glass case, shattering it and the artefacts inside it. His opponent bent and picked up a handful of the finer fragments, closing his fingers on them. He held up his bleeding hand at Nick Tewfell, and gestured.

'Go away. Get out. Go *away*.'

Many years later, when Tewfell was a minister in Tony Blair's government, he would still wake at night and remember that moment, the unbroken box, the bright unbroken beakers, the broken box, the splinters of glass, the dark-faced tall man with his bleeding fingers, the strange dancing light in the room, which was the torches outside, and the flaring behind his own eyes. The odd thing was, that the Vice-Chancellor had never said anything to anyone about who had broken the glasses. And for a few years, he had hated him for that. And then, as he grew older, he had almost loved him. He had, he saw, come in a way to resemble him.

In another part of the campus, Deborah Ritter had led a foray to release the imprisoned creatures. The Zoology Research Centre was built round an internal quadrangle, with a lawn. The rescuers surged into the laboratories and opened cages, and pens. They overturned glass tanks, and undid the collar of a solitary sheep, which snorted, and remained immobile. They worked by torchlight, their small fires bobbing and dancing as they smashed padlocks and untwisted wire. A procession of tufted ducks wandered satisfactorily out on to the grass, followed by various rabbits and hares, white and piebald, lolloping and scuttling. Mickey Impey picked up several jars and shook out colonies of worms and beetles on to the grass. Deborah Ritter, with kaleidoscope eyes, approached various banked tanks of white rats. They peered out at her, their own eyes – come and *see*, she cried – wonderful rosy crystals, opals with crimson fires in fields of white spikes of furry icicles.

Go, you darlings, cried Deborah Ritter, go and live your lives. She tipped them out on to the floor, where they cowered, cringed, and then began to prospect. She poured out a cage of piebald mice amongst them. One rat snarled and several mice bolted. Mickey Impey, opening a box, was met by a shrilling, and a mouthful of yellow teeth, which fastened on his finger. He shook the angry curled creature to the ground. Ten days later his wound began to froth and fester. Then his hand swelled, and his arm and shoulder blew up into bolsters and went blue. He was in hospital for a month, and wrote several poems about night-nurses and moanings in the dark.

Waltraut Ross released several bandaged cats, some of which trotted off sedately, some of which staggered, and one of which fell over and was still.

Flocks of small birds were poked out of cages, and scrambled and fluttered into the night. The birds were the most satisfactory releases, because they were able to get further than the lawn, the courtyard, and the surrounding corridors.

Someone alerted Christopher Cobb, who looked around for help, and found Vincent Hodgkiss and Marcus Potter. When they reached the Research Centre the revellers, or rescuers, were gone. The grass, the lab floor, the benches, were alive. Hundreds of newly-hatched chicks scuttled along the corridors, desperately cheeping. Ants swarmed over the coffee-making machine. There was a sound in the darkness of clucking, quacking and hissing. Christopher Cobb stood in front of his chaffinch cages, and held out his arms to the sky, as though summoning back the vanished singers. Tears stood in his eyes – Hodgkiss did not know whether he was mourning the creatures he knew, or the years of experimental work lost, or both. A brindled cat with a shaved belly went past, with a half-dead black mouse hanging from its jaws.

'Some of this is bloody *dangerous*,' said Cobb. 'God knows where to start. We'll have to kill a lot of these –'

The lights went out. The lights went out in the whole building, which seemed to give a sigh, and settle into blackness. Cobb said

'Stay here. Try not to let anything out, or anyone in. I'll get the fire brigade. Or someone. Don't get bitten.'

Vincent and Marcus, neither of whom was either an animal-lover or physically very competent, asked if they should try to put anything back.

'No. Guard the door. Mind the rats. There was only one snake. I can't see her, but she was harmless, a nice creature.'

He went off.

Vincent and Marcus sat down on the grass, by the door, side by side. They peered apprehensively into the gloom, and listened to the slithers and rustles and squeaks around them. There was a smell of soiled sawdust, and a smell of what Vincent thought was formaldehyde. He stared upwards. Above the courtyard, in the midsummer dark, hung a fine curl of new moon. He said

'I did it all wrong. I should have been draconian. I should have moved them on, at the very beginning.'

'Then they'd have won.'

'But all this – this wreckage –'

'If people want wreckage, it happens, somehow.'

They sat in silence. A very large, very damaged cockerel, white, with a jagged crimson crest and tremulous wattles advanced towards them, and retreated. Its tailfeathers were draggled, but the really disgusting thing was its neck, which was plucked bare, and bright crimson, erect above the pouffe of its breast feathers. It came into the range of their vision, saw them, put its head on one side, staring with mad yellow eyes, and backed off, gobbling.

'A non-aggressive male,' said Hodgkiss, gloomily.

Marcus said that when they were in that state, it was very clear to see that they were related to dinosaurs. The beak and the crest, the scaly bits and the snaky bits. Interesting, he said. He seemed somehow less ill at ease, in the darkness, than Hodgkiss had expected. They didn't try to look at each other, only sat side by side, looking at the grey grass and the vague shapes that scurried across it. Hodgkiss saw something make a movement between a lollop and a waddle. He smiled to himself.

'Is that a duck or a rabbit?' he asked his beloved. He said 'There are all sorts of people and creatures who fall between categories. Duck-rabbits. Cock-dinosaurs. Crowing hens.'

He moved his hand, like a blind, questing creature, over the blades of dark grass, until his fingers met those long, delicate fingers he had watched for months. And in the dark, the fingers neither shrank, nor evaded. They touched, and gripped and held.

'I've been dreaming about you,' said Marcus Potter's light voice, calmly. 'Good dreams. I think – we know in dreams – who we are – what we are –'

'I think we are infinite shape-shifters – in dreams –' said Vincent Hodgkiss, taking a grip on the thin hand, which gripped back. Hodgkiss moved nearer, so that his substantial thigh lay alongside that thin one. He wanted to touch Marcus's hair, but did not want to let go of the hand he had, and thought, this will do, for now. For now, this is enough, and more than I could have hoped.

Wilkie was taking photographs of the fires and the dancers, helped by the TV crew who had been working on the Conference. Frederica, running messages between the wet ashes of the Long Royston show-bedrooms and the chaos of the university administration, saw a large, black-cloaked figure, bent low, running purposefully down the Long Royston drive, away from the building. She thought, let her go, and then thought of Gerard Wijnnobel's face. She began to run herself, but Eva Wijnnobel had a very considerable start, and a surprising turn of speed.

Frederica looked around her, and saw Luk Lysgaard-Peacock. She said, breathlessly,

'She's getting away.'

'Who's getting away?'

'That woman. Lady W.'

'Getting away?'

'She was in it. In the march. She – I'm sure she – set, helped to set, the fires, those skoobs, in Long Royston.'

'Skoobs?'

'He asked us to look for her. To get her to come back.'

'I'll get my car. The police are guarding some of the gates, but there aren't enough of them. They'll let me through. We could catch up with her, and – well – talk her into coming back. You do know she's *mad*?'

'Well, that's why. He's been – extraordinary. It's all – *literally* – falling down round him. We could help him. We could get her back.'

'If you call that helping him,' said Luk Lysgaard-Peacock drily.

By the time his little car swung out of the gate of Long Royston, there was no sign of Lady Wijnnobel. And then, some way along the road, Frederica saw a familiar white van. She said

'That's Elvet Gander. I haven't seen him all night, he wasn't *there*, that's odd.'

Two figures, one black, one shimmering and sparkling, stepped out into the road from behind a hedge, and waved down the van. It stopped. They got in. It turned, and went off, bouncing, up the road into the moorland.

'Now what?'

'I don't know. Where are they going?'

'We could guess. We could follow and make sure. Would you like a night-drive over the moors?'

'Why not?' said Frederica.

'Excuse all the snail-stuff rattling about,' said Luk. 'I've not had much time, or inclination, to keep the car tidy.'

'Not to worry,' said Frederica. Her spirits lifted as they drove away from the flaring chaos behind them.

The white van drove up, and up, on to the high Moor road, followed, at a discreet but obvious distance, by Luk's small blue Renault. If the driver of the van observed the followers, he neither accelerated nor deviated. There were in any case no turnings off the road which ran along the crest of the moorland. Frederica leaned forward anxiously. Luk told her to calm down.

'I don't see what you're going to do.'

'No. Nor do I.'

In the event, the white van drew up at the gate of Dun Vale Hall. Someone got out – the headlights shone on Elvet Gander's bald dome – unlocked the gate, and drove in. He then returned, and swung the gate closed. Luk had pulled up, some distance away. He imagined that Gander inclined his head, with ceremonious irony, before he vanished behind the gate.

'Now what?'

'Now we go back and tell the Vice-Chancellor where she's gone.'

'I've got a better idea. Now we go up to my cottage – which isn't far – and telephone the University. And have something to eat – I'm starving. I don't know about you.'

Luk thought that taking another woman – any other woman, including this one, whom he alternately disliked and felt a kind of armed truce with – to Loderby – would in some way exorcise the painful memory of his – it now seemed to him – absurd wooing of Jacqueline. Frederica thought, because it was the way her life seemed to go, and because she had dreamed it, that perhaps Luk intended to make love to her. These were the new days of sexual liberty, when love-making was more likely than not. Frederica also thought, for she had been there many times, that if this was a beginning, it was the beginning of an ending, that was the way it went. She thought she was sorry, because she had been interested in his lecture and his fierceness, and then gave a little snort of laughter, remembering the subject of the lecture.

'What are you laughing at?'

'I was remembering your lecture.'

'Hah.'

'It was brilliant.'

'Thank you.'

'It should have been depressing, and was the opposite.'

'Thank you.'

They drew up in the dark, and Luk found his keys. He explained that he hadn't used the cottage for some time, and put on some lights. He said he would telephone the University, found a bottle of wine, and poured Frederica a glass.

'Make yourself at home,' he said vaguely, waving a welcoming hand. 'Light some candles, it looks sad with the electric light.'

He sat down by the telephone in the narrow hall, and began what was a long and patient attempt to get through to the beleaguered University. The lines were engaged, or down. He thought laterally, tried Vincent Hodgkiss without success. Behind him, he heard Frederica Potter going into the bathroom. He heard the lavatory flush. He heard her running down the stairs, and striding up and down in his kitchen and study. He wondered if she would or wouldn't, did or didn't. She seemed rather pleased with herself. Cocky. She would do as she pleased. Did he want to be what would please her? He got through to a policeman on a walkie-talkie on the campus, and relayed the message that Lady Wijnnobel had been seen going into Dun Vale Hall. With Elvet Gander the psychoanalyst. And the singer, Paul Ottokar. Yes, he thought that was all he had to say.

Frederica had done nothing feminine to make things comfortable, except, as instructed, to light candles and put out the electric lights. She was prowling up and down, picking things up, the skull, the shells, the feathers, putting them back where they had been arranged. She said

'It's like a bower-bird's bower. I'm sorry, that just came to mind. I *love* the peacock feathers and honesty in the jar on the turning of the stair. They are such very beautiful things.'

'Unlucky,' said Luk.

'You are the one who is against astrology – and superstition – and all that. Peacock feathers are completely improbable, completely beautiful things. I heard what you had to say about Darwin feeling sick every time he saw one. I don't think even you can think up a useful evolutionary explanation for all those colours, and that sheen, and hundreds of eyes. I've seen them put them up in great fans, Crowe had some. They *creak*, and they quiver, and up they go, and they rustle . . .' She laughed. 'They're absurd, and breath-taking. Every time.'

Luk looked at her, thin and bony and energetic, with candle-light in her tangle of red hair. He said

'You are covered with bits of burned stuff, and your face looks
as though you've pushed it in a bonfire. Do you want a bath?'

'Have you got hot water?'

'Of course I have. A gas geyser, instant hot water, I'll light it.
I'll get you a towel. And then, I'll make you a meal. It won't be
much – my emergency rations – but it feels like a week since I last
had food.'

'Me too.'

She was wearing a smart, tight party-dress, shot brown silk. It
was torn at the neck, water-stained and smoke-stained.

'I could lend you a dressing-gown. This is like a bad film.'

'It is, isn't it? That's fun, isn't it?'

Her uncertainty made him confident.

'Oh yes. Go and have your bath.'

He found plastic packs of pumpernickel, a tin of pressed ham, a jar
of olives, a tin of black cherries. He found several bottles of wine,
and busied himself with corkscrews and tin-openers. He heard the
sounds of female flesh in water, of the rattle of his geyser, of the
choked gurgle of his primitive drainage. She came down damply,
in his grey dressing-gown, her hair trailing wetly over her
shoulders, her face thinner, more ordinary, more real without its
spiky mascara and spangled eyeshadow.

'I had to wash my hair. It was full of horrible things.'

'I could rub it for you.'

'I did my best. Thank you. It'll dry out.'

She ate voraciously, hunched in an arm-chair, and would have
eaten more, if there had been any. He remembered his store of
bitter chocolate and Kendal Mint Cake, for his snail expeditions,
and broke off several pieces for both of them. He filled her glass
frequently, and she drank recklessly, which would have been a
good sign if he had been sure what he wanted, or how he wanted
it, he thought confusedly, having drunk quite a lot himself.

He said, 'Well?'

Frederica thought, that is the end of the wooing, and the
beginning of the sex, and the end of the, the end of the, the end.

The sex was good, despite the wine. Luk was aggressive,

successful, and then (reasonably) grateful. Frederica liked him. She liked the excitement of his unknown, new, movements and smell. She liked his hair and his beard. She felt sad. She said, tentatively, her mouth close to his ear, 'I dreamed about you.'

Luk kissed her mouth. 'It couldn't have been anything good,' he said.

She did not answer.

They slept entangled, as though their bodies belonged together. In the morning they were formal and cautious, with that complicated courtesy adult humans use to show they have not been using another human for selfish purposes. There was no milk and no butter, so they had black coffee and more pumpernickel.

Frederica spoke sagely of the felling of Theobald Eichenbaum. She said she had read the pamphlet, and it was of course distasteful, but she felt, many people might feel, there but for the grace of God . . .

Luk said he didn't believe in God, or his grace, and things looked different if you were a European, people had had to make difficult choices, and other people remembered. He said his father had been one of the few Danes who had *really* fought in the Resistance. He had trained with the British Army and gone back – had been dropped by parachute – with the Commandos. He wasn't very tolerant of people who had accommodated themselves – and then claimed that they hadn't.

'Was that how you came to be half-English?'

'Not exactly. He met my mother when they were both Christian missionaries in Ethiopia. That was why he came back here.'

'Are they still alive?'

'Oh, yes. Still very Christian. I didn't take that job in Copenhagen because I can't cope with all that at close quarters.'

He was not looking at her. It was not lovers beginning to share their pasts. She thought he was – fighting some other battle, involved in some other snarl. And he was not interested in her, in Frederica, he had asked nothing about John Ottokar, and nothing . . . nothing . . .

'Wijnnobel is European. He knew Tinbergen, who spent the war in a concentration camp, and refused to be let out as a privilege. Pinsky lost much of his family in the death-camps. They don't forgive, even if they choose to forget.'

'Eichenbaum was a prisoner. He paid.'

'He was a prisoner of the Russians. Because he was in the German army, in the end. There's paying, and paying.'

They drove back again, after breakfast. Luk took Frederica to the door of her parents' house. He said he had better go and help with the damage-assessment. He kissed her very gently and abstractedly. He said

'Thank you.'

Thank you is the end, thought Frederica, going into the house. Thank you. Thank you for the use of your body. Thank you very much.

Vincent Hodgkiss and Marcus Potter ate breakfast in Vincent's flat, and could not stop smiling. Vincent said once 'You're not sorry?' and Marcus said 'You know very well I'm not.'

The Vice-Chancellor appeared at the Academic Board with heavily bandaged hands. He gave a clear, unemotional summing-up of the damage, financial and material. He said errors had been made, not least by himself, and that matters were now, to a large extent, in the hands of the police. Abraham Calder-Fluss said he wished it to be on record that the Conference had – up to the final incursion from outside – been highly successful. This must not be forgotten.

The Professor of Sociology said that, in view of the considerable expense of repairing the buildings, and the very strong feelings of the student body, it would be wise to reconsider the preparatory year of maths and languages. It was anomalous in British education. It was creating ill-will. It should, in his view, be scrapped. A strand of cultural studies could then be offered across the board . . .

Lyon Bowman said 'I see our student representatives are not with us.'

Calder-Fluss said 'I noticed the film people recording some of the – events. Whilst it can certainly be argued that such film will be useful to the police in their enquiries, there were certain unfortunate moments – certain matters – which I hope they can be persuaded not to make public.'

Wilkie said 'We've got her on film. Stomping along in a black cloak with a great *rod*, and waving them on.'

'You can't *use* that,' said Frederica.

'It's a newsman's dream.'

'You're not a newsman. You'll kill him.'

'He got it all wrong.'

'*They* got it all right.'

'It was a campaign, it was planned, there was no good outcome. They've all buggered off, caravans and everything. Struck camp. Buses-full, going back down the A1.'

'They'll boil up somewhere else. Wilkie, *please* don't put her on the telly. He – it was *right* of him to – let her do her own thing. But he shouldn't have to – be punished for it.'

'It's news. The public has a right –'

'No, it doesn't. It just has a hunger for blood.'

'It's an amazing bit of film,' said Wilkie. 'But OK, I'll scrap it. I'll show it to you, first.'

'I don't want to see it. I don't want her in my mind. She's dangerous.'

XXV

Time moved on. The events of the Battle, as it came to be called, settled into legend, and the University began its repair work. Luk published his paper, in *Nature*, and it was taken up by a Sunday paper, which presented him as a bristling genetic predestinarian and moral pessimist. Wilkie said to Frederica that they ought to have him on the programme to talk about it, and Frederica said it was no good, they'd tried that, he thought they were trivial, and wouldn't come. Luk, who was beginning to have some success in public debates and on the radio, was in fact waiting for the television invitation, which did not arrive. Both Luk and Frederica thought from time to time about their night together, in the shadow of the burning. The shape of it changed, in both their minds. Luk felt a sudden compunction, visited by a memory of the damp-headed, naked woman, bent over his snail-shells, and then could not think why, and dropped it into the well of unconscious cerebration. Frederica allowed Agatha and Daniel to think that her unusual diminution of confidence and energy was a result of the *débâcle* of John Ottokar, as indeed it partly was. She bought herself a Liberty peacock shirt, and then did not wear it. She took, without too much thinking about it, to celibacy. She got better at television interviewing, and branched out into other arts' programmes. She was better, as she had originally been good, because she was not anxious, she was not intimidated. She did not quite care.

At the beginning of the next academic year, in late September 1969, she invited Alexander Wedderburn and Daniel to dinner in Hamelin Square. She was in charge of Saskia and Leo, as Agatha had been in charge when she travelled to the Conference. Agatha was away at a conference on examination boards, and the complicated business of assuring parity of judgement. Frederica said to Alexander that she thought their way of life was about to come to an end.

'Why? It seems a good way of life, considering everything.'

'Well – it appears that Agatha is going to be *very rich*. Rupert Parrott told me, *Flight North* is making a fortune. They reprint and reprint and reprint. Everyone reads it. Children and adults. Culture and counter-culture. People remembering their child-hood reading, and kids looking for a story. It's given Saskia and Leo enormous kudos at school. Only I can't see how a woman that rich will want to go on living in this South London desert.'

'I've noticed the gentrification going on. You've got brass knockers and new-old shutters, and window-boxes all round the square.'

Daniel said 'Have you asked Agatha?'

'No. It's up to her.'

'You are a family. An odd one, two women and two children, but you *are* one. She won't want to break that up.'

'Well, I'm not going to be able to afford her life-style.'

'She hasn't changed it,' said Daniel.

Daniel had things preying on his own mind. His son, Will, never a great scholar but always competent, and always pursued by his grandfather's pedagogic vigilance, had quite suddenly failed all his exams. This had been made worse by the fact that the school thought that Mary was showing signs of unusual brilliance – like her mother, Daniel thought – and had been moved on a year ahead of her age-group. He had gone North on receiving this news, and had tried to talk to Will. It had not been a success. Will had glared, and shuffled, and burst out, on one occasion only, with a series of accusations that, Daniel felt, were clearly seared into his mind. Daniel had left him when he was little. Daniel didn't really care what happened to him, he only cared about the down-and-outs in his horrible crypt. Daniel had let his mother die. Daniel was a bad – a bad religious, he didn't really believe in God, he didn't really understand that God was absolute, and came before exams.

This last accusation stung Daniel horribly. He said that what he believed was a personal matter.

Will said, rightly and cruelly, that no, it was not, actually. He had no right to go about behaving like a – religious – since he wasn't one.

Where are you getting all this? Daniel asked his son.

'You don't care where I get anything, or what I get, or what I believe. When have you ever talked to me about God?'

Daniel could not answer.

'Never,' said Will. 'That's when. Never. Never. Never. Only about *fucking* exams, which don't matter.'

'Don't swear. And yes, exams do matter. And, if you want me to, I will talk about God.'

'Well, I don't. It's long past – the time when – that would have been – any use. Why don't you go back to your *failures*, they make you feel better, I *don't*.'

'Will –' said Daniel. But Will's burst of speech was over, and he could not be got to say any more.

Alexander told Frederica that he was going to go North, in November, and put on a play, in Long Royston, in aid of the University's appeal for funds for damage-reparation. He said that his costume-designs for *Astraea* had been damaged in the violence, and the Vice-Chancellor was concentrating the appeal action where → where things had been lost.

He thought he would put on a Shakespeare. His own writing was not going too well, inspiration was burned out. He thought he might put on *The Winter's Tale*. Indoors, of course, it was Winter. A play about rebirth after tragedy. Appropriate.

Frederica said her father had always hated that play.

Why, said Alexander.

For being a wilful device for making comedy out of tragedy by ignoring real feelings. By ignoring the feelings of a woman shut in a vault for sixteen years who then conveniently comes back to life as a statue.

'As we are mock'd with art,' she said, thoughtfully.

Alexander asked Daniel what he thought. Daniel said he didn't know the play, and stared darkly down, through the floorboards it seemed.

'I hope you don't hate it,' said Alexander. 'I was thinking of doing the play the way we did *Astraea* – with a largely amateur cast, and some professionals. I wondered if you'd like to act.'

Frederica hesitated. She handed around a dish of fruit. Dark grapes and pale golden plums, pomegranates and kiwi fruit, tangerines and Chinese gooseberries. No time to cook pudding, these days, she said.

She said she was too old for Perdita, and too young for Hermione, and not fierce enough for Paulina. And had lost the desire to act a part, somehow. Although she granted she might be said to be doing that all the time.

'I had a sudden vision of you as Hermione, and Mary as Perdita,' said Alexander.

'That's meddling with genes in an unacceptable way – sorry, I don't mean to be rude, I'm thinking aloud. It feels wrong. And I don't seem to want to act, any more.'

Daniel thought, something's wrong, but he was too tired to ask what. He picked at the seeds in his fruit. He thought, Will too had Frederica's genes, and belligerent Bill's, in his fiery half. And his own dark, heavy heredity. Damn.

Luk Lysgaard-Peacock, on one of his autumnal surreptitious snail-excursions, crept in through his sawn paling, heard sounds, and stopped. The ground rose, just inside the Pale, at that point. He dropped down, and crawled forward, peering cautiously over a hummock.

The Hearers were gathered on what had been the burned earth of the hen-houses, next to 'his' dry-stone wall. They were chanting. There was a sound of crashing stones.

A figure stood against the wall, a female figure, in a white gown of some kind, pleated. Paul-Zag was sitting on the wall, playing his guitar, and John Ottokar stood beside him, blowing a mournful melody on the clarinet. The Hearers were dancing, shuffling, and filing past, stones in their hands. As they passed, they cast them in the direction of the woman. He did think for a moment that they were stoning her, but then he saw that it was not, not exactly, not that. They were heaping up stones – many of them gathered from the snail-wall – before and beside her, making a kind of cairn, or a loose barrier. She stood and shivered – it was chilly – and they sang.

It was unhappy.

Luk wondered if they were going to hurt her, if he should stay, or get help.

It became clear that they were not. The punishment – if that was what it was – was symbolic only.

Luk retreated, ill-at-ease.

From Brenda Pincher to Avram Snitkin

Well, here I still am, a sacrifice to the cause of true ethnomethodology. I've got no more tapes, so I've got to write to you, as I've got to communicate or I shall get sunk and absorbed in what's going on here. Even if communicating is not the right word, given the one-way nature of this – well, it isn't a correspondence. I won't think about that. I'll pretend you're real, and out there, and that I shall be able to get this message-in-a-bottle *out* to you. Gander still goes out regularly, and Zag occasionally. They do such shopping as is done, and we have to rely on how spaced-out, or not, they are, for what they remember, or don't remember (Loo-paper. Aspirins. Torch batteries) – to bring back.

We work a lot harder and eat a lot less and grow a lot thinner. We clean a lot, but somehow – maybe some of this is subjective – things get grubbier, paint gets scraped off and not put back, blankets fray. We have rituals now. The Manichees worked a lot with mirrors and light and Gander brought back a whole van-full – balancing mirrors on stands, mirrors to screw on walls, old pub mirrors, gilded mirrors out of what looks like redundant cinemas or something. We've got a mirror-room *lined* with the things now, and we do – movements – in there, and – sing, and dance. Also there's a lot of talking. Joshua talks a lot, about light, and emptying out, and self-loss. Eva W. talks a lot, about Rosicrucians, and astrological mysteries, and alchemical transfigurations. I think I'm not the only one that thinks that's all crap, though it's interesting that none of us would ever *say* any such thing to any of the others. This might be a relic of the Quakerly charity, which could be a very severe thing. But it also feels like fear. As though everything's explosive, or potentially so, and no one wants the explosion quite yet. (Some, including me, don't want it *at all*.)

We have got semi-savage chickens running in and out of everywhere, shitting on things, like a Yorkshire version of sacred cows. That adds to the general run-down feeling. We are still allowed to look at the television, oddly, but the programmes are restricted. We get to see Nature programmes – lots and lots of shots of snakes pretending to be leaves, and killer fig-trees in the Amazon – and we get to see children's TV. No News. Can you tell me, Avram (if you ever get this letter) who is Charles Manson, and what has he done?

387

I've been wondering why everyone puts up with Eva W. now she's moved in permanently. She even got what used to be Lucy's bedroom. I've had the idea that she's a kind of lightning-conductor. Because we are all repelled by her – I was going to say, because we all hate her, but that's schoolgirlish talk, we don't, it's more primitive, we are *repelled* and *appalled*, except those who are fascinated (Zag, Lucas Simmonds, Canon Holly) – because we are all repelled by her, except *those*, we somehow draw together, and don't mind things in each other that might have been irritants.

Also, she somehow channels away the conflict between Gideon – sexy, out-of-his-depth, no-longer-charming, grumpy Gideon – and Joshua Ramsden, who grows in beauty, and epigrammatic crispness, and untouchability. He really has got a lovely face. I have to say that. He is *both* repelled by, and in a way I simply don't understand, attracted to Eva W. and her mumbo-jumbo.

I'm avoiding telling you, Avram Snitkin, Avram Snitkin, who have *got* to be real and ordinary (well, you never were *that*) and out there somewhere in an ordinary world – I've been avoiding telling you what has scared me. If we all end up dead, I'd like to have told somebody.

He talks a lot about *stones*, as well as about light, and fruit, and mirrors. He gets them out of the *Book of Joshua* in the Bible, which is one of the really bloodthirsty ones. God and Joshua are always beating people into submission with hails of stones.

Anyway, as we all know, one of the things people were traditionally stoned for, was adultery.

One of the girls – well women – I'm scared to write this, Avram – turns out to be pregnant. It is that Ruth, with the plait dangling, and I *suppose* I assume Gideon is the other party, since no one's suggesting parthenogenesis, though when she's asked, she stares – she stares *stonily* – and says she doesn't know how it happened.

No, we didn't *stone* her. Joshua quoted the New Testament, Let him who is without guilt among you, cast the first stone.

Then he said, we were all guilty, because we were all one, and we would build a commemorative pile of stones.

So we all walked past poor silly Ruth and solemnly added our non-vindictive stone to the heap in front of her.

It was silly and quite horrible.

I want to come out, and must not, for some sort of professional ethnomethodological honour requires me to see it through.

I am not sure, Avram, we shall always stop at symbolic stones. I mean, they were *already* real, she was *already* in a sort of pillory.

They haven't sent for a doctor, or sent her to see one, or anything. I tried mentioning it to Elvet Gander, and he said

'In the fullness of time, dear girl' and snapped his fingers. If we all die, it will be because of his mind-expanders.

It is just possible that Joshua Ramsden is the father. I mean, why does he otherwise not go after Gideon? It is also possible that the whole idea of sex, and everything to do with it, *embarrasses* him, with a religious intensity of embarrassment.

I can't be a very good sociologist if I can't sniff that one out. No, it has to be Gideon. Clemency's past caring, which makes it harder to tell.

They all – including Eva W. – want to be the Maiden of Light. I don't. But I feel I have to say I do.

I want fish and chips, and a Mars bar, and *you*, Avram Snitkin.

From Elvet Gander to Kieran Quarrell

Worry not, worry not, old friend, dear chap, all is under control, or if not under control, expanding splendiferously, producing marvellous fruits and flowers and bursts of fireworks.

Yes, I declare myself a responsible person, fit to watch over Lady Wijnnobel, and yes, I declare this a Therapeutic Community, where she is safe (and yes, if you like, old friend, where people are safe from her). I am sure that – with my own assurances of *personal interest* – will calm the Vice-Chancellor, and the Chief Constable, and all other interested parties. And, whilst I am at it, may I assure you also that your ex-patient, Josh Lamb, Joshua Ramsden, is more resplendently sane than the next man (yours truly) and is conducting, in the fullness of time, a Great Work, which will change utterly those of us who are *in*-volved in it, wound up in it, concentrated upon it.

These persons, who are not patients, and not very patient, are embarked upon a spiritual journey which inevitably takes them – and us – through the Valley of the Shadow – but the Light is visible – and better to travel on than cower in a drugged stupor under hospital blankets.

We are living in a world of perpetually shimmering symbolic Truths which connects with the real world at points of wonder – Rocks, Stones, Trees, Mirrors. I am learning daily the beauties of synchronicity and many-layered coincidences of staggering beauty.

That woman – your ex-patient – Lady Vineyard – is a silly Old Bag, Old Hag, Old Crone – but out of the mouths of Old Crones come the Speakings of true Priestesses. Now and then, and often, I am the first to admit, involuntarily. She is a Conduit, Kieran (oh the horror and the beauty) for celestial and infernal jellyfish and Medusas and blood, sweat and tears.

She discerns upon the white fleece and pale brow of our sacrificial Lamb and vengeful Ram the true bloody Sweat, the rosy dew, of the Proclaimed One. (Or One of Them.) A veil of blood. He is to be the Work, the *Mysterium Coniunctionis*, the Stone, which is the true Mercurius or Psychopomp, born as White Light from the bath of colour, the peacock-tail, the *Cauda Pavonis*. She told us an esoteric creation story in which the God made the Peacock, and showed him Himself in a mirror, and the lovely bird was so amazed at his own beauty that beads of rosy sweat burst out on his brow – and from these, were all other creatures made.

I have been reading and reading in Jung's *Alchemical Studies* and as I read, I see that the veils and threads of colours and connections in the fabric of the unconscious are *more real* than the world of – of – dirty socks, old friend, trouser-flies, nail-clippers, junk like that. I see and know it. But not as Ramsden knows it, who knows it with grace and in both worlds at once. I am either in the coloured veiling, glimpsing the light, or coming round amongst tea-leaves, trash, and toe-clippings. He can see the light in the toe-clippings, and *can get it out.* Have you noticed (but I think you are as yet unconverted to Jung) how Jung says that One of the primary metaphors for the Alchemical Work is *torture*? The flesh must groan to release the spirit, the light is wrung with blood out of the Stone, the veils of flesh are ripped and bleeding so that the Child of Light may come forth and shine.

Listen, Kieran, this is ecstasy, not madness. But it might not help with yr Practical problem wch is who is in charge of yr So-called Patients. (Victims.)

I AM.

OK?

I AM.

A handclasp, dear old Kieran.

Elvet Gander

From Brenda Pincher to Avram Snitkin

Listen, you bastard, I am going to get this letter out to you, and you are going for once in your life to do *something*.

Things have been happening. They aren't funny. I daren't write much.

The baby got born. Nobody fetched a doctor, and nobody had ever consulted one. It was a horrible birth, she screamed for twenty-four hours, I'd guess. Lady W. waved her arms and said all would be well, and burned nasty smelly choking charms. Clemency and Lucy saved the baby, and saved Ruth, I think and trust. There was an awful lot of blood. Gander and Zag were unconscious with something they took. Lady W. said to Ramsden, Come and behold the Work (I quote exactly) and he came. He said he smelled blood. (Well, how could he *not*, it was everywhere.) Anyway, he strode in, looking priest-like, and took one look at her lying there – they had tidied her up – and had a *colossal* epileptic fit, and Lucas S. and Canon H. had to hold him down and do things with his tongue and drag him away to bed. Where he's kind of comatose.

That's bad, but there's something worse.

There is – was – a girl called Ellie. She was pretty sick, in a quiet way. She took the not-eating very seriously, and got thinner and thinner. And thinner. The other day, someone went up to look for her – she slept in a tiny attic. Well, it wasn't *someone*, it was me.

And she was dead. Quite cold, with her mouth and eyes open.

I thought, now they'll have to get a doctor, or the police.

But they buried her, in the garden, with singing and clarinet music.

It was quite respectful, and if you're dead, you're dead, but it's illegal.

And they seemed to think oh well, it was quite natural, she was better off, her journey was over, Gander said.

Avram, I think you'd better tell someone.

Who can I trust with this letter?

I can't think.

What can I do?

Oh, *shit*.

The Winter's Tale was performed in the Great Hall at Long Royston. Alexander had asked Harold Bomberg who had played Gauguin in his London production of *The Yellow Chair* to play Leontes, and had found a Hermione amongst the lecturers in English in the University who had been at Cambridge with Frederica, and was now a mediaevalist. The rest of the cast were university teachers and students, with the exception of Perdita. Perhaps sentimentally, but also because Blesford Grammar School said she was outstanding, he had chosen Mary Orton. For this reason, Daniel, as well as Frederica, Agatha, Saskia and Leo, had come North to see the first night. They sat together in a long row, Bill Potter next to Daniel, Winifred next to Will, who was on the end, Frederica between Daniel and Alexander. The university dignitaries and the county notables were in front of them, including Matthew Crowe, in his own arm-chair, wrapped in blankets.

Vincent Hodgkiss sat, not with the university dignitaries, but with Marcus, further back, behind the row of Potters. Luk Lysgaard-Peacock was with them. He looked to see where Frederica was – deep in family and old friends – and looked away again.

Alexander had had a hand in the costumes. They were vaguely classical, with Elizabethan touches. In the first act, with its crescendo of jealousy and its polarised trial scene, the men wore black, with touches of crimson, and the women wore white, with touches of purple. The boy, Mamillius, wore a miniature version of his father's black robe, standing collar, and tights. He spread the wings of his cloak to tell his ghost story. '*A sad tale's best for winter.*' He told his father '*I am like you, they say*' and went off, to die of grief and humiliation. Gerard Wijnnobel listened with delight and amazement to the tortured syntax, the straining thread of language, of Leontes' agony of jealousy. It was coherently incoherent, beyond bearing, and entirely beautiful.

Luk Lysgaard-Peacock got faintly bored of all these words, and considered the back of Frederica's red head. He had always supposed she slept with Edmund Wilkie – they seemed to be a couple – and he saw her touch Alexander Wedderburn's arm with a sort of intimacy. She was a free woman. He might go and talk to her. Or not.

Marcus suddenly had a complicated idea about the geometry of the physics of nodes of growth forming on the stems of sunflowers. He looked desperately around for a mnemonic.

'*My life stands in the level of your dreams,*' said Hermione.

'*Your actions are my dreams,*' returned her terrible husband.

Frederica wanted to cry, at the closed perfection of those running feet. She remembered her dream of Luk Lysgaard-Peacock. What relation did it have to the now-dreamy nature of remembered actions? There were drinks at the interval. Luk decided he *would* speak to Frederica, made his way across the Hall, and found her with her son and the headmistress. 'You should have been Mamillius,' said Miss Godden, 'if Mary is to be Perdita.' Frederica put an arm round Leo. 'I don't want him to be

Mamillius,' she said. 'Hullo, Luk. In any case, he's in his own school play. He's in *The Wizard of Oz*.'

'I wanted to be the cowardly Lion. But I'm the Scarecrow. I sing, I dance.'

'I must come and see that,' said Alexander. He said to Bill 'How are you bearing up?'

'Oh, the first half's splendid. It's always splendid. The verse, the pace, you've got it very well. It's the damned *statue*. I'm waiting to see what on earth you can have done with that impossible piece of stage machinery.'

'You do have to lend it your imagination.'

'I have never been able to do so. Never once. Just because *he* got old and self-indulgent – is no reason why *I* should –'

Most of this meant nothing to Luk. He said to Frederica 'I saw you interviewing that herpetologist. I noticed you mentioned my research. Quite a lot of people have remarked on it. Remarked on the mention on TV, that is.'

'I'm sorry.'

'No, no, I didn't mean that. It's always good to get recognition. I wanted to say, thank you.'

Frederica remembered the previous thank you. Her face stiffened. Luk drew back. The second half began.

Alexander had dressed the sheep-shearers and pastoral dancers in sharp pinks and blues and yellows – new colours of the 60s, colours of the flower children, dyes that hadn't been created when Frederica played the young Elizabeth in 1953 on the terrace of the House. It was winter, outside and in, and Alexander filled the stage – the space under the minstrels' gallery, under the plaster frieze of marble men and maidens under blanched forest boughs – with an artificial summer of silk flowers – poppies and lilies, roses and delphiniums, marigolds and convolvulus – made by a clever Chinese artist he had found working for tiny sums in Soho.

Mary Orton appeared, in a demure white cotton dress and a floral crown, weightless and intricate. She began to speak Perdita's flower speech.

> O Proserpina
> For the flowers now that frighted thou let'st fall
> From Dis's wagon . . .

393

Daniel was quite unprepared for the effect this would have on him. She was acting a woman a year or two older than herself, and was full of the careful dignity of speaking great verse clearly. She was in her own world, not trying to charm, but enchanting. He saw, not his daughter, but his wife. Only for a moment, but entirely, and remembering life he remembered death, automatically, and his eyes filled with tears. He heard a small sound next to him. Bill Potter was rubbing his cuff angrily across his faded eyes. An audience is one, and many, it is moved separately, and together. Daniel pushed at his own eyelashes, and with his other hand touched Bill's knee, to show he knew they knew.

The play swept on, and broke up into the irritating little runnels of scenes in which the greatest of playwrights evaded the recognitions, reparations, climax, everyone had a right to expect, and fobbed off his audience with *oratio obliqua*, reported speech, when the father met the lovely living daughter who replaced both his dead son, and her exposed infant self, for whom he had mourned for sixteen unstaged years. What a *mess*, Frederica thought, as she always thought. 'I can see why he did it, and we find ways to excuse it, because it is what *he* did, but *what a mess –*'

And all squeezed and rushed and jangled together for the sake of the set piece of the damned statue.

Alexander had done his best, like many before and after him. He had put the woman on a plinth, and had veiled her, in imitation of those virtuoso seventeenth-century marble carvings of metaphorical stone veiling over metaphorical stone flesh. With hidden gold safety-pins he had pulled the fine muslin back over the dead Queen's face, as though a wind was blowing through the twilight of the windless underworld. He had damped it very slightly, and the contours of the face – the nose, the cheek-bone, the eyeballs, the lips and brow, could be seen. They were highlit with a white spotlight – a white of a purity and coldness also unavailable in 1953, a dead white, that made pure shadows.

Paulina, the psychopomp, led the repentant intemperate king, his rage cool, into the vault, followed by his reconciled friend, his daughter, and her young lover.

It is an impossible piece of creaking stage machinery.

Leontes   *See my lord,*
   Would you not deem it breathed, and that those veins

> *Did verily bear blood?*
> Polixenes   *Masterly done.*
> *The very life seems warm upon her lip.*
> Leontes   *The fixture of her eye has motion in't*
> *As we are mocked with art.*

'Mocked' mouthed Bill Potter, silently. Daniel saw. Alexander's lighting changed to rose and gold, which filled the whole space under the minstrels' gallery with a liquid shimmer, in which, to the sound of music, rebeck, hautbois, lute, the veiled figure, its face pressed against its cerecloth, began to flow down off its pedestal and to cross the ground. The stage-vault was heaped with colourless silk flowers, transparent like the discs of honesty, or the operculum which closes a snail-shell in winter. The rose and gold light transfigured these drifts of ghost-petals, making them substantial. Mary–Perdita had one in her hair, which now caught this new light, and shone out like a living flame. The statue – the only moving thing in the dumb-struck gathering – swept on towards the king, and lifted its veil, like a bride, and held out a rose-bathed face for a kiss.

Mocked, tricked, Daniel Orton and Bill Potter wept, and pushed away their tears.

Afterwards, there was the usual rejoicing and celebration. Bill Potter tried to tell Daniel about his revelation – after all, he had shared it with him – but Daniel was pushing through the crowds, looking for his daughter. So he told Frederica. 'I've just *understood*. Never too old. Never too old to understand something. The thing about the late comedies – the thing is – that what they do, the effect they have, isn't anything to do with fobbing you off with a happy ending when you know you witnessed a tragedy. It's about art, it's about the necessity of art. The human need to be *mocked with art* – you can have a happy ending, precisely because you know in life they don't happen, when you are old, you have a right to the *irony* of a happy ending – because you don't believe it. Are you listening?'

Frederica was abstractedly looking for a scientist. Who was putting his coat on, to leave.

Daniel found Mary. He wanted to say, 'Whatever you do, don't die.' He hugged her. She danced, a human girl, within his arms' circle, and said 'I got it *right*, I remembered it all, every word – as though it just spoke itself . . .'

Winifred came up, and said 'Lovely, lovely Mary. Has anyone seen Will?'

'He was sitting next to you,' said Daniel.

'Well, he got up and went out – just after the sheep-shearing scene – and I thought he'd gone to the lavatory – it is some way, in this building. But he didn't come back.'

'Perhaps he went home,' said Daniel. He thought, and then said 'I'll go and look.'

'He's only sulking,' said Mary. She didn't say why. She didn't have to, and was a nice girl.

Will was not at home. He had been at home, it was slowly established, because his anorak and his bicycle were gone, and his desk-drawers were open and tumbled, though nobody knew what had been taken, since his privacy was always respected, and he lived in a horrible mess.

The bicycle was the worrying thing.

It was possible he had just gone out for a long ride and possible he would simply come back. There was also the pit of other possible things. And general uncertainty over what to do. Also, it was a foul November night, and thick mist was rolling in over the Yorkshire moors, making the roads very dangerous, and the sheep-tracks and footpaths treacherous or impossible.

Various small excursions were made into the wall of fog. School-friends were called, and knew nothing. The night went past. In the morning, the police reported that a lone cyclist had been seen by a farmer, riding furiously along the edge of Mimmer's Tarn, in the fog, which had opened briefly, like a curtain, and revealed him in the headlights.

Leo said 'He used to go to listen to that Zag, playing. When there was that tent. He liked his playing. I didn't.'

Daniel drove out with Frederica to Dun Vale Hall, and was told by the long-haired young men on the gate that they had seen no one. And no, he could not come in.

Frederica said that Luk Lysgaard-Peacock went in and out through the Pale, she happened to know, to check on his snails.

Luk arrived at Freyasgarth in his blue Renault. The family was tense and desperate. Mary sat weeping in a corner, feeling that her moment of glory had precipitated disaster, and feeling also, as siblings do, that disaster would *have to be* her fault. Bill was telephoning. Leo was white and shaking. Luk watched Frederica, who paid him no attention beyond a brief welcoming smile, talking to the boy. She was not telling him it would all be right. She was telling him that there were things to do. Her sharp face was concentrated and *grown-up*, with a look Luk had never seen before. When he and Daniel left for Dun Vale Hall she was sitting with the boy in her arms. Both were staring out of the window, grimly composed. They were very like each other.

The moorland fog was still thick when Luk and Daniel went through the Pale. They strode down across heather and fields, towards the Hall, and were able, because of the fog, to come to the back gate of the farmyard unseen. Coils of air and water wound themselves round them, thick and grey. The watchful geese began an invisible honking. Daniel pointed. The bicycle was leaning against an outbuilding.

'Now what?' said Luk.

'Now we fetch him out,' said Daniel.

They strode, a heavy dark man, a brisk, fiery man, across the yard and into the kitchen. The kitchen was full of women who with slowed movements were washing, and preparing food. They all wore the same long pale dresses. The atmosphere was steamy, an indoor fug to match the fog. The room was hung, as with tapestries, with the white on white embroidered cloths, with motifs of suns, moons and stars, sunflowers, melons and grapes. They hung also like banners from the long racks on pulleys which in the old days had carried the laundry. They were spread over the dressers and chests of drawers on which were groups of candles and nightlights. There was a smell of fur and feathers, dog and sheep and hens.

Someone said that visitors were not welcome.

Daniel said he had come to fetch his son.

Someone else said his son was not there.

Daniel said he intended to look for him.

Luk stood in the doorway, poised and watchful.

Daniel pushed through the women and out into the hall. The

house was an old house. It had harboured Puritans and Non-conformists. Wesley had preached from its kitchen table. Daniel stood at the foot of the staircase and looked briefly up at the murky stained glass window which showed, though he could not see it, Christian and Hopeful crossing the Jordan to reach the heavenly City, 'and the trumpets sounded for them on the other side'.

A dark figure stood on the turning of the stair. It was Eva Wijnnobel. She looked, Daniel thought, hunting a word, *mummified*. Her hair was glossy as ever, her eyes painted, her lips red. Her gaze was not fixed. She stared, not at him. She said

'You should not be here.'

'I have come for my son.'

'You may not find him. If he is here, he has, like Mary, chosen the better part.'

'Nonsense,' said Daniel.

He pushed past her, and the embalming smell of her perfumes. She said

'You have no place here.'

'Indeed not. I am going, as soon as I have found my son.'

He went on up, trying doors, looking into dormitories and cluttered cupboards. Finally he opened the door of a long attic and was met by a disorienting glitter of light, like ripples of reflection in underwater caverns, like the streams of sparks off revolving mirror-spheres in dance-halls. There was indeed such a sphere, hanging from the ceiling.

The room was a box of mirrors – lined with mirrors, and mirrors behind mirrors, crazily reflecting each other. There was a television, showing white noise. There were low tables, with candles of all kinds in glass dishes of all kinds. There were huge white cushions or bolsters on which, in white dresses, sat the male Hearers, or some of them. He saw Gideon, he saw Canon Holly, in their trailing white shirts, two dried-up wrinkled old walnuts, with tired eyes. He saw Lucas Simmonds, his cherubic face beaming over his innocent garment. He did not see Will, but he did see Zag, wearing his white shirt over his silver tights, like a crusader's surcoat, lolling on a heap of pillows. He did not see Gander, he did not see John Ottokar.

'I have come for my son.'

'I don't think you'll find him. Here.'

'Then I should like to speak to Joshua Ramsden.'

'He doesn't speak to strangers,' said Zag.

'Then I shall have to go and look for him,' said Daniel.

He had, in fact been consulted by Kieran Quarrell at Cedar Mount, who was troubled over the present state of the Therapeutic Community, and had been sent to Daniel because Daniel had been present at Four Pence, had worked with Holly at St Simeon's, was felt to be a man with his feet on the ground. Quarrell had told Daniel the story of the eleven-year-old Joshua, and the fate of his father.

Daniel lifted up his shaggy head and roared. 'WILL. If you're there, come out, come here. WILL. COME HERE NOW.'

Two doors opened simultaneously, one from a cubby-hole under the eaves, one from behind an avenue or rank of mirrors at the far end of the room. From the cubby-hole Will crawled and stumbled. His face was tear-stained. He stood up, and fell down. He said 'They gave me sugar-cubes, white sugar-cubes.'

'They should not have done that,' said Daniel.

Joshua Ramsden, who had come through the other door, came into the middle of the room, and stood facing Daniel, his hands behind his back.

'I came for my son,' said Daniel.

They looked at each other. Ramsden saw Daniel's dark features in the middle of a series of images of himself, standing at the threshold of an infinity of reflected doors, half-obscured by the veil of blood which spread on the mirrors like a curtain.

Daniel blinked and saw the blood, blinked again, and it was gone. He said

'A bad trip is not a spiritual journey. You should not hurt young boys. He is coming home.'

'Home?' said Ramsden. 'What does that matter in the face of the evacuation and the expulsion? There is a battle going on. He chose to fight it. He may not have been ready, or strong enough.'

For a moment Daniel felt the strangeness, the distance, of the other man, who was far away, in the mental worlds in which the lost, and the contemplative, and the brave, and the foolhardy, wander. It was a place where he had once briefly hoped to go.

The man was a priest, in a way he had not been, and would not be.

He stood, his legs planted apart like an axeman, and confronted the tall, swaying figure with its bent head and white crest.

'You look ill, Joshua Ramsden. It is all going away, like water down a funnel. You are killing yourself. You need rest.'

Joshua Ramsden looked at the mirrors and the light, and the mirrors and the blood and the Light. He moved and spoke in a howling chorus of invisible voices. He heard his father, explaining that the pure fields of white light were just beyond the dissolution, that he had always known that, and had acted in wisdom, as Joshua must now do, having failed to die at the proper time.

'I am a Priest of the Light,' he said, 'and the outcome is uncertain, as Mani knew. It is in the balance.'

'You look very ill, Joshua Ramsden. I think you should get looked after.'

'It will not be long now.'

'You've got a right to kill yourself, but not other people.' He folded his son in his heavy arms.

Ramsden saw the woman's dead mouth, and the slipped false teeth.

Daniel saw Stephanie's dead lip, curled back, as he saw it daily.

They looked at each other.

'Go home,' said Ramsden. 'What is happening here, is happening.'

Daniel gestured at the room, the objects, the robes.

'Don't you see, all this is *only human*? It's bringing out of the cupboards and boxes of the mind what's stuffed in there, and boxing yourself in yourself, and suffocating in yourself. It's *more human* than not being religious at all, and whistling to yourself out there on the moor. But it's *only* human.'

'What do you know? You refuse to see the mystery.'

'I know that humanism isn't enough either. Making any sort of religion out of *being human* is a failure. The Religion of Humanity is a sugary sweet compared to the truth of things. It's just a dummy for babies, you and I are agreed on that. My son says, I'm not a religious. He may be right. I do the things somebody has to do since religion died in the world. Not for "humanity's" sake, but because we are religious beings, and caring for each other is what is left of what we used to know or believe about how everything worked. I am a religious, and God isn't a man, and I don't know what It is. There. Now, I'll take my son.'

Will crouched down on the floor, and shivered and sobbed. Daniel crouched beside him and put his arms round him.

'Listen to me, Will. I worry about thankless down-and-outs, yes and neurotic rich women with drug habits and night terrors, because someone must, because nothing is quite hopeless. It's laid on us, but I don't know what laid it. If you can't see what Mary saw, then you must make do with Martha, who lived with what's solid. That's all there is. All the stones were put on top of each other to make places where people would think about kindness and about what's solid without coming to bits. Which is easy to do, to come to bits, believe me, the difficult thing is not to. Now, come home.'

Will came, staggering, looking with huge eyes at dissolving frames and lintels and receding tunnels. The stairs were a horrible hazard, but the figure on them had vanished, leaving her unmistakable odour. Daniel guided his son back into the kitchen. He saw Ruth, standing by the sink, arrested in the peeling of a carrot.

'And you, Ruth? Are you coming?'

She opened her mouth. No sound came out. She rushed from the room. Luk, still just over the back threshold, felt someone push something into his hand. Ruth rushed back. She pushed a bundle at Daniel, who had to let go of Will to take it. It was a very small, very weak baby, wrapped in a scrap of blanket.

'Take it!' said Ruth. 'Take it away. I'm not coming. I don't want it. Take it.'

'Take her,' said Clemency Farrar's scraped voice.

Daniel, still concentrating on Will, gave the little creature, which moaned and murmured, but did not cry, to Luk. Luk said 'Does she have a name?'

'No,' said Ruth.

'Sophy,' said Lucy Nighby from a dark corner. 'Eva calls it Sophy.'

Ruth said to Luk 'Give it to Jacqueline.'

It took them a very long time to get back to the gap in the Pale, and the Renault. Will kept falling over, seeing precipices in front of him where there was only blackened heather, muttering that there were creatures gathering round with eyes, with little lights, with fires. Luk carried the baby, very inexpertly, and thought that if there was one thing he knew, it was that Jacqueline didn't want a baby. The mist swirled and metamorphosed itself like a huge living creature, clutching the surface of the moor, putting out trailing, probing fingers and inserting stumpy limbs, flowing, condensing, expanding, a breathing, clammy skin. Will sat down again and said he was suffocating, he couldn't go on. Luk said it was water vapour. Will said the heaven was trying to smother the earth. Daniel said, well, it hasn't yet, and it won't.

What had been pushed into Luk's hand turned out to be a letter, addressed to Dr Avram Snitkin, at an address in London. It didn't have a stamp, so one was found (by Winifred) and stuck to it, and it was posted. The English do not open other people's letters. Frederica knew who Snitkin was, but not where he was. Marcus, who had seen him in the Teach-Inn, did not know who he was.

XXVI

Daniel often wondered if he had triggered subsequent events. Two nights later – on a clear night this time – the farmer who had seen Will and his bicycle saw a red light over the moor. The Hearers had been known to light 'bonfires and such' on other occasions, but this was duller, and smokier, and contained exploding lumps of sparks. He reported it, in a stolid way, when he reached home and had had a cup of tea. By the time the fire engine had come out from Blesford, the whole of Dun Vale Hall was going up in smoke and leaping flames. Since there was no telephone, no one had called for help. Various concerned people in various places – including Daniel, Jacqueline, Luk Lysgaard-Peacock and Frederica – piled into cars and drove across the moorland to be of help.

It turned out that Need-fires had been lit, to purify the place. Need-fires, ideally, begin with sparks ignited from wood on wood – impregnated cloth is attached to a wooden frame, through which infected cattle – or in this case, sinful people – are herded. The whirling fire-lighter should ideally be pulled alternately by twin brothers. In this case, it was. This information came from Brenda Pincher, who was the only Hearer, when the fire spread to clothing, bushes and buildings, who ran out of the grounds into the road, to flag down passing cars and ask for help. She came back, however, with the helpers, and rushed energetically, indeed desperately, in and out of burning outhouses, driving the beasts and fowl to safety. It was Brenda Pincher, too, who showed the firemen where the Nighby children slept, so that a ladder could be got up, in time to get them out.

Everyone rushed, sooty, unrecognisable. There was somehow, Frederica thought, as she beat out the dull conflagration on the hind-quarters of Tobias the sheep, a gap between those who had been Inside – who were part of a spectacle, ringed with flame –

and those who were Outside, and had come partly at least because they were drawn by the perennial need to observe someone else's disaster at close quarters. Even if you got hurt, she thought, it wouldn't be the same. Her lungs were bursting simply with running and carrying. She bumped into Luk, in the courtyard, who was struggling with something wrapped in a singed blanket. The faceless thing hopped and spun, struggled out, and turned out to be John Ottokar, his lovely hair burned almost off, his face scorched.

'You've had *enough*,' said Luk. 'Go and get attention, get yourself out of this, you've had enough.'

John Ottokar stood submissively, and appeared to listen. Luk let go of him, and turned to Frederica. 'There are apparently people still in the attic,' he said, looking up at what was empty windows full of scarlet light and billowing blue-black fumes.

John Ottokar suddenly darted away, back into the house.

'*Shit* –' said Luk, and rushed after him.

Frederica pulled at Luk.

'He's mad. You can't.'

She panted. They touched sooty hands and went to fetch help. A fireman was found, armed and ponderous.

John Ottokar came out of the house, howling, and pulling. He had his brother by the foot – a silver-meshed leg shone in the flame-light – the same face, curiously peaceful, was dragged along the ground, with the same burned-off blond hair. The fireman rushed forward with blankets.

Frederica turned to Luk, who held her.

Something inside exploded, and everyone ran for cover.

There were three dead, it turned out. Everyone thought it would have been many more. Joshua Ramsden was found amongst a heap of shattered and melted glass – mirrors, a television – no more than burned bones, recognisable from his bridge-work. Eva Wijnnobel appeared to have died sitting in an arm-chair, staring into what must have been an advancing wall of smoke and flame.

Ruth was a curled heap under a windowsill, her arms over her head, her gold plait scorched but still in one piece.

The Ottokar twins survived, and lay side by side in Calverley

General Hospital's Burns Unit, their faces turned to each other, their bandages and skin-grafts uncannily symmetrical.

Frederica visited them. They did not speak. Their lips were covered with dressings.

Elvet Gander came to consciousness in Cedar Mount, looking into the eyes, very cross, very relieved, of Kieran Quarrell. He was not badly burned, but his lungs were smoke-damaged.

'I blame myself,' said Quarrell. 'I blame myself.'

Gander croaked 'We are all to blame.'

'Some more than others,' said Kieran Quarrell.

Little congealed, burnt-together heaps of books were found, on the turnings of what was left of the stairs, on the landing outside the room where Eva Wijnnobel had met her end.

The newspapers wrote of An Accident Waiting to Happen, of A Terrible Fate, of A Religious Cult in Self-Destruct Mode. One journalist opined that there were no such things as accidents, and quoted D.H. Lawrence, on how everyone made their own fate. Most cults imploded, self-destructed, in the same manner, you could observe it like the workings of beehives and antheaps and battery hens, said this sage observer.

Daniel Orton, who knew very well that there were such things as accidents, went heavily into Freyasgarth Church, to pray for a man whose father had predestined him to die, to save him from a predicted holocaust. Daniel sat inside the man-made heap of stones, and turned it all over, in the light of his own mind. He judged, harshly and clearly. He put aside his judgment, because the important thing was kindness, was Will, was the lost souls who had blundered out of the fire, Lucy and Gideon, Clemency and Canon Holly, the Ottokars and that anxious little person who had seemed, and still seemed, out of place, Brenda Pincher.

Brenda Pincher found Avram Snitkin. He was lying in his caravan in a singlet and some not very nice underpants, snoring. His hair and beard fanned out over a dirty pillow with no case. He was almost the only remaining person in the Anti-University. The tents were gone, the cottages were empty and disinfected. The

University had asked him to go, and he had said 'Sure, sure' but had not yet gone.

She shook him awake.

She said 'Where are my letters?'

He snuffled and mumbled. He reached under his bed-settee and pulled out plastic bag after plastic bag, full of unopened letters.

'Bills,' he said. 'Persecutions. Unrealities.'

Brenda Pincher looked around for a weapon. She took Talcott Parsons, and smote Avram Snitkin across the shoulders. She hit him and hit him, weeping and laughing, and he parried the blows, wincing and smiling.

Later, after her important *Hen Parties: a Study of Female Interfemale Chat*, she published *Group into Cult: an Ethnomethodological Analysis of the Development of a Belief-structure*.

After the burning, Luk took Frederica back to Loderby. They phoned Freyasgarth and ascertained that Leo was still soundly asleep. Luk opened a tin of tomato soup, vegetable red and creamy-sweet, and they sat on the terrace in the cold night, clutching hot black mugs. They looked at the stars, and the black ridge of the moor on the blue-black sky, and talked. Luk wore his hooded anorak. Frederica was shivering. He fetched his quilted eiderdown, and coiled it round her in a rough cone, with a trailing foot. The cloak of feathers was light and warm. Frederica rested her sharp chin on top of it. The outside was scattered with paisleys, a design she had never liked, because it was too common. These were crimson, and scarlet, and orange. Some had frills like sea-slugs, and some had tails like tiny whales, and some had fine branching patterns, like veins or ferns, inside them. Frederica was in that state of exhaustion where everything seems very sharp, and clear, and transparent. She thanked Luk for the warmth, and remarked on the pattern.

'Paisleys have some sort of Eastern symbolic meaning which escapes me,' she said. 'I've always not liked them. But when you look properly, they are an extraordinary example of pointless and delightful human ingenuity.'

Luk said he didn't like symbolic meanings. He said some of the paisleys reminded him of the patterns you saw on the retina if you closed your eyes and pressed lightly on the lids. They both tried this. Frederica got blue pools, and Luk got trains of bright sparkles.

Luk said, the thing the paisleys now irresistibly reminded him of was a magnified photo of a female mite which he had once been shown by Bill Hamilton. I used it as an example in my lecture, you may remember. I do, said Frederica. The mite lived on fungus threads in rotting oak. She contained two different kinds of unhatched female and a smaller number of males, who copulated with the females, before the mother burst. Some of the hatched impregnated daughters were a special 'dispersal morph', with claws like lobsters, which they used to cling to the hairy forelegs of insects flying away from the oak tree. The males, said Luk, were never dispersers.

Frederica huddled inside the paisley quilt and said he made her see the whole world quite differently, which was true. They looked up at the stars. Frederica, who accepted the poetry of astrology, could identify nothing but the three stars of Orion's belt. You could just see Gemini, said Luk, and that was Aries over there, and the Triangle, and Taurus, and the Whale. Looking at them, he couldn't even begin to see why they had been given these names. Did Frederica realise that we can only see the night – the dark – because the universe is expanding? If it was not expanding, wherever we looked, our line of sight would end at a star. It would be like looking into a forest of trees. The whole sky would be the surface of a star, and shine with perpetual starlight. But because the universe is expanding, we have darkness. The expansion degrades the light from distant stars and galaxies, and turns them into points. I like the dark, said Luk, sitting darkly on his terrace wall, his hooded head thrown back, his sharp beard silhouetted dark on dark.

They did not speak much of what had happened at Dun Vale Hall. The place was becoming already, in their minds, a closed form, a wall of flame enclosing disintegrating walls of stone, inside which were unimaginable aspirations, and destruction and pain. It was a separate thing. Frederica said cautiously that she could not begin to understand it. Religion had been left out of her, indeed knocked out of her, by her father, who was *fervently* anti-religious. Luk said, looking away over the moor, that he could understand it, because he had once been religious. He had had experiences, which he had believed fitted into the pattern of – Christian explanations. Then he had had – other experiences – it had come to him with a saner version of the same – certainty – that it was all untrue. All made up. All wrong. He said 'Much more light, so to speak, flooded in the second time. The world became real.'

He stopped and thought, still staring out over the earth.

'There are all sorts of words I mistrust, because of those two experiences,' he said. 'Reality's one. Authenticity. Creation. Love. Words that have become meaningless.'

Frederica in her feathers kept still and silent, watching his shadow on the night.

'"Creativity", for instance,' he said. 'My Danish religious forebears knew that only God creates, and I think I avoid the word out of a vestigial religious respect. But also – I haven't really thought it out – because I think current uses of it have got hidden religious roots, and they cause us not to think clearly. Is there any real difference between a really intelligent piece of work and a *creative* piece of work? I don't think so. I saw your programme on the notion, with Elvet Gander and Pinsky. I hated it.'

Frederica shrank into her covering.

'For personal reasons,' said Luk. 'Oh, with hindsight, we can see that poor old Elvet Gander was wandering off towards Jungian mysticism and whatever led to what's just happened to those poor creatures. Pinsky was OK. I suppose this story is against myself, because it could be said to be about synchronicity and coincidence, in which I don't believe.'

He told Frederica, then, about Jacqueline and the child that never was, Pinsky's retailing of Freud's tale of the associations of 'aliquis', his own disappointment and rage. He said, rage. He said it hadn't actually been *helped* by Frederica's discussion of female matters on the Free Women programme.

'I wasn't talking to you.'

'You don't know who you're talking to. And I was watching.' He said 'Anyway, Jacqueline is now potentially a very successful Free Woman.'

Frederica shivered.

'I'm sorry. I sound cross with *you*. Which would be ludicrous. What are you thinking?'

'I was thinking about bower-birds. I was thinking about peacocks' tails, and your lecture, and the peacock feathers and honesty in your jar. The horror Darwin felt at the excess of the peacock's tail – he was right of course, to try to get rid of the idea that God made it for Man's delight in Paradise. But theories of sexual selection don't explain why human beings find peacock feathers beautiful. Or for that matter why *we are interested* in the bower of a bower-bird. We like bower-birds because they are an image of us. They use the feathers of the Bird of Paradise – you said in your lecture – with other blue flowers and shells and things – you said they were a kind of prosthesis for attracting female bower-birds. But you didn't say why bower-birds attract naturalists and aesthetic theorists, or why peacocks attract men and women, who see metaphorical eyes where none are.'

Luk laughed. 'My curiosity, and your aesthetic pleasure, according to strict Darwinian theory, would both be fantastic elaborations of something originally adaptive. Like the tailfeathers, if you like. I have a hunter-gatherer's need to notice how things function. Snails and birds. You are trained to discriminate between more and less perfect eyes and feathers.'

'You make metaphors yourself. I saw you wore a peacock scarf to give your peacock lecture on the irrelevance of peacocks. Freud thought everyone was implicated in their own name, which they hadn't chosen. What's your star-sign, unbeliever?'

'Libra, the Scales. The one inorganic, man-made sign.'

'You see. You're proud of it. You make the meaningless connection. You're human.'

'I never said I wasn't.'

'You're an artist, like the bower-birds.'

'Bower-birds are particularly nasty to female bower-birds. They tempt them in, trample them, and beat them up, and drive them out. To make space for the next female.'

'That's very unpleasant.'

'It's natural. It happens. And it isn't a good analogy. Hodder Pinsky would warn you against it. Human beings aren't bower-birds, though I imagine we may have an enormous number of identical genes. Come to bed?'

They were gentle, because of exhaustion, and considerate, because of a new respect for each other, and therefore, as happens between men and women, felt the fact of the strangeness – the fact that they were, essentially, strangers – more intensely than the first anonymous time. Frederica thought of Jacqueline, and felt – for the first time in her life – a stab of pure sexual curiosity about another woman, and then a stab of jealousy. She was interested in this. Maybe jealousy was an important part of normal sexual behaviour – it was certainly so in novels – and therefore significant. You do not know another person, even when his sleeping face on the pillow, very close to your own, has a small, pleased smile on its mouth.

Over breakfast, they talked of their separate futures, with cautious respect. Luk said the new developments in electrophoresis were making rapid nonsense of years of patient research in population genetics. Science was like that. Things became untrue, disproved overnight. There were greater differences being found between neighbouring groups of snails than between humans and cows. He needed to move on. He was thinking of American labs – and some in Japan – where work was being done on relations between mammals which showed where creatures diverged under pressure of natural selection. Molecular clocks were eliminating natural history, he said. He wanted to be in on it.

Frederica said she wished she was as sure of anything. She said she would go back to London and go on with the television. She said it was every girl's ambition to be an air hostess, and now she was an air hostess. Whereas what she wanted, was to *think*.

What about? asked Luk, out of sexual contentment, thinking of the energy of her wiriness, in bed and out.

Frederica said she had wanted to think out the nature of metaphor. She had thought of writing a thesis, once, on religious metaphor in the seventeenth century. This was interesting, because seventeenth-century religious poets – and allegorical storytellers – used all sorts of elaborate metaphors – scientific, sensuous, philosophical – to describe a state of heavenly contemplation that was none of these things, that was said explicitly *not to be* able to be figured.

Luk the heir of Grundtvig and Kierkegaard was interested in this. She said

'I had the idea – it wasn't mine, it was very common in the 50s – that the seventeenth century was when people really *stopped believing* as they once had. When all those words – like creation, like real – became riddles. I thought, if you looked at the metaphors you could trace the thinking processes, you could see how the mind works.'

She said 'I wanted to find a place to start understanding

everything. Including why certain forms of language appear to be so perfect and beautiful. I've not got a first-rate mind. I shan't think up a new problem, or a new language. But it may not matter, because language is something we all have, with a long history, it's *in common*.'

She stopped, confused.

'Well —' said Luk. 'You could go back to universities.'

'That's what John said. It would make more sense for Leo. But then I saw, I don't *want* to be in an English Department, stuck with Eng. Lit. I saw that when you were talking, when Hodder Pinsky was talking, I saw the world was bigger. In my air-hostess cabin I can have Simon Moffitt explaining the Amazon flora and fauna — and Pinsky — and you, if you weren't so cross. Explaining genes, and chromosomes, and the language of the DNA. You know, the *new* metaphors, the ones now, are in that box. Wars are in that box, and beliefs, and persuasion, just as they were in *Paradise Lost* but infinitely more so.'

'And a lot of nonsense, and a lot of mind-twisting, and advertisements, and political haranguing —'

'Yes, but it's interesting, it's *what is* —' She drew circles on the breakfast table with a finger. 'I'm simply confused, that's what I am. I'm a mess.'

'I don't see why. What about Edmund Wilkie? He's respected by perceptual psychologists. And he puts things in your Pandora's box.'

'It's harder for a woman.'

'And so? You must just whistle harder. Louder. You won't do either perhaps quite as successfully as you would have done a straight university "career". But you'll *know more*.'

'That's what matters.'

'Of course.'

And if he had said, you are lovely, and if he had said, I want you exclusively to be *mine*, and if he had said again, 'thank you', Frederica would not have been so perturbed in body and mind. The laminations were slipping. Fire was re-arranging them in new patterns. She was full of life, and afraid.

XXVII

January 1970

Frederica sat in the basement in Hamelin Square, methodically and ruthlessly stripping the petals – one by one – from a huge and handsome hothouse chrysanthemum, a ruddy bronze one, given to her by the poet Hugh Pink, with whom she had set up a group to read *Paradise Lost* and *The Faerie Queene*, in winter evenings. The bruised petals gave off the winter smell, the funeral smell, of those flowers.

'To bleed, not to bleed,' said Frederica. She glowered at the flower. 'To bleed, not to bleed.'

Leo came in. He said '*Don't* do that. It was beautiful. Don't do it.'

His head was a shining bronze mass.

'I'm sorry. I was worrying about something.'

The plucked flower had a forlorn coppery crest.

'The flower hadn't done anything. Hugh gave it to you.'

'Hugh hasn't done anything. Nobody has. It's OK. Go to school. You'll be late.'

When Leo had gone, Frederica finished the dismantling. It ended on 'To bleed'. Like most oracles, it was wrong.

Frederica's life had appeared to be taking on a new, fluent, elegantly provisional shape. She had started work on a series of programmes on painting, for educational television, with Alexander and Wilkie. This meant interesting journeys to Amsterdam, to see Van Gogh, to Madrid, to see Velázquez, to Venice, to see Titian. She was working again on the metaphors. She was discussing making programmes about the chemistry of thought, with Wilkie and Lyon Bowman. There was Luk Lysgaard-Peacock. She discussed him with no one, and he and she did not discuss themselves in relation to each other. They were wary, they were pleased to meet, they survived separation equally. They did not use those words, *love, in love*, which both, for different reasons, felt to be dead words. It did not occur to Frederica to think of sleeping with anyone else, or to want anyone else. She had space to breathe and be – and so had he – and they met eagerly and happily. That would do.

She and Leo had gone North for Christmas, and Luk had come to Freyasgarth, and Frederica had said nothing to anyone. He was her private life. Marcus had made even more elaborate Christmas decorations, explaining the Fibonacci series to Leo and Saskia, drawing sunflowers and fircones. Marcus was happy. He was going to Cambridge, where he had a Fellowship in mathematics at St Michael & All Angels. Vincent Hodgkiss was also going to Cambridge. He had resigned as Dean, after the invasion, and had been given a Readership in Philosophy. He had bought a small house in Newnham village, which he and Marcus were to share. He was not present at Christmas – he was not in any sense part of the family. But Marcus said 'Vincent says –' with almost complete ease, and everyone smiled encouragement.

Jacqueline Winwar came, too, with Daniel. Daniel and Luk had discussed whether or not to tell her that Ruth had, so to speak, bequeathed her the baby. Luk said roughly that it would be cruel to do anything of the kind, and he was having no part in it. The baby, who was suffering from malnutrition, exhaustion, and various after-effects of its difficult birth, was in Blesford Hospital, in the wards where her mother had once been a nurse. Daniel visited her. She was very quiet. He decided against telling either Gideon or Clemency Farrar where she was, unless they asked, which they did not. They had moved away, no one knew where.

He did, however, go to see Jacqueline Winwar. He told her what Ruth had said, and where the child – who seemed not to have shaken off the name, Sophy, given to her by Eva Wijnnobel – was. Jacqueline, who had had a good Christian upbringing, stared out of the window with a set face, and then stared at Daniel.

'Why me?'

'You were her real friend. Outside that place.'

'Then I *ought –*'

'She made bad choices for herself. She can't impose one on you, unless you want it.'

'I want to do what's right.'

'And it's hard to think that what's right, might be what you want *for yourself*, because the world we grew up in said, always put others before yourself. You don't want this child.'

No, said Jacqueline, she wanted to go to Paris and work with French neuroscientists on the electricity and chemistry of memory. That is who I am, said Jacqueline. She said, more anxiously, that she had also *got* to get away from Lyon Bowman. Who treated his lab like – like a harem, who stole results, who – who was good at the science, and full of energy, and kept giving her things, like giving her *sugar-plums* – things like an introduction to Pinsky's Filaments group – but she wanted to be herself, herself alone, which meant, Daniel must understand, not thinking about *herself*, but about the work, the experiments, the synapses and the axons that did the thinking. I *can't do that* with a baby, said Jacqueline, her face white. Poor Ruthie. How *silly*. I suppose Gideon . . .

'No one knows for certain,' said Daniel. He said, he supposed Gideon might know. He said, he didn't propose to talk to Gideon, and Jacqueline said that was wise. She said 'It isn't your baby, it isn't your problem –' Daniel said, it was his problem, he had been given it. So to speak.

'If you have, I have.'

'No. Because what I do, is deal with intractable problems. What you do, is neuroscience.'

I don't want to be a human being, said Jacqueline, feeling suddenly that she was very lonely in the world, that her choice of work had deflected or distorted her unthinking life.

Daniel did what he never did, and put his arms round her. Jacqueline thought, he doesn't *do* that, he's the opposite of Gideon.

'Listen, it's *your life*,' said Daniel. 'My son says I'm not a religious, and as a not-religious, I say, be who you are. You've changed. I like you as you are.'

Jacqueline put her face up to be kissed. Daniel kissed her. He knew a woman who was breaking up a good marriage because she could not have a child, and the adoption authorities considered her too old. She might be kind to Sophy.

'I'm glad you told me, though,' said Jacqueline. 'I wouldn't like not to have known –'

'No, you like to know things,' said Daniel. 'I know.' He kissed her again, less gently. He was not quite sure what he was doing, but nothing seemed to hold him back.

Neither Jacqueline nor Daniel said anything about any of this, in the Christmas family gathering. Frederica watched Jacqueline and Luk talking, and felt an almost-pleasant prickle of jealousy. Jacqueline and she herself were part of a new world of free women, women who had incomes, work they had chosen, a life of the mind, sex as they pleased. It was interesting. She preened herself. Luk, despite his polemic about redundant males, appeared to be preening himself also. She would take that as it came. She had time, she thought.

And now, suddenly, she had no time. She was afraid she was pregnant, and then sure she was pregnant, and she had no idea what to do. Pregnancy disturbs the balance of body and mind, and is hard in any case on women like Frederica, who do not give in gracefully, who cannot let slip the habit of logical thought, who do not slumber easily. Her fight against bodily vagueness made her wild, without making her decisive. She went over and over possible courses of action, and all of them appeared impossible. Uncertainty is a terror to women like Frederica, and is paralysing.

She thought of telephoning Luk, of writing to him, and did not know what she wanted to say, or what she wanted to happen, or what he would want to happen. She wanted to be clear before she said anything, and she was *not* clear, and time went by, and time went by, as it does in pregnancy, slowly, slowly, but inexorably.

Luk had wanted to marry Jacqueline. He had never said anything, ever, about wanting to marry Frederica.

Moreover, she herself had been quite sure she did not want to be married again. This second pregnancy brought back banished memories of the first, the terror of being trapped by her own body, by two other people's bodies, of being *shut in*.

There were practical things. The television. People did not employ pregnant women to look like Alice in Wonderland on or in the Box.

And the exhaustion to come, and the sleeplessness, and the closing jaws of the trap of caring for someone as she cared for Leo.

In both senses, cared for. Looked after, as best she could. Loved. Oh yes. Loved.

Leo and Luk, Luk and Leo. They had nothing to do with each other. She could not ask Luk to care for Leo. She could not break Leo's present strange family-structure. He was happy with her and Agatha and Saskia. She thought about families. All the recent movements – the student Left, the dreamier counter-culture, the religious communities, had seen the nuclear family as a static thing, a source of oppression, the wrong kind of social forms and structures. Who is the father was an outdated Victorian question.

She did not talk to Agatha, who was away more frequently, possibly because of the success of her book. Frederica believed she should think it out for herself, and could not think.

The obvious answer was, the logical answer was, to stop it now, quickly, and stop thinking.

Frederica did nothing. Not exactly nothing. She played fair, minimally fair. She went to a clinic, not to her own doctor, she bought some vitamins, she felt stupid.

The cells divided energetically. They streamed in purposeful sheets, contracting and expanding. They put out filopodia which attached to the wall of the blastula. They made a neural tube.

Frederica felt sick. The biological clock ticked with the tides and layering of the cells.

Because she could not think what to say to Luk, because of what she was more and more frantically and obsessively *not* saying, she did not say very much. They had kept in touch with carefully casual phone-calls and letters. These dwindled. Frederica thought that if Luk really minded the dwindling, he might ask about it. He didn't. He sent bits of news about the rebuilding of the University and asked if she was coming North.

Not in the foreseeable future, said Frederica.

She was dully angry.

She disliked her body.

She smiled well enough on the television. She had to.

If you don't look at it, it isn't there.

It divided, and increased. The clock ticked.

The person who was looking at her, Leo, said he didn't know what had got into her.

Frederica said, neither did she.

In April, she went with Alexander and Wilkie to Holland, to film paintings. They went to the Van Gogh Museum, and filmed Van Gogh's *Reaper*, blue in the gold field of corn ready for cutting. They went to The Hague, on a train, to film Vermeer's *View of Delft*, which Frederica knew from reproductions, and from Proust's descriptions of the death of Bergotte in front of it, but had never seen. She was bundled in an anorak, over a useful shapeless tunic in navy blue. She sat on the Dutch train, and thought it would not be long before Wilkie noticed, Wilkie was astute, Wilkie was quick. Wilkie was excited by the idea of the *View of Delft*, which he believed had been painted with the help of a *camera obscura*, a mirror-lens in a dark space, so that the drops of water painted on the painted side of the painted boats appeared as perfect spheres, which from that distance they could not have been.

On their way into the Mauritshuis, they stopped on its dignified steps, to look at the dark water of the moat, which perfectly reflected the white swans sailing placidly on it. The camera crew had gone ahead to set up. A man, a woman and a child, a girl, were leaning on the stone balustrade, considering the swans. The man had his arm about the girl's shoulder. The woman stood with her body pressed slightly against his. A family. And then they turned, and the tall man straightened, and Frederica and Alexander recognised them. Agatha and Saskia Mond, smiling, and Gerard Wijnnobel, the Dutchman. A family.

There was a moment when Agatha clearly thought of pretending not to have seen them. Then she looked up at Gerard Wijnnobel, who smiled.

'So you see,' she said.

'I see,' said Frederica.

'It was too early to say anything. We needed time –'

Stories raced through the minds of both Alexander and Frederica, stories they could never substantiate or deny, stories of committee-journeys, meetings, *what* had been said to Saskia, when, of the death of Eva Wijnnobel, of the lovers meeting, talking . . .

No one spoke.

Wilkie said 'We've a film to make.'

Wijnnobel said 'What are you filming?'

'The *View of Delft*.'

'A mystery of survival and renewal. They say it has been so much restored that the brush-strokes Bergotte so lovingly traced on the little patch of yellow wall are no longer the ones we see. But it is still there.'

He gathered his family, bowed to Frederica and Alexander, and they walked off.

Filming is long and tiring, the lights are hot (even if the great *View* is protected from them) the repetitions which must look more and more spontaneous are exhausting. Frederica asked Alexander sprightly questions about the still panorama, and he spoke of what it had meant to writers – to Proust – something that endured – great art which lasted longer than life. Frederica struggled with a haze of female somnolence, and thought the 'petit pan de mur jaune' was sandy, was almost orange. It was partly because she was tired – and making the effort not to think about Agatha until later – that they had to record so many versions of what would be reduced to an amiable ten-minute chat. The paintings brooded and shone around. Shadowed seventeenth-century gilded faces under fantastic hats and helmets. Huge impossible vases of flowers, striped and spotted, red, blue, white, pink, tiger-gold, against heavy stone windows opening on glimpsed paradisal depths of plain and forest. Wilkie and Alexander went off to look quickly at other rooms, whilst the crew packed and removed the cameras. Frederica sat on a long leather seat in front of the *View of Delft* and went to sleep. She went into a very deep, very brief sleep, a drowse of defeat.

And woke, and for a moment did not know where she was. She was in a calm place where golden buildings stood above dark water, where the sky was blue and still, the stone was pink, time was very quietly arrested. She stared at the *View*, which has the quality of being so wide that the eye must travel along it to see it. She saw it as though she was in it, and saw, simultaneously, the perfect art with which each element had been considered, and understood, analysed geometrically, chemically, so that the colours could be reconstructed, and harmonised. This artist is not present in the traces of his hand – no flamboyant brush-marks make his signature, though Proust and Bergotte were wise in envying the spontaneity of the yellow strokes where the sun strikes. Delft is not, and was not, Paradise. It is, and was, a temporal city, with its own burghers, in the middle of a tempestuous history, for all its calm. What Frederica remembered was the momentary illusion of reality – the light in the dark room had appeared to be coming from the painting, had indeed come liquid through the window and been reflected off its surface. And beyond that, the adequate intelligence of the Master. Who had set himself problems only he could solve, and had solved them, and made a mystery.

Leo said 'I've got to talk to you.'

'Well?' said Frederica.

'You're not telling me something, and I'm not stupid, I notice things, and I know.'

Frederica looked up, a little haggard, from her desk.

'I want to know what you're going to do. I mean, it does concern me too. But that's not why. It's because you're so horribly miserable. I can't bear it. Tell me what you're going to do.'

'I don't know, Leo.'

'Babies have fathers,' said Leo. 'I've got *one* other family already. And Saskia. I wanted to tell you about Saskia. She minded most dreadfully, all those years, not knowing who – who her father was. We talked. She used to imagine all sorts of things. She never said any of them to Agatha. They didn't talk about it. It doesn't mean *she didn't think*. That's what I've got to tell you.'

Frederica considered her son. There were two of them, and he was ten, and having to be the man, since a man was needed. But he was a boy.

'I just wondered – because of Saskia – if he knows?'

'No,' said Frederica. She began to cry. 'I didn't know what to say. I don't know what to do. I shouldn't put all this on *you*.'

'I exist,' said Leo. 'So does – this – baby. So does Luk.'

She saw that he was afraid, whether of her wrath, or of his having got things wrong. She held out her arms.

'I've been silly, I love you. You're right. We must tell him. Then we can think what to do.'

'Telephone –' suggested Leo.

'I *can't*.'

'Well then, we'll go there. Come on. We can go.'

They arrived on a May morning at the North Yorkshire University to find that Luk was neither in his laboratory, nor in his apartment. An interested neighbour in the Evolution Tower said she rather thought he had gone on a field trip to Norway. She added that he had been talking of going to Japan.

Frederica said they should try Loderby. She drove out across the High Moor, filled with a desperate sense of urgency, as though she had left everything too late. Leo sat stolid and alert, staring around him.

Loderby too appeared to be deserted. The shutters were closed, there were plastic bags of rubbish stacked by the terrace wall, and a broken bunch of honesty thrown on the compost heap. Frederica sat down heavily on the terrace wall. Leo went round the house, and came back to report an open window, in which there was a stone jar, full of freshly cut yellow gorse.

'*Come on*,' he said. 'He's still here. We must look for him.' So they drove over the moor – there are very few roads – looking for the blue Renault, or the fiery-headed man.

The gorse was out, and spread like a sea of fire, along the sides of the road, across the heather. It was bright, bright, sun-yellow, with flecks of scarlet and crimson. It was full of movements in the turmoil of the air, it bowed, and flickered, and lapped with vegetable flames at the sooty roots of the heather and ling. Frederica drove unthinkingly towards where she had once, with John Ottokar, found the snail-seekers, round the thrush's anvil. The sky was full of huge white heaped cumulus, which piled forwards like castles on the move, like flocks of fleecy monsters, like sails.

Leo saw the blue Renault, parked at the edge of a track, almost obscured by the swaying golden bushes.

They stopped, and set out on foot, down the track, and then across the open moor, like hunters or beaters. Leo leaped over the bushes, his hair blazing in the blaze of flowers. Birds started, insects scuttled, brown moths rose like dust. Frederica ran slowly but purposefully. She thought about her life. She found herself thinking about *Paradise Lost*, which seemed to float beside her mind like a great closed balloon of its own colour of light, a closed world, made of language, and religion, and science, the science of a universe of concentric spheres which had never existed, and had constructed the minds of generations. It was part of her. She thought of the *Faerie Queene*, and Britomart the female knight, who saw her lover in the magic glass sphere made by Merlin, which was also a tower.

She looked at the earth under her feet, and the cobwebs and the honey-scented gorse, and the peat, and the pebbles, and thought of Luk's world of curiosity. She thought that somewhere — in the science which had made Vermeer's painted spherical waterdrops, in the humming looms of neurones which connected to make metaphors, all this was one. And in front of her, another creature, another person, contained in a balloon of fluid, turned on the end of its cord, and adjusted to the movement.

Leo crashed over the brow of a hill into a small decline, and found Luk, walking, in fact, towards him.

'*There* you are —' he said. 'We were looking for you.'

Luk looked up, and saw Frederica standing on the skyline. She was wearing an odd garment, in fact one of her Laura Ashley dresses from *Through the Looking-Glass*, which she had put on simply because it was made of a heavy cotton and had no waist, fanning out from below the breast. It was cream-coloured, sprigged with pink flowers, and olive-green leaves. It had long sleeves, and a kind of ruffle round her long neck. It ended below the knees and Frederica's long thin legs, striding purposefully, were naked. The wind from the sea tangled her hair, and blew the folds of the dress back around her belly, making her state perfectly visible at first glance. One or two startled sheep trotted in front of her. She looked like an absurd shepherdess.

Luk walked up through the gorse, and Frederica stepped carefully down. Leo kept his distance. He watched them meet, and heard raised voices. Luk shouted. Frederica shouted. The wind rushed in their clothes and hair and shouted. Then Luk put his arms round Frederica, and Leo knew it was all right, and continued up the hill, to join them.

They stood together and looked over the moving moor, under the moving clouds, at the distant dark line of the sea beyond the edge of the earth. In the distance, the man-made Early Warning System, three perfect, pale, immense spheres, like visitors from another world, angelic or daemonic, stood against the golds and greens and blues. Frederica said to Leo 'We haven't the slightest idea what to do.' Everyone laughed. The world was all before them, it seemed. They could go anywhere. 'We shall think of something,' said Luk Lysgaard-Peacock.

FINIS

Acknowledgements

I am grateful to many people in many ways for help with this book. Steve Jones and Frances Ashcroft have been patient with my queries about snails and genetics, physiology and cognition, and have been creative with their suggestions. Jonathan Miller and Richard Gregory aroused my interest in vision, memory and cognition in the early sixties and have been frequently helpful since.

I am also grateful to Steven Rose, Helena Cronin, Robert Hinde, Pat Bateson, Matt Ridley, Richard Dawkins, John Maynard Smith, Antonio Damasio, Semir Zeki, Marion Dawkins and Arnold Feinstein for help with science, to the Reverend Mark Oakley, and Dr. J. S. Fountain for help with religion; to David Caute, Martin Asher, Jeff Nuttall, John Forrester and Lisa Appignanesi, and Carmen Callil for help with the culture of the sixties. Mike Dibb and Leanne Klein were helpful with television, and Leanne's film of gorse was a useful delight. My interest in the possibilities of television was aroused in the late 1960s by Julian Jebb. Clara Sodrê Gama was helpful about dyslexia. Daniel Fabre's ethnological work on birds has been invaluable. I read Charles Lindholm's splendid book on charisma at a crucial moment, and am grateful for his email discussions. Judy Treserder long ago started me thinking about groups and group therapies. John Wren Lewis and James Mitchell, both now dead, started me thinking about religious culture in the sixties.

I owe much to my translators, and have discussed this work with Jean-Louis Chevalier, Anna Nadotti and Melanie Walz. Claus Bech has provided both endless interesting facts and words, and extraordinary understanding.

I could not have written the book at all without Gill Marsden, who kept my life in order, typed the pages, understood my problems, and understood the novel.

My publishers, Alison Samuel and Caroline Michel, have been both warm, wise and patient, as has my agent, Michael Sissons. My editor Jenny Uglow is the editor all writers hope for – clear-minded and enthusiastic, a true reader.